Claimed by the Rogue

Hope Tarr

Many thanks for hanging out for our Lady Janes Blog.

Samhain Publishing, Ltd.
11821 Mason Montgomery Road, 4B
Cincinnati, OH 45249
www.samhainpublishing.com

Claimed by the Rogue

Print ISBN: 978-1-61922-401-8
Digital ISBN: 978-1-61921-736-2

Editing by Amy Sherwood
Cover by Angela Waters

First Samhain Publishing, Ltd. electronic publication: March 2014
First Samhain Publishing, Ltd. print publication: March 2015

Acknowledgements

Publishing a book truly does take a village, and how fortunate I am that mine is filled with so very many generous and gifted people. I name but a few of them here.

To my editor, Amy Sherwood for her patience in waiting for the novel to be born as well as for her artful stewarding of the work from the first draft onward.

To my agent, Louise Fury of The Bent Agency, for being so unfailingly smart, supportive—and well, great.

To Tom Wareham, Curator of Maritime and Community History, The Museum of London, for his kind and comprehensive responses to my emailed questions on maritime routes between England and India during the Regency as well as his enormously helpful explanations on sundry and fascinating aspects of London's Docklands. Any errors here are, of course, wholly my own. (To wit, Regency enthusiasts will no doubt note that the Serpentine Bridge in Hyde Park was erected in 1826, six years after the start of my story proper).

Also, to my former research assistant and always friend, Julie—Jules—Kendrick, I will always cherish the memories of our days of historical fact-finding online in the pre-Google era.

Finally to my family, both biped and quadruped, for putting up with my disappearing into my office for hours—sometimes days—on end. As much as I adore hanging out with my swoon-worthy heroes and intrepid heroines, no creature of fiction can begin to touch my joy in spending time in the Real World with all of you.

Prologue

The East India Docks, Blackwall, London, April 1820

Home, finally I'm home.

Captain Robert Lazarus, formerly known as Robert Bellamy, stood on the ship's bridge. A hand upon the rudder, he steered the East Indiaman through the narrow neck of waterway leading into the harbor, prompting cheers of "Land, land!" and much waving of caps and brawny arms among his men. Once they'd made Spithead, he'd dismissed his pilot and taken the tiller himself. This was his last voyage, his swan's song upon The Swan—or so he hoped—and he'd felt a deep need to pilot her into his home port himself.

Ahead, the lock gate lifted. Beyond it, the bustling diorama of the London Docklands unfolded. Merchantmen similar to his craft crammed the berths, their cargo of sugar and spices, tea and Madeira wine offloaded under the watch of armed militiamen wearing company coats, the burly stevedores bearing their burdens toward the warehouses fronting the quay. Everything seemed busier than he remembered and vastly bigger. Was it truly so? He couldn't for certain say. Six years away had muddied his memory, erasing all but the most vital details—the silken feel of Phoebe's skin beneath his fingertips, the way her eyes mirrored the shifting hues of the London sky, the tangy taste of her tears when last they'd kissed, a kiss meant to convey not farewell but a brief goodbye.

And now he was finally home, home to England and, please God, home to Phoebe too, assuming she would have him. His welcome was in no way certain, his homecoming entirely unannounced. The letters he'd meant to send before setting sail from Madras had all perished before posting, crumpled balls of contrived explanations and tangled, torn-asunder half truths tossed missile style upon his cabin floor. Just as well. How *did* a man go about informing the woman he loved, the woman who'd waited not for the promised six months but instead six years that he wasn't drowned, dead, after all?

He would discover soon enough. Once he saw her, he would have his answer not from her lips but from her eyes. Phoebe's lips had been known to tell a fib or two in the service of saving someone's feelings, but her eyes never lied. Needing to see them now, he reached up and tugged his neck cloth free, fingertips feeling for the silver chain buried beneath the stock, the padlock-shaped locket housing his beloved's portrait in miniature resting against his breastbone. The keepsake, a match for the one he'd given her before leaving, had not left his person for six years barring the one terrible time when it had been torn from his throat.

"She's a pretty piece, your woman." Beneath the black satin mask, the corners of the pirate captain's mouth lifted. "What's her name?" he asked, toying with the locket lying open in his gloved palm. Though the band he led was Malagasy, his voice carried the vowels of Northern England.

Trussed, Robert managed to twist his head away from the slimy cabin wall. "I wouldn't have you foul it with your tongue." He gathered what precious little spittle he had left and spat, striking his tormentor square in the eye.

Not even the swathe of mask could conceal his captor's welling rage. The pirate wheeled about to the deckhand wielding the whip. "Lay on him and see you don't let up until he surrenders the slut's name or his last breath."

Fifty lashes in Robert broke. "Phoebe Tremont, Phoebe Tremont, Phoebe Tremont," he called out again and again, singsong fashion, almost as if he were a child reciting a nursery rhyme. Having finally succumbed to betraying her, he couldn't seem to stop. Laughing, they cut him down, dragged him back to his cell, and tossed him inside. Fevered and bleeding, he lay belly down on the filthy straw-strewn boards, his back on fire, the fractured remains of his half-mad mind fixed on a single thought.

I deserve to die.

Robert gripped the ship's wheel hard, squeezing the smooth wood until his tanned knuckles turned white, willing the damnable memory to retreat. Utter erasure, he owned, was an impossible dream. But there was one dream yet left to him, one that was as yet pure and untainted and unequivocally good.

Phoebe.

He slid the chain over his head and used the callused edge of his thumb to pry open the locket's hinged casing. His beloved's weather-spotted miniature stared up at him, the oval-shaped face by now as familiar as his own if not more so, the quicksilver gaze gentle yet direct, the high brow and aristocratic nose softened by a rosebud mouth parted in the slightest of smiles.

"So you won't forget what I look like," she'd said on their last day together in London before he'd let stubborn pride and the sea carry him away.

Swearing seamen's curses, Robert snapped the case closed and slipped the chain over his head. What a bloody idiot he'd been to even think of leaving her, an absolute fool to have done so. But he had. And now the dewy-eyed boy Phoebe had once loved enough to want to wed was every whit as dead as if he were indeed buried at the bottom of the sea. The man returning in his stead might wear his face and bear his name, yet he was a different beast entirely. A man who'd survived torture and near death to be sold at market like so much chattel, who'd labored as a beast of burden for more than two years before a kinder enslavement intervened, and had managed to survive it all, battered but not broken, dented but not done in. Could

Phoebe learn to love *that* man? Would she be willing to try?

Hoping so, Robert steered them into the dock basin. The lock lowered behind them, the barrier blocking off any last possibility of a hasty, reconsidered retreat. For a brief, dizzying moment he once more knew what it was to be caged, not by pirates or slavers or sinking ships but by the finality of his own irrevocable choices. In a few short hours he would stand face-to-face with Phoebe, not her silent, inanimate portrait but the living, breathing *her*. The thought sufficed to suck the moisture from his mouth, leaving his lips and tongue dry as sun-bleached bone. And yet in the midst of his mayhem, he allowed he wanted neither to retreat nor run, not now, not ever again.

The vacant berth lay just ahead. Resolved, he steered toward it. As he did, he felt a familiar presence at his back.

Without turning, he said, "Home, Caleb. This is my home, or at least it was."

The turbaned Arab approached, more than six feet of bronze skin and broad shoulders and communicative dark eyes; the latter served for the tongue the torturer had cut out. Since meeting in a granite quarry in Madagascar, they'd shared a food trough, a slop bucket and a mutual responsibility for one another's lives.

Joining him at the rail, Caleb acknowledged the statement with the barest of nods. Having met after Caleb's muting, Robert couldn't be certain of how much English his friend knew, yet the sympathy in the dark eyes meeting his seemed to say that "home" was understood.

Robert turned his gaze back to the harbor. It had been years since he'd prayed but now he sent up his silent plea to the heavens, to whatever deity yet might bide there.

Dear God, let her be well.

Dear God, let it not be too late.

Dear God, let her want me still.

Chapter One

Hanover Square, London

Phoebe poked another pin into the coil of wheat-colored hair at her nape and regarded her reflection in the cheval dressing glass. "Why Aristide must have a masque for our engagement ball baffles me utterly."

The costume ball may have been her betrothed's idea, but casting the entire Tremont family as personages from the Elizabethan era was her mother's doing. Phoebe's ensemble, a brocaded Italian silk meant to convey the character of the Scots Queen Mary Stuart, was proving to be both cumbersome and confining. The crinoline bolstering the bell-shaped skirt would make dancing a misery.

A dramatic sigh rose from the bed. "I think it's dreadfully romantic." Sprawled belly down on the quilted counterpane, her baby sister Belinda absently twirled the costume wig whilst from the floor Phoebe's spaniel Pippin monitored the spinning hair with rounded eyes. "I don't see why Mama must be such a stickler and banish me from attending. I *am* almost seventeen."

Phoebe studied the mutinous face in the mirror. With her honey-colored tresses and golden brown eyes, Belinda was a coltish beauty on the cusp of womanhood.

At times such as this she was also a royal pain in the rump.

Reaching for patience, Phoebe answered, "You should be counting your kind fortune. This costume is perfectly miserable. You could take my place for all I care."

Belinda's gaze lit. "Do you mean as Queen of Scotland or Countess of Beaumont?"

"That is the outside of enough. And by the by, do stop tormenting my dog."

Belinda snorted. "Egads but someone's touchy."

Phoebe turned back to her flushed reflection, alarmed by how Belinda's teasing had rattled her. Despite Aristide's pressing, she had yet to settle on a wedding date. Once their betrothal was announced at midnight, she would not be able to put him off any longer. She asked herself why she should wish to do so.

Because you're in love with a ghost, her inner voice answered for her.

Robert. Her heart hitched, the pain every whit as knife-sharp as it had been on that terrible day six years before when a representative from the East India Company had materialized on her doorstep bearing tidings of her beloved's demise. Robert's ship, The Phoenix, had foundered somewhere off the Comoros Islands. Her last correspondence from him had come by way of Capetown.

But time sallied forth, or so her mother never tired of telling her. Her little sister, Belinda, was little no longer. The girl would make her come out the next season. It was difficult to fathom. Phoebe's own presentation to society felt as though it had taken place merely yesterday for all that it had been eight years. How brimming with hope she'd been back then, how certain that a fairytale future was hers. Only the fairytale had ended the day Robert had boarded the doomed ship at Gravesend along with the Company's other new recruits, troops and supplies.

With two broken betrothals behind her, the courtship of Aristide Bouchart, Count of Beaumont, was greeted as a godsend and not only by her mother. They'd met at Almack's during the Little Season. The dashing French expatriate had settled his dark gaze upon her, forded a path across the crowded assembly room to where she'd stood holding up the wall with the other long-toothed misses and eagle-eyed matrons, and bespoken a dance. *'Tis my fortune he's after,* she'd told herself even as she'd allowed that the solid warmth of his hand at her back had felt uncommonly fine. Her mother's hasty conference with one of Almack's senior patronesses had laid that fear to rest. Unlike so many French émigrés fleeing Bonaparte's despotism, the count had managed to bring much of his wealth with him, which he'd invested in a profitable wine-importing venture. Strictly speaking, he'd gone into trade. But even a notorious snob such as Lady Tremont had been willing to overlook that less than desirable detail in the service of saving an elder daughter from spinsterhood.

Snarling sent her spinning about. Belinda let out a gasp and leapt off the bed. The sisters' gazes met and then fell to the rose-patterned carpet. Pippin stood on all fours, the very picture of pride, Phoebe's wig locked within his jaws.

"Naughty Pippin, give it over *now*," Belinda demanded, wagging her finger beneath the black button nose to no effect.

"I'd rather say you're the naughty one. You've been baiting him the entire time." Phoebe reached down to pull the thing free, but Pippin had his back arched, his ears pinned and the wig wedged between his canines. The resolve reflected in his chocolate-brown eyes assured her he was not yet prepared to relinquish his prize. Straightening, Phoebe blew out a breath. "You know he cannot be trusted with hair. Like as not he thinks it's another animal."

Belinda shrugged. "It's not my fault he's so badly behaved. You're the one who's spoiled him."

Spoiled—if that wasn't the pot calling the kettle black, Phoebe couldn't say what was. She fixed Belinda with her best imitation of their mother's glare. "He is as well behaved or better than certain bipeds I know. He may attack hair but at least *he* holds his whining to a minimum."

As if sensing he was no longer the center of attention, Pippin dropped the wig and hopped up onto the four-poster. Black lips pulled back in a yawn, he subsided onto his side, his brown and white head dropping like a stone to the fringed pillow.

Belinda stooped to pluck up the sodden, mangled mess. “Ewww.” Pulling a face, she dropped the ruined wig as if it were a hot coal.

Phoebe shook her head, which would remain wig-free for the evening. “Oh, bother it! I shall simply have to be a blonde Mary Queen of Scots.”

A sharp rap outside the chamber barely preceded the brass doorknob’s turning. Signaling Belinda to silence, she kicked the wig beneath the ruffled duster just as the door opened and their mother marched inside.

Fixing on a faux smile, Phoebe folded her hands and straightened. “Mama, how splendid you are.”

She nudged Belinda, who piped up, “Indeed, Mama, you look a picture.”

A picture, indeed! Wearing an elaborately teased and curled red wig and heavy face powder and rouge to portray the Tudor queen, Elizabeth, Lady Tremont sailed toward them, brocade skirts swishing.

“Phoebe, whatever can you be thinking to stand about woolgathering when your guests will be arriving at any moment?” Her scowl, fixed on Phoebe, threatened to crack the patina of face paint.

Phoebe paused, searching for an excuse that would skirt blaming both adorably spoiled dogs and peevish little sisters.

Before she could, Belinda broke in with, “Mayhap I could go below and greet them…that is, until Phoebe finishes dressing.”

Their mother shifted to Belinda, her gaze narrowing. “How many times must I tell you that you may not appear at evening events until your come out?”

Belinda’s face fell. “But Mama—”

“No buts.” Lady Tremont cut her off with a sharp look. “Now off with you. Your governess informs me you have lessons yet to finish. No man wishes to marry an ignoramus.”

"Yes, Mama." Belinda shuffled toward the door, her ordinarily proud carriage slipping.

Though mere moments ago Phoebe had felt like throttling her sibling, seeing Belinda so dejected had her ready to do battle. She waited for the door to close before starting in with, "Really Mother, an ignoramus? That was beyond harsh. She only wants to be included. Why not allow her downstairs for the first hour at least? It would mean so very much to her and it *is* my engagement ball."

"Stuff and feathers," Lady Tremont snorted, nostrils flaring as though the suggested breach of propriety had released a noxious odor into the room. "I won't have it said I allowed Belinda to run amok *too*. No man wants a wilding for a wife."

Phoebe was well aware her mother considered her to be a black sheep and yet the implication that she might have harmed Belinda's chances hurt. "An ignoramus and a wilding—good gracious, what a pair Belinda and I are! Poor Mama, to be saddled with such derelict daughters hardly seems just."

Lady Tremont sniffed. "Really, Phoebe, your sense of humor grows queerer by the day. I suppose it's no wonder given the low company you keep at that horrid hospital."

Even considering the source, the barb stung. Phoebe had begun volunteering at the London Foundling Hospital for something to do, as a reason to rise, bathe and dress in a world that no longer held Robert. Helping to put a smile on the face of a formerly forlorn boy or girl had proven the very best medicine for her grieving heart. Her tutoring and fundraising work had catapulted from a crutch to a raison d'être.

"Quite, Mama. Fraternizing with orphaned children is terribly shocking, is it not? Can frequenting brothels be far behind?"

Even her mother was wise enough to admit defeat upon occasion. Turning the topic, she dropped her gaze to Phoebe's throat and scowled. "Must you wear that trifle tonight of all nights?"

Phoebe covered the padlock-shaped locket, Robert's parting gift, with a protective hand. "It is not a trifle to me, Mama," she said, throat thick.

Indeed, it was one of the few mementos she had of her first and still only love. That Robert's drowned body likely still wore the mate bearing her miniature might seem morbid to some, but the notion had brought Phoebe comfort even on her darkest days. She only regretted that there hadn't been time before he sailed to have him painted as well. Instead she'd made do with a lock of his hair.

"It is *silver*," her mother hissed as though the metal was something foul. "A lady should never lower herself to wear less than gold."

The locket was summarily removed and whisked away. Brisk strides carried her ladyship to the dresser atop which Phoebe's rosewood jewelry case sat. Without asking, she lifted the lid, dropped the maligned locket inside, and rifled through the velvet-lined compartments. An "Ah ha" announced she'd located the object of her search. She closed the case and whirled about, the heavy gold chain bearing Aristide's betrothal gift, a ruby ring set in gold filigree, resting in her gloved palm.

She stepped behind Phoebe, their full skirts battling for space. "You really must find a moment to have this fitted so that you may wear it properly."

Ornate and unwieldy, the band swam upon her finger. Handsome piece though the betrothal present was, Phoebe had never cared for it. Or perhaps it was what it signified that she didn't care for—giving herself to a man other than Robert.

For now, she settled for a dutiful nod. "Yes, of course, Mama."

The gold chain, another gift from Aristide, was heavy upon her breast, the ring resting just above her cleavage. A snap announced the clasp's closing.

Her mother crossed to Phoebe's front. Features relaxing now that she had won her way, she cupped Phoebe's chin. "You are fortunate, my darling. You have been spared spinsterhood and given a rare and precious second chance to lead a normal life as a wife and mother. Cease mooning for a man who never came close to worthy of you and instead count your blessings: a titled fiancé who adores you, a house filled with guests to celebrate your engagement and a mother who has labored tirelessly all these many years to see you happily settled." She dropped her hand and stepped back. "Now put on your wig and come downstairs before your guests arrive. Aristide awaits you."

Phoebe opened her mouth to confess the wig's ruin and then clamped it closed. What would be the point? "I shall be but a moment more."

Seemingly satisfied, Lady Tremont turned to go. Watching her depart, Phoebe fingered the ruby. Though she quite liked rubies, this particular gemstone never failed to bring chills skittering the span of her spine. Resolved, she reached both hands behind her. After several tries, she got the clasp open. Freed, she carried the chain and ring over to the dresser and dropped the lot inside the case.

I may marry, Mama, but I shall do so on my terms.

Yes, she must ford into her future but doing so need not mean that the past be buried entirely. Robert and their love would always hold a permanent place in her heart. Considering the momentous step she was poised to take, she needed to feel as though she carried a part of him with her. Putting his padlock locket back on, she almost fancied he was near enough to watch over her.

Outside the Tremont townhouse, Robert handed over his horse to a liveried footman and joined the crowd of masked guests pouring out onto the torch-lit walkway. Carriages clogged the square, the queue backing up traffic to the main road. A ball, a masque, was apparently underway. Witches and warlocks mingled with kings and queens in the throng making its way toward the classically columned entrance. Orchestra music wafted out the open windows, the front rooms lit to a high glow. So much for the poignant private reunion he'd planned. Glancing down at himself, he was suddenly conscious of the mud caking his boots and the road dust clinging to his clothes. Other than the anise he'd chewed on the way over to calm his nervous stomach and freshen his breath, he was scarcely in a fit state for mingling in society.

An older couple dressed in the powdered wigs of the previous century sidled up. "Must we really leave so soon?" the woman whined, her scowl causing the velvet heart-shaped patch below her mouth to droop. "Everyone knows the engagement is to be announced at midnight."

Engagement! Robert's heart picked up pace. When he'd left England, Phoebe's brother Reggie had been a gadabout bachelor and her baby sister Belinda not yet eleven. Then again six years had passed. Either sibling might well be wedding, yet another marker of how much time he'd lost. He cocked his head to the side, straining to hear more.

"I can't abide that crush a moment more, let alone 'til midnight. This damnable wig has me scratching like a hound with fleas." Pulling off his black felt mask, the gentleman swiped a gloved hand across his sweat-beaded brow.

Plucking at her gown's panniers, the woman sighed. "Very well, Herbert, I suppose you must win your way. It's not as though she's a chit fresh from the schoolroom. Given her age and history, Lady Phoebe should count herself fortunate to have snared any offer at all."

Phoebe...marrying! Robert's heart skidded to a stop.

"To my thinking," the man replied, "the poor gel's due for a bit of happiness even if the bridegroom is a Frog."

A Frog! Phoebe was wedding a Frenchman?

"Aristide Bouchart, Count of Beaumont sounds very grand, don't you think?" The woman's approving tone implied it wasn't a question. "They say he comes from one of France's ancient lines only his family lost their lands and most of their fortune to the Terror."

An aristocrat, bloody hell!

"He's made a good bit of it back—the fortune, that is."

"By going into trade." The woman's shudder sent the flesh of her bared shoulders wobbling like a pudding released from its skein.

The pair paused, eyeing him with open admiration. Edging toward Robert, the man cleared his throat. "Bloody good costume, that."

The matron nodded. "There's another pirate within, but he can't hold a candle to you."

Another...*pirate*?

Since putting into port, Robert had found himself the recipient of similar stares though at first he'd assumed the interest must be directed at Caleb. Now he understood otherwise. From what he'd so far seen riding through the city, men's fashion had sobered substantially since he'd last seen London. With his scarlet silk, flowing sleeves and broad-brimmed hat festooned with feathers, he must stand out like a peacock—or a sore thumb.

Mastering himself, he found his tongue. "Thank you." Thoughts churning, he divided his gaze between them. "The only article my...*costume* lacks is a mask. By the time I realized I'd left it behind, it was too late to turn back." He focused on the man pulling at his periwig. "I don't suppose you might be persuaded to part with yours? I would of course compensate you for its worth."

The man shoved the mask into his hands. "My good fellow, I will gladly give it over for the pleasure of never having to wear it again."

"You are too kind, sir." Robert accepted the beribboned black felt with a bow. Straightening, he glimpsed the wilted square of vellum in the man's gloved hand. "The dashed thing is

I've left my invitation behind as well."

The husband, Herbert, broke into a broad grin. "In that case, take ours." Ignoring his wife's warning look, he added, "Ordinarily I would not think to hand it over to an unknown person, but I can discern from your speech and manners that you are a gentleman of the utmost character and breeding." Leaning in, he confided, "But I must warn you 'tis hot as Hades in there, a most damnable crush. Are you quite certain you're up for it?"

Robert tucked the vellum inside his breast pocket. "Indeed, sir, I don't think I've been more ready in all my days."

Phoebe accepted a glass of iced lemonade from a circulating footman and passed it to her father. "Here, Papa, drink this. It will revive you."

Accepting the beverage, Lord Tremont swiped a crimson-slashed sleeve across his perspiring brow. "The only thing that will revive me is release from this bloody costume." Between the starched lace riding high at his throat, heavy doublet coat and skintight hose, he was the very picture of misery as well as a less than convincing Lord Robert Dudley. Phoebe felt sincerely sorry for him.

"You could well do so, but I believe there is already one Lady Godiva in attendance," she quipped, hoping to tease him into a better humor.

He spared her a brief smile and then twisted inside his ruff to look about the room. "Your mother is adamant on holding off on serving supper until after the announcement is made. I cannot fathom where that fiancé of yours has got to."

Aristide had partnered her in the opening reel and promptly repaired to the card room. She more than suspected he was as yet there, savoring his beloved brandy and cheroots, oblivious to the passage of time.

Heart in her throat, she patted the top of his arm. "Do not fret, Papa. I shall find him directly."

She turned away before he might see how close to crying she was. How different this was from her other betrothal ball held in this very room six years before. How young and in love she and Robert had been, how eager he to maneuver her out onto the balcony so that he might entreat her to elope. If only she might relive that night, she'd gladly follow him to Gretna Green, Calcutta or the Earth's end. But, alas, one couldn't go back...

Eyes welling, she headed for the balcony to collect herself before seeking out Aristide. Dodging well-wishers, she gained the suite of French doors. Stepping out, she closed them behind her with very real relief.

The garden lay below, lit by torches and strings of Chinese lanterns much as it had been six years ago, the breeze sweetened by early blooming roses and the honeysuckle intertwining the trelliswork. She crossed to the rail, reaching it as the first angry tear splashed her cheek.

Oh, Robert, if only...

The costuming, the music and collective chatter, the ceaseless press of people wishing her happy when she felt anything but, was suddenly all too much. Feeling as though she might suffocate, she pulled at her mask, the surprisingly sturdy ribbons resisting snapping.

"Bloody, bloody, *bloody* hell."

She tore the accursed thing off, hauled back and pitched it over the ironwork, the force straining her gown's seams. Breathing hard, she gripped the ironwork and looked over. The fit of temper, better worthy of Belinda, had reaped the intended and instantly regretted result. Beyond reach in the thorns, her mask was as good as gone.

"Whoa! Whoever he is, he's not worth it."

Phoebe let out a gasp and spun about, her backside

bumping the balustrade.

A tall man costumed as a pirate pushed away from the plasterwork column against which he must have been leaning. "You would fare far better with a lover who makes you laugh than one who makes you curse—and cry," he added, stepping into the cone of colored light.

Beyond mortified, Phoebe dashed a quick hand across her damp eyes, hoping he might at least miss that much of her shame. "Sir, you should have made your presence known."

One dark brow arched upward. "I believe I am doing just that."

A gentleman would apologize for the intrusion and excuse himself to go inside. He, however, showed no sign of budging. Arms folded over his broad chest and legs akimbo, he stood his ground, raking her with his gaze. Stunned by his boldness, Phoebe studied his lantern-lit face. Who did he imagine himself to be? More importantly, who *was* he? His broad-brimmed hat with its extravagant plume and form-fitting doublet coat were not the standard fare found in costuming shops. He must have taken the invitation's call for authenticity seriously indeed, for his leather breeches and riding boots wore a cannily real-looking coating of dust.

As foolish as she felt, still she forced her shoulders back and her chin high. "I do not care for being spied upon."

Beneath the hat, his brow beetled. "Spied upon?" He let out a guffaw. "I've been standing in plain view all along."

Phoebe hated to admit it, but he had fact on his side. Given the way she'd barreled out, it was a mercy she hadn't plowed into him.

Still, she refused to be cowed. "You are forward, sir." She lifted her chin another notch. "And rude."

And handsome as sin, or so he seemed from what she'd so far surveyed. The throat of his silk shirt lay indecently open, the undone buttons revealing a muscular neck banded by a fine silver chain similar to hers. Even in the low light, she marked the darkness of his skin. Gentleman though he undoubtedly was, he must spend a great deal of time out-of-doors.

"You wound me, lady." He fell back, pantomiming pulling an invisible dagger from his pectoral. In contrast, the wicked-looking curved sword tucked into the crimson sash at his waist looked frighteningly real. "You'd be better served to save your ire for another—the one who made you weep."

Robert. Robert made me weep. And yet she could hardly fault a dead man for being dead any more than she could a living man for failing to live up to him whom she so dearly loved.

A square of snowy linen appeared in one bare, broad-backed hand. "Please," he said, passing it to her, his eyes no longer mocking but softened by what seemed to be concern.

Phoebe hesitated and then accepted the handkerchief, acknowledging the courtesy with a small, silent nod. He was barehanded, highly irregular considering the formality of the affair. Their fingertips brushed and gloved though she was, still she felt a tiny tremor trill through her.

"All brides cry," she snapped, blotting at her eyes with the hankie, the cotton so soft and finely woven as to be Egyptian. "It's...*tradition.*" The latter was a lame excuse but she couldn't think of what else to say. Indeed, with his eyes fastened upon her, she could scarcely think at all.

His smile froze. "I wouldn't know. I've never had the pleasure of being leg-shackled."

So he was a bachelor. That tidbit of intelligence lifted her spirits far more than it ought. "In that case, you're hardly in a position to be offering romantic advice."

"I suppose you are correct on that count." Framed by black felt, his bold gaze perused her, the thorough inventory beginning and ending with her eyes.

Handing back the hankie, Phoebe eyed the sword at his

side and a hopeful thought struck her. "Perhaps you might employ your weapon to retrieve my mask from those bushes below. I…dropped it," she added, the bald lie brought on by his steady stare.

His crack of laughter flared heat into her face. "The devil you did. You tossed it over the rail out of pique." Phoebe opened her mouth to protest, but his chuckle cut her off. "By the by, you've an impressive arm for a woman. Beyond my sister, I've never seen the like on any female." One corner of his mouth, his full, sensuous mouth, curved upwards. Phoebe's heart hitched. She hadn't seen a smile like that in…a very long time.

More put out with herself than him, sharply she asked, "Will you help me or not?"

"Since you implore so charmingly, how can I refuse?" He turned to the rail, braced both hands atop and peered below.

Coming up beside him, Phoebe tried not to notice how ungodly good he smelled. Not like Aristide, who had a heavy hand with bottled scent, or the other gentlemen of her acquaintance, but rather like leather and sandalwood and the musk of male sweat. And his breath bore the faintest aroma of what must be licorice. "It's just there," she said, pointing to the thorny bower upon which it perched, her shoulder inadvertently brushing his side.

He nodded. "Aye, I see it." One hand on his sword hilt, he took a step back. "Stand away," he ordered, gaze no longer on her but on his quarry.

For the first time in years, Phoebe obeyed without question. As soon as she'd moved, he unsheathed his weapon and stabbed it into the bushes below, neatly hooking her mask on the tip.

He pivoted, presenting the mask with a bow. "Milady."

Phoebe hesitated and then plucked the mask from the sharp blade point. Amazingly, the fabric had escaped so much as a tear. "You have my gratitude, sir," she said, meaning it. Her life seemed to be filled with a surfeit of men of words but standing before her was, at long last, a man of action.

Straightening, he sheathed his sword. "If there are other articles of clothing with which I can assist, please do not hesitate to ask." A roguish smile accompanied the wicked offer.

That smile seemed to suck the breath from Phoebe's lungs. "You are most adept with your sword, sir, but I believe that shall suffice." Dear Lord, had she really said that?

A flash of even, white teeth greeted her gaffe. "For now, perhaps, but should you desire another...demonstration, I shall be happy to oblige."

Horrified, she hastened to add, "Your costume is quite impressive. Are you meant to be a pirate or a privateer?"

His gaze anchored to hers. "Is there a difference?"

If there was, her suddenly swimming thoughts were no longer capable of deciphering it. Instead she directed her gaze to the blade hanging from his hip. "Pirate or privateer, you look frightfully authentic. Have you experience at sea?"

He hesitated as if weighing his words. "Some." He tilted his head and studied her, his gaze traveling over her yet again, taking in every detail of the hideous costume and, she suspected, mentally mapping the body beneath. "My schoolroom days were long ago. I cannot think who you are meant to be."

A pearl of perspiration slid between her breasts though the night air was cool. "Mary Stuart, the Scots queen."

She held back from saying more, wishing she might stop imagining how lovely it would feel to have his rough-looking hands free her from her stays, wondering how, after six years of feeling so very frozen and fallow, a few flirting exchanges could warm her into a wanton.

He frowned. "Poor student though I was, still I recall that lady as being a redhead. And yet your hair is as fair as the moon above."

He reached out and lifted a stray strand from her shoulder.

Tucking it behind her ear, his fingers brushed the line of her jaw. It was a glancing caress, a whisper of a touch, and yet Phoebe caught her breath, liquid warmth sliding the length of her spine.

Throat dry, she answered, "I had a wig, but it too met with a...mishap."

"Did you hurl it into the bushes as well?"

"No. My...my dog ate it." She sounded more of a dimwit by the moment, and yet she'd begun enjoying herself far too much to care.

He chuckled. "I would have thought a dripping beef bone would be more to Pippin's fancy."

Phoebe's breath stalled. "How do you know my dog's name?" Whoever he was, he must be more than a passing acquaintance.

"I have known the beast since he was a whelp." His gaze scoured her face. "Can you not look past this mask and see me for who I am?"

She searched her muddled memory. In most cases, the men's costumes provided only the thinnest veneer of disguise. Earlier she'd easily recognized the portly Bacchus as Cubby Whitebridge and the tall Cupid as Lord Percy. Might he be one of her brother Reggie's friends? Despite his flirting and bad manners, he hardly seemed a fit for that libertine lot.

Shaking her head, she admitted, "I am afraid I am at a loss. I must accept defeat if only until midnight."

His mask made it hard to tell for certain, but she thought he frowned.

"What happens at midnight?"

She hesitated. Thinking of her soon-to-be-announced betrothal, she was alarmingly loath to end this lovely interlude by owning it. "The call will be given to unmask and the guests will go in to supper."

"And if I decline to part with mine?"

"You must. It is the rule."

He reached for her hand. Feeling as though she'd slipped into a trance, Phoebe surrendered it. "I despise rules."

Gaze locked on hers, he carried her hand to his mouth. His lips brushed along the line of her gloved knuckles, the light contact stirring an all but forgotten fluttering. Phoebe sucked in an uneven breath. "You, that is we should not—"

He turned her hand palm up and pressed a deeper kiss to the pulse point inside her wrist.

Feeling the graze of teeth, she snatched her hand away. Dallying out-of-doors with a stranger, allowing him to fondle her, what had overtaken her? "As soon as my fiancé can be found, my father will announce our betrothal."

Scowling, he demanded, "And does your fiancé often desert you at such monumental moments?"

The remark struck uncomfortably close to the truth. Stiffening, she answered, "He is in the card room along with my brother and a great many other gentlemen."

He leaned in as though to share a confidence. "Were you my bride, Lakshmi herself could not lure me from your side."

"Lakshmi?"

"The Hindu goddess charged with doling out wealth and good fortune." Smiling, he hesitated. "Lady Luck, if you prefer."

His breath was a balmy breeze against her cheek, his lips a promise waiting to be fulfilled. Alarmed by how easy it would be to tip her face and match her mouth to his, she lifted her mask. "I must go back inside before I am missed." Assuming her mother had not raised the hue and cry already. Since she'd stepped out, time had seemed to halt.

"Must you?" His hand wrapping lightly about her wrist stayed her. "Aren't you forgetting something?"

Phoebe hesitated. Other than her morals, what had she possibly forgotten?

"I retrieved your mask. What favor shall I claim in

repayment?" His gaze slid to her mouth, bringing a burst of heat blooming in her lower belly.

"Handsome as sin" took on sudden new meaning. Legs wobbly, Phoebe stepped back, nearly tripping on her heavy train. "A good deed is its own reward, is it not?" She'd been mistaken earlier. He wasn't a pirate or a privateer. He was Mephistopheles, the Devil incarnate.

"Is it?" He flashed another blindingly beautiful smile. "Mind you, I *am* a pirate."

The ballroom doors opened. Sound and light poured onto the patio. "Ah, *chérie*, I have found you at last."

Heart plummeting, Phoebe pivoted toward Aristide as he stepped out.

He made his way over to join them, his black domino catching on the breeze, the sight putting Phoebe in mind of a bat rather than the raven prince he was meant to portray. An elaborately plumed mask covered all but the lower third of his face. The muscle jumping in his jaw confirmed he was not happy with her.

"It is nearing midnight. Your father is most eager to announce our betrothal."

Feeling oddly bolstered by the stranger bearing up behind her, she answered, "Yes, I know. I have searched the four corners for you."

Aristide's gaze bore into her. "And yet I find you not within but out...here with..." He gestured with his gloved fingers rimmed in rings to indicate the pirate who'd stepped up to her side. "Will you not introduce our guest?"

Heart thrumming, she waited for the pirate to announce himself. Surely he didn't mean to adhere to some silly midnight rule. Rules, for this man, hardly seemed to exist.

Instead he stayed silent. Left with no choice, Phoebe admitted, "I am afraid I have yet to persuade this gentleman to give up his name."

Aristide's sanguine smile slipped. "Let us have done with this farce. Unmask yourself, *monsieur.*"

Ignoring him, the pirate turned to Phoebe. His gaze locked upon hers, trapping her in a private world that seemed to contain only the two of them. "You are quite certain you do not know me...*Phoebe*?"

The unsanctioned intimacy rocked Phoebe to her core. More jarring still was how very right, how very *familiar* it felt to hear her name on his lips.

Gaze holding hers, he removed his hat and set it upon the post. Wavy dark hair stirred in the breeze, the unfashionably long tresses curling about his collar. From his left ear, a diamond winked like a small star. Brawny arms reached up to untie the silk ribbons holding his mask in place. The felt fell away.

Colored light splashed familiar chiseled features: a high brow, slightly crooked nose, full mouth and squared jaw that Phoebe knew not only by sight but by touch. But it was his eyes to which she kept returning. A dead man's eyes, a ghost's eyes...

Robert's eyes.

Eyes that despite the darkness she knew were the color of amber. Like a fly caught in that sticky resin, she was powerless to move or so much as look away and yet her numbed lips somehow managed to murmur, "This isn't real... You are not...real."

The specter shook his head. "This is real. *I* am real, a living man forged of flesh and blood," he swore, his breath, his *living* breath, brushing across her lips, his eyes not the hollow, flat gaze of a ghost but enticingly warm.

There was but one way to be certain.

Phoebe lifted a trembling hand to his cheek. Sandpapery stubble grazed her fingers, a day's worth of beard. His scent and warmth were wrenchingly familiar, the white scar splitting his chin a foreign thing. Too caught up to question how he might have come by it, she traced its thickness with her thumb. He flinched.

"Do I hurt you?" she asked, drawing away.

Expression stoic, he shook his head. "No, you but undo me with your gentleness." His own hands remained solidly at his sides though the heaving of his chest, broader than she remembered, suggested that the self-restraint exacted a toll she couldn't begin to comprehend.

Aristide stepped between them. "Phoebe, *arrêtez*!" The admonition to stop came in a whoosh of hot, brandied breath.

But Phoebe had no intention of stopping. If this was a haunting, she hoped with all her heart it might never end. Ignoring him, she moved to trace her ghost lover's mouth, the lips that once had matched hers to perfection. Everywhere she touched felt neither airy light nor marble cold, but warm and solid and thrumming with life.

Letting her hand fall away, she took a step back, aware that not only her limbs but her whole body had begun shaking. Her ghost lover was no ghost at all but a flesh-and-blood man.

"Robert," she said, almost a whisper, as if she were at prayer. In a way, she was.

He swallowed, a long ripple traveling the muscled column of his throat. "Aye, 'tis I, and I've sailed many a league to make my way back to you."

He reached inside his open shirt and drew out a silver chain. Hanging from the end was yet another object she'd thought never again to see, the locket fashioned in the form of a padlock, its engraved casing an identical match to hers.

Phoebe took a wavering step away, the stone floor seeming to suck at her slippers, the night exploding into a swirling chaos of stars and stabbing lights. Suddenly the balcony seemed to be spinning.

"Phoebe!" Robert's call came from a faraway place, an echo

from the storm-tossed abyss into which she was fast falling.

For the first time in six years, Lady Phoebe Tremont fainted.

Chapter Two

Robert caught Phoebe against him. Hairpins pinged onto the stone flagging as he lifted her into his arms, her lithe form as slack as a sack of feathers. Head resting against his shoulder, she released a sigh.

The fiancé threw back his domino and tore off his mask. He wore his black hair fashionably cropped, the fringe combed low over his forehead, framing a florid-featured face more arresting than handsome. A stubborn mouth curved into a sneer. Deep-set dark eyes raked over Robert. He fixed his gaze on the Frenchman and glared back. Standing toe-to-toe, they took one another's measure. Robert didn't move save for the telltale muscle in his jaw which had begun ticking fiercely. Likewise the hairs at the neck of his neck stood at full alert. Phoebe's fiancé was a stranger and yet Robert couldn't shake the sense that they'd met before. That was ludicrous, of course. He could count upon the fingers of one hand the Frenchmen he knew. This one he would have remembered.

"So you are the brash young lover returned from the dead?" the Frenchman finally said.

"And you are the devoted fiancé returned from the card room," Robert shot back, not a question.

"Aristide Bouchart, seventh Comte de Beaumont." Black-shod heels clicked together. "I will take my bride now, if you please." He stretched out arms which were well built but not particularly powerful.

Robert had no intention of relinquishing Phoebe, not now, not ever. "And if I do not please?"

A strained smile answered the challenge. "Then, *monsieur*,

we find ourselves...at odds."

"A score I shall look forward to settling in the very near future," Robert assured him. If pistols at dawn proved the sole solution to securing Phoebe's freedom, then so be it.

"Unhand my daughter, you rogue."

The strident female voice ended their standoff. Both men turned to see the balcony doors once more opening.

Costumed as Elizabeth, the Virgin Queen, Lady Tremont stepped out onto the terrace. A pudgy Elizabethan-era courtier followed, drawing the doors closed behind them. Apart from the red wig and white face paint, she was exactly as Robert recalled her—straight-backed, iron-eyed and fire-breathing.

Supporting Phoebe in his arms limited his salutatory courtesies to a spare nod. "Your ladyship will forgive me if I do not bow. Or ought I to say Your Highness?" he added in deference to her costume. Trust Phoebe's mother to use her daughter's betrothal as an opportunity to ascend to sovereign status.

Her penciled eyebrows shot to her wig's hairline. "Bellamy, can it be you? But...you were to have drowned!"

He nodded. "Indeed, madam, it pains me to once again disappoint and yet I am quite alive as you can see. I am gratified to find you likewise hale and hearty."

Her gaze narrowed. "Don't think to cozen me with your honeyed words. You've never given a fig for my health and well I know it." Her gaze dipped to Phoebe's head resting against his shoulder. "Nor would it seem you greatly care for my daughter's; otherwise you would not have intruded to spoil her chances once again." Her gaze flickered to Bouchart and an anxious look eclipsed the scowl.

The Frenchman answered with an oily smile. "*Au contraire,* the present unpleasantness only fortifies my resolve to make your daughter my bride." He glanced over at Robert. "That is, provided *Monsieur* Bellamy can be persuaded to part with her."

Lady Tremont shifted to Robert. "Unless a surfeit of seawater has rendered you deaf, you heard well enough. Hand over my daughter or I'll have my butler set the dogs on you."

There'd been a time when the flimsy threat would have cowed Robert, but not so now. "I very much doubt you keep hounds at your town residence, milady. Now pray direct me to where we are least likely to encounter your guests...unless, of course, you do not care about what scandal broth is stirred," he added, well knowing she dreaded social disgrace as others did plague and pestilence.

Silent ere now, Lord Tremont stepped up to them. He hesitated and then laid a hand on either man's shoulder. "Let us defer any further argument until we can be private. I've bid my butler summon the guests into supper. As soon as the room is emptied, we shall bear Phoebe within and upstairs to my study. It is the one chamber kept locked at all times."

Sincerely grateful for his lordship's calm composure and sound sense, Robert nodded. "Thank you, milord."

They stood in strained silence a moment more, waiting for the music to cease. It did, and seconds later a bell sounded. Several minutes more passed, taken up with shuffling footfalls, collective conversations punctuated by the occasional exclamation or titter and the swish of fine fabrics as the guests were herded away.

Wilson, the Tremont butler, poked his graying head out onto the balcony. "The room is clear," he said in a low monotone. "I have posted two footmen outside the supper room doors with strict instructions to see that no one is permitted to leave until you have passed."

"Good man, Wilson." Lord Tremont turned back to Robert. "Shall we?"

Robert inclined his head. "Lead the way, my lord."

Wilson held the door, and they filed inside. Other than the musicians packing their instruments, the chamber was deserted. Following Lord Tremont, Robert cut across the columned ballroom, Aristide and Lady Tremont bringing up the rear, their heels clicking on the parquet floor. The pier glasses interspersed among the four walls reflected their tense faces as they whisked past. A dollop of wax from the crystal chandelier caught Robert on the forearm. Lest Phoebe be similarly splashed, he stepped swiftly to the right.

The sudden jolting sent Phoebe stirring. Throat knotting, Robert dared a look down. When he'd first arrived, he'd glimpsed her from the breadth of the ballroom. Despite her mask and the densely packed crowd separating them, he'd known her on sight. Standing on the outskirts of the dance floor whilst she waltzed by in the arms of her fiancé had tested his fortitude—and his temper. The meeting on the balcony hadn't been entirely contrived. He'd sought refuge there to clear his head before approaching her. Once she'd stepped out, it had been too dark to discern her in detail. Now, beneath the bright light of the massed candles and with no cover to conceal her, for the first time in six years he looked upon her in plain view.

She hadn't changed, not really. Her face was the same flawless oval the miniaturist had captured so cannily, her complexion paler than he remembered but every whit as petal-smooth. Her bow-shaped mouth looked as luscious and kissable as he recalled it; likewise her cheekbones were the same high arcs, her chin somewhat less rounded. The only discernible difference was her hair. The cropped curls had grown into waist-length waves that slid over his forearm like a skein of wheat-colored silk.

Coming up behind him, Lady Tremont hissed, "I cannot imagine where or how you have been keeping yourself these past years, but once you set my daughter down, you are never to lay your paws upon her again."

Dropping his voice, he replied, "That is for Phoebe to decide."

A brace of footmen stood guard outside the supper room. Laughter and collective conversation filtered out from behind the barred doors. Robert had been a guest sufficient times to have a basic memory of the interior, and he remembered a certain side door used by servants for moving unseen and unheard between the private and public rooms. Lord Tremont headed toward it. Grabbing a candle from a bracketed wall sconce, he ducked inside the passageway and started up a steep flight of bare wooden stairs. Robert followed, keenly aware of the gazes boring into his back and the footfalls trailing his heels.

They came out into an open hallway. A swift look below to the tiled foyer showed it to be empty of all but two family footmen. Seemingly satisfied that they remained unobserved, Lord Tremont continued toward the arched door at the opposite end of the hall. Coming upon it, he reached inside his padded doublet and produced a cluster of keys. The click of the lock and the creak of the opening door struck Robert as deafening amidst the hush. Holding the door, Lord Tremont stood back for him to enter. Brushing past his lordship, Robert rushed Phoebe inside.

Apart from the new tooled leather paper-hangings, Lord Tremont's study was as Robert remembered it, the same floor-to-ceiling bookshelves, the substantial Chippendale desk with its green baize blotter, the aroma of cigars marking it as the sole masculine sanctum in a house otherwise filled with fragile porcelains, dainty furnishings and prim pastels. He'd seen the inside of this room only once before, six years earlier, when he'd first sought Phoebe's hand. The man-to-man interview had gone far better than Robert had dared hope. Setting aside his reservations concerning Robert's lower birth and lack of fortune, his lordship had granted them his blessing, much to his wife's chagrin.

Hopeful of ending this evening with a likewise-happy result, Robert crossed the Turkish carpet to the velvet-covered sofa. Stooping, he settled Phoebe onto the cushions and slid his arm free from beneath her. As if sensing his withdrawal, she shivered. Subsiding onto his knees beside her, he battled a piercing sense of loss. Though he'd held her but briefly, his unburdened arms felt abysmally empty.

Leaning over, he cupped the sweet curve of her cheek, inwardly cursing the wretched calluses that kept him from fully feeling the satiny texture of her skin. "Phoebe, love, awake," he coaxed, willing her eyelids to lift.

Once she revived what might her feelings be? The few words she'd spoken before her faint had been those of a woman deep in shock. With her wits returned, might she feel less than tender toward him? Lest he forget, she'd been poised to promise herself to another.

"Step aside, you scalawag." Pushing past, Lady Tremont produced a small vial from her gown's hidden pocket. She pulled out the stopper and Robert rocked back upon his ankles. The reek was reminiscent of rotted egg and ammonia—smelling salts.

She passed the bottle beneath Phoebe's nose. Coughing, Phoebe came awake, her eyes shooting open. "Have done, Mama, I p-pray you." Batting the bottle away, she pushed herself up on one elbow. Her watery gaze alighted on Robert, widening if not in delight then certainly in surprise. "So I wasn't dreaming."

Heartened, he braced his hands upon the sofa side and leaned closer. "No, love, you were not."

Lady Tremont whirled on him, her stiff skirts clipping him on the chin. "How dare you address my daughter as though she were your doxy! She is the nearest thing to a married woman. Now leave us and see you do not darken our door ever again."

Rising to his full height, Robert glared down at her. "I'm not going anywhere, not until Phoebe and I have spoken—in private." Seeking support, he looked to Lord Tremont but Phoebe's father had taken refuge behind his desk and was making an intense study of the jade paperweight in his palm.

Her ladyship sniffed. "If you are suggesting we leave our

daughter sans chaperone and quite alone with you, it is out of the question."

"No, Mama, it is not." All heads, including Robert's, turned to Phoebe. "Now leave us. *All* of you," she added, her quicksilver gaze settling on her mother. She might appear as fragile as a hothouse blossom, yet Robert sensed a steely strength in her that had not shown itself before.

Aristide shoved away from the wainscoted wall and sauntered over toward them. Once again Robert was sensible of a sharp stab of something more than rivalry—wariness. "You are as yet in shock, *ma petite.* Permit yourself to be guided by those who have your best interest at heart." The dagger glare he shot in Robert's direction signified his exclusion from that select circle.

Phoebe brought her feet to the floor and sat upright. Smoothing her skirts, she lifted her face to Bouchart. "I thank you for your concern, my lord, but pray you be assured I do not require guiding."

A muscle jumped in the Frenchman's jaw; otherwise he appeared perfectly composed. "I suppose it would be cruel to refuse such a touching reunion." His hooded gaze flickered to Robert. "Provided it is in the service of saying *adieu*, I shall not interfere further."

Lord Tremont put down the paperweight and crossed to the desk's front. "They have not seen one another for six years. I for one mean to give the lad a chance to say his piece. Without an audience," he added, casting a meaningful look to his hovering wife.

"Really, Tremont, I—"

"Come along, m'dear. Taking firm possession of her elbow, he towed her toward the door. One hand on the brass knob, he turned back inside. "Given the highly unusual circumstances, Bouchart, you will understand that I must delay announcing your betrothal."

A stormy look greeted the paternal pronouncement but,

catching Robert's eye, the Frenchman swiftly assembled his features into an affable mask. "But of course you must do as you feel best, *mon père*. Phoebe and I shall be guided by your wisdom."

Sickened by Bouchart's unctuous display, Robert turned to Phoebe's father. "Thank you, sir. Your faith in me will not prove misplaced."

Keeping an arm about his wife, Lord Tremont met his gaze with a nod. "I should hope not, Bellamy. I entrusted my daughter to you once before. Try to do better this time, eh?"

"Quite, sir."

Bouchart bent and placed a peck upon Phoebe's brow, the proprietary gesture boiling Robert's blood. "*Ma petite*, I shall cede to your wishes for now, but know that I keep watch from the corridor. Cry out, and I will be by your side in an instant." He touched the ornamental sword at his side, a toothpick compared to Robert's cutlass, before following Phoebe's parents out.

Robert waited for the door to close behind them before turning back. Phoebe's gaze met his, as yet unreadable but not overly warm. At a loss as to how to proceed now that they were indeed alone, he wracked his brain for some source of occupation.

"Your Frog fiancé is correct on one count. You've had a shock."

So had he. Finding her in the midst of a betrothal ball—hers—hadn't been among any of the possible scenarios he'd spun.

"I'll pour us a brandy," he added though of the pair of them, he allowed it was he who could do with the drink.

He'd expected her to refuse—the Phoebe of his memory hadn't been much of a tippler—but to his supreme surprise she pointed him to a mahogany and bird's-eye maple spirits cabinet. "Please."

He made his way toward it. The hinged door had been left unlocked. Opening it, he took a swift inventory of the interior shelves and located what must be brandy and two dusty if otherwise clean glasses. Tucking the decanter into the crook of his arm, he carried it and the glasses back over to where Phoebe sat waiting. Aware of her gaze going over him, he poured out the drinks, a small one for her and a brimming one for himself. Setting the decanter down on the marble-topped side table, he handed her the glass.

She took it with a murmur of thanks, her gaze alighting on his left wrist and the thick carved ivory band he wore over it. "That's a most unusual bracelet. I don't recall you wearing such adornments before you...left."

Her eyes veered to his pierced ear, and he availed himself of the distraction to slip down his sleeve. "I've worn your locket every day since we parted, albeit concealed beneath my neck cloth." Every day save one—the day his torturer had ripped it from his throat. "Of all the jewels that have since come into my possession, none can touch your token in its worth." Eschewing several nearby chairs, he seated himself on the cushion beside her, his thigh brushing hers.

She slipped over as if to make room, and even after all these years, Robert knew her too well to misread the gesture. Those few millimeters separating them might as well have been a chasm.

Regarding him over the rim of her glass, she remarked, "And you've grown out your hair."

He reached his free hand toward her tumbled tresses and clipped a curl between his thumb and forefinger. Testing its silkiness, he said, "So have you."

She pulled back and rather than press her, he let his hand fall to his lap. "After you...died, I hardly cared for keeping up with fashion."

Robert stiffened. "And yet you've managed to land yourself a lord for a husband." Admittedly it was a boorish way to begin.

Beyond her flashing eyes, she didn't answer, nor did he blame her. "Forgive me. I should not have—"

"No, you should not have. Six years you've stayed away without a word, allowing us all to believe you dead. One line from you, Robert, one bloody line, and I wouldn't only have forestalled marriage plans. I would have *lived* for your return." She stopped there, waiting.

The condemnation in her face and voice was deserved, he knew—he'd more than earned it. And yet as tempted as he was to rise up and defend himself, how could he possibly foul her ears with the truth? That until six months ago, he'd let himself believe it would be kinder, nobler, to let her and all the rest go on thinking him dead? That though his body might be healed, his mind was as yet too shattered to trust himself in her society, let alone her bed? That months of wandering and later those at sea had seemed to halt time to a standstill, the hope of "someday" floating before him like an elusive golden grail he could never quite commit to, let alone reach out and grasp? What would have been the point in writing only to let her know that, for the foreseeable future, he must as yet remain away? Instead he'd waited until he could trust himself not to fall apart in front of her, until Caleb's soothing herbs and other healing ways had hushed his inner demons to a muted roar, their salivating jaws and snapping tails banished to his nightmares and no longer his waking. And, it now seemed, he'd waited too long, acted too late.

"And now you've returned. What did you bloody well expect, a hero's homecoming?"

Phoebe Tremont, Phoebe Tremont, Phoebe Tremont...

Him heralded as a hero? The mere suggestion had him awash in shame. He fought his way back to the present—and sanity—by focusing on minutia, notably her expanded vernacular. The Phoebe of his recollection had never once uttered any oath bolder than "What fustian!" or "Stuff and feathers!" The outraged female facing him now was fully capable of cursing a blue streak if provoked, he felt certain of it. The stark shift might be damnably disconcerting, but it was also undoubtedly...arousing.

Fantasizing other, more pleasurable pursuits to which her rosebud lips and sharp tongue might be put, gamely he said, "I'd settle for a smile—and a kiss."

Her gaze narrowed. "And I'll settle for answers."

"It's a long story," he warned, taking a swig of port to buoy his courage.

She stared at him askance. "Fortunately I find myself with some time."

Setting his glass aside, Robert steeled himself to repeat the script he'd rehearsed so many times in his mind. "We put in at the Comoros Islands to replenish our water and perishables. The islands lay off the southeast coast of Africa between the continent and...Madagascar." Someday pray God he'd be able to speak the latter without sickening, but he wasn't there yet, not nearly.

"I'm well aware of their location."

Her clipped tone caught him off guard, as did her confident assertion. The Phoebe from six years ago had been barely able to locate England on an atlas.

"The islands are a desirable stopping-off point for ships, including those that sail under the black flag."

"Pirates, you mean?" Her eyes widened with what he took to be concern—finally! "Were you...set upon?"

Heart drumming, he nodded. "With easily half of the crew ashore, we made an absurdly easy target. By the time we spied their approach, we were trapped. Despite our superior guns, they had surprise on their side. Their broadside attack left us leaking like a pudding cloth." A well-aimed chain shot had taken out their main mast and most of the rigging. "They boarded our quarterdeck and the battle, though valiantly fought, was short-lived. The captain and most of the crew were cut down inside of an hour."

Those of lesser luck had survived to serve as sport for their drunken captors and, later, to be sold as slaves.

"Were you wounded?" Her gaze slid over him as though searching out potential peg legs and other wooden appendages. Thankfully for him, she couldn't begin to suspect the ugly sight his clothes concealed. Given what they'd done to him, he would wear a nightshirt to their marriage bed.

"I'd been confined to my cabin with a fever," he admitted, the bald truth though it hardly painted him as a hero. "By the time they got around to finding me, they'd looted anything of value and their bloodlust was waning along with the Madeira and porter."

Her hold on the glass tightened. "How did you escape?"

Now came the hard part. Robert braced himself to repeat the bold-faced lie he'd rehearsed in his head. "I hid in one of the hatches, waited for darkness, and once it arrived, used its cloak to make my way to land." In reality, when he'd next trod upon terra firma, he'd done so as a prisoner in irons. "There I waited for the next ship to make port. Once it did, I begged my passage to the mainland."

She brought the wine to her lips with a trembling hand. "Thank God you were spared," she said with feeling, the first to warm her voice since she'd revived.

Watching her closely, he answered with a nod, wondering what it would take to thaw her. Alone though they'd been left, she'd yet to meet his overtures with anything approaching affection.

She lowered the glass. "And afterward?"

Robert hesitated. "Eventually I made my way to India," he said as if the two intervening years spent as a slave in a Malagasy granite quarry had never happened. Would to God that might be so! "Once arrived at Fort William, I learned that my post had been long since filled, myself believed to be dead, drowned along with the others. My attempts for an interview with the commander were received with contempt. Rather than expend time and breath attempting to convince my superiors that I was who I claimed, I left and took a new name, Robert Lazarus, and commenced my maritime training with the Company with an eye to captaincy."

"You changed your name? To *Lazarus*?" she emphasized, lobbing him a look as though he'd added blasphemy to his sins' mounting heap.

He shrugged, the burden of subterfuge weighing upon his shoulders as once the slave yoke had done. "Given my circumstances, the Biblical reference seemed fitting." A swift swig of port served to clear some of the emotion thickening his throat. "Altering my identity was easier than you might think. What valuables and money I'd sailed with were either pilfered by the pirates or sacrificed with the sunken ship. Without so much as my packet of orders to commend me, I had no means of proving my identity. It wasn't long before I resolved that a career at sea, not land would prove the more profitable course."

The privilege of pursuing one's personal trade had drawn many an ambitious man to East India Company service at sea. As a ship's captain, Robert was entitled to carry his own cargo as well as that belonging to the Company.

She slammed her glass down upon a marble-topped table, sending sticky liquid slopping. "What of my aspirations, my hopes and dreams, most of which perished once I thought you dead?"

So he hadn't imagined it. She was well and truly angry, her standoffishness a subterfuge to screen her seething—thank God!

Grateful for the thaw in her—he far preferred fury to the previous prickly politeness—he nonetheless crafted his response with care. "I'd survived the ship's sinking, but nothing had changed, not really. I still had nothing to offer you." Not even his life, which overnight had become the property of another man. "Staying dead whilst I sought my fortune seemed the kindest course. It's taken me the devil of a long time, but I've become a man of means, deucedly rich."

It was no idle boast. Coffers of gold and silver, silks and precious gems, and East India Company coin had been his reward for foiling an attempt on the life of the silk merchant, his final master. His first purchase as a free man had been Caleb. Liberating his friend had still left him with wealth beyond his youthful imaginings. The spices and silks from the present voyage alone should more than suffice for setting his Sussex estate to rights, the home to which he meant to take her once they were wed.

The glare she gave him might have melted iron. "How nice for you."

"Not for me but for *us*. It's taken me a while—very well, bloody long, but I'm finally in the position to take proper care of you."

Her eyes darkened, the pupils all but obliterating the silver-blue irises. "Do I look as though I'm in need of caretaking?"

The girl he'd left behind had been both softly spoken and sweetly disposed. The woman to whom he'd returned was prickly as a porcupine and bitter as carbolic, her resemblance to the Phoebe he'd known and loved limited to her fair looks.

"I only meant I am able to provide the life you deserve." Patience nearing its end, he drained his glass. Setting it aside, he swiped the back of his hand across his mouth, freezing when he saw how her lip curled. "Bloody hell, what does it matter where I've been or how long or even why? I'm here now. I'm here to stay."

Weary with waiting, he reached out and took her face between his palms. Her skin was silken as he remembered but marble-cold. He searched her beautiful eyes, but they were cold too.

Resolved to resurrect the light in them, in *her*, he added, "If you believe nothing else, know this: there was not a single day or waking hour that I did not think of you."

"Ha!" Phoebe surged to her feet. "Tell me, in the throes of all that...*thinking*, how could you not trouble yourself even once to put pen to paper and let us know you lived?"

The torturers hadn't only rent his flesh. Appalling as his scars might appear, the very worst of them were on the inside. Even after he'd won his freedom, it had taken a year before he'd been able to stand the sight of himself in a mirror; closer to two before he could bear a hand upon his shoulder without flinching. Even now, the slightest human touch upon him tended to make his flesh crawl. How could he have come to her like that, broken, a wreck? Kinder to allow her to remember him as he'd been than to foist the leavings upon her, a shell empty of all but pain and horror, until death did them part. But now he was better, so very much better if substantially less than perfectly fine, and wholly resolved to reclaim his life—and his bride.

He rose up beside her, nearly tipping over the table. Tall though she was, he topped her by nearly a head. "I did...the best...I could," he ground out, thinking of the crumpled paper carpeting his cabin floor. As if of their own accord, his hands took possession of her shoulders. His fingers firmed, digging into her gown's rich velvet. "I've never stopped thinking about you—" he paused to suck down more air "—or loving you."

"Leaving me to mourn you for dead isn't love. At best you're in love with the idea of me." She braced both palms against his chest and shoved.

Her puny push couldn't begin to budge him, but her hard words crashed into him with the power of a pugilist's punch. "Damn it, woman, we have a chance to be happy, a second chance such as few ever receive. Can't you see how deucedly rare, how bloody precious, that is? Do you really mean to cast it all away for the sake of your wounded pride?"

"*My* pride! Why, you puffed-up popinjay, you insufferably selfish lout! You made your choice. You chose to remain dead.

You chose not only for yourself but for all of us who lost six years mourning you. But this time it's not for you to choose. It's mine."

Feeling as if his heart were cradled in clutches of ice, he demanded, "Phoebe, what are you saying?"

Her steely gaze struck his. "I want you to leave, Robert Bellamy or Robert Lazarus or however you style yourself these days, not only this house but London. Go back to whatever godforsaken port of call you make your home and forget I exist."

Rage ripped through Robert, freeing him to think—to act. "You cannot mean that."

She glared up at him, her anger a match for his. "Oh, but I do."

All at once the cork he'd kept upon his feelings blew. "In that case, allow me to make it memorable."

Though the thought of her touching him anywhere below the neck still sufficed to send him sweating, the reverse no longer held true. He slid his hands down her arms to her wrists. Before she might move away, he shackled them to her sides.

Her breath caught. "What do you reckon you're about?"

Humbling you, teaching a much-needed lesson, claiming my bride.

A gentleman would have released her and walked away, but Robert was hardly that, not anymore. Heedless of her recent faint, he hauled her hard against him. Predictably she struggled, the doomed effort bringing her breasts chafing his chest—and his manhood firming.

"Don't you wish to cry out for your Frenchman?" he taunted, holding her pinned hands behind her. Her wrists were so slender he needed but one hand to bind them.

She wasn't cold now. Her cheeks flushed and her eyes blazed. "Don't tempt me. I may yet."

Robert let out a mirthless laugh. "Pray do. I welcome the opportunity to gut him."

"You would, wouldn't you?" Defiant, she lifted her chin. "Do what you will. I'll not see Aristide murdered because I was foolish enough to entrust myself to your honor."

"What a perfect little martyr you make," he remarked wryly, thinking what scant notion she had of how very breakable human beings could be.

In the past he'd treated her as if she were fashioned of Dresden china, but those bygone days were done indeed. She was a flesh-and-blood woman, *his* woman, and he meant to claim her in every way he could.

He angled his face to hers. "Don't even think of biting me," he warned.

Her eyes flared, confirming she'd contemplated doing just that. "And if I do?"

"I'd be obliged to bend you over my knee and paddle your pretty posterior until it glowed rosy."

The prospect made his palm tingle—and his cock thicken. Initiating Phoebe to the sensual pleasures shared by couples in the Orient, including light striking, biting and even bondage, wasn't something he'd considered when his image of her had been one of peerless purity—but he did so now. The spirited woman before him wouldn't shrink from his darkness, he felt sure of it. But first she had a lesson to learn—and he a long-overdue kiss to claim.

Her blackening eyes betrayed her, her dilated pupils all but blotting out the silver-blue irises. Whether she owned it or not, she badly wanted to be kissed, conquered, *claimed.* But if she needed the pretense of force, Robert was only too happy to oblige her. He'd wager his ship and all its holdings that beneath the folds of heavy fabric her nipples were hard—and her sex moist. Nor was she alone in her arousal. His hardened manhood pressed tautly against his trouser front. His balls felt tight and tender, heavy and aching. For a few fraught seconds, the primal desire to sheath himself inside her and well and truly claim her as his nearly eclipsed all morality or reason. But despite years of living less as a man than as a beast, he was no rapist. He hardly meant to become one now with the woman he loved, royal bitch though she was being.

Phoebe's face was a hairsbreadth from his, so close he could see the flare of her nostrils, feel the brush of her breath. "You wouldn't dare."

The question smacked of a challenge. Meeting it, Robert smiled his first true smile since her faint. "Try me."

Stilling, she looked up at him as though seeing him for the first time. "You're an animal."

Robert didn't deny it. Brushing his mouth over her ear, he dropped his voice to a whisper and asked, "Shall I show you what a beast I can be?" He bit lightly down upon her lobe.

Phoebe shivered. Likely she'd steeled herself to endure a swift, brutish assault. If so, she'd soon find herself sorely mistaken. Instead he took his time, nibbling kisses along the shell of her ear, the line of her jaw, the pulse point striking the side of her swan-like throat, the very throat that had inspired his ship's renaming.

Laying a hand along her cheek, he turned her face to his. Ever stubborn, she locked her lips, but Robert refused to be daunted—or defied. He brushed his mouth over hers, whisper-soft strokes that sent her breath catching and her lips parting. Ravenous, he ran his tongue along the seam, urging her to grant him her bounty. Another sharp inhalation and her body's slackening signaled her surrender. She opened and Robert delved in. She tasted of the spirit she'd sipped and the lemon-flavored comfits he suddenly remembered her fancying. The hungry lips opening to his were no longer those of an endearingly awkward girl but of a woman well accustomed to kissing. Her obvious loss of innocence both infuriated and aroused him. He should have been the one to school her, but instead that pleasure and privilege had fallen to another. Now the chaste embraces with which he'd satisfied himself six years ago belonged to another lifetime.

Like the pirate she'd accused him of being, Robert possessed, pillaged, plundered. She fought him, not that he'd expected otherwise. Their tongues met, warred, melded. Robert entwined his with hers, driving her hard. Her utter submission—nothing less would suffice. With his free had, he sank greedy fingers into her hair, gathering the thick silk into a fist. He tugged, bringing her head back and her breasts and pelvis jutting forward. Holding her flush against his body, he drank in her every breath and moan as once he'd quaffed water, fed on her fear-laced lust as a starved man might fall upon a feast. Insatiable, he drew the bruised fruit of her bottom lip into his mouth, suckling the delicate flesh, savoring the tangy, raw sweetness.

Lifting his lips from hers, he looked into her heavy-lidded eyes. "Tell me you still mean to marry your Frenchman."

As soon as the words were out, he owned that uttering them had been an enormous mistake. Phoebe turned to stone in his arms. "Given my age and history, I count myself fortunate he would have me. After all that has transpired tonight, I only hope he still will."

Catching the quaver in her voice, Robert let his hands slip away. Matured though she might be, she'd never before been kissed like this, not by Bouchart, not by any man. Robert felt both certain and glad of it. He also, for the first time since they'd started sparring, felt a wrench of guilt. Be she frosty or warm toward him, foul-tempered or sweet, she was still Phoebe, his Phoebe, his first and only love, and despite her bold words and bravado she was trembling like a wind-shaken leaf—because of him.

Fearing she might faint again, he laid a guiding hand on her arm, thinking to steer her back to the sofa, but she shook him off. "Don't dare to ever lay hands on me again."

Taking in the tangled hair tumbling about her shoulders, the darkened eyes and kiss-swollen lips, he allowed he'd never seen her lovelier—or so angry. "Spare me your hypocrisy. You wanted this every whit as much as I. You still want it. You still want *me*. No, want is too paltry a word. You *crave* me."

He barely saw the blow coming. Phoebe hauled back and struck him—hard. Her hand sang across his cheek. Her fingernails, though no longer bitten to the quick, were at least trimmed short. Focusing his watering eyes upon her, he spied the tears spangling her lower lashes. She was near to breaking though not in any way he might want.

"I wish you'd never returned," she said with feeling, backing away as though she expected him to return the blow.

The paltry violence brought the benefit of clearing his head. "Have a care what you wish for, milady. You may come to rue the day your wish is granted—as I have."

Chapter Three

Robert's lips, the same lips that had plundered Phoebe's mere moments ago, curved into an infuriatingly smug smile. "For now, I bid you goodnight, milady." Stepping back, he offered her a brief bow, the gleam in his gaze making a mock of the mannered civility.

Even now, after all the years and all the hurt that lay between them, she couldn't look at him without remembering how good it once had been to hold and be held by him, how perfectly her head had settled against his chest, almost as if they were twin halves of a Chinese puzzle box that only when fitted together formed a whole.

He turned on his heel to go, the motion sharp, crisply efficient, almost military. Phoebe watched his departure in mute fury. Swaggering steps carried him to the study door. He opened it and stepped out. She quickly turned away lest Aristide or her mother glimpse her as she could only imagine she must look—flush-faced and trembling, her cheek bearing the brand of Robert's day-old beard.

From the corridor, Aristide's raised voice reached her. "You have made your goodbyes and now you have no reason to return. Do not come near my bride ever again."

Phoebe curled her hands into fists, deliberately digging her nails into her palms, the petty violence the very least she deserved. While she'd comported herself no better than a common harlot, Aristide had stood guard as he'd sworn to do. The show of loyalty prompted a stab of guilt. Her betrothed might not be the most constant of lovers, but unlike her former feckless fiancé, at least he kept his promises.

Robert's voice rose in response. "Until she's your bride in truth, I shall see her as I please. Stay out of my path, Frenchman, or prepare to answer for the consequences."

The implicit threat shot a shiver down Phoebe's spine, for she now understood that the cutlass Robert carried was no more a costume contrivance than any other article on his person. Considering the roguish life he'd led, she suspected the blade was seasoned with the blood of more than one victim who'd crossed him. She must warn Aristide to have a care, she must...

The first thing she must do is steer herself back to the sofa—and sound sense. Self-control had been her watchword for the last six years. Observing it had served her well. No more clandestine meetings in the mazes of moonlit gardens, no more impetuous engagements made for love alone. She'd put away that part of herself as she had her bridal gown and wedding china, both wrapped in cotton wool and buried at the bottom of her marriage chest. Or so she'd supposed.

Running a finger along her tender lower lip, she sank onto the seat. Robert's kiss, and her surrender, seemed to have fed him in some way, curbing his anger and fortifying his resolve. She instead felt hollowed out and drained, boneless as an eel and with scarcely more wit or will. Alas, his boast that she wanted—*craved*—him wasn't baseless braggadocio. It was the shameful truth. The kiss he'd stolen hadn't been stolen at all.

Lowering her hand, she took note of the faint bruise blooming on her right wrist bone and sought a steadying breath. Though she'd sooner devour dirt than admit it, having him bind her had appealed to a primitive part of her. Being forced to bend not only to his body but also to his will had made her throb with longing.

But even as Robert's breath-stealing kisses and mastering touch had stoked her banked desires to flaming life, she'd felt empty and unanchored. Emptier even than she had on the day she'd received word that The Phoenix, and Robert, were lost.

For six years, her grief had grounded her—that and the assurance that once she'd known a pure and perfect love. Now she saw that all had been a lie.

The man whose memory she'd cherished and kept alive in her heart all these years didn't exist. The pirate who'd returned in his stead might not be a specter, but he was most certainly a stranger.

A dangerous stranger she'd do well to avoid.

Oh, she knew his amber eyes darkened to burnished brown whenever his temper or his passions became aroused. That his hair grew out from his temples in soft ripples. That when pondering a puzzle he was prone to jiggle his knee and toy with his timepiece. But beyond those small and rather inconsequential details, she didn't know *him,* not really, not in any way that mattered. The sun-bronzed adventurer who'd swaggered into her life might have the look, manner and even scent of Robert, but in every way that most mattered, he was a stranger.

Like a splinter left to fester, anger worked its way to the surface and with it a wrenching sense of betrayal. How callused he must be to have pursued his seafaring life for six years whilst back in England all who loved him believed him dead.

She picked up her all-but-forgotten glass and gulped the remainder of the brandy as though it were water. Throat on fire and lips stinging, she choked down a cough, feeling as though she'd just cauterized a wound. In a way, she had.

Robert Bellamy had stolen six years of her life. Six *years*! And not any six years, but those commonly accounted to be a woman's prime. In society's eyes, a woman was valued on par with a loaf of bread or a pitcher of cream, a perishable commodity that must grow moldy or sour with time whilst a man was considered to age in the manner of a fine wine. Before Aristide had come along, she'd been considered to be on the shelf, almost a spinster.

Phoebe reached up and tore the locket from her throat. Her

hand fisted about it, her arm shaking with the force of her fury. As of now, this very moment, she was done with crying, done with mourning what might have been, done with waiting to live her life because the present couldn't possibly live up to the past's rose-colored perfection. To prove it, she hauled back and cast her former treasure faraway across the room.

Because of Robert Bellamy, she'd wasted six years. She'd be damned if she'd give the blackguard one bloody day more.

In the course of the past six years, Robert had fantasized about his and Phoebe's reunion many times, so often that he sometimes felt as though he'd lived it. A modern-day Odysseus, he would return to England young yet wise, seasoned yet whole. Like that mythical Greek warrior's devoted wife Penelope, Phoebe would have held all her would-be suitors at bay. Waiting, she would wear one of her simple pale gowns, her shorn golden locks stirred by the slightest springtime breeze. A mellow English sun would beam benignly down upon them, a swathe of manicured lawn their sole separation. Feeling his gaze upon her, she would look up at the very moment he stepped out from behind a stand of trees, a hedgerow or some such conveniently concealing foliage. Their gazes would connect, collide. Seconds later, she'd pick up her skirts and fly toward him. They'd meet in the midst of all that cool, lush countryside, and she'd launch herself into his arms, already open to embrace her. They'd kiss, a kiss to end all kisses, and when they finally broke apart, laughing and breathless and giddy on gratitude, he'd lift her high against his chest and swing them both 'round and 'round until there was no telling where the earth stopped and the sky began.

How very far removed from fantasy the recent episode within had proven. And yet her response to his kiss lent him hope that she might be brought around. At the very least, his impromptu reappearance had forestalled any announcement of a marriage. He had no way of measuring how much time tonight had bought him, but he meant to put every precious minute to its most potent use.

Stepping out from the Tremont townhouse, he marked that most of the guest carriages had not budged. Like crows picking over carrion, the ton would linger as long as possible, feeding on the succulent scandal of an unannounced betrothal. Robert had no stomach for it. Unhitching his horse from the post, he allowed that though he had succeeded in postponing Phoebe's betrothal, he was as yet far from seeing it broken. But he could do no more tonight. Arguably he had done more than enough already. His rough handling had crossed a line, giving Phoebe further fodder for seeing him as a rogue and a bounder. In contrast, Bouchart had maintained the mien of a consummate gentleman, behaving impeccably throughout the interlude. In forcing himself on Phoebe, had he played into the Frenchman's hands?

Furious with himself, he swung up into the saddle and headed for Berkley Square, anger making a blur of Mayfair's tidy tree-lined streets, classically styled townhouses and elegant shops. The temptation to seek out a public house and get stinking drunk was enormous. Resisting it, he rode on. Before he did anything, including deciding whether the remedy for what ailed him was brandy or rum, there was one other to whom he needed to make his return known—his sister Chelsea.

Chelsea and her husband, Anthony Grenville, Viscount Montrose, bided at 12 Berkley Square, one of a terrace of fashionable Palladian-style townhouses faced in pink stucco and fenced in black ironwork. For the first time it occurred to him to wonder why he hadn't seen them at the ball. Even masked, with her flamboyant flame-colored curls Chelsea would have been impossible to miss. Surely such high-ranking near-neighbors would have made it onto Lady Tremont's guest list even if the viscountess bore the taint of having him as a brother. Then again, Anthony had once been affianced to

Phoebe. Though ending their engagement had been a mutual choice, in Lady Tremont's eyes her daughter had been as good as deserted at the altar.

Light shone from a second-story window; otherwise the house was dark. Grateful for the profusion of street lamps—not the case in lesser areas of town—Robert dismounted, tethered his horse to the post and crossed to the gated residence. He let himself in, the well-oiled hinges opening near soundlessly, and followed the stone path bisecting the patch of manicured grass known as "the area." A slender set of marble steps led up to the fan-lit facade.

Starting up, second thoughts assailed him. Ought he to have curbed his eagerness and waited until morning? And yet were Chelsea to learn he was alive through a third party, he would never forgive himself. Nor, he felt certain, would she. Resolved, he reached for the brass knocker fashioned in the form of a pineapple, the international emblem of hospitality. Hoping he would find that most welcome sentiment within, he brought it down with a bang.

A salvo of solid strikes brought the door finally opening. A lanky manservant of late middling years appeared on the threshold dressed in a drooping nightcap, striped cotton robe and bearing the countenance of one rudely awakened. Holding a taper aloft, he peered at Robert over its fledgling flame.

Heartened to see a familiar face, Robert reached out and seized the butler's bony shoulder. "Chambers, old sod, you're a sight for sore eyes. You look splendid." Indeed, the butler seemed to have shed a good decade.

Chambers dropped his gaze to the cutlass hanging from Robert's side, and his bleary gaze bugged. "My father retired to Bath nigh on five years ago," he said, a tremble to his tone.

Chambers...*Junior*? Robert withdrew his hand. Until now he'd supposed the man had observed him through the peephole, recognized him and only then opened the door. Seeing that was not so, he made a mental note to have a word with his brother-in-law about the lax state of his household's security. Montrose might have chosen to play fast and loose with his life in his bachelor days, but now he had Chelsea and the twins to consider. For their sakes, if not his own, the viscount was duty-bound to do better.

"Pray convey my regards when you next visit. And see that in the future you make better use of that peephole," he added, jerking his chin toward the small opening above the knocker. "For all you know I could be a cold-blooded killer out to murder you all in your beds," he added deliberately, stroking the cutlass hilt.

The statement had the desired effect. The thin hand clutching the taper began to shiver like a ship with sails all in the wind, causing the candle to sway. "Lord and Lady Montrose are abed. If you'd care to, er...leave your card, I shall be happy to present it in the morning."

"Leave my card, a pox on that!" The butler's dropping jaw reminded Robert that his rough seaman's bearing wouldn't do for London. Modulating his manner, he added, "I assure you her ladyship will receive me despite the hour. I am her relation recently returned from...abroad."

He stopped short of claiming kinship as a brother. The disastrous reunion with Phoebe had shaken his faith, making him cautious about presuming his return would be greeted as wholly happy news.

"W-what...name shall I g-give?"

Robert thought for a moment. "Tell her Sir Robin awaits." He hadn't invoked the childhood pet name since leaving England. Saying it aloud felt both foreign and bittersweet.

"Very good, sir." With his free arm, he reached behind and fumbled for the knob.

Forcing his way within would have been child's play, but Robert held back, allowing the door to be closed in his face. From within a bolt struck home. The belated nod to caution had him shaking his head. Shifting from foot to foot, he waited. The minutes ticked by. A church bell tolled a single chime. From nearby a night watchman called, "One o'clock and all is well," the voice rusty and slightly slurred. While well lit, the tony neighborhood was still shockingly vulnerable. Knowing firsthand the dangers of dropping one's guard, Robert cursed beneath his breath. To prove his point, he considered leaving his post and trying the tradesman's entrance. He'd wager half his personal cargo that it had been left unlocked. Before he could confirm for certain, the door reopened.

"Her ladyship will receive you." Shaking but mildly, the butler stepped back to make room for Robert to enter.

Robert stepped inside the hushed house. Lamps had been lit. Grateful for their reassuring glow, he followed the fellow through the foyer and into a well-appointed side parlor. Brocaded floor-length draperies were drawn against the night. A settee and several chairs were arranged in an amiable semi-circle. Set on the far side of the room, a chess table with a painted-on board showed a match in mid-play. A pianoforte held pride of place in the room's center, a branch of lit candles atop. Aware of the butler retreating, Robert stepped up to the instrument and lifted the case. Eastern music utilized a variety of string, percussion and wind instruments, but nothing with a keyboard. He hadn't set eyes on a piano in his six years away. Then Montrose had been in the throes of renovation, the present room a shambles of plaster dust and scaffolding, the furniture buried beneath Holland covers—another reminder of how much, everything, had altered in his absence.

Rustling from the hallway had him whipping about. "Chelsea!"

His sister stood in the doorway, a hand cupping her mouth. Mussed copper curls tumbled about her shoulders. Ruddy color rushed her cheeks. A silk dressing gown, obviously donned in haste, clung to the swell at her midriff. The thickening answered his earlier question of why she hadn't been at the betrothal ball.

He was to be an uncle again!

Her hand fell away from her face. "Bloody hell, it *is* you," she said, eyes shimmering.

Montrose materialized beside her, tucking in his shirttail. Sighting Robert, his aristocratic jaw dropped. "Good God, Bellamy, can it really be you?" he demanded, wrapping a protective arm about his wife.

"It is I." Robert walked toward them. Training his gaze on Chelsea, he asked, "Can a prodigal brother hope for a hug?"

Smile wobbly, she stretched out her arms. "Oh, Robert, I'd hoped and prayed and yet..." She swayed, her eyes rolling back.

Anthony caught her before she folded to the floor.

Looking on, Robert allowed there was no help for it. For the second time in as many hours, he'd felled a woman he loved.

Lying abed in one of the guest chambers, Robert wasn't surprised to hear a soft tap outside his door. "Psst, are you awake?"

Bolting upright, he made a grab for his shirt which he'd shucked off upon retiring but as always kept within arm's reach. He hauled it over his head and quickly did up the buttons. "No, I'm fast asleep. Out like a light. Of course I'm awake. Don't be a goose. Come in."

The door opened and Chelsea, taper in hand, padded inside. Pulling the door closed behind her, she admitted, "I couldn't sleep. My brain is abuzz with excitement and...questions."

"I'll answer them all," he lied, moving over to make room on the mattress. "Provided you promise not to go fainting on me again."

She set her candle on the lamp table and lowered herself onto the bed. "It's the babe. Most days I'm a woozy watering pot. Anthony has been a saint to put up with me."

Robert snorted. Before wedding Chelsea, Anthony had been renowned as one of London's most notorious rakes, with good reason. Had love and marriage so utterly transformed him? For Chelsea's sake, Robert hoped so.

"Reformed rakes truly do make the very best husbands," she answered, as if reading his mind. Given how close they were, Robert deemed that to be entirely possible.

After a carriage accident had claimed the lives of both their parents, they'd only had each other. When a neighboring squire's treachery had landed him in the custody of kidnappers, Chelsea had resolved to do whatever was required to raise his ransom, including highway robbery. Waylaying Montrose's coach had shortened her criminal career considerably. Though betrothed to Phoebe, Anthony had taken one look at the flame-haired felon and fallen head over heels. When the same henchman who had Robert also kidnapped Phoebe, he'd soon found himself fallen similarly smitten. As in a Shakespearean comedy, their romantic entanglements had been sorted to the supreme happiness of all parties—or so it had seemed.

Chelsea's face, more radiant than any candle, proclaimed her to be a well-satisfied wife. "Married life must agree with you," he conceded. "You're more beautiful than ever."

She let out a laugh. "At the moment I only know I feel large as a house. You, on the other hand, look as though you've lost a stone." Shifting to face him, she poked a finger in the vicinity of his belly.

He fell back against the headboard. Two years' enslavement in the granite quarry had chiseled away anything of him that was soft or surplus, firming his will to survive along with his body. "Mind you don't let Caleb hear you say that. He takes great pride in having fattened me up." It was thanks to Caleb's regimen of strengthening herbs that Robert could no longer count his ribs or feel the knobs of his vertebrae when he lay abed.

"Who is Caleb?"

He hesitated. How to explain the complexity of their relationship in terms his very English sister might understand?

"Caleb is my manservant, though our relationship is more complex than that. We are bound in ways no European master and servant would ever be. I saved his life and now he insists that it belongs to me. For what it's worth, I consider him a friend, almost a brother."

She reached out and gave his hand a squeeze. "I shall look forward to meeting him. For the moment, you'll forgive me if I can't seem to think much beyond my next meal. Come below with me, and we'll raid the pantry as we used to when we were children. You can regale me with your adventures," she added as though speaking of his travels and travails were some sort of inducement.

Quite the opposite, Robert had hoped to postpone the inevitable questioning at least until the morrow. "Anthony won't have my head for keeping you up?"

Already on her feet, she laughed. "Not if I tell him it was all my idea, which happens to be the truth. At this stage, I only sleep in snatches. The poor man can only profit from a few hours' freedom from my tossing and turning."

Whereas most couples of their class slept separately, an adjoining dressing closet serving as a discrete portal for conjugal calls, Chelsea and Montrose must still share a bed. Once Robert had taken it for granted that he and Phoebe would enjoy a similarly passionate, unconventional union. Now he was no longer so certain.

Tucking in his shirttail, he followed her over to the door. "Very well, lead the way."

Like the truant children they once had been, they tiptoed through the corridor. A servant's passageway and a steep set of plain back stairs brought them to the basement, a spare, tidy space of flagstone flooring and plain plaster walls. Few ladies of rank would condescend to come in to this humble area of the house, but Chelsea had always abided by her own rules, not those of society. She navigated the low-ceilinged labyrinth with the foot surety born of familiarity, steering them through scullery, laundry, china pantry, larder and lastly into the kitchen.

"Sit." Crossing to the meat safe, she motioned him to the planked pine table bracketed by backless benches, but Robert stayed standing.

"You'll pardon me if I don't fancy being waited upon by my pregnant sister."

Ignoring her fussing, he found the flint box and set to work resurrecting the banked fire. The parlor and other rooms relied upon coal for heat, but Chelsea's kitchen followed the English culinary tradition of cooking over wood. Though he hadn't much occasion for fire-making in the Orient, he'd hardly forgotten how. He'd soon raised a cheerful blaze and set the kettle on the hob to heat.

Sometime later they sat across from one another, crumbs all that remained of their impromptu feast of Stilton cheese, crusty country bread and thinly sliced roast beef. Robert hadn't thought he was hungry, but once the cold collation was set out, he'd tucked in as though starved. After the years away, the simple English fare was ambrosia.

Hands laced about her earthenware mug, Chelsea sighed. "When one of the children is ill, I often come down here late at night and fix myself a cup of tea."

Dusting his hands atop his trousers, he asked, "Daphne and Tony are well, I trust?"

His twin nephew and niece must be coming on seven. When he'd left, they'd been babes in arms. And now there was a third child on the way. Once again he was reminded of how very much he'd missed.

A beaming smile answered his tentative query. "They remind me of you and I when we were children. Daphne would rather play with frogs than dolls. Tony allows her to bully him dreadfully though she's the eldest by mere minutes."

"I'll have a look in at the nursery in the morning, if I may."

"You'll see them at breakfast. Other than a nursery luncheon, the children take their meals with us. I like to keep my family close," she added with a wink. "But mind me prosing on like a fat, happy housewife when it's you I want to hear all about. How have you been keeping yourself all these years? *Where* have you been keeping yourself?"

He hadn't expected his reprieve to go on indefinitely; still he tensed, anticipating all the questions to come. "Calcutta, Bombay, Ceylon, parts of Arabia, oh, and one voyage to Canton." Once he'd been greedy to see the great wide world, but now his dearest wish was to find contentment in one small corner of it—England, with Phoebe.

Predictably her eyebrows shot to her hairline. "That's...a great deal of exploring. However did you manage it?"

Breaking into a smile, he admitted, "I'm a captain in the Honourable East India Company."

She slanted him a smile. "So that explains the sun bronzing and the earring and that frightful-looking cutlass I saw you wearing earlier."

"It does in part." Laboring in the granite quarry had toughened his hide in more ways than one. By the time he'd found himself free, he was berry brown and inured to burning. "My ship, The Swan, is harbored at Blackwall," he said, and despite how abysmally things had gone with Phoebe, he felt his chest swell. "She's a grand lady, gilded and festooned, for all that she likely has but one more voyage left in her."

An East Indiamen typically was good for four, no more than five, voyages. The Swan was built of English oak, not the Bombay teakwood that afforded a longer lifespan but also prohibited berthing in a London dock. Unloading the cargo and overseeing its transport to the Company's warehouses in Cutler Street would occupy him for the following few days, and then afterward the vessel would require a thorough overhauling before making the return voyage to India. Whether she did so with or without Robert at the helm depended wholly upon Phoebe.

"Dare I hope that means you'll be staying on?"

His gaze wavered away. "That rather relies upon Phoebe."

Her smile faded. "You've seen her, then?"

He nodded. "I have. I came to you directly from her betrothal ball. It seems I chose a damnably inconvenient time to come back from the dead," he added, unable to keep the bitterness from his voice.

She set down her cup with a sigh. "Don't judge her overly harshly. She mourned you for...a very long time."

"Six years, the same span for which I stood steadfast. She, quite clearly, cannot lay claim to a like constancy."

She cut him a look. "She draped herself in black crepe and bombazine for a full year as though she were your widow in truth. There were times when we feared she might take her own life."

Suicide, surely not! He snapped upright in his seat. "Good God, she didn't try—"

"We watched her closely."

His gaze dropped to the ivory bracelet banding his left wrist. Turning it about, he found himself confiding, "While I was...away, the resolve to find my way home to her was all that sustained me. More so than fouled water or maggoty meat, it was what kept me alive."

She reached across the table and took hold of his hand. "Have you told her that?"

"Our privacy was...limited." Thinking of Bouchart holding out in the hallway, he picked up his knife and stabbed it into what remained of the wedge of cheese. "Tell me more of this Frenchman. Can it be she loves him?"

She hesitated. "Love is a strong word. I believe she is...fond of him. In many ways, Aristide's courtship brought her back to life. It and her work with the orphans gave her renewed zest."

He set aside the knife and looked up. "Phoebe *works*?"

Chelsea's gaze narrowed. "Yes, she does, and quite indefatigably. That surprises you?"

It did. The Phoebe he'd known had rarely risen before ten. It wasn't that she was indolent, more a matter of her having nothing of any pressing import to do. Like most gently bred young ladies, she'd filled her hours with shopping, making the social round of roués, soirees and musicales, and perfecting her needlework, watercolors and pianoforte playing. Still, how taxing could it be to wipe a few snotty noses and sing a lullaby or two? Rather than say so and risk inciting Chelsea's wrath, he asked, "What sort of...work does she do?"

She thought for a moment. "She reads to the younger children, tutors the older ones in history and literature, science, mathematics and geography."

"Geography?" When he'd first announced to Phoebe that he'd bought colors in an East India Company regiment bound for Calcutta, he'd had nearly to drag her over to the globe in her father's study.

Ignoring his interruption, Chelsea continued, "She also devotes considerable time to organizing social functions to raise funds—lectures, art auctions, the occasional charity ball. Last autumn she approached the Foundation Members of the Royal Academy of Arts and persuaded them to make a loan of some of their collection's finer works. The special exhibition fetched nearly seven thousand pounds."

"Phoebe does all that?" Robert shook his head, struggling to reconcile the pampered miss of his memory with the industrious and capable woman Chelsea described.

Chelsea nodded. "She does indeed though sometimes I think she'd rather pay a visit to the tooth puller than accept praise for her accomplishments."

"She's not terribly keen to accept praise or anything else from me at the moment. She told me in no uncertain terms that she expects me to leave London—and her—well alone."

Brow furrowing, Chelsea shot him a hard look. "Really, Robert, did you expect that she would sit by for six years stitching her sampler whilst you were off...adventuring?"

"Adventuring!" There it was—that word again. He was half-tempted to tear off his shirt and show her just what his *adventuring* had brought him, but he held back, settling for blowing seaman's curses beneath his breath. "Damn it, Chelsea, I expected...well, I didn't expect her to take up with some Frog exile. Arachnid, what the bloody hell kind of name is that anyway? Sounds like a damned spider."

"It's *Aristide*, and if we're going to talk about...him, we're going to need this." She reached into her robe pocket and brought out a monogrammed silver flask. Passing it over, she admitted, "It's Anthony's, but he won't mind."

"Thanks." He uncapped the bottle and took a long pull, the brandy burning its way through the pain. "What do you know of Bouchart?"

That he was Phoebe's betrothed made him Robert's enemy, but there was something more, something endemic to the man that didn't settle, something lurking beneath the surface that had caused Robert's gut to tighten and the hairs at the back of his neck to bristle.

She hesitated. "Not all that much, I'm afraid. His family is an old one, quite ancient actually. Before the Revolution, they had an estate and vineyards in Normandy. During the Terror, they lost their lands and nearly their lives along with so many others. Aristide joined with the British to fight against Napoleon. He served in Nelson's navy for more than two years. Afterward he settled in London and established a successful wine importing business."

"Since when does Phoebe's mother accept a tradesman as a son-in-law? I was at least landed and yet she treated me scarcely better than a chimney sweep." The inherent injustice made Robert hard-pressed to hold back from grinding his teeth.

Chelsea sent him a measured look of sympathy. "He still

holds the title if not the lands and, well, Phoebe is coming on twenty-six. I suspect her ladyship is relieved not to have a spinster on her hands especially as she still has Belinda to bring out."

It was the second time that night Phoebe had been consigned to near-spinster status, the first such assertion having been made by Phoebe herself. Beyond frustrated, Robert brought his fist down upon the table, scattering crumbs to the four corners. "This isn't some grizzled, bent-backed crone of whom we speak. It is Phoebe, and if she isn't tenfold lovelier than when I last left her, then by God, I haven't eyes. As I see it, she and I are still betrothed. I still mean to marry her, but first I need to break whatever hold that Frog dandy has upon her and persuade her to marry me instead."

If only matters might be made so simple. The bungled reunion forced him to acknowledge that winning Phoebe back would be less of a single battle and more of a prolonged campaign.

Unruffled by his display of temper, Chelsea looked at him askance. "Oh, is that all? First things first—I want to know why you've stayed away all this time without a word."

Unfurling his fist, Robert hesitated. How much to reveal, how much to hold back and, dear God, where to begin? The earlier recitation to Phoebe should have made answering easier—only it hadn't. "You know The Phoenix floundered off the southeast coast of Africa?"

She nodded. "The shipping log showed you'd last put into port at Capetown, but there was no record of after. Was it foul weather?"

He shook his head. "Pirates."

Her eyes rounded. "But The Phoenix was en route to India, not returning. What cargo could she have carried worth plundering?"

"Cargo is not limited to precious metals and gemstones, textiles, saltpeter and spices." Rather than risk revealing more, he quickly added, "We carried arms and munitions bound for Fort William."

In reality the ship's hull filled with flintlocks and gunpowder hadn't been what the pirates were after. Slavers in Tripoli, Tunis and other locales in North Africa and the Western Indian Ocean relied upon pirates to supply them with a steady stream of stock, both African and European. An able-bodied young man fetched a hefty price at market—even one with putrid wounds running blood and foulness down his back.

To his relief, she moved on to ask, "Were there other survivors?"

He lifted his mug and took a swallow to sooth his throat's sudden cinching. "A handful of us survived to be sold as slaves. Our captain and most of the crew were killed in battle as I would have been had I not been too ill to rise from my berth."

Who would have guessed that a bad bout of seasickness would save his life? Preoccupied with puking, he hadn't realized anything was amiss until he'd heard the cannon boom. By the time he'd staggered on deck with his pistol, the battle was done, the planks blood-soaked, the fallen officers dying or dead, the few survivors, most of them injured, corralled like cattle and marched toward the cargo hold. Robert had found a cubby in which to conceal himself and stayed hidden there for hours, ears ringing with the pirates' soused singing—and the screams of those apparently deemed too wounded or weak to be put upon the auction block. Eventually he too had been found. The cocked pistol clapped to his chest had forestalled any fancies of running. The nightmare that had ensued had eradicated any hope of a swift or even foreseeable homecoming.

Chelsea clearing her throat carried him back to the present. "What happened after—"

"I'm back now," he barked, suddenly aware he was perspiring though they sat some distance from the fire. "Let's leave it at that, shall we?"

"Must we?"

He rested his elbow atop the table and fitted a hand to his brow. “Chels, please don’t press me for more. I simply...can’t give it, not now, perhaps not ever.”

“All right, we’ll leave sleeping dogs lie—for now.”

“Thank you,” he said, lifting his head to look at her. The sweating had subsided, but he still felt the telltale trembling in his limbs as though he were once more hung out to dry from the pirate ship’s masthead, so sun-blistered and thirsting he’d feared swallowing his tongue. “Thank you. I mean to go to the Admiralty and make my report. Perhaps I’ll let you read it someday, though I rather think not.”

“You do realize you’re going to have to tell Phoebe the whole truth, not only the bits you’ve made due for me?”

Much as he now meant to make Phoebe his bride, he wasn’t prepared to stoop to winning her with pity. “There are other ways of wooing,” he said, thinking of earlier when for a precious few moments he’d succeeded in melting both body and her will. He swung his legs over the bench and stood. Turning back to her, he asked, “Where precisely does Phoebe engage in this worthy work of hers?”

Brow furrowed, she looked up at him. “The Foundling Hospital on Guilford Street but why?”

Rather than reply, he took a moment to reconstruct a mental map of the city. “That’s in Bloomsbury, isn’t it?” He held out a hand to help her up.

Waving it away, she braced her palms upon the table and pulled herself up. “It is but barging in unannounced won’t endear you to anyone, least of all Phoebe.”

For the first time since he’d discovered Phoebe was betrothed, Robert found his smile. “Who’s to say I haven’t grown a sudden passion for philanthropy myself?”

Chapter Four

Three Days Later

Standing behind the lectern, the schoolroom slate mounted on an easel behind her, Phoebe did her best to pretend that it was any ordinary day, as if Robert's turning up at her betrothal ball after six years "dead" hadn't upended her world. That he hadn't sought her out since was as much an occasion for pique as relief. First he set her life at sixes and sevens and then he ignored her, the audacity!

Then again, she had been the one to send him away—this time.

Placing the peeled hardboiled egg atop the narrow-necked beaker as she had many times before, she looked out onto the classroom. "As you can see, children, there is positively no way this egg shall ever fit through this bottleneck...or is there?"

Hoping to instill some small appreciation for the "magic" of science, she stopped to survey the fascinated faces staring back at her from the queues of classroom benches. Ordinarily such a fine spring day saw her staving off pleas to forsake lessons for forays out-of-doors, but Newton's classic illustration of the relationship between matter and space rarely failed her. Even eight-year-old Johnnie, a terrible fidget, had abandoned his nose picking to attend to the lesson.

Satisfied that she'd allowed the suspense to sufficiently build, she removed the egg, picked up a flat wooden stick and lit it from the lamp. She tossed the stick into the beaker, replaced the egg atop the glass mouth and stood back. A sucking noise, a tremor of motion and *voila*, the ovum slipped through, landing at the bottle's bottom with an audible plop.

Predictably, her pupils squealed with surprised delight. Phoebe hid a smile.

From the rear of the room, a boy hissed, “Bleedin’ parlor trick, that’s all ’tis.”

Peering out to the final queue, Phoebe traced the caustic comment to fourteen-year-old Billy slouching upon his bench. She might have known. The source of spiders set upon her chair and ink poured into her tea mug, Billy required more of her time and patience than the other children en masse.

Reining in the reprimand that rose to her lips, instead she called out, “Are you quite certain of that, *Billy*?”

As if startled at being singled out, Billy bolted upright. Shoving a hank of hair out of his eyes, he answered, “Aye, I am. Just because we’re poor and no one wants us don’t make us daft.”

Phoebe had long suspected that surliness was the boy’s defense against being born with a lazy eye and a foster father who’d squandered his Hospital stipend on gin. “So you believe this was a magician’s trick and that the egg will fall back out?”

He nodded. “Aye, I do.”

Heartened by his uncharacteristic interest, however rudely displayed, she pressed on, “In that case, why don’t you come up and have a try?”

Red-faced, he stood. “All right, I will.”

By now, all heads were turned to Billy. Hands stuffed into his trouser pockets, he loped up the aisle to the front of the class. Phoebe picked up the beaker and held it out. He hesitated and then took it.

He tried upending the vessel to dislodge the egg, shaking it vigorously, but by now the glass had cooled. “Blimey, it’s really stuffed in there,” he said, lifting sheepish eyes to Phoebe.

She suppressed another smile. “Indeed it is. As Newton’s experiment demonstrates, altering one’s environment can make the seemingly impossible possible. Exposing this bottle to heat caused the glass to expand just as exposing ourselves to new thoughts and ideas broadens our minds. But tell me, what made you so certain I was out to dupe you?" she asked, reaching out to reclaim the bottle.

Handing it over, he shrugged. "You're the Quality, ain't 'ee? Besides, bleedin' lessons is for children with parents, not for us lot," he added, kicking at the desk leg.

Phoebe set the experiment aside. "Nonsense, learning is for everyone. Sir Isaac himself hailed from quite humble circumstances. His father was a farmer who couldn't so much as sign his name, but mind the success his son made of himself through education."

He slanted a skeptical look. "That true?"

Phoebe nodded. "Entirely and by the by, I am here to teach you, not trick you. Now take your seat, and in the future kindly preface your remarks with the raising of your hand."

"Yes, miss." He gifted her with a goofy grin and reeled away.

Feeling as though she'd just won a significant victory, she picked up her chalk stub and turned to face the board. "Sir Isaac's experiment proves an important premise put forth centuries earlier by the Greek philosopher, Aristotle: 'Nature abhors a vacuum.'" In big block letters, she wrote the sentence upon the board. "Now, who can tell me the meaning of *abhor*?"

Uncharacteristic quiet met the question. Phoebe turned about—and found her pupils riveted on the rear of the room, only this time the instigator wasn't Billy.

It was Robert!

A capped floor matron ushered him in, and Phoebe's heart caught in her throat. The bottle-green frock coat, starched lawn shirt and buff-colored breeches he wore must be borrowed—they were far too tasteful to satisfy his new flamboyance—and even the most nimble-fingered of tailors would require more than a mere three days to turn out such a splendid ensemble. Still, the clothing molded to his broad shoulders, trim torso and muscular thighs as though fashioned for him. A beaver hat replaced the previous evening's extravagant plumage. The jaunty smile he flashed on catching her eye was, however, wholly his own.

Phoebe's hand holding the chalk clenched, snapping the stick in twain. "Children, be seated," she called out, though of course it was too late—hopeless, really.

They broke ranks, jolting to their feet like jack-in-the-boxes. Teddy danced on his toes like a performing bear at Astley's. Fiona twirled like a top. Johnnie's nose-picking ratcheted to a mining expedition. Only Billy kept to his seat, watching the newcomer's approach in sullen silence. Apart from the hospital directors, gray-haired and dark-suited, adult males were almost an exotic species, and even in his sobered attire Robert stood out as more exotic than most.

She bit back an oath and crossed to the front of the desk, her pounding heart keeping time with his approaching steps.

Robert Bellamy, this puts you well and truly beyond the pale.

And yet her treacherous heart trilled at the sight of him, her mind awhirl with petty fancies. Had she bothered to smooth her hair after removing her bonnet that morning? She didn't think so. And why oh why hadn't she selected her gown with greater care? Belinda was likely right. The pale patterned taupe did nothing for her.

A sharp tug on her skirt drew her gaze downward. "A papa!" lisped five year-old Lulu, the baby of the group and newly brought to town from fostering the country.

Succumbing, Phoebe bent and lifted Lulu into her arms. Though she shouldn't show favoritism, in Lulu's case she couldn't help herself. That the child regarded any adult male as a potential father, a papa, wrenched her heart.

The matron ushered Robert up to her. Balancing Lulu upon her hip, Phoebe steeled herself. The other evening she'd been taken utterly surprise, but she couldn't very well faint every time she faced him.

"How may I assist you, sir?" she inquired coolly as though they'd never before met.

"Lady Phoebe." He followed the address with an overblown bow. Straightening, he turned to the matron. "Since my return from abroad, my sister has done little else but sing this teacher's praises, so much so that I find myself impatient to witness all her good works with mine own eyes."

Phoebe forced her gaze to his, any pretense to civility shrinking on par with her patience. "We are in the midst of a lesson."

Gaze glinting, he glanced from her to the carafe and then back up. "How fortuitous I arrived in time to witness its enthralling conclusion."

The matron cast Phoebe a pleading look. "What Lady Phoebe means to say is that she shall be delighted to take you about anon." Phoebe opened her mouth to refuse again when the matron's elbow found her side. "Potential donor," she hissed beneath her breath. "Sister's a viscountess."

"Never fear, I am in no rush," Robert said affably as though oblivious to the byplay. "I am prepared to wait all day if need be." As if to prove it, he pivoted away and made for the benches at the very front.

"That is indeed fortunate," Phoebe called after him. "For you may have to."

Subsiding onto the wooden seat, he waved a sun-bronzed hand in her vicinity. "Don't mind me, carry on."

She set Lulu down and wheeled about to the matron, scarcely caring whether or not her high whisper reached him. "Surely there is someone else, another instructor, available to lead a tour?"

Leaning in, the matron whispered, "He was most specific that his guide be none other than you."

"I wish to see the institution through the dedicated eyes of its sole volunteer teacher," Robert piped up from the bench, leaving no doubt that he'd overheard their every word. "She who reaps no reward save for commendation to Heaven." As much as his prosing, his steady stare and smug smile assured Phoebe he didn't intend to accept any answer save yes.

"Surely one of the senior students can mind the class whilst you show this fine gentleman about," the matron added, giving Phoebe a nudge.

With no choice but to capitulate, Phoebe sought out the tall, solemn girl, the eldest of the group, and beckoned her over. "Mary, pray lead the class whilst I am showing our...visitor about. It is to be mathematics next. You may commence with simple sums." She handed her the broken chalk.

"Yes, milady." Mary took the stub and bobbed a promising imitation of the curtsey Phoebe was taking pains to teach her.

Apparently satisfied that the matter was settled, the matron excused herself to go.

Lulu raced to Robert. Wrapping chubby arms about his leg, she stared up at him with worshipful eyes. "Papa!"

Phoebe spotted the scarlet scoring his cheeks and surmised he must no longer care for children, yet another change in him for the worse. The Robert she'd known and loved had sworn he wanted a score of babes. The nursery, he'd assured her, would be the very first suite of rooms in his ramshackle estate he'd set to rights once they were wed.

In six months, a year at most...

Swallowing against her throat's thickening, Phoebe hurried over to them. "This gentleman isn't your papa, pet," she said gently, taking Lulu by the hand and leading her away. "But if you are very good for Mary, I'll read you a story before I leave tonight."

Bottom lip trembling, Lulu sent Robert a last longing look before turning back to Phoebe. "*Dick Whittington and His Cat*?"

Phoebe settled her hand upon the child's crown. Hospital

policy forbade the keeping of pets by students, which Phoebe considered to be a great pity. The cook, however, kept a mouser, and Lulu and several others snuck away to visit it whenever they could contrive to do so.

"Whichever you fancy, poppet. For now, settle into your seat like a good child and mind Mary." She handed Lulu over to the senior student and turned back to Robert. Despite having regained his earlier equanimity, his tanned cheeks still bore the telltale pinkish brand. Wishing it were her slap that had made it so, she leveled him a look. "Where do you wish to begin?"

Rising, he replied, "I rather think I shall leave our route entirely to you."

"How refreshingly modern of you," she shot back, a deliberate mock. If she had her druthers, she'd lead him directly to the latrines—and lock the door behind him.

"Lead the way, milady."

Meeting his gloating gaze, she answered, "Very well, I shall."

She turned on her heel and headed down the aisle toward the door, leaving him to follow. Stepping out into the hallway, she drew the door closed behind them. "How dare you sabotage my class! Passing yourself off as a potential donor to bamboozle your way inside, you should be ashamed."

He had the audacity to pretend puzzlement. "I've bamboozled no one and for what it's worth, I didn't set out to sabotage you. The students bolting from their benches was utterly unforeseen."

"If that is even half true, you obviously know nothing about children."

His eyes dimmed. "Perhaps you can enlighten me. Why was that child so insistent that I must be her father?"

The question, though unexpected, struck her as genuine. Grudgingly she explained, "Not her father but *a* father. Other than the occasional visit by one of the directors, men are a rarity here. For most of these children, fathers are either violent ogres or, in Lulu's case, a fairytale fiction."

Silence met that assertion. Vulnerability washed over his chiseled features, affording her a fleeting glimpse of the softhearted boy she'd once so madly loved. Gaze raw, he finally said, "Chelsea and I lost our parents when we were young. That was hard, damnably hard, and yet I count myself fortunate to have had them for as long as we did. Neither of us ever had the slightest doubt that we'd been born wanted—loved. I cannot fathom being motherless and fatherless from one's very first memory."

It was an inordinately feeling thing to say, a sentiment utterly at odds with the selfish, callused adventurer she'd made him out to be. For her sanity's sake, she needed to still see him as that man—that pirate—who'd broken her heart and stolen her life, or at least the last six years of it.

Resolved not to weaken, she lifted her gaze to his. "Why have you come?"

Inscrutable mask back in place, he shrugged. "I am given to understand this institution was begun by a charity-minded sea captain by the surname of Coram. Who knows, mayhap I am cut from the same philanthropic sailcloth."

The late Captain Thomas Coram was second to a saint for Phoebe. Hearing Robert speak of himself in the same breath, even in sport, boiled her blood. "I'm sure this will be difficult if not impossible for you to comprehend, but my work here brings me great peace, even joy. I won't stand for anyone making mock of that, especially you."

He scowled as though she were the one of them in the wrong. "Must you paint me so black? I am a man of considerable means. I may well allot a measure of those means to this institution—provided I see firsthand how the funds are spent." He paused, locking his gaze on hers. "Would a donation of say...one hundred pounds a day make up for any disturbance to the peace?"

One hundred pounds. A day. Her mouth fell open. "But that's a bloody fortune. And bribery!"

"Correct on both counts."

"Are you quite certain you wish to go to such lengths for the privilege of following about another man's betrothed?"

His smile froze. "You scarcely behaved as a betrothed woman the other night."

Just like a rogue to taunt her with her lapse. "I had been...drinking."

He rolled his eyes. "If you're referring to that sip of spirit I poured you, you are reaching far indeed." Bending to her ear, he added, "By the by, you're flushed, not only your face but your lovely throat as well."

"Of course I'm flushed," she snapped. "I'm that angry."

He hoisted a black brow. "Are you certain anger is the only cause?"

"Don't flatter yourself."

"Very well, I shan't. Only answer me this—do we have a bargain or not?"

Feeling as though she were poised to make a pact with the Devil himself, she paused. "What precisely do you want in return? Know this—I shan't go to bed with you for it."

His crack of laughter had her ears burning. "Methinks milady holds a very low opinion of me—and a mighty high one of herself."

Mortified, Phoebe found herself wishing the floor might swallow her whole. "I didn't mean...I only thought...after the other night—"

"I have never paid for fornication, and I don't intend to begin with you. When you come to me, and come to me you shall, you shall do so of your own accord and wholly free of all commerce and custom."

He ran his gaze over her, a slow, thorough perusal that gnawed at her nerves and chipped away at her resistance. It didn't require a great deal of imagination to see what he was about, mentally stripping away her clothes layer by layer, her gown and petticoat, stays and shift, until she was as bare as the day she'd been born. Not that he need rely on imagination entirely. Six years ago she'd granted liberties beyond the handholding and kissing that a betrothed man might claim as his right. Recalling one night in particular, their last night together before his leaving, she looked sharply away.

"I couldn't help but notice that little Lulu looked to be in need of new shoes. I expect she's outgrown her current ones. I'll wager they pinch her toes fiercely. And Mary's smock looked a bit threadbare."

Phoebe swung her head back to him. Her hands curled into fists. Never had she wanted to throttle someone as she did now. "You, Robert Bellamy, are a rogue of the first order, a shiftless scamp, an unconscionable cad."

He grinned. "And those are my better qualities. Shall I assume we've come to terms?"

She set her fisted hands upon her hips. The stance was better suited to a fishwife than a lady, but she reminded herself that she didn't care what he thought of her, or at least she shouldn't. "As I recall, keeping your promises isn't precisely your strong suit. If you should renege—"

"I shan't." Reclaiming her arm, he folded it into his. "Shall we get on with our tour? Time is, after all, money, and I shall expect my hundred pounds' worth."

"Don't you ever rest?" Robert asked some time later, trailing Phoebe down yet another labyrinthine passageway. So far they'd visited the governors' courtroom, chapel, girls' dormitory, boys' dormitory, sundry classrooms and even the morgue, all of it at a brisk to breakneck pace.

She glanced back at him over her shoulder. "I haven't the

need, but don't let me hinder you from doing so."

"No, I'm fine. I was only concerned for you."

"Hmm," was all she said before darting down another white-walled corridor.

Lengthening his stride, he found himself wondering how it was that such a graceful woman managed to move so swiftly. The indolent maid of his memory seemed to have acquired the gait of a racehorse, not that he considered complaining of it. Admiring the hind view of those slender, swaying hips made for a deucedly pleasant pastime even if the reek of turpentine and lemon oil was beginning to block his nose.

They ended their tour at the infirmary. The strong smell of vinegar permeated the vicinity. A glass-front apothecary cabinet containing myriad meticulously labeled clear jars, a washing bench outfitted with a bandage roller and stacked bedpans, and a leather-bound ledger presumably for recording the circumstances of patients comprised the long, narrow room. Phoebe's hushed conference with the attending nurse secured their admission. Robert followed her along the queue of narrow cots, all but one of them unoccupied.

"Feeling a bit better today, Sally?" Phoebe asked, pausing to rest her hand upon the child's brow, her swollen jaw banded by a camphor-soaked cloth.

The girl, Sally, shook her head, wincing. "Tooth hurts terrible."

Phoebe stroked a hank of brown hair back from the girl's forehead. "I'm sure it does, poppet, but at least your fever's down. Once the foulness finishes draining, you'll be right as rain."

Dull eyes looked up into hers. "Yes, miss."

Most in Phoebe's position would have moved along, but instead she lingered. "I was going to give this to you later, but now shall serve." She reached into her gown's pocket and pulled out a cloth-covered doll.

The fevered little face lit. "Oh, miss, thank you!"

Phoebe tucked the doll into the crook of Sally's arm and straightened. "Not only a doll, but a *magic* doll. Whenever your tooth troubles you, squeeze upon her and she'll help keep the pain away."

Looking on, Robert felt his heart give a powerful pull. Phoebe had the makings of a marvelous mother. The earlier scene in the classroom and now this strengthened his resolve to do all in his power to ensure that her future children would be his, not Bouchart's.

Seeing her about to turn back to him, he quickly made a mask of his face. "You needn't fear infection," she said archly, misreading him yet again. "Mostly we treat minor injuries, sprained ankles and, in Sally's case, toothaches. More serious cases are transported to St. George's."

"My constitution is that of an ox," he answered, no idle boast. Given the fevers and pestilence to which he'd been exposed, an abscessed tooth and a few runny noses hardly seemed of note. Stepping away from the beds with Phoebe, he asked, "How did you come to volunteer here?"

She hesitated. "In an odd way, I have you to thank for it."

"I?" Even strongly suspecting he would regret it, he had to ask, "How so?"

"After we were told you were...lost, I wasn't entirely certain what to do with myself, how to go on. Coming here began as a crutch, a reason to rise from bed each morning. Over time I began adding days, heartened that it was in my power to do some good."

His kitchen conversation with Chelsea came back to him. *She draped herself in black crepe and bombazine for a full year as though she were your widow in truth. There were times we feared she might take her own life.*

"How does your mother feel about your manual laboring?"

She lanced him a look. "You mean my *eccentricity,* or so

Mama calls it. She's pinning her hopes on marriage proving the cure. To be fair, I should admit that she is hardly alone in her censure. Barring Chelsea and Anthony, most members of the *ton* think I'm daft to spend my days fraternizing with orphaned children, whom they're convinced will amount to nothing more than cutpurses and prostitutes."

Watching her closely, he ventured, "And Bouchart, what does he say?"

She hesitated, the pause telling or so it seemed to Robert. "Aristide tolerates my employment for the time being, though he too assumes I'll give it up of my own accord once we're wed." She paused, her quicksilver gaze honing onto his. "He's mistaken."

"I admire you for following your passion."

She looked at him askance.

A renegade curl clung to the side of her cheek, which was neither pale nor waxen as it had been after her faint but a healthy, becoming pink. Resisting the urge to reach out and brush it back, he shook his head. "No, really I do."

Admire her though he did, he was in no way inured to how enticing she not only looked but smelled—vanilla from the milled soap she'd always favored, lavender from the eau de cologne she preferred to perfume and some spicy citrusy scent he didn't recall from before but badly wanted to sample.

A baby's bawling drew their attention outside. Robert joined her at the window overlooking the front lawn. Fifty-odd women and children, the latter of various ages from infancy to adolescence, stood in queue extending from the arcaded entrance gate to the circular drive. The group had multiplied since Robert had arrived. Passing them by, he'd seen more than one cheek tracked with tears, but aside from the occasional wailing infant, they'd waited in stoic silence. It seemed they waited still.

"Good God, there are so many of them."

Letting the curtain drop, Phoebe sighed. "I know. Every Monday brings the same sad sight. I'd thought by now to be accustomed to it, but after five years it still breaks my heart."

"Have the London parish houses grown so lax in dispensing relief?"

Her arch look told him he'd said the wrong thing—again. "They've not come for alms but to petition that their children be taken in."

"All babes, I see."

Expression somber, she nodded. "Only infants of twelve months or younger are accepted, and the mother must stipulate that the child is both born out of wedlock as well as the fruit of her first fall."

"I gather if those conditions are unmet, mother and child are turned away?"

Eyes suspiciously bright, she sighed again. "It sounds heartless, I know, and in a way it is, but we haven't beds for them all. Truth be told, we haven't room for the ones we do take. Presently we're at four hundred and ten and that's with several of the younger boys and girls sleeping two to a cot."

He'd thought himself inured to sad, suffering sights, but apparently he wasn't as hardened as he'd hoped. "What will happen to them?"

"Once they pass the medical examination, they're sent to the country for fostering. At four or five years of age, they're brought back here as Lulu recently was, the boys to learn a trade, the girls to train for domestic employment. When the boys reach fourteen, the governors arrange indentures for them; many end up enlisting in the army. Settling the girls is more difficult, but every effort is made to find them suitable situations."

Like a surgeon probing a wound, he had to know. "And what of those who are turned away?"

She shrugged, but once again her eyes confirmed how very

deeply she cared. Silver-blue irises awash in unshed tears—if only she'd look upon him kindly again Robert would happily dive in and drown in them. "Some will be abandoned. Others will starve alongside their mothers. Still others will seek refuge in the workhouses or...worse." A pained look crossed her face. "Last winter a newborn was discovered in a...rubbish bin behind the hospital kitchen. He'd been dead some hours of exposure, or so the resident physician judged." She turned her face away.

He reached around her and braced a hand upon the sill, bringing their bodies ever so slightly brushing. "Surely something more may be done? What of the fathers? Haven't they any say in whether or not their children are surrendered?"

She turned back to glare at him, her quicksilver gaze once more sharp as Damascus steel. "Do you honestly believe that even one of those women standing out there would give up her child if she might choose another course, if she herself hadn't been abandoned?"

Abandoned—so there it was, the crux of Phoebe's philanthropic passion. Clearly she felt an affinity with these women who'd been left by their men to fend for their offspring and themselves.

"I only meant that it seems a father should have some rights, some say at the very least. Conceiving a child requires both parties, after all." Gaze on hers, he owned how very much he wanted to make love with her and babies with her, the yearning so fiercely primal he felt a sudden aching in his loins.

"One of the prerequisites for petitioning is that the father must have *deserted* both mother and child. *Deserted*, Robert. I'd think you of all people would understand that."

He swallowed against the pain pushing a path up his throat. "I didn't desert you."

She answered with a sharp laugh. "You chose to stay away and leave me to think you dead. If that's not desertion, what is?"

"I chose to *return* when I knew I might be a fit husband for you in every way."

Her gaze narrowed. "And now you are too late, for I have a husband, or at least I shall before the season's end."

Before the season's end! Robert felt as though an invisible fist plowed his solar plexus. In the past, controlling his reaction to the pain, pretending to no longer feel or care, had served as his best defense, his strongest weapon.

Calling upon that hard-learned stoicism now, he summoned a smile. "What a coincidence, for I too will be embarking upon my next voyage then as well, but not before I have the pleasure of seeing you as a bride, I hope."

Phoebe's smile dipped.

"For now, I am afraid I must away. I have another appointment to attend."

"Pray do not let me keep you from your pressing business," she retorted, sounding much like her mother.

Judging from her planted stance, he gathered she didn't mean to see him out. Just as well, he supposed for he needed some time to regroup from the crushing blow she'd dealt.

Heading for the door, he turned back. "What ungodly hour shall I arrive tomorrow?"

She shrugged. "Anytime or not at all, as you wish."

"If you treat all your benefactors in such a shrewish fashion, 'tis a mercy you have a roof and four walls," he answered, a deliberate reminder that he was, in point, paying for her company if not her goodwill.

Releasing a sigh, she capitulated, "Oh, very well, nine o'clock sharp, and mind if you're late I shall bar the classroom door and you may wait out in the hallway until the session finishes."

"My dearest Phoebe, I wouldn't dream of being late."

Stepping out into the hallway, Robert considered that six years was quite late enough.

Given the ticking clock he faced, he didn't mean to waste so much as a single second more.

"You're late." Reclining in a banyan and slippers despite the midday hour, Aristide looked up as his henchman-cum-manservant entered.

Dragging sand and reeking of rum and stale fish, Payne offloaded his brimming satchel. "Sorry, I got...tied up. Or ye might say I were busy tyin' someone else up." A cackle punctuated the comment.

Judging from the booting spilling out onto the carpet, the mudlarks and lumpers employed to steal from moored ships had been industrious that week. Pawning the ill-gotten articles sufficed to keep Aristide in his suite of let rooms in Knightsbridge—and the appearance of style—for now.

"Spare me your excuses." Aristide picked up his cheroot. "I need you to follow a certain East India Company captain."

Payne wasn't much for ironing newspapers or blacking boots, but when called upon he was a wonder at making "inconveniences" such as Robert Bellamy disappear. Whether or not such a permanent "solution" would be called for remained to be seen. Certainly Bellamy's unforeseen return had made a hash of Aristide's perfectly plotted plans. The six hundred pounds a year Phoebe's father had agreed to settle upon her was but the beginning. Once Aristide had her in his clutches as his wife, her doting papa would pay dearly to ensure his poppet was gently treated. If he balked, a few well-laid bruises on Phoebe's fair skin should bring him swiftly around. In the interim, every day Aristide must continue their courtship put a pinch on his purse—and his patience.

"I'm all ears. Who is 'e?"

Aristide took a long drag of his cheroot, exhaling before answering, "Robert Bellamy, lately known to the Company as

Robert Lazarus. His ship, The Swan, is berthed at Blackwall amongst the import vessels. According to my fiancée, he is likely biding with his sister and brother-in-law in Berkley Square." Eking the information out of Phoebe had proven on par with straining pudding through a skein, but in the end her guilt had proven his ally.

Picking at his gold-capped front teeth with a blackened fingernail, Payne appeared to weigh his latest "assignment". "Berkley Square, eh? Fambly must be top drawer."

Aristide tapped ashes into a pewter bowl. "His sister made a fortuitous marriage, as I mean to do. For now, find out his familiars, his habits, where he sleeps, with *whom* he sleeps."

Sucking on his teeth, Payne asked, "What do you want me to do with him—or should I say *to* him?"

Aristide ground his cheroot to ash. Imagining it was Robert Bellamy whose light he snuffed, he replied, "Nothing—for now."

Upon leaving Phoebe, Robert headed for the Board of Admiralty, where Phoebe's brother Reggie served as a clerk in the service of the Lords Commissioner. Among its mandates, the Board was charged with enforcing the Piracy Law and keeping a record of violations thereof.

Walking his horse through the classically styled entrance screen, Robert called on his courage to do that which had been delayed for far too long. He dismounted, turned his mount over to a porter and headed up the steps of the U-shaped brick building.

Reggie's suite of offices was on the uppermost floor. Upon stating his purpose to one of the guards posted inside the entrance, Robert ascended the grand staircase. Stepping off the landing, he passed the boardroom, its floor-to-ceiling windows looking out onto Whitehall, and continued through the warren of intersecting corridors and enclosed offices to Reggie's door.

You can do this, Bellamy. You must do this.

Several sharp raps brought the door opening. Bleary-eyed and brandy-breathed, Reggie stood back to admit him. "Bellamy, splendid to see you. Sorry if I've kept you waiting."

"Not at all," Robert lied, doing his damndest not to mind the guiding hand Reggie laid upon his sleeve. "How is civil service treating you?" Stepping to the side, he moved beyond arm's reach.

Reggie closed the door behind him and turned about. Catching a strong whiff of spirits, Robert studied him. Six years ago they hadn't been friends, but they hadn't been enemies either. Blessed with the same thick blond hair and slate blue eyes as Phoebe, once Reggie might have passed for her twin rather than her senior sibling. Now he looked nearer to forty than thirty. Judging from his pink-shot eyes and high color, his rakehell ways were more than fleeting youthful folly.

"Nothing near as noble or colorful as I venture to say your years away have been. My days are an odyssey of endless minutia—reports, meeting minutes, correspondence that must be answered and filed—utter enslavement."

Biting back the temptation to inquire if Reggie might prefer splitting rocks instead, Robert said, "I regret that I must add to your burdens."

A gentleman born and bred, Reggie shrugged aside the suggestion. "Sit, please," he said, waiving him toward a high-backed chair covered in leather.

Though Robert would have rather said his piece standing, he reminded himself that he was no longer aboard ship. On land and in London, there were proprieties to be observed, implicitly understood rules of engagement every whit as codified as the protocol for a sultan's court.

"So," Reggie began, observing Robert overtop his tented hands, hands marked by a slight but telling tremble. "I suppose felicitations on your resurrection are in order."

Robert inclined his head. "I fear your mother is less than elated."

Reggie did not dispute him. "I marvel your ears haven't singed to cinders from her rant at breakfast the next morning, not to mention the clamor across the St. James's clubs. You should know that you've been officially entered in the betting book at White's."

"That's one way of getting in, I suppose," Robert remarked. How ironic that the club that once had declined him as a member should include him now in their infamous book. "And what, if I may ask, is the nature of the wager?"

Reggie hesitated. "Whether you'll, er...win Phoebe back to you or leave London with your, er—"

"Tail between my legs in deep disgrace?" Robert finished for him.

Reggie had sudden difficulty meeting his eyes. "Something along those lines, yes."

"And which outcome have you wagered upon?"

Toying with the feather of his quill, Reggie answered, "This once I have laid my money on the same outcome on which I've set my heart—on you and Phoebe—though I warn you, it shan't be easy. As the savior of my sister's prospects, the Frenchman can do little wrong in our household. The other evening's farcical masque is but one example of the sway he holds and not only over Mama."

Robert's back stiffened. "You speak as though Phoebe is a wizened crone." Was six-and-twenty truly so damnably old?

Reggie shrugged. "Not wizened, but tarnished to be sure. Two failed engagements, first to Anthony and then to you, are a lot for a woman's reputation to weather."

Phoebe had said as much the other evening and Chelsea had echoed her, but ere now, Robert had been too angry and hurt to give the complaint much credence. He did now. An unwed Englishwoman might enjoy greater freedoms than her female counterpart in the East, but her worth was every whit as weighted by her chastity and breeding capability. For the first time he fully owned the severe social straits in which his six years away had stranded Phoebe.

"Granted it's not very sporting to slip out on your sister's betrothal ball," Reggie continued, "but the truth is even before you returned I wasn't overly keen on her choice of husbands, at least not this time 'round." He added the latter with a crooked smile that likely had persuaded many a misused mistress to forgive him his faults.

So there was at least one Tremont who was less than enamored of Phoebe's Frenchman. Tucking away that bit of intelligence for later, Robert came around to his purpose. "I haven't come to speak of your sister, but to make my official report. As the sole survivor of The Phoenix to make his way back to England, that grim duty falls to me."

What had taken place aboard the doomed East Indiaman wasn't only Robert's story. He shared it with men like the ship's portly purser, Bob Snow, who'd suffered the hacking off of all ten fingers and toes, one digit per hour, before blessedly bleeding out. He shared it with the ship's middle-aged cook, Nate Blount, who'd met his end submerged headfirst in a boiling cauldron of his own soup. Deemed too fat or old for enslavement, their screams and pleas for mercy would haunt Robert until his dying day. They were his brethren now, their kinship steeped in suffering and bathed in blood. It fell to him to stand as their witness.

He drew a bracing breath, calling upon his courage. "The Phoenix wasn't sunk by foul weather as is commonly credited. She was done in by pirates."

Reggie's ruddy complexion drained. "Piracy, bloody bad business that." His gaze went to an adjoining door, which Robert surmised led to an interior office. "I'll just call in my secretary, and he'll jot this all down." He pushed back from the desk and started up.

"No!"

Robert's command, issued in a tone similar to the one he used aboard ship, sent Reggie sinking back into his seat. "But I've a dashed dodgy hand and—"

"I make my report to you alone or I walk away." It would be challenge aplenty to say what he must to Phoebe's brother. He'd yet to begin and already his chest was tightening as though leather straps once more cinched him. The prospect of baring his blackened soul before some likely bespectacled, beetle-browed stranger was beyond conceiving.

Reggie reached for a sheaf of paper. "Very well, as you wish." Dipping his pen's nub into the ink well, he looked up. "Let us begin at the beginning, shall we?"

"Mark me this is my official report which I am making to you in your official capacity. You're not to speak a word of it outside this office." Robert stabbed a finger into the space separating them.

"Not even to Phoebe?"

"*Especially* not to Phoebe."

Focusing his gaze not on his confessor's countenance but on the wavering pen, Robert began. Unlike his previous two expurgated recitations, this time he held nothing back. The beatings by fists sheathed in brass knuckles and boots bearing razors at the tips, the whippings and brandings, the mastheading and starving, the sundry psychological tortures used to break his will whilst leaving sufficient of his body intact for the slavers, all poured out of him.

Five sheets of paper in, he finally finished, sweat sheathed and shaking. Only then did he dare lift his gaze from the quill feathers to Reggie's face. The clerk's cheeks had gone as chalky as the Cliffs of Dover.

Reggie raised his shocked gaze to Robert's. "Good God, man, I'd no notion."

Robert rolled his shoulders, willing the bunched muscles to

ease. "Why would you?"

"How much does Phoebe know?"

"Beyond the ship sinking, nothing—and I mean to keep it that way."

"You should tell her. It would...that is to say it might make all the difference."

Adamant, Robert shook his head. "My sister made a similar case, and my answer to her was the same as it is to you. No. And you are not to tell her either. Breathe a bloody word that's on those sheets, and I'll have you before your superior."

Reggie put down the pen. "Draw it mild, old boy, I shan't say a peep, not to Phoebe nor anyone beyond official channels. But should you change your mind—"

"I won't." As much as Robert wanted her back, the possibility that she might return to him out of pity was beyond his ability to stomach.

"Still, old sod, give it a think. Despite the stiff upper lip she's grown, Phoebe's still got the same dashed soft heart. If you don't believe me, you should see her with those ragamuffins she's taken beneath her wing, especially that recently arrived little blonde imp. Her 'working' is all but driving our mother to Bedlam, God bless her. Takes some of the parental vigilance from me," he added with a grin. "Otherwise I might find myself disowned."

Robert stood to go, legs as shaky as though this was his first footing upon land after a long sea voyage. He'd kept the truth bottled up for so long that, having released it, he wasn't certain what to do about the sudden sinking emptiness.

Reggie rose as well. "Now that you've sworn me to silence, is there anything I can do for you, anything at all? If so, you've only to name it." Crossing to the front of the desk, he clapped a hand to Robert's shoulder.

Robert fought the urge to knock it off. Pinning Phoebe's arms the other evening hadn't been solely from anger. Earlier on the balcony, allowing her to touch him had been a test he'd passed but barely. And yet despite the disastrous turn their reunion had taken, there was no denying that kissing her had fed the starved space inside him.

"There is something you can do, though I shan't hold you to your promise."

Dropping his hand, Reggie said, "Name it."

"I should greatly appreciate being made privy to your sister's social calendar for the following fortnight."

Chapter Five

Almack's Assembly Rooms, King Street, One Week Later

The ball and art auction to benefit the Foundling Hospital was a veritable crush. Persuading all seven patronesses of Almack's to open their hallowed hall for other than the weekly Wednesday night subscription dances had required patience on par with pushing a bill through Parliament, but Phoebe had persevered. The club's cachet virtually guaranteed success despite the rooms being drafty and lukewarm lemonade the sole beverage served; still, with its floor-length velvet draperies, inlaid pier glass wall panels and double-tiered crystal chandeliers, the great room made a magnificent sight. Standing on the outskirts of the dance floor greeting guests, her arm linked with Aristide's, Phoebe conceded that her last-minute "guest" deserved much of the credit for the unprecedented crowd. Robert's return was the preeminent topic of gossip in every West End drawing room. She'd even heard a rumor that there was some sort of wager going at White's, though Reggie refused to confirm or deny it.

Yet again her gaze strayed to Robert. Positioned on the far side of the dance floor almost directly across from her, he stood stoic in the face of the goggle-eyed stares and high whispers directed his way. So far as Phoebe could say, he hadn't budged since his arrival, barring his eyes, which seemed to follow her everywhere. One arm folded behind his back, he looked stiff and out of sorts—and breathtakingly handsome. With his unruly waves tamed by pomade and combed back from his square-jawed face and his brawny body sheathed in expert tailoring—he'd even worn the requisite knee breeches!—he stood apart from the other gentlemen and not only because of his sun-bronzed skin or the diamond ear stud he still stubbornly wore.

Phoebe suppressed a sigh, full knowing she was far from the only female to notice him. Like peahens, any number of ladies both eligible and a few wed had found excuses to flock toward him, cooing over his crimson coat and toying with the dance cards dangling from their waists in unmistakable invitation. So far he'd politely but pointedly rebuffed them all—so far.

Not for the first time he reached up to slip a finger beneath his elaborately wound neck cloth. Between it and the starched shirt points standing at attention on either cheek, he looked supremely uncomfortable.

It served him right.

For the past week, he'd put himself in her path in every way possible and not only at the Foundling Hospital. Be it Lady Winifred's musicale with Aristide on Tuesday, Wedgewood's show rooms on Thursday where with her mother she'd perused the latest china patterns or Gunter's Tea Room where just the other day she'd treated Belinda to a lemon ice, it was as if he knew where she would be before she did. As much as she might like to believe those meetings were pure happenstance, she knew better. One of the servants in her household must be in his pocket. It was the only conceivable explanation. Were she to root out the blather box, she'd see him or her turned out without tuppence. She had a suspicion the culprit might be Betty, her new lady's maid, though without proof there was little she could do about it.

It was beyond annoying. And yet were she honest, she'd admit to selecting the cream-colored muslin tamboured in gold thread, her evening best, with not Aristide but Robert in mind.

Catching her eye, he lifted his lemonade glass in a silent salute, smile bold and eyes smoldering. Phoebe's heart kicked into a canter. Her pulse quickened, her flesh flushed. Beneath her gown, she felt a telltale tingling. Beginning at her breasts, it trickled all the way down to her...

She looked sharply away. The cut direct—she'd learned it at the knee of her mother and yet ere now she'd never thought to employ it in earnest, certainly not upon Robert. Doing so wasn't snobbery. It was self-preservation. Even with the breadth of a ballroom between them, being in proximity to her erstwhile betrothed made her knees watery and her heart stumble.

"This is insufferable," Aristide spat into her ear. "Is it not enough that you must bear his boorish company during the day? Must he stalk you by night as well? I have had enough of this foolishness!" Unlinking arms, he took a determined step forward.

Panicked that there might be a scene or, far worse, the prelude to a duel, Phoebe caught at his arm. "Please, it is such a lovely evening. Let us not spoil it by fretting over Robert Bellamy. Beyond all, it is attention he craves. Why not do as I do and simply ignore him? He will move on to greener pastures soon enough," she added, though a lump lodged in her throat at the very thought.

He relaxed fractionally. "As you wish, *ma petite*, though should he presume to press himself on you tonight, I will not stand for it."

She released the breath she hadn't realized she'd been holding. "Thank you."

He answered with a curt nod and looked away, affording Phoebe the opportunity to study him without subterfuge. With his black-brown hair, dark eyes and impeccably tailored evening wear, her intended cut a fine figure indeed. And yet why was it she couldn't seem to summon so much as a flutter when she stood in his proximity as she did now? As much as she might wish to pawn off her apathy to his peevishness, in her heart she knew there was greater cause.

Robert.

Since his return, she hadn't been able to summon a single sane thought. The wellspring of feelings flooding her had her second-guessing everyone and everything, most especially herself.

Aristide shifted back to her, barely bothering to conceal his openmouthed yawn. "How soon may we leave?" he asked though the ball was barely beyond its first hour.

Knowing Robert stood within eyeshot emboldened her to say, "As the hostess, I must see the evening through to its end, but you need not stay."

A stormy look quelled the suggestion. His mouth twisted into a sneer. "Ah, *oui*, I am sure the good captain would be most happy to take my rightful place. Perhaps for all your protestations, you prefer his society to mine?"

"That is not true by half," she protested, mindful of the watchful eyes wending toward them.

His dark gaze narrowed. "Is it not? You certainly seem to spend sufficient time in his company."

Rather than deny the obvious truth and risk stirring a scene, she said, "I only meant that I do not wish to keep you from—"

She paused. Where did he go on the nights they spent apart? Most men might be found at their club, but to her best knowledge he didn't belong to any. Was it a gaming hell or, far worse, a brothel that he frequented? If so, his nocturnal revelries must have brought him crossing paths with Reggie though her sibling had never spoken of seeing him. Then again, Phoebe supposed that hell-raking habits weren't something a man, even a scapegrace such as Reggie, took up with his sister.

"Wherever it is you go, I shouldn't wish to impose upon you. I can find my way home with Reggie and Mama." Indeed, the prospect of unfettering herself from him, if only for the night, brought a giddy sense of freedom.

Aiming a dagger look Robert's way, he dug in his heels. "I will stay. To the bitter end, as you English say."

The ungracious remark prompted a decidedly unwelcome

and unflattering comparison. Whilst Robert appeared content to wipe her chalk slate and follow her unflaggingly from classroom to ballroom, her betrothed was put upon to attend so much as a single social event.

But perhaps she was being unfair. Robert's return had muddled her mind, resurrecting old feelings better left buried. Unlike the love-struck chit of six years ago, this time 'round she must employ sound sense. Robert was her past, Aristide her future. They were to be married. Why was it she didn't feel anything close to content?

"It seems greener pastures have arrived," Aristide remarked, sounding almost jovial.

Curious as to what had brought about his sudden shift of humor, she followed his gaze across the dance floor. Robert stood, no longer alone but cheek to jowl with Phoebe's old rival from her debutante days, the recently widowed and undoubtedly delectable Lady Morton.

Monitoring Phoebe from the corner of one eye, Robert made a point of dipping his head toward his companion despite finding her perfume—and person—cloying. After the past week's chilly standoff, Phoebe's glare felt like sunshine upon his face. By day at the Foundling Hospital, she'd treated him with icy civility. Outside of it she'd simply refused to acknowledge him. Flowers, confectionary, an abysmally written sonnet—none of his courtship tactics had found the slightest chink in her armor.

Desperate times called for desperate measures, or so Chelsea was fond of quoting.

The one tactic he hadn't so far tried might prove to be the very one that worked.

Jealousy.

He turned his gaze back to the curvaceous blonde, the former Miss Leticia Blakenship, forcing himself to stare as though she were Aphrodite incarnate rather than the witch who, six years ago, had cut him socially. If he lived to be one hundred, he'd never forget her caustic comment which he'd chanced to overhear at his and Phoebe's betrothal ball.

"The on dit is that it's a love match, but I venture to say it's her six hundred pounds a year that he holds most dear."

"Tell me, my dear Miss Blakenship, how is it that a diamond of the first water such as you has managed to remain unattached? The men of London must be blind idiots indeed." He deliberately dropped his gaze to her gown's low neckline.

Predictably she preened, sailing a gloved hand through the air. "Oh, but you have it all wrong, sir. I am Lady Morton now and, sadly, a widow," she said, not seeming sad of it at all.

A widow—her mauve-colored gown made sudden sense. "And yet you have come out of mourning to attend. How...stalwart of you."

"Half mourning," she corrected, face flushing. "I set aside my grief in support of the orphans...and Lady Phoebe, of course."

Robert choked back a bitter laugh. "Your selflessness is an inspiration to us all, milady."

She nodded solemnly. "My late husband was a great contributor to the Foundling Hospital."

Amidst her prattling, Robert shifted sufficiently to glimpse Phoebe glaring in his distinct direction. Encouraged, he turned his brightest smile on Lady Morton. "Forgive my impertinence, but your husband must have passed on a most happy man."

"Oh, gracious, sir, your courtly compliments have me flushing most fiercely. And may I take the opportunity to say how very happy I am that you are not indeed dead?"

Another sidelong glance confirmed that Phoebe had bit on the bait. Leaving Bouchart behind to hold up the wall, she appeared to be making her way toward him.

Bending his head to Lady Morton's, he said, "That is by far

the kindest remark that has been made to me all week."

She turned so that her lips brushed the outside of his ear. "Allow me to assure you, sir, I am prepared to be a great deal kinder."

A throat clearing had them pulling apart. Robert turned to Phoebe, who'd joined them. "Lady Morton, there you are," she trilled, as though she hadn't had them in her sights the entire time. "You must think me a poor hostess indeed for failing to find you earlier."

Lady Morton sent her a baffled look. "Find me? But I have been in plain sight—"

"The bidding for the art auction is about to begin, and recalling your late lord's generosity, I took the liberty of reserving a seat for you in the front." She shifted her gaze to Robert. "A single seat, I'm afraid."

Smile slipping, Lady Morton said, "But I was only—"

"No buts," Phoebe broke in yet again. "I am resolved that the Hogarth shall go home with no other than you." She slanted a look Robert's way. "I shall endeavor to entertain Mr. Bellamy until your return."

"Well, if you're certain—"

"Quite. Now off with you or you shall lament losing your prize," Phoebe warned, wagging a gloved finger beneath the other woman's nose.

Defeated, Lady Morton turned back to Robert. "Shall I see you at supper, sir?"

"I should not miss it," Robert swore. "Mayhap we can resume our most delightful...*conversation* then." Though he'd as soon break bread with Bonaparte himself, the pink pooling in Phoebe's cheeks more than repaid any sacrifice.

Left with little choice, the widow dipped a curtsey and whisked away to follow those wending toward the auction room.

Watching her head off, Phoebe cast Robert a sideways look. "Have you no decency? She's in mourning."

He smothered a laugh. "Half-mourning, and you'd do better to remind her of that. But tell me, why should you care?"

She swung about to face him "Who says that I do?"

"Your face gives you away. Your complexion has gone quite green."

She sniffed, and her injured air sent his hopes soaring. "Are you intimating I am jealous of Lady Morton?"

Feeling on firmer footing than he had been all week, he leaned back against a Palladian pilaster. "Are you?"

"What nonsense, of course I am not. I only hate to see you play the poor woman for a fool. Given her recent loss, she is certain to be in a most vulnerable state of mind."

Robert had never encountered a less vulnerable female than Lady Morton. She was clearly on the prowl for her next conquest. He doubted she would require much persuasion to cast off her widow's weeds in favor of wearing his bedsheets.

Rather than voice such a crude if clearly correct conclusion, he settled for, "A woman such as Lady Morton is more than equipped to care for herself." He looked out onto the dance floor where couples were queuing up for a quadrille. "Tell me, are there any other ladies present whom I should take pains to avoid?"

Phoebe's gaze narrowed. "Myself, for one."

He snapped his gaze back to hers. "I might point out that 'tis you who forded the floor to reach me."

Her eyes flashed. "Do you deny you have been deliberately following me all the week? I have come to think I may not even take my sister for an ice without you spying?"

"I do love a good ice," he answered with a wink. "And I've taken quite a fancy to that quaint if over-crowded little teashop. As I find myself biding nearby, I cannot promise you will not see me there again—soon."

"So you're staying on then?"

Wishing she might sound more pleased about it, Robert

shrugged. "As I said before, I have until the month's end to decide whether to accept new orders or resign my captaincy."

"Don't you mean Robert Lazarus has the month to decide?" she asked archly.

He forced a shrug. "A rose by any other name."

She sent him a dour look. "So this week was no aberration merely to plague me. You mean to circulate in society."

At times such as this she sounded nearly as starchy as her mother. "Mayfair has always been rather incestuous, an elite pond of familiar faces. We are bound to continue to run into one another with some frequency. Why spend those occasions in awkwardness or aiming daggers at one another? Why not strive to be civil or, better yet, friends?"

"Friends?" She stared up at him as though the suggestion had never once occurred to her.

He felt his smile softening and with it his heart. "I recall our beginning that way."

They'd first met as fellow captives in the cellar of an East End tavern. By the time Phoebe had joined him in his dark, dank prison, he was weak from starvation and delirious from the daily drug dosing. Drifting in and out of consciousness, he'd mistaken her for an angel and kissed her. And Phoebe, who'd later confessed to never before much caring for kissing, had liked it very much indeed.

She swallowed hard. "That is all in the past."

"Is it?" he asked gently.

She sealed her lips as if suddenly afraid what sentiments might slip out.

Torn between exasperation and amusement, he blew out a breath. "Come now, is the sight of me truly so off-putting? I realize I am not the smooth-cheeked youth with whom you first fell in love, but I am hardly a monster." So long as he kept on his clothes, the statement might remain a true one.

Light brown brows snapped together. "If you're fishing for

compliments, I am sorry to disappoint. As a betrothed woman, I cannot go about remarking upon the countenance of every peacock that puts himself in my path."

"Peacock, egads," he said, enjoying himself despite all that stood at stake. "Shall I gather from that remark you don't care for my coat?"

She raked her gaze over the wine-colored wool, admittedly a standout in a sea of crow's black. "Surely Anthony wouldn't own something so vulgar."

"I'll have you know this is newly made." When he'd brought the bolt of fabric to the tailor and explained it was meant not for a waistcoat but for the coat itself, the poor fellow had nearly dropped his false teeth. "Though were you to accompany me on a shopping expedition, I'd promise to cede to your good taste and sound sense."

She sent him a shocked look. "I cannot be seen shopping with you for something so intimate. I might as well declare myself your mistress."

Leaning in, he whispered, "Delightful as that sounds, I'd much rather have you for my wife, but at this juncture I'll take what I can get."

Color high, she stepped back. "Would it not cause a scene, I would slap you soundly for that revolting remark."

"Would you now?" Recalling the fervor and feel of her strike on their reunion night, he felt himself thickening, a state that his cutaway coat could not conceal. Leaning ever closer, he snared her gaze and whispered, "Have a care, milady, I might well put you to the test." Out of the corner of his eye, he caught a familiar figure approaching and choked back an oath. "But, alas, your ever vigilant keeper is on his way over to reclaim you, forcing us to adjourn this invigorating badinage until a more private time."

Fierce-faced, Bouchart strode up to them. "Monsieur Bellamy, like the bad penny, you turn up yet again."

Robert met the Frenchman's quelling look with one of his own. "It's *Captain* Bellamy, and as tonight is a public ball, I purchased a ticket as is my right."

Bouchart opened his mouth as if to reply when they were interrupted by a wigged server circulating a silver tray of lemonade. The Frenchman made a face. "*Mon Dieu*, more lemonade! I wonder we are not all afloat in it." Expression mortified, Phoebe shushed him but to no avail. Pitching his voice higher, he demanded, "May a man not be provided a proper drink in this godforsaken place?"

Robert hid a smile. Almack's choice of beverage was the one thing on which he and Bouchart could agree, though he wasn't about to make his complaints quite so public. "Doubtless you would prefer a glass of Calvados?" he said, recalling that Bouchart hailed from Normandy, where the apple-flavored brandy was almost exclusively produced.

For a split second, the scowl was replaced by an expression of pure puzzlement. Recovering, Bouchart turned back to the waiter. "Have you no champagne?"

"Nay, milord, not a drop, I'm afraid," the man answered and then scuttled away toward the next grouping of guests.

Robert waited for the servant to leave before pursuing the topic. "Calvados is from your native Normandy, is it not? I should think you would leap at the opportunity to sample the nectar of your homeland, especially after so long an exile."

The Frenchman hesitated. "It was a spirit much drunk in my father's day, but it has fallen out of fashion."

Robert scrubbed his gloved knuckles across his chin. "You don't say?"

Bouchart's color rose. "Enough! I am in no mood to educate you on the subject of fortified wines."

Robert's heart stilled—and his hopes rose. Calvados was brandy, not wine. A Frenchman from Normandy who was also a wine importer would be well acquainted with the spirit—unless

Bouchart was not who or what he seemed.

"As you wish." Making a mental note to take up the topic at a later time, Robert returned his attention to Phoebe. "I was about to bespeak the next dance. May I?"

Having earlier committed the evening's program to heart, he recalled it was a waltz. He hadn't danced in six years, not a waltz or any other. The close contact would once again put him to the test. He couldn't very well pinion her arms on the dance floor as he had in her father's study. Nor could he continue shunning the very touch he craved. Phoebe wasn't the only one of them mired in the past. His hopes of claiming her hinged upon his moving forward as a whole man.

She opened her mouth to reply, but before she could, Bouchart broke in with, "I am afraid you are too late yet again," a nasty jab intended to recall the six years of separation. "It is promised to me, as are all my bride's dances."

"All of them, you say?" Robert reached out and lifted the dance card dangling from Phoebe's slender waist. "And yet your name appears but once." Dropping the card, he looked up to Phoebe. "The ladies' dances tonight are in the service of charity, are they not?"

The question was intended as rhetorical, but she answered nonetheless. "Ten pounds for each dance to benefit the Foundation."

"Ladies selling dances as if they were favors, it is a disgrace," Bouchart spat.

Phoebe's lips slid into a wry smile. "As you can no doubt ascertain, Aristide does not precisely approve." She rolled her lovely eyes, looking more like her old lively self than Robert had yet seen.

Heartened, he smiled back. "So I gather."

Flinging his gaze between them, Bouchart snorted. "I am afraid my fiancée is that most annoying species of female, a do-gooder or so you English say."

They both ignored him.

Gaze locked upon Phoebe's, Robert felt as if they were the only two in the room, co-conspirators, friends—lovers—once more. "What if I were to triple the ten pounds to thirty?"

Her put-upon sigh was for Bouchart's benefit, Robert felt sure of it. The desire in her eyes, which kept returning to his, was too plain not to read. Nor did he miss the telltale moistening of her lips. A signal from six years before, it meant she wanted him to kiss her.

She cut a look to her fiancé's furious face and swallowed hard. "As it is for the foundlings, I can hardly refuse." Her gaze dipped to her dance card. Lifting it and the nub of pencil dangling from its silk ribbon, she prepared to write in Robert's name.

"Forty pounds."

Phoebe's head shot up. "Forty pounds? But Aristide—"

"Be silent," he ordered and hearing the snappish tone in which he spoke to her, Robert was hard pressed not to call him out on the spot.

Instead, he retorted, "Fifty."

Aristide's fuming gaze met his. "Sixty."

From the trellised balcony above, the orchestra struck up a waltz. At this rate, they would all sit out the dance. Resolved to forestall further haggling, Robert said, "One hundred pounds."

He looked to Bouchart, but the blazing eyes and tight lips told him that no counter offer was forthcoming—so much for the Frenchman's pretense to riches. Adding that suspicion to the other, he turned back to Phoebe. "Milady?" he said, offering her his arm.

She took it, and this time there was no mistaking the gleam in her eye for anything other than what it was—excitement. Bouchart's glare following them out onto the dance floor added a fillip of triumph.

"That wasn't nice," she said, laying her gloved hand on the

outside of Robert's upper arm.

He steeled himself not to flinch, but the familiar flesh-crawling feeling never came. He tucked her right hand into his, reassured by how bloody good the contact had him feeling. "Perhaps not, but it was effective." Laying a glove upon the small of her back, he drew her closer. Through the silk and minimal undergarments, her waist felt supple and small.

"I'm not a mare on the auction block at Tattersall's, you know."

He pulled back to look down at her. "Of course you are not. For one thing, you smell too good. For another, the proprietor of Tattersall's prides himself on his stock's sweet disposition."

She tilted her head and slanted him a look. "Is this how you woo, with insults?"

"Who says I'm still out to woo you?"

Fresh color flooded her face, but to her credit she didn't back down. "You've followed as closely upon my heels as Pippin all this week. If not wooing, than what are you about?"

Hearing himself likened to her lapdog was hardly flattering. Beneath the tightly wound stock, his neck heated. "Perhaps I am seeking to make amends."

She let out a soft snort.

"Six years ago I hadn't a farthing to my name. I couldn't give you even a fraction of all the things I wanted to. Christ, the purchase of your locket all but beggared me."

Gaze going to her throat, he saw that she no longer wore it. The observation prompted a pang. Not for the first time he wished me might exchange places with his younger, purse-pinched self. He might be possessed of a fortune now, but the true treasure, the pearl beyond price, Phoebe, belonged to another. So far since his return, he'd only succeeded in borrowing her.

Blue-grey eyes lifted to his face, eloquent in their sudden starkness. "Didn't you know I only ever wanted you?"

Emboldened, he bent his head to the silk of her cheek. "You have me now, or you could. Say the word and we'll leave this instant, sail away from here, anywhere you'd like."

Stiffening, she shook her head. "You don't give up, do you?"

"No, I do not, not when the prize is as worthy of winning as you are."

Her gaze shuttered. "I'm not a possession to be won or claimed. I've a heart and mind the same as you and both are now set on another. It's too late for us. The sooner you accept that as fact, the better off the both of us shall be."

Exasperation had his hold tightening. "Why too late? I'm here. You're here. We're both young still." *I still love you.*

Casting a cautious look to the other circuiting couples, she dropped her voice to barely above a whisper. "It's taken me six years to pick up the pieces of my life and forge some sort of future for myself. Do you honestly expect me to toss that all away simply because you've sailed back into my life? Even if I were foolish and dishonorable enough to break my promise to Aristide, what guarantee have I that you wouldn't leave again when the fancy strikes you?"

Robert's fingers firmed on her waist. "One word from you and I'm here to stay—on land, in England. Cry off with Bouchart right here, right now, and I swear to you I'll head for East India House in Leadenhall Street at first light and resign my commission. What more will it take for you to trust me again?"

She shook her head, expression vehement. "There is nothing you can say, nothing you can do, that could possibly lure me to ever trust you again."

"As I've remarked upon before, never is a damnably long time." If she carried through with becoming Bouchart's wife, he would have no choice but to cede the field and leave her be. But that dark day hadn't yet come. If Robert had his way, it never would.

The music segued to a stop. He let his hand linger in the curve of her back a moment more, a delicious dalliance that would no doubt be remarked upon and not only by Bouchart. “We shall see, milady, which of us wins their way, but for now allow me the privilege of seeing you back to your escort.”

Upon depositing Phoebe on the edge of the dance floor, Robert could bear the ball no longer. As the son of a mere country squire, he hadn’t belonged to her fashionable world six years ago. He belonged even less now. More to the point, she hadn’t wanted him there.

The first article of clothing to go was his gloves. Shucking them off, he exited through a side door and stepped out into a back alley leading to the mews. Desperate for air, he tore at the confines of his cravat. Crumpling the blasted thing into a ball, he shoved it into his coat pocket and cut across to the stable.

The groom who led his horse over to the mounting block was a different fellow from the callow youth Robert recalled from earlier. Stubble-jawed, gin-breathed, and well into his thirties, he seemed an odd choice to wait upon Almack’s persnickety patronesses and their elite subscribers. But then servants were meant to be invisible and despite his lack of couth, this one couldn’t be faulted for his manners.

“G’night, guv,” the groom said, touching his forelock and treating Robert to a gold-toothed grin.

Eager to be on his way, Robert took the reins and handed over a few quid in gratuity. Walking his horse out of the stable yard, he turned onto St. James’s Street and headed northwest toward home. The quarter known for its gentlemen’s clubs fell somewhere between bustling and somnolent, the hour far too unfashionably early for any self-respecting member of the ton to risk being seen returning home. Later lacquered carriages would glut the thoroughfares, but for now most of the traffic was limited to single riders and those on foot. Resolved to make use of the room, Robert picked up pace. Cantering over the cobbles, he consoled himself that Phoebe wasn't wed to Bouchart yet. From Reggie he knew that she'd yet to agree upon a date. There was yet time—and hope. The jealousy splashed upon her face when she'd spied him with Lady Morton hadn't lied. She still felt something for him. All he need do was stay the course, and she would come around. She had to.

At Piccadilly, a phaeton whipped out in front of him, jarring him back to the moment. Veering to avoid it, he turned his horse's head sharply right—and felt the saddle slipping.

Thrown sideways, he knew surrender was his sole hope. Sliding his feet free of the stirrups, he leaned into the fall. He struck the street hard, his right shoulder bearing the brunt of the impact. Head tucked and knees tented, he rolled away from the horse before the hooves might do deadly damage.

The temptation to simply lie on his side in the gutter and catch his breath was enormous, but doing so risked trampling. After all that he'd so far survived, dying in a London ditch wasn't how he meant to take his earthly leave.

Covered in filth, he crawled onto his knees and pushed himself upright on skin-scoured palms. Grabbing hold of a hitching post, he came to a slow but steady stand. Grateful that no limbs seemed to be broken, he looked to his mount a few paces away, tail lashing the air, the bridle held by a lad in livery.

Eyes bugging, the boy walked the horse over to him. "Gorm, that was a close one," he said, holding out the saddle.

Reaching out to take it, Robert didn't disagree. A less experienced horseman might be seriously injured or dead. Not for the first time, he thanked Providence for his pastoral upbringing. His right shoulder throbbed like the very devil and the eye on that side was rapidly swelling closed, and yet compared to what might have been he'd gotten off lucky.

"You all right, guv?"

"Never better." He dug a hurting hand into his pocket,

scooped out several coins and handed them over. “I thank you for your aid.” Looping the reins about bashed knuckles, he turned away and limped over to the pavement.

What the bloody hell had just happened? Sucking on his split lip, he ran his hands over the animal, searching for signs of soreness or other injury. But beyond being spooked, the stallion seemed to be hale and fit. Likewise the tacking, newly purchased, was in pristine order. He’d checked the cinching on the girth himself before heading out that evening. And yet there was no discounting what had happened, which begged the question of how—and why—it had come about. Turning the saddle over, he saw he had the first half of his answer.

Two of the three leather billets had been cut clean through.

Chapter Six

Phoebe often slipped inside the Hospital's Court Room when she required respite to think. Grand and vast, its walls hung with paintings by such great English artists as Hogarth, one of the founding governors, beyond the occasional board meeting it was rarely used. Pacing its four corners, the echo of her steps ringing from the high plasterwork ceiling, Phoebe tried telling herself that Robert must have overslept. But when the clock atop the chimneypiece chimed noon, she forced herself to own the truth. He wasn't coming.

Her behavior the previous evening at Almack's must have served as the final straw for him, and now he'd tired of their cat-and-mouse match.

I should feel relieved—no, not only relieved, but elated.

After not quite a fortnight of demanding that he leave her alone, apparently he'd deigned to do just that. Alone, that was what she'd wanted—wasn't it?

Their tiff had blown up like an unexpected summer storm. One moment she'd been melting into his arms and the next she'd been hard put not to stomp upon his foot or deal him a swift kick in the shin. She hadn't meant to argue with him. As soon as the thought crossed her mind, she owned it as the very worst of self-deceptions. She'd wanted them to argue, she'd wanted it rather badly. She'd been spoiling for a fight since the first shock of his return had waned. She wanted it still.

She'd moved through her morning classes restless and snappish, her thoughts scattered and her patience worn thin by the slightest disruption. Myriad worries assailed her. What if an accident had befallen him? What if he'd been set upon by footpads? Even on a darkened street, that claret-colored coat could scarcely be missed.

Or perhaps he'd met up with Lady Morton following the ball. After several minutes of making herself miserable by imaging them lying intertwined in Leticia's bed linens, she dealt herself a brisk mental shake. This was absurd. This needed to cease. It wasn't as though Robert owed her an accounting of his whereabouts, let alone his fidelity. And really, why should she give a fig how or with whom he amused himself, let alone care so very keenly? After his desertion, surely she couldn't be softening toward him...could she?

Yet again her thoughts circled back to their waltz. Fleeting though the interlude had been and marred by her harsh words, it had felt uncommonly good to be back in his arms almost as if...she belonged there.

A voice from the hallway broke into her brooding. "Hopefully the truant will find a warmer welcome than that shown to the prodigal scarce a week ago?"

Robert!

Heart lifting, Phoebe spun about to the doorway. Whatever caustic comments she'd meant to make withered at the sight of him. "Dear Lord, what happened?"

Bruised and bloodied, his right arm resting in a makeshift sling and his eye swollen halfway closed, he tried for a smile. "I took a tumble from my horse."

Phoebe found that difficult to fathom. Robert had grown up in the country. While accidents might happen to anyone, he had an excellent seat. "Were you...racing?" He wouldn't be the first young buck to bolt through Rotten Row on a wager and find himself the worse for it; still, the man who'd returned seemed beyond such boyish behavior.

Crossing toward her, he shook his head. "My horse threw a shoe. At least allow me to hold onto what dignity I have left by not pressing for a full recitation of the humiliating details."

Phoebe met him partway. Taking in his set jaw, swollen yet undeniably firmed, Phoebe surrendered the subject—for now. Instead she said, “You look a fright.”

He grimaced, fingering a gash on his chin that would likely turn to a scar as had its predecessor. “Just when I thought I couldn’t possibly become more handsome.”

He’d made some similar disparagement of his looks the night before at the ball. Staring into his face, sinfully handsome despite the bruising, she wondered why he seemed intent on seeing himself as some sort of freak. The night before she’d assumed he must be trying to trick her into admitting how very much she still wanted—craved—him, but suddenly she wasn’t so certain.

It struck her that he hadn’t really told her all that much about himself. How had he fared these past years? More to the point, how had he kept himself? The narrative he’d sketched had been vague on details, timelines especially. The few times she’d tried drawing him out, he’d found a way to turn the topic. She thought of how they’d once told one another everything and her heart lurched.

Determined to protect that vulnerable organ against further assault, she sought refuge in sarcasm. “I suspect Lady Morton will still have you.”

He had the audacity to nod. “I suspect she will, only it isn’t Lady Morton I want, and we both know it.”

Rather than follow him down that well-trod path, she asked, “Have you seen a physician?”

He shrugged, wincing as the movement pained him. “Chelsea tried to persuade me to let her call one, but I told her the same as I am telling you—I am fine.”

She shook her head. Some things hadn’t changed. “What you are is as stubborn as ever, too stubborn for your own good.”

“I don’t care for being fussed over.”

The snort she let out would have mortified her mother. "You adore being fussed over, or at least you used to."

His gaze bore into hers. "It rather depends upon who does the fussing."

The pull to envelope him in her arms was a powerful force. Battling it, Phoebe reminded herself that she was another man's betrothed. Beyond that, battered as he was, she wasn't certain where it was safe to touch.

She settled upon his forearm. A comforting stroke such as she would have bestowed upon Lulu or Mary or any of her pupils, it meant nothing—or so she told herself. And yet the slight contact brought heat prickling her palm, the sensation akin to playing with an electricity machine—dangerous, forbidden. Robert must have felt it too. He flinched.

Phoebe drew back her hand. "I'm sorry. I've hurt you. I didn't mean—"

"It's nothing." His gaze raked her face, raw in a way that physical pain couldn't entirely account for.

"You should be abed."

The corners of his mouth lifted, his eyes no longer pained but decidedly devilish. "Is that an offer? If so, I accept."

She reached out to bat him but, mindful of his injuries, thought better of it. Instead she laid light fingers on his slinged shoulder, careful not to touch anything more than fabric. "You should come with me to the infirmary where you may be properly looked after."

He jerked away as though she'd proposed taking him to a torture chamber. "The devil I will."

"Very well, then I shall have a look at you myself." She reached up her two hands to undo his top shirt button, but before she could, he backed away, bumping up against a roundel painted by Thomas Gainsborough.

She dropped her arms to her sides. "When did you grow so modest?" she asked, frustrated but also genuinely perplexed.

Six years ago he hadn't given a second thought to shucking off his shirt for a bare-knuckle boxing lesson at Gentleman Jackson's or, more scandalously, sea bathing at Brighton wearing no more than his smallclothes. She'd used to tease that he was more at home out of his clothes than in them. That too seemed to have changed.

His gaze shuttered. "It's not a fit sight for a lady." As if determined to put as much distance between them as he could short of departing, he shoved away from the wall and walked over to the far side of the room.

Phoebe followed him over to the globe ensconced in a footed brass stand by which he'd stationed himself. "I assure you, a few bruises and cracked ribs won't drop me to the ground. Since volunteering here, I have seen far worse."

He opened his mouth as if to dispute her, and then closed it. Holding his peace, he reached out with his unfettered hand, giving the sphere a spin.

Wondering if it was only his hurts that made him so quick-tempered and melancholy, Phoebe resolved to change the subject—for now. Coming up beside him, she said, "You never did tell me which lands you visited."

Gaze on the globe, he hesitated. "Africa, the northeast coastline mostly, sundry archipelagos and islands, and India, but then I suppose that's a given. My first stop was Madras. It's situated in the south of—"

"I am well aware where it's situated, along with a great many other ports you put into or would have had your ship continued upon its route. I made it my business to know, to memorize your itinerary, after... " Exasperated, she let her voice trail off. She hadn't meant to snap but his apparent assumption that she must be some sort of ignoramus was too grating to suffer, certainly not in silence.

He dropped his hand and stepped away. "I'm sorry, I didn't mean to play schoolmaster. It's only that you never used to show much interest in geography."

Phoebe let out a sigh. Would he ever cease seeing her as that foolish chit he'd left behind? "Or in mathematics or politics or, indeed, any subject that might be considered less than ladylike, yes, I know. But I was interested—fascinated, really—by all of it."

The span of his stare was far from flattering. Six years ago she'd apparently played the part of the empty-headed miss over well. "You never told me."

"Of course I didn't. I didn't want to frighten you off, now did I? I wanted you to be interested in me—even if it meant coming into Papa's study after the house was abed and sneaking books back to my room or creeping into the breakfast parlor in the hope he'd left behind his copy of *The Times*. Once Mama caught me with newsprint on my thumbs and made me do without luncheon, but I didn't care. It was worth it."

Robert shook his head as if doing so would help the revelation sink in. "Did you honestly believe that knowing you cared for reading beyond fashion plates in *La Belle Assemblée* and penny dreadfuls on loan from Mudie's would have made me any less *interested* in you?"

"Mama, Aunt Tottie, Mrs. Whitebridge and her set all assured me that men were put off by women who speak their minds too freely or show themselves to be overly clever. I'd like to say they were wrong, but I'm not so certain they were. In truth, when I recall my coming out and our courtship, I cannot recall all that many men enthusing over the machinations of my mind—you included."

He shot her an exasperated look. "Certainly I never expected you to simper and pout, to pretend to lose at cards or laugh when my jokes fell flat."

The portrait he painted was the farthest thing from flattering. It was also deserved, or at least it had been. And yet despite his protestations, Phoebe remained skeptical. "Are you quite certain?"

"If you must know, it annoyed the hell out of me."

His admission was akin to a slap. Clearly she hadn't been the only one of them playacting six years ago. He'd read his role equally well. Just how much of what they'd had had been real versus artifice? Presently it was impossible to parse.

She shook her head, which had begun aching. But instead of seeking cloths soaked in lavender water and soothing cups of tea as once she would have, what she sought now was the truth. "Why didn't you tell me so? Never say you feared to injure my feelings!"

"In part," he admitted. "And because all the things I loved about you, the qualities that were so inestimably wonderful so far outweighed the paltry few annoyances that it would have been unconscionable to complain."

The latter sufficed to take away some of the sting, but only some. Wistful, Phoebe sighed. "What a pair of pretty fools we were. And now we meet again after all these years almost as strangers."

He shot up his head to stare at her. "How can you say that? How can you *know* that? We've scarcely had time alone to find out."

She shrugged. "Our lives have taken such separate courses. You've traveled, had experiences...taken lovers," she added, a shameless fishing expedition and yet suddenly she had to know. The man who'd flirted so smoothly with Lady Morton the other night at Almack's was clearly well at ease with women.

The ruddy color running into his cheeks proclaimed the answer to be precisely that which she didn't wish to hear. "In the Orient, it's not unusual for a man to have more than one wife and several concubines."

A wise woman would let the topic die, but Phoebe had never been that, not where Robert was concerned. Determined to draw him out, she trailed a finger along the edge of the Chippendale library table. "Surely it's no affair of mine, and yet I can't help but wonder. Have you ever...seen the inside of an actual...harem?"

Out of the corner of her eye, she caught his half-hidden smile. If her prurient question amused him, so be it. "Barring eunuchs, men are not allowed within—and I assure you, my curiosity does not extend nearly so far. But I did have the pleasure of making the acquaintance of one of its inmates, the Princess Nadia, the sultan's favorite daughter. I blush to say it, but she developed a *tendre* for me."

She brought up her head so swiftly she wouldn't have been surprised to find it flying off. "Do...that is to say, did you...return her sentiments?"

He paused as if pondering. "Princess Nadia's charms *were* considerable. I cannot say I was indifferent to her, but there could be no notion of our marrying."

Phoebe dug her nails into her palms. "Because of you being a commoner? Certainly with you and her papa, the pasha, being such chums, you might have found a way 'round that."

Gaze honing on hers, he said with seeming sincerity, "Princess Nadia may be a royal princess but you, Phoebe, have always been the queen of my heart."

Refusing to be so easily mollified, she shot back, "And was I still the 'queen of your heart' when you were...disporting yourself with the princess?"

Robert's straight face suffused with laughter. Great guffaws burst forth from his chest, obliging him to brace a hand upon his no doubt cracked ribs.

Blushing profusely, or certainly it felt as though she must be, Phoebe pitched her voice above the din. "I fail to see what is so amusing."

He lifted his good hand and scoured it across his damp eyes. "Princess Nadia was... Well, to be fair, she did have a sweet face if the missing front teeth might be overlooked."

Wondering if she might have misheard, Phoebe echoed, "Missing front teeth?"

He nodded. “The ones she’d kept were various shades of brown—she’d a great fondness for chewing tobacco.”

Phoebe rested her hands upon her hips to keep them from pummeling him. “Do go on.”

“Well, hmm, let me see. As I recall, her considerable *charms* owed to her being rather a large lady overall.”

“How large?”

“Were I to hazard a guess, I’d wager fifteen stone, give or take.”

She swung away to the mantel. Snatching an arrangement of roses from one of a brace of urns, she turned about and struck him atop the one body part that had heretofore escaped hurt—his head.

Ducking the shower of petals, he said, “Ouch, what was that for?”

“For you being a rogue and a bounder. I thank my lucky stars you left before I could make the biggest mistake of my life.”

No longer laughing, he asked, “If that is indeed the case, then why are you so angry?”

“Because...because I’ve let you gull me yet again.”

Brushing away bruised buds, he tossed the broken bouquet to the floor with a curse. With his good arm, he reached for her. Phoebe might have moved away in time only she didn’t. Melting against him, she laid her cheek against his chest and let him hold her.

His sigh rose above her head. His lips pressed against her scalp, which like the rest of her felt tingling—alive. “It wouldn’t have mattered if Princess Nadia had the body of Venus and the face of an angel. She could have performed the Dance of the Seven Veils beneath my very nose, and it wouldn’t have made a bloody bit of difference. Yours is the only face I see before I close my eyes at night, the only one I want to wake up to every morning.”

She lifted her face to look up at him. "You make very pretty speeches."

"It's no speech—it's the truth—even if you do scowl overmuch."

Caught by surprise, Phoebe drew back. "I do not." Perpetual scowling was her mother's province, and above all Phoebe had sworn to herself she would never, *ever* follow suit in becoming like her mother.

"Oh, but you do." He traced his thumb along the curve of her bottom lip, drawing a shiver. "It seems to me these very pretty lips don't smile nearly enough."

Wary, she searched his face for signs he might be toying with her. Finding none, she said, "Has it occurred to you that perhaps I haven't had all that much to smile about?"

"I could change that...if you'd give me leave." Gaze holding hers, he added, "Give me leave, sweet Phoebe. Give me leave to make you happy again."

Tears pricked her eyes. She inhaled his scent, that of six years before and yet subtly changed, and suddenly she wanted nothing more than to kiss and be kissed by him.

As if sensing the shift in her, he laid a hand along her nape, guiding her to him—only Phoebe didn't require guiding. She angled her face to meet him, her mouth a hairsbreadth from his, their breaths an invisible comingled cloud. She could all but taste the anise he always took after meals in keeping with the Eastern custom, the exotic scent yet another bittersweet reminder of that part of his history to which she would never belong.

The past was fixed, irreversible, done, the future a foregone conclusion. Eventually she would return to her senses and wed Aristide and Robert would sail away to his next adventure. Whatever they were, whatever they felt, belonged to the present, this glorious, fleeting meantime moment, a moment that suddenly seemed far too rare and precious to waste on words alone.

Knocking from outside saw them separating. Smoothing a hand over her hair, Phoebe darted a look to the door. "Come in," she called out, hating that her voice hitched, shaky and uncertain.

The door opened, and Mary entered. Stopping on the threshold, she took in the scattered petals and bent stems, her eyes widening. Saucer-like gaze going back to Phoebe, she said, "Lulu and Fiona were playing outside, and Lulu fell on the oyster shell path and cut her knee. I tried to comfort her, but she only wants you."

Guilt struck Phoebe. While she'd dallied with Robert, one of her charges had fallen and hurt herself—and not just any student, but her dear little Lulu. Feeling more a mother than a volunteer schoolmistress, she sidestepped Robert and hurried toward the door. "Take her to the infirmary directly. I'll join you straightaway."

"There you are, sweetheart, all finished," Phoebe soothed, spreading salve on Lulu's skinned knee. If only a hurt, confused heart might be as easily sorted. "And now we shall seal that cruel cut with a kiss," she added, blowing a buss in the vicinity of the wound.

Seated at the edge of a straight-backed chair set close to the sink, Lulu lifted her tear-streaked face to Phoebe's. "Boo-boo throbs, but not as bad."

"Good," Phoebe said, feeling relieved. Not for the first time since walking into the infirmary and scooping a wailing Lulu into her arms, she reminded herself that sustaining scrapes and bruises were childhood rites of passage, and yet...

The salving had been the easy part. Cleaning out the dirt and debris had tested Phoebe's courage as much as it had Lulu's. Even though the little girl had been admirably brave and mostly still, hurting her even in her best interest had been hard on Phoebe.

Robert shoved away from the corner to which Phoebe had banished him and came forward to join them. "It will stop soon enough, poppet."

He'd followed her to the infirmary, not that Phoebe had asked him. Whether she needed him or not, whether she wanted him or not, he seemed determined to be there for her.

The problem was she did want him, apparently too bloody much to trust herself alone in his presence.

Stiff though he was, he went down on one knee, putting himself on eye-level with the child. "I took a tumble myself the other day, and my...*boo-boos* hurt like the dev...dickens, but I'm feeling ever so much better today."

"Did milady kiss you all better too?" Lulu asked with the utter innocence of children.

Angling his face to Phoebe's, the smile Robert sent her was anything but. "Not quite yet, but I remain...hopeful."

"Since you're here, you might as well make yourself useful and hand me that bandage roll," Phoebe snapped.

Not bothering to hide his smile, he did as she bid.

Watching her wrap the child's knee in the clean linen, he added, "Lulu, if you could have anything you wished for, what might it be?"

Lulu didn't as much as pause. "A mummy and papa."

Robert blanched. Looking up from tying off the bandage, Phoebe shot him a look. *What are you doing!*

Recovering smoothly, he said, "I was thinking something more in the way of a treat, a reward for being such a brave child today."

Sucking on her lip, this time Lulu hesitated. "I should like a picnic like little children sometimes have in the storybooks."

"A picnic, that sounds simply managed. Let's have one, then."

"Truly?" Lulu asked.

"I can't see why not." He shifted to Phoebe. "Are there any

rules against holding picnics?"

She hesitated. "Honestly, I shouldn't be surprised if there were."

Standing stiffly, he answered, "In that case, tell those fusty directors of yours that your latest benefactor absolutely insists upon it."

"Please God, no more. No more!"

Robert's voice rasped from a throat left raw from thirst and screaming. Blood from his reopened wounds dripped onto the cabin floorboards. Tomorrow they would make port in Madagascar. Once there, he would be taken to market and sold. In light of that, he'd assumed they must be finished with torturing him. Stripped of even his smallclothes and strung up like a beast to be gutted, he felt fear turning his bowels to water.

In giving up Phoebe's name, he'd proven himself less than a man. Was he now to be unmanned in truth? He'd heard of brawny men being made into eunuchs so that they might serve as harem guards. Not for the first time, he cursed the ship's doctor who'd stitched and bandaged the wrist he'd used a rusted bit of razor to rent.

The pirate captain turned away from the fire, his features bathed in flickering flames and engulfed in shadow. "Alas, my friend, giving more *is what I do best." His dark, waist-length black curls brushed Robert's cheek as he came around to his front.*

Seeing what he held, Robert struggled against his shackles. "No, not that."

Thick lips pulled into a pretend pout. "Indeed, I am afraid it is necessary."

"Aaaaaaaaaahhhhhhh."

Pain seared Robert's right thigh. His skin sizzled, the charring stench invading his mouth and nostrils.

Drawing back, the pirate captain sent him a satisfied smile. "Now there will be no question tomorrow that you are my property and you, mate, will have a permanent memento to remember me."

Not until later, when a vinegar-soaked sponge carried him back to consciousness, did Robert look down to the initials blackening his outer thigh.

AT—Arthur Trent.

Robert bolted upright, the sudden motion driving a shaft of pain into his battered right side. Cursing, he eased back against the headboard, swiping a bandaged hand across his sweat-beaded brow.

Another nightmare, and just as he'd begun hoping he might finally be free of them.

The evening at Almack's culminating in the fall from his horse had dredged up all the old anxieties. Feeling powerless even for an instant invariably hauled him back to that hellish time of being tortured and trussed, taunted and denigrated. Likely it always would. But he was stronger now. He couldn't control the nightmares, but he could control his actions in their aftermath. Unlike the times before, he wasn't going to bury himself beneath self-pity or piles of blankets. He wasn't going to get drunk. Now that he had Phoebe to fight for, he was going to persevere, to push through the mental anguish and physical pain for her sake as well as his own.

Resolved, he lowered his stiffened legs over the bedside and stood. Shuffling over to the washstand, his bruises made him move like an old man, but he swore to shake off the temptation to slacken. Rather than ring for hot water, he made do with cold. Sluicing his swollen face, he allowed that the cuts would likely mean eschewing shaving for another day. Still, he dressed with care, making himself as presentable as he might before heading downstairs. The savory scent of sausage and kippers and coddled eggs steered him to the breakfast room.

Seated at the cloth-covered table, Chelsea looked up when he entered. Unlike the previous day, she barely blinked at the black-and-blue sight of him. “Children, bid your Uncle Robin good morning.”

Two bright-eyed imps looked up from pushing food about their plates. “G’morning, Uncle Robin,” they chorused, staring at him as though he were a carnival curiosity.

“Children.” Favoring his right side, he approached the table and dropped a kiss atop each tousled crown.

“How are your boo boos, Uncle Robin?” Daphne asked, her blue eyes mirrors of concern.

“Much better today, thank you, poppet,” Robert answered. Looking over the child’s crown of copper curls, he shared a smile with her mother.

Daphne was the very image of Chelsea, while Tony’s brown hair and acorn-colored eyes favored his father. Seeing them looking like miniature adults brought home yet again just how very much he’d missed. But now was not the time to indulge in maudlin musings. He made his way over to the sideboard. Lifting the lid on the first of several chased silver rashes, he found it brimming with bacon. Of all the foods he’d missed during his years away, English bacon crowned the list. Ever since his return, he couldn’t seem to stuff himself with sufficient. He picked up a juicy slab and folded it into his mouth.

From the corner of his eye he caught his sister scowling. “Why not make yourself a plate and sit down with the rest of us?” She cast a pointed look to Tony and Daphne, regards riveted on his greasy fingers.

Sucking his glistening thumb, he accepted the napkin she passed over. “You sound just like Mother used to.” Locating the coffee urn, he poured himself a cup. Finding it strong and black, just as he liked it, he took a bracing swallow.

Tony piped up, “When I’m grown, I’m going off to sea and be a pirate like you, Uncle Robin.”

Robert nearly spat coffee onto his shirtfront.

Shooting him a warning look, Chelsea turned to her son. "Your uncle is a merchant, not a pirate. They're two different occupations entirely, aren't they, *Uncle Robin*?"

"Er, quite."

"I don't care what 'tis called so long as I can go to sea." Gaze mutinous, the boy put down his fork, picked up the remains of his sausage and crammed it into his mouth.

Expression alarmed, Chelsea's reached across to wipe his mouth. "Don't be silly, darling. You're going to stay on English soil with Mama and Papa and the other normal people. And by the by, use your cutlery as Mama has taught you."

Lower lip protruding, Tony announced, "But being a landlubber is *boring*."

Dodging Chelsea's dagger look, Robert choked back a chuckle.

"May I at least wear an earring, Mama?" Tony persisted, staring pointedly at Robert's. Despite his concessions to London's more subdued men's fashion, keeping his earring proclaimed that "Captain Lazarus" wasn't entirely dead and buried.

Chelsea clanged her teacup in its saucer. "Not while I live and breathe, my precious."

Daphne, quiet until now, dragged her gaze from Robert to her mother. "I want to be a pirate—pardon, Mama, *merchant*—too. Only he—" she lanced her twin a barbed look "—swears I can't on account of being a girl." She swiveled her curly head back to Robert. "There are girl pirates, too, aren't there, Uncle Robin?"

"Indeed there are," Robert replied, dodging Chelsea's dagger looks. "There was Grace O'Malley and Anne Bonny, both Irishwomen who did quite well for themselves, certainly for a time. But by far the greatest female pir—er, *merchant* was a beautiful Chinese woman by the name of Cheng I Sao. Ten years ago, she retired from the trade richer than Croesus despite starting out as a lowly prostit—"

"Children, that will serve," Chelsea broke in, pinning Robert with a gimlet gaze. "Your uncle has an important engagement and you have lessons with Nanny. If you've finished your breakfasts, you are excused."

The twins set aside their napkins and scooted out of their seats. Padding toward the door, Daphne turned back. "Shall we see you at tea, Uncle Robin?"

Robert hesitated. If all went as he planned, he would be sharing the midday meal al fresco with Phoebe. "I'm afraid I have an appointment to attend."

The children's smiles dipped.

"But I shall see you for supper," he put in swiftly. "And afterward, I shall tuck you in and tell you a story—one that meets with your mama's approval, of course," he added, shooting his sister a wink.

Spirits restored, the twins padded out. Once their footsteps had faded, Chelsea said, "I fancy I now know how Mother and Father must have felt when I announced my plans to decamp to Epsom and earn my bread as a jockey."

"A case of tit for tat, indeed," Robert agreed. "You were about their age, I believe, and Mother and Father not much older than we are now."

She arched a roan-colored brow. "Wait until you have a family of your own, and then you'll—" She stopped in mid-sentence. "Oh, dearest, I am sorry. I didn't mean—"

"It's fine." He set his half-drunk coffee down, the beverage suddenly seeming to have turned bitter. "I do want a family, but that rather depends on Phoebe."

"And if she won't be dissuaded from this marriage to Bouchart?"

He shrugged though he felt the farthest thing from nonchalant. Bouchart was at best a bounder after her fortune, at worst something far more dangerous. “I’ll go back to sea, I suppose. Salt air’s wonderfully good at healing wounds.”

Visibly bristling, Chelsea shot him what he was coming to think of as The Look. “So that’s the plan, is it? Live out your vagabond life as little better than a pirate until your luck runs low?”

“I believe the proper term is *merchant*, but yes, that’s the basic notion. And why the devil shouldn’t I go where the trade winds blow me? If Phoebe won’t have me, what’s left for me here?”

Chelsea slammed her teacup into its saucer. “Thanks a bloody lot. What of your niece and nephew, the babe on the way, me for that matter? Are we mincemeat?”

“I didn’t mean... Christ, Chels, don’t you be angry with me too. You must know I worship those children and...well, as sisters come, I suppose you’ll do.”

Her scowl eased. “Then why not stay on with us? The children adore you. Despite that ridiculous earring, I’m rather fond of you myself. As for Anthony, the two of you appear to be growing upon one another.”

“And so we are. It’s only that—”

“Yes, yes, I know, land is *boring*. But then perhaps you’ve yet to give terra firma a fair chance, hmm? Surely playing hazard with your life by haring off to parts unknown must become boring, too, after a while?”

Torn between exasperation and amusement, he shook his head. Once Chelsea fixed her mind upon something, in this case keeping his prodigal feet planted on English soil, she was implacable as a boulder. Then again, he supposed the same could be said of his resolve to reclaim Phoebe.

“I appreciate the invitation, Chels, and I love you for it, but I won’t feed you false hope. If Phoebe goes through with this marriage, I’ll be pulling up anchor as soon as the ship is provisioned. Staying on and crossing paths with her as another man's wife would be beyond bearing. Surely you of all people can comprehend that?"

Exhaling heavily, she nodded. "Years ago when I thought Anthony had gone through with marrying Phoebe, I couldn't think beyond getting clear of London as quickly as I could, so yes, I do understand. That doesn't mean I have to like it. Or," she added, brightening, "give up hope of changing your mind."

"You, give up! Perish the thought." Shoving away from the sideboard, he reached out and gave her shoulder a squeeze. "It's early days yet, sister dear, and mark me, I mean to use every weapon in my arsenal to win Phoebe away from that Frog fop."

Chelsea nodded. "Barring kidnapping, I'll help you in any way I can and not only for your sake. Phoebe doesn't love Aristide, I know it. As for the count, though I've no reason to disparage his character, I only know I cannot like him."

He studied her. "Why is that?" Something about Bouchart had never set well with him either, but until recently it had been a simple matter to fob off his ill feelings as bias born of their rivalry.

She shrugged. "'Tis nothing I can lay my finger upon, more of a sense I have that won't go away. Anthony teases me about my 'woman's intuition', but I've never been able to bring myself to trust the man. I fear he may try to provoke you into an open quarrel or worse."

Robert thought back to the other night at Almack's. His cinch hadn't cut itself. Someone had tampered with his tack, a deliberate act meant to see him injured or worse. Beyond Aristide, who in London had cause to wish him out of the way? Phoebe's mother came to mind, but much as he disliked the woman, he couldn't see his way to laying such a foul deed at her feet.

Nor could he accuse Bouchart openly. The Frenchman had been in plain view all evening. But men such as the count didn't soil their hands themselves. They employed others to do their dirty deeds for them. Not for the first time, Robert recalled the gold-toothed groom. His gallows face was more in keeping with an inmate of Newgate Gaol than a servant in St. James's. Robert would wager The Swan that the man was no stableman but a henchman planted there to make mischief. When he'd returned to Almack's the previous day to inquire more closely, none of the footmen or groomsmen on duty could recall ever seeing a groom fitting that description anywhere about the premises.

Eyeing him, Chelsea said, "You never did say how you came to fall the other night."

Robert shrugged. "It was a careless accident. I took the turn too fast, nothing more." Another lie, this one in the service of sparing his pregnant sister undue upset.

She hesitated, biting her lip as though she were the one of them holding something back.

"What is it?' he asked, glimpsing tears gathering.

She paused, taking a long, trembling breath. "I never told you this, I thought it best not to, but the carriage accident that took Mama and Papa from us was no accident at all. Before he died, Squire Dumfreys admitted to soring the lead horse."

Besotted with Chelsea to the point of obsession, the squire had been the one behind Robert's and Phoebe's kidnapping six years ago, but he'd never considered that the man's treachery might extend to murdering their parents. Had poison not already placed the villain beyond his reach, Robert would have gladly made murdering him his life's mission.

Once again he was too late.

He scraped a hand through his hair, belatedly recalling his bruises. "Dear God, I had no idea. Why didn't you tell me before?"

She swiped a hand over her eyes. "What was the point? Telling you wouldn't bring Mama and Papa back. And you'd been through so much already with being kidnapped and held that I thought you deserved a chance at being happy."

Emotions cinched his throat—shock, anger, *betrayal.* "They were my parents too. I had the right to know." Were it not for her pregnancy, he would have said more.

She hesitated, blinking back fresh tears. "I suppose I was trying to protect you. I only bring it up now because... Well, you're an awfully good horseman to lose your seat as you did the other night."

He opened his mouth to admit the cut girth when his gaze alighted on her protruding belly. "My tumble the other night was an accident and nothing more. Pray put it from your thoughts."

"You're quite certain?"

She wasn't the only one who could keep a secret in the service of love. Lying to her face was damnably difficult but given the circumstances it was also the right thing to do. "I am. Be that as it may, I'm stiff as a board and gamey as a geezer. Might I borrow your carriage for the day rather than ride?"

Her expression eased. "Of course, it's yours for as long as you like. Given my girth, I shan't be making any social calls."

"And your pantry—might I purloin it in the service of a good cause?"

"Have Cook pack up whatever you like."

Grateful that she didn't grill him, he nodded his thanks and turned to go.

"Robert?"

One foot in the hallway, he turned back. "Yes?"

She cast him a careworn look. "Promise me you'll take care?"

"I shall," he said, the sentiment sincere. He had Bouchart's measure now. For Phoebe's sake as well as his own, he'd not drop his guard again. "If the past has taught me any lesson, it's to keep a weather eye open no matter how mild the sea on its surface may seem."

Chapter Seven

Standing on the Hospital's columned portico with Mary, a leashed Pippin at their feet, Phoebe fought to put her finger on the source of the girl's obvious distress. Before the week was out, Mary would be en route to a promising post with a respectable family in Cornwall. Likely her pallor and tear-tracked cheeks were nothing more than a bout of cold feet. Still, when she'd begged for a word in private, Phoebe hadn't hesitated to grant it. She'd gathered her bonnet and gloves and bid them step outside.

Expression anguished, Mary shook her head. "I shouldn't have brought you into it. Please, milady, forget I ever mentioned it." Shoulders bowed, she turned to go back inside, but Phoebe laid a staying hand upon her shoulder.

"Brought me into what, my dear? You're speaking in riddles." Turning her gently back around, she searched the misery-laden face for clues. "I wish you would tell me plainly what's troubling you. Whatever it is, you have my word it shall remain between us."

Mary kept mum.

Very well, a fishing expedition it was to be. "Does it have to do with your leaving?"

Eyes welling, Mary nodded. "In a way..."

"If you don't feel ready, if you'd rather wait and seek a position closer to London, you've only to say so. I'll gladly speak to the directors on your behalf."

Mary dismissed the offer with a vehement shake of her head. "Oh no, it isn't that. I shall miss my friends and you especially, milady, but I've a mind to see something of the world beyond these gates."

The journey from London to Cornwall could be accomplished in two days by post chaise, closer to one were the traveler able to procure a seat on a Royal Mail Coach—hardly a grand tour, but given how small her world had been kept, so it must seem to Mary. Then again, Phoebe had scarcely traveled herself. Bonaparte's bullying had precluded excursions abroad. She'd always assumed that once the war was over, she and Robert would go off on the grand honeymoon voyage they'd talked about, but he had forged forward and had his adventures without her. Despite their near kiss the previous day, despite that more than once since stepping outside she'd caught herself casting her gaze out over the lawn to look for his approach, the old bitterness bubbled to the surface.

Baffled, Phoebe asked, "Then what is amiss?"

The child cast a cautious look over her shoulder. Turning back, she dropped her voice to a whisper and admitted, "It's my mother, milady."

"You've kept in contact?" Phoebe asked quietly.

Shamefaced, the girl nodded. "Oh, I know 'tis against the rules, but we meet sometimes, always on a Saturday in Russell Square. Only the last few weeks she didn't come and now I'm to leave in a few days with no means of letting her know where I'll be or how to reach me."

"Can you not write her?" Phoebe asked gently. Her prize pupil, Mary possessed very pretty penmanship. Her spelling left something to be desired; still, she read and wrote far better than most domestic servants.

Mary darted another look about before admitting, "I have, only I'm loath to mail it. Mum likely won't have the coin to pay the postage to receive it, and even if she does, I'd be as good as taking the bread from her mouth." She slipped a folded letter from her pocket and passed it to Phoebe.

Chastened, Phoebe took it. Despite her years of working at the hospital, she still sometimes lost sight of how privileged she was. Of course Mary's mother would be among the many for whom receiving correspondence was accounted a luxury.

Turning her back upon the building façade with its many windows, she tucked the letter into her skirt pocket but not before giving a cursory glance to the recipient's direction: *Mistress Sally Fry, No. Six Church Lane, St. Giles Parish, London.*

Phoebe felt her courage curdle. The quarter was notorious as a haunt for criminals of every order, from petty pickpockets to commissioned cutthroats. Even among East Enders, the collation of crumbling tenements known as The Rookery had a deserved reputation as the very worst of the city's stews. Still, she'd made her promise to her pupil, and she meant to keep it.

"Do not to fret yourself, my dear. I promise to do all I can to ensure that this—" she patted her pocket "—is laid in your mother's hands before you leave and her reply returned to you. I shall send one of my family's most trusted footmen to undertake the task this very evening." Whoever went she would make sure he carried a loaded carriage pistol.

She'd hoped her promise would set Mary's mind at rest but, if possible, she only looked more forlorn. "That is too good of you, milady, but Mother can't read or write beyond making her mark."

Comprehending the predicament, Phoebe suppressed a sigh. Mary's sad situation was not as uncommon as she might wish. Illiteracy ran as rampant in the British Empire's capital city as it did elsewhere, a close companion to poverty and despair. "In that case, you will require someone to read the letter aloud to her and then wait and transcribe her reply. Is that correct?"

Mary nodded. "Mother keeps an oyster stall in Billingsgate Market. You might tell your man to seek her there first."

The Market might be a vast improvement over St. Giles's, but still Phoebe dare not venture there without an escort, someone whom she could trust to keep their secret. Aristide would never consent to such a scheme. He might well try to prevent her from undertaking it. Other than Reggie, notoriously unreliable and not always the most discrete, who might she ask? More to the point, who might she *trust*?

The clatter of carriage wheels had her looking once more out to the crushed oyster shell drive. A bright green carriage trundled toward them, the sun striking off a copious amount of gilded trim. Plumes danced atop the headgear of the team of matched blacks. A turbaned Arab, seemingly torn from the pages of the *Arabian Nights*, sat on the driver's box. *What a perfectly vulgar vehicle*, Phoebe thought, curious to see who would alight. The conveyance halted, the door opened, and Robert climbed down.

The sling was gone. Scouring him with her gaze, Phoebe marked that the swelling had gone down in his face. His right eye was black-and-blue but thankfully fully open.

Tipping his hat, he greeted them with a jaunty smile. "Good afternoon, ladies," he said, stopping on the step below.

Mary dropped into a low curtsy. "My lord," she said so solemnly Phoebe had to smother a smile.

Robert grinned, his split lip stretching to its limit. "I'm not a lord, Miss Mary. I'm as much a commoner as you. I just happen to be a rich one," he added with a wink. Holding out his hand, he helped her to rise.

"Whatever you are, you are late," Phoebe put in, painfully aware of how peevish she must sound. That she'd fallen into the habit of waiting for him irked her to no end.

He swung his gaze back to her. "If I didn't know better, I'd say you must have missed me."

"You would be mistaken," she snapped, feeling her pulse quicken.

With Aristide she was ever on tenterhooks, weighing her words before she spoke them, but with Robert she was free to speak her mind. Even her deliberate rudeness didn't seem to put him off. If anything, he seemed rather to like it.

The corners of his cut mouth cocked upward. "If I'm late, and admittedly I am, 'tis in the service of procuring Lulu's picnic luncheon."

So he hadn't forgotten. "It's the middle of the day—the *school* day."

Her weak protest didn't begin to put him off. "Unless English custom has altered drastically in my absence, midday is the time when picnics take place. Morning classes have concluded, have they not?"

"We don't resume until three," Mary volunteered, face brightening.

Phoebe shot her a look.

The rogue had managed to win over even her loyal Mary! But then that was the magic of Robert Bellamy, a testimony to the easy charm he exuded. She almost fancied an invisible cloud of fairy dust swirled about him, enveloping everyone within his sphere. Fairy dust or not, the simple truth was that he drew people. Despite their history, he drew *her*.

Behind them, the main door opened. Children spilled out onto the porch. The scamps must have availed themselves of her absence to take to the windows. Shouts of "A picnic, a picnic!" chorused through the group.

Breaking away from the others, Lulu ran toward Robert with open arms. "Mister Papa, you didn't forget!"

"Forget my promise to a lady? Perish the thought." He swooped down and picked her up, easily settling her atop his broad shoulders though doing so must hurt him mightily.

Seeing him thus, it was impossible not to think what a wonderful father he'd make. Aristide, Phoebe felt certain, would wish to keep their future children tucked out of sight in the nursery.

Robert turned back to Phoebe. "I've brought food enough to feed an army."

Clearly she was outnumbered. Aware of the children

watching her, she gave way with a shrug. “I haven’t an army, but growing children certainly eat like one.”

Divested of both hat and coat, Robert rested his back against the tree trunk. Shirtsleeves rolled to his elbows and legs stretched out in front of him on the blanket, he lounged as best his injuries would allow. Phoebe, however, had remained primly upright and fully buttoned throughout their luncheon, her skirts secured about her ankles, the ubiquitous lace fichu folded into her gown’s neckline.

Pleasantly replete, he swallowed a yawn. “Admit it, this was a good idea.”

“You’ve gone to a great deal of trouble,” she conceded, looking over at him. “And brought joy to not one child but twenty odd. Thank you.”

Her unexpected praise had him feeling uncharacteristically at a loss. “Anthony and Chelsea keep a well-stocked larder and pantry. I did nothing more than bespeak the items I desired from their cook.”

Growing children could indeed consume prodigious quantities. Little was left of the cold roast chicken, bread, fancy olives and cheeses, gooseberry tarts and fresh fruit. Even the bananas he’d brought were duly devoured once he’d demonstrated how to pull back the thick yellow peel to the soft, succulent flesh.

Once they’d chosen their spot, Caleb had taken charge of laying out their picnic beneath the bower of a large chestnut tree. At first the children other than Lulu kept their distance, but curiosity and hunger had overcome any trepidation and they crept closer. The tall, turbaned Arab far outstripped Newton’s science experiment in capturing their collective imagination. Likewise Pippin was so fascinated with his new friend’s headgear that at least once so far he’d leapt up, caught one end of the fabric in his mouth, and nearly torn the turban off. Looking from Caleb at play with his new admirers to Phoebe sitting beside him on the blanket, Robert felt a rare peace roll over him. For an afternoon at least it felt good to pretend that peace might indeed prove possible.

He shifted his gaze to Phoebe. Not for the first time he caught her gaze going to the building. They picnicked in plain view of any number of windows. "Are we violating some draconian dictate by being here?"

She hesitated. "There are a few stuffed shirts among the staff who've made it known they don't approve of my so-called 'modern methods.'"

He shrugged, biting back a wince as pain pulsed through his sore shoulder. "I would think they would allow you all the leeway you could wish for given how good you are with the children and not only Lulu." Her special fondness for the little girl was impossible to miss. Far from the first time, he considered what a splendid mother she would make.

Her raised eyebrows suggested his compliment had caught her off guard. "I wasn't always. First I had to win their trust."

There is nothing you can say, nothing you can do, that could possibly lure me to ever trust you again.

Summoning what he hoped would pass for a casual tone, he asked, "And how did you do it...win their trust, I mean?"

She paused for a moment. "I suppose I...listened."

"You listened?"

She nodded. "I did."

Robert gestured to the space beside him. "This trunk is broad enough for the both of us. Why not share it with me?" She hesitated and then scooted back to join him. "Better, thank you." Gaze holding hers, he swallowed hard. "Go on, I'm listening now."

She released a heavy sigh. "Sometimes I feel as if all I ever do is fight—with Mama, with the hospital governors and now with you."

Liking the casual intimacy of her shoulder resting beside his, he said, "It doesn't have to be that way. Why not call a permanent truce and start afresh?"

She shook her head. "You've always possessed a talent for making matters sound simple, when they're not."

In six months, a year at most...

He stiffened. "And you for making them out to be far more fuss than they need be."

For a fleeting moment he thought she might reach for the pitcher of lemon water and upend it over his head, but then her features relaxed. Instead, she rested her head back against the tree and sighed. "Oh, dear, we're fighting like cats again. What has it been, all of forty minutes?"

Robert reached for his timepiece, pretending to consult it. "More like thirty to my reckoning. Shall we try this again?" At her nod, he lifted his water glass from the grass. "A toast—to friendship renewed."

"To friendship." She touched her tumbler to his and took a sip. Setting the water aside, she said, "But mind you, anything more is out of the question."

"I shall lower my expectations accordingly." Was she, like him, thinking of the other day's near kiss? He bloody well hoped so. But as he couldn't very well kiss her here before an audience, sparring would serve as a close second best.

She hesitated. "Seriously, if we're to be friends, we should agree upon some ground rules."

He felt his smile slip. Rogues and rules hardly went fist-in-glove. "What have you in mind?"

Clearly she'd given the subject considerable thought, for she didn't so much as pause but launched directly in. "Firstly there shall be no kissing."

So she was indeed still thinking of their near embrace—excellent! "Very well, I agree not to *initiate* kissing you."

"Secondly, heretofore there shall be no speaking of the

past—*our* past."

"That suits me well enough. I'm far more interested in the future—ours."

Ignoring that remark, she continued, "Lastly, there shall be no provoking a quarrel with Aristide."

At the mention of the bilge rat's name, Robert felt his blood boil. "I quarrel with him! 'Tis he who—"

"He and I are to marry," Phoebe put in reasonably, so reasonably that he could not possibly argue. "If you are sincere in seeking my friendship, you must honor him as my intended—and my choice."

Despite the muscle ticking in his jaw, he nodded. "Very well, I shall not provoke a quarrel with Aristide—but should he see fit to challenge me, I shall see the thing through." Were he to find a way to prove the Frenchman was behind the severing of his horse's cinch, he would cede no quarter, none at all.

Seemingly satisfied, Phoebe nodded. "I suppose that shall serve."

He folded his arms across his chest. "What, no other stipulations? Perhaps a provision for an armed guard to accompany us with orders to shoot me on the spot should I fall afoul of rules one, two or three?"

Her lips twitched as though she fought a smile. "Don't tempt me."

He cast a sidelong glance her way. Flatter himself though he might, he'd yet to see her so bright-eyed and pink-cheeked with Bouchart. More worrisome still was her fiancé's suspect background and questionable character. A man who'd tamper with another's tack couldn't be trusted, certainly not as a husband.

"You know, 'tis oft said that those who craft rules do so in the main to govern themselves." He'd made the remark purely to goad her, but belatedly it occurred to him it might be true.

Phoebe narrowed her eyes. "I have never heard that."

"I suppose it's just as well we're having our picnic in plain view. You shan't have to worry about trusting yourself alone with me."

The tweak had the predictable—and desired—effect. Phoebe swiveled to face him, nearly bringing them to bump noses. "What a perfectly arrogant remark to make. In your years away, your good opinion of yourself seems to have grown apace with your hair."

Rather than dispute it, Robert laughed. "The Bible counsels that the meek shall inherit the earth, but I've yet to see any evidence of it."

"I can see you've added blasphemy to your heathen habits." She glanced toward Caleb, still tearing about the lawn with the children. Changing the subject, she asked, "Should we perhaps make him a plate?"

Robert shook his head. "You'd only insult him. Taking care of me is his life's purpose, at least until he feels he's repaid his debt."

"Is he indentured to you, then?"

Robert shook his head. "Where Caleb comes from, indenture as we know it doesn't exist."

Her gaze narrowed. "Don't tell me he's your...*slave*." She pronounced the latter in a voice hushed by shock and rife with disapproval.

Her question pulled him from his good humor. "Trading in human flesh is the vilest of acts, altogether the very worst evil man visits on his fellow man. I've seen not only men but women and children too led near naked and chained to auction blocks in markets throughout the Orient. A prize horse at Tattersall's is granted greater dignity, I assure you. Caleb stays with me of his own accord. Though he won't accept wages for his services, I set aside a certain sum every month. When the time comes for him to strike out on his own, he will not do so as a pauper."

She glanced back to Caleb, riding Fiona on his shoulder.

"Why does he feel indebted?"

"I once helped him to escape...a very bad situation, and he believes he owes me his life."

"Does he speak any English?"

Robert hesitated. "Speak it, no, but I believe he comprehends quite a bit."

"What is his native tongue?"

"None now."

Phoebe's eyes snapped back at him. "I may not have traveled farther than Scotland, but that does not make me an ignoramus. All humans have a spoken language. I'm certain Caleb's people are no exception."

"He was brought up speaking Persian as well as some Hindi and Malagasy, but he hasn't uttered a word of either in years."

She cast him a quizzing look. "Did he take some sort of vow of silence?"

"Not quite." Robert paused and then admitted, "He hasn't a tongue."

Her hand flew to her mouth, her eyes popping. "How awful!"

He let out a laugh. "There's no need to hide the cheese knife. I wasn't the one to cut it out."

Dropping her hand, she said, "I never thought—"

"The devil you didn't."

"Well, perhaps for a moment," she admitted. "That cutlass is a frightful-looking thing," she added, casting a look to the blade he'd earlier removed and set within arm's reach beside the blanket. "Must you still carry it?"

"London can be every whit as dangerous as Calcutta," he said, thinking again of the other night's *accident*. "And yet I've missed it, all of England, really."

"What have you missed particularly?" she asked and her guileless gaze forestalled any hope he'd had that she might be fishing.

He pointed to the remains of the wedge of Stilton. "The food, for one."

"Is there no cheese in India?"

"There's no *English* cheese nor bacon nor Christmas pudding and a thousand other small things one takes for granted because they were always there—the way the spring air smells just after a rain shower, the crunch of snow beneath one's boot soles."

Leaning forward, she rested her chin on tented knees. "But only think of all the exotic sights you've experienced, people and places that most of us only know through newspapers and books." Her wistfulness wasn't lost on him nor had he forgotten the grand plans they once had made.

"The East is a different world entirely, beautiful in its way, but brutal too."

"I'd like to see it someday," she said, turning back to look at him.

Looking into her lovely face, for this moment as open as those of the children playing upon the lawn, it occurred to him that the present moment presented the ripe opportunity for which he'd been waiting. He should snatch his chance and snare her with bedazzling tales of swashbuckling exploits, and then reel her in like the prize carp that as a boy he'd caught fishing with his father and Chelsea at Framfield. Though their father had sworn it was vain waste, in the end he'd let Robert mount the blasted thing on the study wall rather than turn it over to their cook. But he couldn't bring himself to do it. For all those daring adventures and golden moments were intertwined, painfully and inextricably, with the horror and the humiliation.

"The sky is clouding." He shifted onto his knees and made a show of dusting crumbs from his trousers. "If I recall anything about England, that means we should expect a shower at any moment." Stiff-legged, he stood and offered her a hand.

She hesitated and then took it, her slim fingers threading through his as they'd used to. In light of the lovely lunch, the small gesture further buoyed his hopes that their bond might yet be repaired.

Gaining her feet, she abruptly let go and shook out her skirts. “I rather think I should be helping *you* up.”

“I’m not *that* bad.” He motioned to Caleb to come forward and begin repacking the hamper.

Looking on, Phoebe hesitated. “Before we go in, might I make a request?” She pressed a hand to her pocket, the unguarded action making him curious about what she might have in there.

“A favor, you mean?” he asked, wondering what she might want, hoping beyond all that it would prove within his power to provide.

“Very well, yes, a favor. Between *friends*,” she added pointedly.

“In that case, ask me anything.” Christ, if she’d expressed a desire for him to change out the sun for the moon, he’d give his bloody best to doing it.

She drew a deep breath. “If I asked you to escort me somewhere, somewhere a lady ought not to be seen, would you do it?”

The circus at Astley’s Amphitheatre, the pleasure gardens of Cremorne and Vauxhall and the seller stalls at Bond Street Bazaar had been her preferred haunts six years ago. Clearly this time she had something more serious than a pleasure jaunt in mind.

Intrigued, he answered, “Where is it you wish to go?”

Her dubious look sent his heart sinking, for it confirmed her trust was not yet his. “First I’ll have your word that you’ll take me—and without telling.”

That didn’t sound good. Still, Robert nodded. “Name your pleasure, milady. By now you must know that your wish is my command.”

"What business can you possibly have at a fish market?" Robert demanded, seated in the carriage opposite Phoebe. In the spirit of prudence, she'd waited to reveal their destination until they'd passed through the Hospital's arcaded entrance.

"My own." Now that they were underway, she subsided back against the leather squab.

He choked back a laugh. "Fair enough, but why so secretive? Once we arrive, I shall discover it soon enough." His gaze darkened. "If I find that Frog fiancé of yours has sent you to do his bidding, I'll have Caleb turn the carriage straight about."

Rather than be cowed, she chuckled. Really, he had the most absurd fancies sometimes. "I very much doubt that Aristide has ventured east of the Strand—he has men for that—and he certainly wouldn't sanction my doing so. I am his betrothed, not his lackey."

He didn't bother to conceal his relief—or his triumph. "In that case, wild horses could not keep me from accompanying you."

She hesitated. "By the by, are you still paying for my time?"

"Cheeky chit. Yes, your orphans will have their hundred pounds and you your pound of flesh from me." He grinned, his pirate's smile crinkling the tanned flesh at the corners of his eyes. "Only mind you don't repeat our arrangement in public. One of us still has a reputation to uphold."

"No thanks to you," she couldn't resist pointing out.

He answered with a laugh and then leaned forward, close enough that she could all but taste the anise he'd taken following lunch. The prospect of savoring its flavor in a kiss stoked a tingling heat low in her belly. "But mind I've upheld my part to take you anywhere you might wish even though ere now you'd kept me in the dark as to our destination. Will you not return my faith in kind and at least tell me why we're bound there?"

Meeting his earnest eyes, Phoebe relented. "I promised one of my students I would see a letter delivered to her mother."

He raised an eyebrow. "Isn't that what the mail coaches are for?"

"Even within the city proper, paying the postage required to receive a letter by Royal Mail is beyond the means of many."

Apparently chastened, he sat back in his seat. "Of course, please go on."

She quickly recounted Mary's situation. "Though her mother was never able to raise the funds to reclaim her, they've kept in touch all these years, contriving to meet on Saturdays in Russell Square. Now Mary's been found a position as a scullery maid in a household in Cornwall. She's to leave within the week."

"Cornwall is hardly the ends of the earth," Robert remarked with a shrug.

"It might as well be. For Mistress Fry to pay the postage on a letter coming all the way from Launceston would amount to taking bread from the mouths of her other children. I've promised to deliver this last letter, which includes Mary's direction, and to faithfully take down her reply."

"It seems an innocent-enough endeavor. Why the stealth?"

"Once a mother has surrendered her child, further communication is forbidden."

His handsome face registered surprise. "That seems harsh."

She nodded. "The intent is to act in the best interest of the child, but in practice it is not always so. Were she to be discovered, poor Mary could find herself turned out. Without a letter of reference from the Hospital, I'm sure you know what sort of position she could hope to obtain."

An orphan girl on her own without references to recommend her would be forced to beg her bread or, worse, sell her favors to make ends meet.

"And what of you, Phoebe? Were you to be discovered

abetting her, what would befall you?"

Her gaze dropped to her lap. Folding her hands over her reticule, she admitted, "I would likely be dismissed."

"And yet you risk your place to help them. Why?"

She edged her gaze up to his. "Perhaps because I know what it means to love someone and believe you've lost them forever."

For a charged moment, they stared at one another, so intensely that for the span of several heartbeats Phoebe was insensible to the carriage bumping along, to the streets streaking by, or to the dubious odors wafting inside the window, anything save Robert. Staring into his eyes, reading the raw pain etched upon his handsome face, in that moment she understood in part what he must have been trying to say these past weeks.

Despite the adventures he'd had and the wealth he'd amassed, he truly did regret leaving her.

Breaking their silence and spelled state, he asked, "Did the girl say where in the market her mother has her stall?"

Phoebe hesitated. "I didn't think to ask. Is it a very large market?"

He stared at her askance.

"The city's main fish market, quite." Summoning what optimism she might, she said, "Well, I'm, er...certain we shall discover her readily enough."

He opened his mouth as if to demur when the carriage struck a rut. Phoebe lurched forward, her bottom slipping off the seat. Robert caught her against him. "Are you all right?"

Pressed against that powerful chest, Phoebe managed a nod. "I should ask the same of you. You're the one with the sore shoulder."

Her solicitude seemed to amuse him. "This body has weathered many a buffeting. A sylph such as you shall scarcely put any new dins in me though for such a slight woman, you do have an impressive grip," he added, a smile in his voice.

Drawing back, she saw that he hadn't been the only one of them to reach out. Her hand curved about his biceps, the muscle beneath his coat feeling nearer to granite than fleshed bone. Recalling the expert ease with which he'd pinioned her on that first night back, she felt a frisson of that same dark, lingering excitement and eased her hand away.

Phoebe cleared her throat. "You may release me now."

Gaze slipping to her mouth, he asked, "May or must?"

"Must."

Holding steadying hands to her shoulders, he set her back against the squabs. As soon as she was secured, his hands fell away. Phoebe felt their loss as though a part of her own body had suddenly gone missing.

He sat back with a begrudging air. "As you wish, *friend*."

From thereon, it felt infinitely safer to turn her head to look out the window despite the unprepossessing scenery. As they headed farther east, the streets grew narrower and more labyrinthine, the crooked thoroughfares and alleys as squalid and stinking as Phoebe remembered them from her brief glimpse six years ago. It seemed as though every block bore the same sort of ramshackle lodging houses and nefarious tradesmen—rag-and-bone shops, pawn shops and on every corner a gin palace announcing *Drunk for a penny, dead drunk for tuppence, clean straw for nothing.*

Catching a strong whiff of the foulness wafting up from the open ditches, she ducked back inside and snapped the leather curtain closed.

"Mind this was all your idea." Arms folded, Robert appeared unaffected.

She regarded him with watering eyes. "I...n-never said it wasn't." A fit of gagging threatened to bring up her luncheon.

Apparently taking pity upon her, he reached into his breast pocket, pulled out his handkerchief and passed it to her. "Use this to cover your nose and mouth until you've become accustomed to the odors."

"T-thank you." She accepted the square of snowy linen with genuine gratitude. "But I doubt I shall ever become accustomed to...this."

"You'd be surprised what one can learn to live with," he said, more to himself than her, and even in her current state, she wondered at the bitterness lacing his voice.

Once they turned onto Lower Thames Street, the breeze picked up, the smell of fish overtaking all others. Seagulls and various birds of prey circled low, keeping a keen lookout for their next meal. Caleb drew their team to a halt. He climbed down from the box, opened the door and lowered the carriage steps. Robert stepped down and then turned back to offer her his hand. She took it, alighting amidst the mayhem.

"I'll just have a word with Caleb," he said, leaving her side.

"Of course," she said.

Leaving the two men to converse, Robert in a mixture of English and some exotic foreign tongue and Caleb through intricate hand gestures, she took the opportunity to get her bearings amidst the hubbub. Admittedly, the market was larger than she'd anticipated. She'd been naïve to think she might simply walk up and locate Mary's mother straightaway. In addition to a large shed that must serve as the main market, there was an open area on the north side of the dock sprinkled with a number of booths and huts. Myriad people moved betwixt and between it all, hawkers with their baskets, costermongers with their three-legged handcarts, the latter loading up treats of jellied eels and freshly shucked oysters to sell elsewhere in the city. Men pushing carts heaped with fishes and other sea creatures bustled between booths.

Rejoining Phoebe, Robert explained that only licensed porters were permitted to move fish through the market. Cockney curses filled the air, some good-natured, others less so, all various shades of blue.

Fighting blushing, Phoebe turned to Robert. "I know Mistress Fry sells oysters. Does that help?" In truth, she wasn't at all certain where to begin.

"We'll try the main market first." Taking her hand, he moved them toward the large shed backing onto the wharf. Approaching the entrance, he firmed his hold on her hand. "Stay close to me," he warned, pulling back on the entrance door.

The din within was ear-splitting, the traders all crying out their wares with full force of their lungs, each man or woman claiming to possess that which was most stupendous and savory. Stepping inside and slipping into the sea of sweating faces and buffeting bodies, Phoebe felt momentarily overwhelmed. Looking from left to right to get her bearings, she allowed she'd never felt more a fish out of water in all her life.

Fortunately Robert seemed entirely at home. He towed them along one straw-strewn aisle after another, occasionally pausing to inquire if one of the vendors was acquainted with an oyster woman by the surname of Fry. Dodging jamming elbows and buffeting hips, Phoebe struggled to keep pace beside him. Booths and stalls piled with fish of every conceivable kind and quality lined the four walls and formed aisles between. Along with fishmongers, there were vendors selling cooked foods and cakes, fruits and vegetables, saloop and beer. Pinch-faced children and skinny cats prowled the stalls, scrounging for scraps.

A sharp cry of "Halt, thief!" preceded a scrawny boy whizzing past, an enormous fish tucked beneath his arm. Two sellers in stained aprons hared after him in hotfooted pursuit. Robert grabbed hold of Phoebe and hauled her out of their path before one or more might barrel into her.

"I told you to keep close," he warned sharply before letting go and, shaken, Phoebe didn't require telling a second time.

"Pearls o' da sea, 'alf dozen fer tuppence, full dozen fer a dime," called a voice from the aisle opposite them.

Phoebe and Robert exchanged looks. Had they found their Mistress Fry? They trailed the singsong chanting to a half dozen stalls at the back of the building, each displaying oysters banked upon a bed of salt. Going down the line, Phoebe saw that only one of the sellers was a woman. By silent assent, she and Robert headed over.

Behind the booth, a woman sat upon a stool working away at the hard shells with a short, wicked-looking knife. Weathered and white-haired, she glanced up as they approached.

"Pardon me, but might you be Sally Fry?" Phoebe asked.

Resuming her shucking, the seller shrugged. "That depends. Who is what wants ter know?"

"My name is Phoebe Tremont," she said, deliberately leaving off her title. In light of the hardscrabble lives most here seemed to lead, the title seemed more a silly affectation than pertinent information.

Cutting her a look, the woman snorted. "Unless you're buyin' oysters, what's i' ter me?"

"I'm a schoolmistress at the Foundling Hospital."

The knife stilled. The woman's head jerked up. "My girl, me Mary, is she—"

"She is quite safe and well," Phoebe hastened to assure her. "She asked me to bring you this." She reached inside her pocket and brought out the letter.

Rising, the woman made no move to reach for it. Hanging her head, she admitted, "I never learned me le'ers."

Mary had prepared Phoebe for as much. "I shall be happy to read it to you and to take down any message you might wish to return to Mary." She paused, casting a sideways look to Robert. Holding several paces back, he made no attempt to interfere.

Turning back to Mistress Fry, Phoebe asked, "Is there somewhere we can be private?"

Mary's mother jerked her chin to a curtained-off area

backing up the booth. “I sometimes tuck inside ter put me feet up. It’s not much, two stools, not at all what a lady such as yahrself is used ter, but—”

“I’m sure it shall do splendidly.”

Again she glanced over to Robert. The approving smile he sent her warmed her to her toes. She tried to imagine Aristide here instead but couldn’t. Her betrothed would never condescend to enter a market, not even to ensure that a mother and daughter remained reunited. But Robert would. More to the point, he *had.* Whatever else he might have had planned for the day, he’d set it aside to see her safely here and home.

She thought back to her earlier skepticism about their rekindled friendship and felt a stab of remorse. True, he hadn’t kept faith with her six years ago, but did it necessarily follow that he couldn’t be trusted now?

Since his return, he’d proven himself to be a friend in need and deed. Her rules aside, in her heart of hearts she owned that she wished he might be so very much more.

Chapter Eight

Though Mistress Fry appeared to be exactly what Robert had hoped, a mother who dearly loved her daughter despite their precarious past, Phoebe was far too precious for him not take precautions. It was far too easy to spirit a person away, especially on the water. Back stairs leading down to cellars or out to the docks, opiates and other drugs that could render a body senseless, the grave robbers known as resurrection men who sometimes helped the living to an early demise—the scenarios his mind spun chilled him. Though ordinarily no eavesdropper, he kept an ear cocked toward the curtain. The voices carrying out were held too low to make out their meanings, but they sufficed to confirm that Phoebe remained both well and within.

Several passersby cast him curious looks and one of the oystermen grumbled that he was blocking the view to his stall, but otherwise he was left alone to wait. Eventually the curtain was drawn back. Phoebe emerged, her arm linked with that of Sally Fry. Both women's cheeks appeared damp. Stepping out onto the aisle, they embraced, looking more like longtime friends than minutes-old acquaintances.

"Tell me girl I love 'er," Mistress Fry sniffed. "And that I'm proud, terrible proud o' da fine bird she's become...thuff 'tis no thanks ter me."

Heedless of the seller's stained apron and coarse homespun brown dress, Phoebe hugged her hard. Stepping back, she said, "I shall see Mary later today and give her your message, but please know how very important you are in her life and always will be."

The woman nodded solemnly. "There ain't many o' yahr stashun what would put 'emselves aht fer da likes o' us. If I live ter be one an' one 'undred, I'll never forget yahr kindness."

Phoebe shrugged aside the praise. "If you ever find yourself in need, or if you wish for my help in getting another message to Mary, you are to let me know at once." She opened her reticule and handed over one of her cream-colored calling cards.

If Robert hadn't loved her already, he would have fallen hard and fast in that moment.

"It was lovely meeting you." Phoebe turned toward Robert.

Mistress Fry called her back. "Hold!" She whisked behind the booth, picked up her scoop and began shoveling shells onto a sheet of waxed paper. "The best o' da lot, freshly shucked," she said with obvious pride. Bundling it with string, she passed the present over the counter to Phoebe.

Whilst Phoebe had nibbled upon many an oyster patty served at buffet suppers, Robert doubted she'd ever come close to eating an uncooked bivalve. Expression alarmed, she drew back. "Oh, no, I couldn't possibly."

Robert stepped forward. "We would be delighted." Before Phoebe could protest again, he snatched up the bag.

The oyster woman's gaze flickered back to Phoebe. "Is that yahr man?" she asked Phoebe as though he weren't standing all but under her nose.

Curious as to how she would answer, Robert forced himself to stay silent.

"We are friends. The best of friends," Phoebe added, keeping her gaze trained on Mary's mother.

Dividing her gaze between them, Mistress Fry grinned. "If I'd 'ad a *friend* like yahrs instead o' da bilge rat what knocked me up, me life might 'ave gone differently."

Blushing prettily, Phoebe turned back to Robert. "We should be getting along."

Heart fisting with the force of all the love he felt but for now must hold within, he smiled down on her. "In that case, milady, your carriage awaits."

Feeling safe by Robert's side, Phoebe exited the market shed in a sort of happy haze the likes of which she'd not known for years. Despite the errand keeping them away longer than she'd planned upon, she couldn't wish it otherwise. Meeting Mary's mother had been deeply moving. As it happened, Mistress Fry had missed the last two Saturday afternoons in Russell Square through no fault of her own. The woman who typically minded the oyster stall on Saturdays had quit and Mistress Fry had been forced to take over those shifts in addition to her own. Her unenviable choice had been to miss seeing her daughter or risk losing her employment.

The mission of mercy had turned into something of an adventure. Despite living in London year-round for the last six years, the present was Phoebe's first excursion to an actual market. Europe's largest fish market had not disappointed. Once she'd become accustomed to the hubbub, she'd found herself fascinated. The sights, the noise, even the smells were all foreign to her. Not, however, to Robert.

Glancing over at him, not for the first time she marveled on how confident and at ease he seemed here, far more so than in the assembly rooms of Almack's or even her parents' small ballroom. Though she'd rather eat...raw oysters than admit it, the ease with which he'd navigated them through the crush, the sense of being utterly cherished and protected by him, was more than a bit thrilling.

And then there was his compassion, which he showered so freely upon all, including Mistress Fry. In hindsight Phoebe saw that, if left to stand, her refusal of the oyster woman's gift might have been interpreted as snobbery, undoing much of the goodwill sewn during her brief visit. Fortunately Robert had understood—and acted. His swift intervention had saved face and feelings for everyone. She glanced to the tied parcel he carried by its string and wished she'd made more of an effort to overcome her squeamishness.

Swinging the parcel, he turned his rogue's smile once more upon her. "Oysters are accounted to be an aphrodisiac. Are you certain you won't try one?"

"Quite." An aphrodisiac—as if Phoebe was in want of such a thing when Robert was about. Despite the conditions she'd earlier imposed upon their "friendship", she found herself wishing she might cast caution to the wind—along with Rule Number One.

She wanted to kiss Robert. She wanted it rather badly. The angry embrace they'd shared on his first night back had become a source of near-constant obsession.

Only, wanton creature that he'd made her, she wouldn't be satisfied with stopping at his mouth. She wanted to touch her lips and teeth and tongue to the whole of his big, lean, beautiful body. Imagining what it might be like to unbutton first his waistcoat and then his shirt and kiss a queue from his muscle-corded throat to washboard-flat belly and beyond had kept her awake for much of the previous night. She could but imagine how beautiful he must be beneath his well tailored if gaudily colored garments.

Unfortunately, she had no recourse but to imagine. In contrast to his former freeness, he'd kept himself scrupulously buttoned since his return. Other than the glimpses of hair-dusted forearms she'd dared during their picnic, she had to make do with memory. From the few times she'd touched him since his return, she'd gleaned an impression of lean muscle and steely strength. Though he certainly sought out every excuse to lay hands upon her, he seemed to have developed a dislike of being touched himself. The Robert of six years before had begged for back rubs, so much so that she'd teased he rivaled Pippin in pandering for pets. The man who'd returned in his stead stiffened to stone if she so much as laid a glove upon his shoulder. The odd aversion was yet another reminder that the boy with whom she'd fallen so madly in love was no more.

Lost to daydreaming, she scarcely registered them reaching the carriage until they were upon it. Glancing up, she saw that Caleb hadn't budged from his seat on the box. Perhaps it was only her imagination, but the body beneath the loose-fitting robes seemed to have shrunk since their leave-taking. Rather than climb down and open the door for them, he stayed put. Reminded of the hand-and-foot way he'd waited upon them during their picnic, his sudden sloth struck Phoebe as strange. Tearing around the hospital lawn with the children and Pippin in pursuit must have worn him out indeed.

Out of the corner of her eye, she caught Robert's frown. He reached for the door, opened it and paused. From habit, Phoebe held out her hand in preparation for being handed up.

Instead of doing so, he turned away and backed up with a view to the box. "Ho, Caleb, I've brought you your favorite delicacy, freshly shucked oysters."

Face covered, Caleb pivoted fractionally toward him.

Robert hauled back and lobbed the parcel at the manservant. Hands, narrow and pale, shot out to receive it, catching it neatly.

Robert backed up a step, slanting Phoebe a warning look. Not that he needed to. Like a phantom ship, her happy haze had vanished. Hairs pricked her nape. Dread sent her stomach sinking.

The carriage dipped as a second man, dressed as a dockworker, leapt down from the footman's rest where he must have lain in wait all along. "What fine fortune, for I fancy oysters meself." Advancing to close the gap between them, he flashed a gold-toothed grin—and the primed pistol he held down at his side. "Now be a good girl and gent and climb inside. We're going for a little ride."

Heart pounding, Phoebe backed away, edging closer to Robert. Wordless, he stretched out a hand toward her. She took it, and his fingers closed firmly about her palm.

Turning to her, he shouted, "Run!"

Skirting the wharves, they tore past Custom House toward Tower Hill, Robert hoping to lose their pursuers in the warren of winding streets and alleys. What followed was a blur of crooked lanes, concealed courtyards and rubbish-strewn alleys. Six years away had muddied his memory and in truth he'd never known the eastern environs terribly well. Unlike Reggie and others of his set, forays into the city's seedier sections had never appealed to him. Even so, his experiences whilst away had honed his survival instincts to a fine point. Ducking beneath lines of laundry strung between rabbit-hole-sized windows, he urged Phoebe forward.

They darted across Rosemary Lane, the footpads hot on their heels, the dockhands, doxies and denizens barely sparing them a second look, as though two people running for their lives was a commonplace occurrence. Perhaps it was. Had he been alone, Robert would have gambled on his ability to outrun them, and to cut them down with his cutlass if they caught up, but having Phoebe with him placed both possibilities out of the question. Despite the admirable pace she'd so far kept up, she was hopelessly hampered by her gown and soft-soled slippers. A fleeting look at her face confirmed she was flagging. Searching out a temporary sanctuary in which to hide, he drew her toward the back of an abandoned building. They entered the alley and despite the acrid odor she neither coughed nor choked.

They'd scarcely drawn a breath when shuffling feet announced their pursuers' approach. Robert motioned Phoebe to silence. Breaths bated, they stood side-by-side, backs flattened against the crumbling wall as the pursuers passed by their hiding place.

"Do yew see 'em, mate?" one called out.

"Naw, they're not 'ere. C'mon, let's move on. Stinks somethin' terrible."

Signaling her to silence, Robert unpeeled his damp back

from the stones.

Phoebe peered past him to the alley entrance. "Fancy we gave them the slip?" she whispered.

Improbably Robert found himself fighting a smile. "I think they've passed on, if that's what you mean, but to be safe we'll bide here a few minutes more. By the by, where did you pick up street cant?" They hadn't been at the market all that long.

"Sorry. I suppose my students have rubbed off on me."

"Don't be sorry," he said, more impressed than he was willing to admit. "Given where we're bound, it might prove useful."

Her gaze sharpened. "Where *are* we bound?"

"We can't return to the carriage just yet. They'll be expecting us to do just that. We'll need a haven to hide for a few hours until our trail cools and they abandon their pursuit."

She nodded. "I agree, but where?"

"I may know someone who might be prevailed upon to take us in. One of my crew has a...*friend* with a lodging house on Well Street." Sandy was a Cockney to his core, having drawn his first breath within earshot of the Bow Bells. His reminiscences of home were so detailed that Robert had felt as if a mental map had been drawn. For Phoebe's sake as well as his, he hoped to God that were true. "But before we continue on, we need to render some...alterations to your appearance."

Phoebe glanced down at herself, then back over at him. "I wasn't aware I required altering."

"A scalawag such as I shall slip in without eliciting a second look, but you, m'dear, are too conspicuously top drawer for your own good." *As well as far too beautiful.*

"Are you quite certain I am the one who is conspicuous?" She cast a pointed stare to his latest colorful frockcoat.

"You are for this end of the city."

"Very well, what improvements do you recommend?" Despite their dire straits, she managed a smile.

"You can start by taking off those gloves."

Phoebe lifted her hand to her forehead in a mock salute. "Aye, captain."

"Most amusing, now get to it."

Phoebe did, beginning with her left hand and pulling at the fabric tipping each finger. She used her teeth to hasten things along, nibbling the seams of the soft cloth, and Robert felt his mouth go dry. Were they anywhere besides a filthy alley, the act would be inordinately erotic. Even under their present pressed circumstances, it *was* erotic, arousing as hell. He made a mental note to have her repeat the act for him one day soon—in private though not in an alley.

She peeled off the right glove and passed him the pair. "What next?" she said, the glow to her gaze making him wonder if she weren't perhaps a whit aroused herself.

Stuffing the gloves into his coat pocket, he lowered his regard to her breasts, modestly covered. She wouldn't like it a whit, but the fichu filling in her gown's bodice would have to go.

Hoping she wouldn't fight him on it, he waived a hand toward her bosom. "No East End doxy would be caught dead looking so prim and proper."

She glared at him. "But I'm not a...doxy."

"No, you're not," he agreed, thinking how infinitely simpler his life might be if she were. "But for the next several hours, we need to make you look as much the drab as possible."

Even in the shadowed alley, there was no missing the blush branding her cheek. Turning slightly away, she slipped a hand inside her bodice. Robert's mouth went dry again. Even though he knew she only felt for the pins, watching her touch herself there had his body heating.

Facing back to him, she handed the lace over in silence.

Robert took it. Slender though she was, she'd filled out since he'd departed. Her breasts were fuller, her hips and buttocks fully fleshed and subtly curved. His regard riveted on her bosom, twin alabaster slopes that rhythmically rose and fell as if taunting him to touch her. Well-remembering their texture and taste, the way her coral-colored nipples had danced upon his tongue, Robert was tempted to do just that—and more.

But the present life-and-death scenario precluded indulging such salacious thoughts, let alone acting upon them. He snapped his gaze safely back to hers. “The bonnet, if you please.”

Reaching up, she pulled out the long hatpin, removed the headgear and handed it over. As if realizing the pin’s potential as a weapon, she held onto it, and then slowly and carefully slid it inside her bodice—clever girl!

He dropped the hat to the dirt and crushed the crown beneath his heel.

Phoebe winced. “I just purchased that...at Harding, Howell & Company, no less.”

He picked up the wreckage and dropped it in the nearest bin. “Once this is over, I’ll buy you the shop if you like. For now, muss your hair a bit more.”

She let out a huff and bent headfirst, ruffling her hair between both hands, shedding pins onto the cobbles. Fortunately, haring away from their pursuers had helped in that regard. Even though she’d managed to hold onto her hat until now, much of her hair had worked free of its moorings. Straightening, she said, “Well, say something. Shall I do?”

Robert nodded. “Barely but yes.” Short of knocking out a few of her pearlescent teeth or blackening an eye, there was nothing he could do to blunt her beauty. “Once we step out onto the street, mind you hunch your shoulders.”

Phoebe stared at him aghast. “Why? Will you being hunching yours as well?”

Drawing a deep breath, Robert called for patience. “The way you carry yourself marks you as a lady far more than any finery.” He extended his hand toward her. “Shall we?”

She hesitated, and then slapped her slender hand into his. "Lead on."

Picking a path through rubbish and broken glass, Robert brought them to the opposite end of the alley. He released Phoebe and stepped out, casting his gaze up and down the street.

"Coast's clear," he whispered, beckoning Phoebe to join him.

She did, falling into step beside him. Though the natural urge was to forge ahead to safety as swiftly as possible, doing so would draw undue attention. Tamping down his impatience, Robert forced them to hold to an amble.

Well Street was the next over from Rosemary Lane. Though their pace seemed maddeningly slow, still it didn't take them more than a few minutes to reach it. Quiet and tucked away, the lodging house was ideally situated for their fugitive purposes. Swinging above the door, a hinged sign read: *Lodgings for Travelers.*

Phoebe hesitated. "Are you certain this is the place your friend recommends?"

Robert wasn't certain of much these days, but he flattered himself that his powers of reason hadn't yet deserted him entirely. "It looks to be the only lodging house here." His boatswain might not have the most refined tastes in women or rooms, but at the moment their pressing need was for four walls and a roof, preferably with a door that might be bolted from within.

Robert opened the door for her to enter. "Follow my lead and let me do the talking." Her plum-in-the-mouth speech would give her away as surely as her ladylike deportment.

He dealt her a light shove and followed her inside. The door falling closed behind him cut off most of the light, barring the scant rays admitted through the smeared panes of one narrow window and the tallow candles set in wall brackets throughout. The air was close, thick and reeking. Several patrons slumped on bare wooden benches, puffing upon pipes and swigging glasses of what must be rum or gin. One old salt sprawled full-body across the seat, snoring loudly. A dirty-faced child played in the filthy straw while a woman, presumably her mother, looked on with bleary eyes.

The blousy brunette pulling pints from behind the bar must be Sandy's Bess. Roping an arm around Phoebe's shoulders, Robert steered them over. "Good day, mistress."

She looked them up and down. "I'd say that's a matter o' opinion. Name your pleasure—gin, porter or ale?"

Bespeaking all of the above was not without appeal but getting foxed wasn't a luxury that Robert could presently afford. He lowered his voice. "I'm a mate of Sandy's—his captain, in point."

Bess's eyes narrowed. "If that's even half true, then why hasn't he been around to visit me?"

Robert thought quickly. "The Swan is in dry dock at the moment. I'm afraid I've kept him and the rest of the crew busy with breaming her. I'm sure he'll come calling as soon as he can."

Bess slammed a foamy pint down upon the bar. "He'd better."

Treading warily, Robert gestured toward a crooked set of stairs in the back. "He mentioned you had rooms for let above-stairs." He glanced over to Phoebe. Slack-jawed and slump-shouldered, she made for a reasonably believable slattern barring her eyes, which seemed to bore holes in the side of his face. "My wife is newly breeding, and I was hoping she might rest for an hour or so."

Wife, breeding—the lie rolled smoothly off his tongue, no doubt because he dearly wished that circumstances were indeed so. Phoebe, however, seemed less than pleased. He heard her sharp intake of breath and tightened his hold on her shoulders.

Bess cracked a laugh. "Your wife is it? Blimey, that's rich." She looked over to Phoebe. "Sorry, I don't let by the hour and even if I was to, we're booked."

Robert looked about before reaching for his money clip. Flashing it discretely, he asked, "Would this be of help in securing a vacancy?"

Chewing on her lip, she appeared to prevaricate. "Well, there is one room that might suit. A dress lodger lets it, but she won't be back until later."

Catching a sideways glimpse of Phoebe's face—her shocked, horrified, *furious* face—Robert remarked, "How fortuitous."

"'Tis a fiver for the hour."

Phoebe spoke up, "That's highway rob—"

"Most generous, we'll take it." Robert flipped through the wad of notes and took out two. "Only let's make it a tenner, and perhaps you could see your way to sending up some soup and a bottle of your best port?"

Snatching the bills and tucking them into her bodice, Bess broke into a gap-toothed grin. "I knew you for a gentleman the moment I clapped eyes on you...Captain."

A sharp elbow slammed into his side, the very spot where the bruised ribs were just beginning to heal. Swallowing an oath, he turned to find Phoebe glaring up at him.

Syrupy smile at odds with her narrowed eyes, she cooed, "Dearest, a word with you, if I may."

"Can it not wait until we are settled, my beloved?" Until he secured her behind a bolted door, he couldn't begin to feel safe.

"No, it cannot."

Lest another jab drive home her point, he took hold of her elbow and steered them out of Bess's earshot.

Dropping any pretense of smiling, she leaned in and whispered, "I can't go upstairs with you—to a...*prostitute's* chamber. I'll be ruined beyond redemption."

Ruined—was that all? He gestured to encompass their fellow patrons, all in various states of inebriation. "Do you honestly imagine anyone here has plans to report back to the patronesses of Almack's or your mother, for that matter? Beyond all, if that lot catches up with us—and they could walk in here at any time—you may find yourself spending eternity at the bottom of the Thames and me with you."

Judging from her widening eyes, that last bit brought her around. Taking her hand, he backtracked them to Bess at the bar. "If you would be so good as to see us up now, I would be most grateful."

She grabbed a ring of keys and ducked beneath the overpass. Joining them on the other side, she said, "To be sure it ain't what your *wife* is accustomed to, but the bed is made and the sheets changed every other month."

She led them up. A narrowed hallway and three closed doors comprised the uppermost floor. After some confusion over which key fit which lock, she got the desired door open. Not sure what they would find within, Robert entered first. It was a simple chamber, sparsely furnished with a rope bed, wardrobe, washstand and a small table set with two straight-back chairs. Though the furniture had seen better days and the air was tinged with stale spirits and sour sweat, all in all it was cleaner than Robert had dared hope. A single window faced onto the front, affording an unobstructed view of the street. He walked over to it and looked out.

"I'll just leave you love birds to your roost," their hostess said with a laugh. "I'll send up refreshments anon."

Joining him at the window, Phoebe asked, "I am curious. What about the footpad on the box made you so certain he wasn't Caleb?"

"The oysters."

She stared at him. "The oysters? How so? You remarked they were his favorite food."

Hoping that his friend yet lived, he explained, "Caleb is a

Shiite. His Halal diet forbids consuming crustaceans other than shrimps and prawns. He wouldn't defile himself by touching a single oyster, let alone an entire parcel."

"So it was a lie to draw them out."

"It was."

She sent him a fleeting smile. "It seems Mistress Fry's gift saved us—as did you."

That was as near to praise as he had so far come with her. Pressing his momentary advantage, he pointed out, "Those men were no common footpads but professional murderers."

She lifted her eyebrows as though never before considering such a thing. "Your powers of reasoning must run deep indeed. How, may I ask, do you deduce this?"

"Most criminals are simple souls as well as lazy. Once a mark gives them the slip, they merely move on to another. This lot is entirely too intrepid for robbery to be their primary motive. They didn't choose us by happenstance. Someone hired them to kidnap you and most likely murder me."

"Who would wish to do either?"

"Perhaps Aristide has hopes of hastening the wedding?"

Her gaze shuttered. "That is perfectly absurd."

Once again he found himself in the thrall of powerful emotions pulling him in polar directions. He wanted to shake her until her skull rattled, but he also wanted to kiss her until she swooned—a direct violation of her first rule.

"Is it? The fall from my mount was no accident. Someone severed the cinch."

Surprise supplanted her skepticism. "You should have told me."

Finally something he'd said seemed to have sunk in. Grateful for it, he answered honestly, "I didn't think you'd believe me."

The next few seconds slipped by in silence.

Stepping into it, Robert continued, "The gold-toothed villain from the market today bears a startling resemblance to the Almack's groom who handed over my horse."

Her mouth firmed. "That does not prove Aristide hired him."

Phoebe was one of the most loyal souls he'd ever known, and the Frenchman was as yet her fiancé. He couldn't fault her for taking Bouchart's part no matter how much hearing her defend him might rankle—or hurt.

"No, it does not," he admitted, tamping down his frustration. Were Phoebe not with him, he wouldn't be the one in hiding—prey. The gold-toothed villain would be. But once again, he couldn't—wouldn't—risk her. Bringing her into this section of the city had been sufficient foolishness to last him a lifetime.

He reached for her hand. To his surprise she gave it. "I am sorry to have distressed you. My only worry is your well-being. Until we—I—get this sorted, have a care about Bouchart. If he is capable of even a fraction of what I think, he is a dangerous man."

She hesitated, and then nodded. "Very well, I shall bear in mind all that you have said—provided you have done with hiding secrets. Whatever you discover of him, whether it damns or exonerates him, promise you will tell me the truth?"

He smoothed his thumb over the inside of her wrist. "I promise." Though the prospect of being touched still tested him and perhaps always would, caressing her in even the slightest of ways brought him inordinate pleasure. Craving more, he lifted her hand and brushed his lips over the spot where his digit had stroked.

Phoebe released a trembling breath. "Mind the first rule is no kissing."

Smiling against the striking pulse, he said, "I believe that was meant only for mouths, otherwise I should not have agreed to it."

"Robert, we cannot—"

"Hush, or perhaps I shall impose a fourth rule of my own invention—no talking," he said, only teasing in part. Since his return, words always seemed to land them in deep dun territory, whereas their bodies communicated in perfect accord.

His gaze fell upon her throat. Long, elegant and cream-colored, it was fashioned for kissing. Angling his head to the side, he trailed his mouth along the slender column and then touched his tongue to the heated hollow above her clavicle. The exertion of eluding their pursuers had salted her skin, deliciously so. Robert closed his eyes and breathed her in. Musk mingled with the other scents she wore—vanilla and lemon and some light floral fragrance he'd never been able to name but which belonged intimately to her.

And then there were her breasts. He'd seen them bared but once, six years before on his last night in London when they'd exchanged the lockets. It had been dark, lit only by the moon and the lantern he'd brought. She'd been shy then, of the light, of *him*. Afraid of frightening her off, he'd let her stay to the shadows, worshipping her with his mouth and tongue and hands. He remembered her as small but shapely, with nipples that budded to life in his palms—and tasted of apricots on his tongue.

She pressed a staying hand to his chest. "We mustn't."

He lifted his head to look up at her, gloriously unbothered by her palm pressing upon his pectoral. "Mind I've seen you before."

She bit her lip. "I remember."

Snaring her gaze, he resolved to be unsparing for both their sakes. "That night in the garden when I slipped your gown from your shoulders and drew you into my palms, I only knew that I liked touching you, and I hoped you liked it too. But beyond coaxing a few kisses from country girls, I'd had no other experiences, good or bad, to compare. Instinct was my only guide, and I was desperately worried it wouldn't be enough."

A wistful smile sifted across her lips. "As I recall, you had…very good instincts."

"Pity I didn't trust them. Christ, I'd even talked myself into visiting a brothel beforehand so I wouldn't make a hash of our wedding night. I probably would have gone through with it too, had Anthony not intervened."

Her eyes widened at that. "*Anthony* stopped you!"

He nodded. "He dragged me to his club, sat me down with a bottle of port and gave me a lecture I'm not likely to ever forget."

"What did he say?"

"That he'd bedded more women than he cared to count, some whose names he'd never even bothered to ask let alone remember. But that no matter how much pleasure the carnal act brought, it couldn't begin to make up for the loneliness that followed when you awoke and saw that the head on the pillow beside yours was that of a stranger. But what truly persuaded me to abandon my plan was when he swore that he'd never made love to a woman, truly made love, until Chelsea. In every way that counted, she was his first and only as you would be mine." He stopped, gauging her reaction.

She lifted her hand and touched his cheek. "Oh, Robert, I wish you'd told me then so that I might have reassured you how terribly honored I was to be your first, as you would have been mine."

Yet another regret—only Robert was done with nursing them. "If the past six years have taught me anything, it's that there's no time to waste. Let us make a fresh start, today, this moment. Only don't confuse me with the smooth-cheeked boy of your memory. I've told you he's gone. A ghost."

Her hand slipped away. She shook her head as though he'd said something foolish indeed. "What of it? Do you think me the same naïve miss who bid you bon voyage in her parents' garden?"

He shook his head. "When I look upon you now, I hardly

see a girl. I see a beautiful woman who tempts and torments me in ways that girl couldn't begin to."

Indeed, there was nothing naïve or missish about her. In the years since he'd left, her prettiness had ripened into a beauty of face and form that stole his breath and stirred his blood. Even clothed, the musk of her arousal reached him, the mouth-watering scent spinning his senses and wrecking his reason. But of one thing he was certain: her body was every whit as ready, as willing as his. And ready he was. His penis was granite hard, his balls heavy and aching. All the second-guessing, the waiting, the ruminating over the past—such obstacles suddenly seemed trifling in the face of his need.

Resolved, he used his free hand to feel for the buttons fronting his trousers. Beneath the buff-colored fabric, the hard ridge of his arousal thickened and thrummed. All he need do was open the front flap and Captain Robert Bellamy could finally and forever claim his lady.

Phoebe rested her forehead against his. "I haven't had an attack of the vapors in six years, and now it seems I'm to have my second in a fortnight."

Smiling, he lifted her into his arms as he had on his first night back only now there was no disapproving parent or fuming fiancé flanking them. Owing to their brush with Bouchart's henchmen, for the next hour or so they were entirely, blissfully on their own, Phoebe not only wholly conscious but fully aware of his need and his love. And, it seemed, prepared to return both.

Slowly he bore her toward the bed, willing himself not to rush. "Go on and faint if you will. I shall catch you. From this moment forward, I'll always be here to catch you."

Chapter Nine

The close air, the overall meanness of the little room, even her anger at being manipulated by Robert yet again receded to the far reaches of Phoebe's mind. Wrapped in his arms, she forgot to breathe, forgot to resist, forgot why she was even supposed to resist. For the first time in six years, she closed off her gainsaying mind and allowed herself simply to feel. And feel she did. Sensations rippled through her, physical desire resurrecting a young girl's buried hopes and dreams.

"Robin," she murmured, dragging a hand through the soft mass of his hair.

The pet name, one of the many memories she'd thought to forever put away, slid off her tongue as sweetly as clotted cream or honey. Like the biblical Wall of Jericho, the barrier she'd spent the last weeks upholding came crashing down, freeing her body to welcome him as neither her mind nor heart yet dared do.

He set her upon her feet beside the bed, and she slid her palms along his biceps and upward to embrace the breadth of his shoulders, refusing to be put off by his barely perceptible stiffening.

His stark gaze fastened upon hers. "Be forewarned, Phoebe, unlike six years ago I shan't rest content only to look upon you."

The remark was no revelation and yet still Phoebe paused. Could she truly break faith with Aristide? And yet how could she not? It wasn't as though Robert was someone she'd met but recently. She'd spent the past six years pining for him. The nights she'd lain awake imagining what their lovemaking might have been like didn't bear counting. And then there were those other nights, nights when her fevered fantasies had led her to do more than imagine, when she'd surrendered her last shred of decency and succumbed to finding release by her own hand. Finally she had the chance, a golden and perhaps even God-given opportunity, to live out her fantasies for real. After six years of desperate yearning, was it so very wicked to be with him this once?

Reaching for her courage, she whetted her lips and admitted, "I don't want you only to look."

His mouth eased into a smile. "Then, milady, we are of a mind."

He slid a hand upward, his sailor's hands worked deftly at her tapes and laces. In a matter of seconds he had her gown's bodice open. Beneath it she wore only short stays and her shift, the fine lawn gossamer as gauze. With each bated breath, her breasts rose and fell. The motion seemed to mesmerize him. He lowered his head and took one coral crown in his mouth, laving her through the linen.

Phoebe's fingers caught in his hair. Unlike the episode in the study, she arched against him of her own accord, a silent plea for more, for all. He gave it, palming her other breast and suckling her through the fabric until the dampened linen molded to her like a second skin.

"Please," she moaned, clasping a guiding hand atop his, not as a lady would ever dream of doing, but more the actions of the doxy she was playing at being—only now every action, every sigh and catch of breath was nothing less than wholly true.

His fingers curled about her breast. Holding her gaze, he took her nipple between his thumb and finger and gently rolled it. Phoebe bit her lip against crying out as pleasure pooled inside her. When he slid her shift off one shoulder, baring it along with her breast, she was too fevered and fraught to feel anything but grateful.

A firmer pinch had her gasping. Before she could cry out,

his suckling mouth moved in to ease the bruising. The flick of tongue, the pull of lips and the light grazing of teeth brought about a beautiful, terrifying trembling. She was beyond containment or control, utterly lost to Robert and her body's too-long-ignored needs. Looking down upon his burnished dark head, she had the strangest sense that the world had stopped or at least suspended. Reality reduced to the four walls of their unlikely bower, to the scents of musk and sweat and sin rising up from their plastered-together bodies, to her own salacious surrender as she stood as still as she could whilst he fed upon her moist, quaking body.

He reached down and lifted her gown's hem. A hand stole beneath, a warm palm and knowing fingers trailing circles along her thighs from front to back, stroking inward with maddening slowness. The pantaloons she wore opened at the front, the lacing held together by a single slim ribbon. Robert's fingers fastened upon it. A gentle pull had the tie loosening. The unlaced flap fell open. What must be his knuckle scrubbed along her sensitive seam. She supposed she ought to stop him from going further, from going *there,* but then she was very weak. And very wet. And Robert's fingers felt so very good as they slipped inside the epicenter of her throbbing, the delicious blunt pressure filling and opening her.

A knock outside the door stayed them. Cursing beneath his breath, Robert withdrew his hand and straightened. Phoebe's hemline whispered back down over her legs to her ankles. Only then did she realize her spread-legged stance. Frustrated and aching, she pressed her thighs tightly together, belatedly aware of how damp she was, the honey of her arousal making a plaster for her skin.

His grimace assured her he was no happier about the interruption than she. Pulling her shift back in place, he said, "That would be the meal I so stupidly bespoke."

"Leave it," she begged, catching at his arm, loath for the protective cocoon they'd spun about themselves to risk unraveling.

"I can't." Robert set her from him with a heavy sigh and went to answer it. A moment later, he returned carrying a tray. A tureen of soup, an unappetizing half loaf of near-molded bread and the port—the proprietress had profited well this day.

He set the tray upon the table, his gaze veering from her to the bed. Standing outside his arms, she saw their bower for what it was—a narrow ledge covered with threadbare and grayed sheets.

"We can't do this, not here." His voice called her back to sanity, only Phoebe was not yet willing to return there. She'd lived by her own rigid rules for the last six years. Never had she imagined that casting them aside could feel so freeing.

"I don't mind." Throbbing, she took a step toward him.

He held out a staying hand. "But I do. We've waited six years for this moment. As much as I want you—and God knows I want you—I'll not have our first time on a strumpet's soiled sheets."

"Then where?" she demanded, too eager and aching to care what a wanton she sounded.

"I want our first time to be in a bed, *our* bed. Thereafter, variations on the basic theme will be not only welcomed but encouraged." A smile skated across his lips. Despite the regret in his eyes, she saw that he was resolved.

"I still have not consented to wed you. Indeed, I am not free to do so."

A betrothal was a legally binding contract. If Aristide was even half the villain Robert made him out to be, he would not hesitate to bring a suit against her for breaching their terms. Along with ruining what remained of her reputation, he might well retain all or part of her dowry.

But such pragmatism was superseded by the one question that still stuck like a splinter in her mind.

Why had Robert allowed her to believe him dead for six

years?

Until that was answered, wholly answered, she might be his lover, but she could never be his wife. Borrow her body he might, but she would never grant him her heart.

Doing up her buttons, she said, "We still have another hour or so before Mistress Dress Lodger returns with her next conquest. How do you propose we spend it?"

Robert looked from her to the abandoned meal tray and back again. "I propose we eat."

Anthony was out with the children and Chelsea napping in their room when Robert returned with Phoebe and Caleb to Number 12 Berkley Square that evening. Upon leaving the lodging house, he'd called upon a hackney coach to take them back to the market. There he'd found Caleb, bloodied and wandering but otherwise none the worse for the robin's-egg-sized knot upon his head.

"We've had a...mishap, Chambers," he announced without preamble. "Lady Phoebe will require a bath, a change of clothing—and your absolute discretion. As for my friend here—" he looked over to Caleb leaning heavily upon his arm "—is there a physician, a discrete one, you may call upon to have a look at his wound?" Cutting a sideways look to Caleb, face a mask of mortification and broad hands madly messaging, he added, "Though as you can see he's possessed of an uncommonly hard head, so like as not he's fine."

The butler nodded. "I shall send a footman to fetch him straightaway." He peered past Robert to the empty foyer. "If I may be so bold, sir, where, er, is Lady Phoebe keeping at present?"

Girding himself, Robert admitted, "I've taken the liberty of loaning her my chamber."

Not surprisingly, the butler's jaw dropped. "*Your* chamber, sir? Are you quite certain—"

"I am. Whoever draws the bath shall believe it is for me. Lady Phoebe shall conceal herself within the dressing closet until they have gone."

Risky as it was to have brought her back disheveled and unchaperoned, returning her to her parents' half-dressed and reeking of rubbish hadn't seemed precisely prudent, either.

"Shall I have a chamber prepared for...overnight?" Given the potential for scandal implicit in the inquiry, the older man mustered an impressive degree of sangfroid.

Shaking his head, Robert hastened to reassure him. "She should not be staying much beyond the hour, and when we depart, it will be by the tradesman's entrance. I trust I can count on your help in seeing the area clear of servants?"

"I stand at your disposal, sir."

Satisfied, Robert sailed on, "As Lady Phoebe and my sister are of a size, or so they were, perhaps she can borrow one of my sister's gowns?"

"I will make an inquiry of her ladyship's maid—discretely, of course. Will there be anything else?" he added, looking almost afraid to have asked.

Robert thought for a moment. "As a matter of fact, there is. When my brother-in-law returns, please inform him I wish to speak with him at his earliest convenience."

The day's events had decided him. It was past time he put both the past and his pride aside and took Montrose into his confidence about Bouchart. It was one thing to endanger oneself, but Robert now understood it wasn't only him at risk. Phoebe might have been injured or worse. Putting her in harm's path again was unthinkable. For her sake, he was prepared to eat humble pie and crow both. Between his tactical experience gained from fighting as an officer in the Peninsular Campaign and his current contacts in the War Office, Anthony would be an admirable ally. Beyond all, Robert was coming to realize that he could do with a friend in his corner.

He had but to take the first step and ask.

Luxuriating in the hipbath of now-lukewarm water, Phoebe thought back over the day. Her emotions had veered from direst fear to most exquisite ecstasy. Time spent in Robert's company was certainly never boring.

The knock outside her door, or rather Robert's door, vaulted her to high alert once more. Surmising it must be the servant returning to replenish the hot water, she stretched out a hand for the robe she'd set out within her reach—or, as it suddenly seemed, a hairsbreadth beyond.

As Robert was wont to say, *bloody hell.*

Instead of a servant, Chelsea called through the door, "May I come in?"

Bloody hell indeed. Phoebe rose, wrapping the robe around her. For a fleeting few seconds she considered dashing back inside the dressing closet, but doing so seemed a coward's course. Chelsea wasn't only Robert's sister and Anthony's wife. She was Phoebe's dearest friend. Despite their rocky start of misaligned engagements, their shared grief over losing Robert had forged a bond between them. Before Robert's return, Phoebe would have sworn their connection was implacable, but now she was no longer so certain.

Heart pounding, she crossed to open the door, leaving a trail of damp footprints in her wake. Opening it fractionally, she met Chelsea's shocked eye. "Surprise?"

Judging from her friend's stunned face her presence was that and more. Backing up, she beckoned her inside.

She gave Chelsea a moment to recover. Garbed in a loose-fitting house gown in the Japanese style, Chelsea quickly entered. "This had better be good," she whispered, reaching behind her for the doorknob.

Phoebe waited for the door to close before blurting out, "It isn't at all what it seems." Admittedly it was a lame beginning, but strictly speaking, it was also the truth. Still, thinking on how close she'd come to letting Robert bed her inside of two hours ago, she allowed she was in peril of becoming that most detestable of creatures—a hypocrite.

Chelsea walked over to the bed, thankfully still respectably made and without so much as a crease in the counterpane. Lowering herself onto it, she said, "I am the last person to ever judge you, *either* of you. I only hope you've taken care not to be seen."

Arms crossed, Phoebe subsided onto a cushioned stool across from her. "So far only your butler knows of my presence and now, of course, you."

Chelsea's expression eased. "Good, let's ensure that it remains that way."

Phoebe satisfied herself with a nod. Alone with Chelsea, she berated herself on multiple counts. Foremost, she'd been a horrible friend. Confined though Chelsea was, Phoebe hadn't called upon her in more than a fortnight, not since just before Robert's return. Until now she'd told herself she was acting in her friend's best interest. Blood was thicker than water, or so it was said, and by rights Chelsea must side with her brother. Rather than put her in the middle, it had seemed infinitely simpler to stay away. Now it occurred to her that in doing so she'd been a self-serving coward. There were no real sides to be taken, none save that of love.

"How are you feeling?" she asked, gaze going to her friend's burgeoning belly.

Chelsea broke into a smile. "Big." She laced her hands over her middle. "Depending upon whether this little one elects to be tardy or on time, I may or may not miss your wedding."

Feeling a sudden chill, Phoebe clutched the dressing gown tighter.

"You do still mean to marry Aristide, do you not?"

Phoebe hesitated and then admitted, "Honestly, I'm not certain."

Rather than rush to put forth Robert's case, Chelsea kept her peace, studying her for a long moment. "May I speak frankly?" she finally asked.

Relieved, Phoebe nodded. "I wish you would."

"For some time now I've witnessed the way Aristide treats you. Since you agreed to his suit, he seems to regard you more as a possession than as a person."

Phoebe opened her mouth to defend him, but really, what was there to say? "He holds to a very traditional view of marriage," she finally murmured.

"Regardless of whom you marry, if you let a man treat you this shabbily before the wedding, there'll be no living with him afterward. Whomever you marry, you must command your future husband's respect as well as his heart; otherwise, your ship is as good as sunk before it's left harbor."

Phoebe couldn't help smiling at the nautical metaphor. It seemed Robert was rubbing off on them all.

"You don't much like Aristide, do you?"

Chelsea shrugged. "What does it matter whether or not I like him? I'm not the one marrying him. Do you like him? Most importantly, do you *love* him?"

Again Phoebe hesitated. Certainly Aristide was handsome. He could be most charming when he chose to be. In the early days of their courtship, more than once she'd caught him deliberately mispronouncing a word to win her smile. The times he'd kissed her, she felt a not unpleasant tingling, but was that love? Phoebe didn't think so.

Dodging the question, she replied, "He was the first person to make me laugh after Robert—"

"Disappeared," Chelsea finished for her. "I know you've struggled to forgive him. I sense you're struggling still. Do you love him? And by the by, I'm not speaking of the boy who left six years ago but of the complicated man who's returned to us."

Phoebe drew a bracing breath. "I believe I may."

Tilting her head to the side, Chelsea regarded her. "Admittedly I am biased on behalf of my brother, but knowing that, would you care for my advice as a seven years' married woman who is more passionately in love with her husband than ever?"

Phoebe unfolded her arms. "Yes, I should like it very much."

"Until you have your answers, firm answers, don't marry either of them."

Phoebe couldn't have been more shocked.

"Better no marriage than one in which you feel anything less than a full partner, let alone chattel or worse, a prisoner to your husband's whims and wishes."

Phoebe bit her lip. "Aristide says that once we're wed, he means to keep me barefoot and breeding. He may be teasing about the barefoot part, but not about the other." Even before Robert's return, her fiancé's frank emphasis on her fertility had weighed heavily upon her mind.

Chelsea rolled her eyes. "That's absolute rot. Conjugal relations should be foremost about sharing pleasure with your beloved. You don't have to have a baby every year, not if you don't wish to. There are many midwives and physicians who advise it is far healthier to space out one's family." Cocking a brow, she asked, "Why do you think Anthony and I waited six years before having another child?"

Phoebe had wondered about the gap, but until now she'd assumed it must be happenstance, a fluke of nature. "It was deliberate?"

Chelsea nodded. "Entirely so. We wanted time to enjoy the twins as well as each other. There are ways to prevent conception or at least to lessen its likelihood. A device worn by the man is made of sheepskin and secured by a drawstring. Oh, but I'm too frank. I'm embarrassing you."

Privately, Phoebe allowed that her flushed face could not be blamed upon the soaking in warm water. "No. Well, perhaps a bit. But I'd rather be embarrassed than ignorant, so please do go on. I want to know these things. Really, at my age, I think I should."

As much as she longed for a child, having one with Aristide would bind her to him more irrevocably than any vows spoken in a church. Every time she tried conjuring the image of the black-eyed, raven-haired babies they'd have together, their eyes softened to hazel and their hair to russet brown. Robert's eyes. Robert's hair.

Robert's babies. Robert's and hers.

"Consider it food for thought. Speaking of which..." Chelsea pushed to her feet. "I'd ask you to stay to supper, but I'm not certain even I could come up with a plausible story to explain your presence."

Phoebe shook her head. "I need to make my way home anyway. My mother will be wondering where I've got to and that is never good."

Having had her own run-ins with Phoebe's mother in the past, Chelsea smiled knowingly. "I'll find you something to wear."

Phoebe rose as well. "Thank you," she said, suddenly impatient to be on her way.

More so than supper with her family, she had a great deal of thinking to do.

The hallway clock struck six when Anthony ushered Robert into the library. Brandies were poured and cigars summarily offered and refused.

Settled into the armchair facing Robert's, Anthony asked, "How may I be of service?"

Hands laced about his snifter, Robert regarded his brother-in-law. Along with being an erstwhile rival for Phoebe, Montrose was a decorated war hero of the Peninsular Campaign. The wounding he'd sustained at the Battle of Albuera had left him with a permanent if slight limp. He was a solid ally to have on one's side—assuming Robert could convince him that the danger Bouchart posed was real and not a fiction fabricated from jealousy.

Rather than waste words on preamble, Robert came directly to the point. "I believe Bouchart is a bounder out to marry Phoebe for her fortune."

Expression inscrutable, Anthony answered, "Much the same was said of you six years ago."

"I am aware." His determination to disprove the rumors by seeking his fortune abroad had driven the disastrous departure from England. "Only in Bouchart's case, the accusation isn't false."

He thought back to the night at Almack's and the impromptu bidding war he'd begun to win his waltz with Phoebe. If the Frenchman were as wealthy as he wished to appear, he wouldn't have backed down. For the sake of honor, he would have matched Robert's most outlandish price without pause.

And then there was the bit about the Calvados, not damning on its own, but in the context of everything else that had occurred, another nail in the coffin of Aristide's character. For a Frenchman from Normandy, such ignorance of the local apple-flavored spirit was exceedingly suspect.

Encouraged by Anthony's silence, he went on, "What's more, I believe he is willing to go to great lengths to accomplish his goal."

Cloaked though it was, the accusation was met by a boosting of brows. "Go on," Montrose prompted.

"When I was thrown from my horse, I afterward discovered that someone had cut the girth. This afternoon Phoebe prevailed upon me to take her to the...waterfront, and we were set upon by footpads."

Anthony shot upright in his seat. "Is she all right?"

Thinking of her soaking in his hipbath above their heads, he nodded. "She is."

Scowling, Anthony eased against the chair back. "What were you thinking to take Phoebe to such a seedy section of town?"

Robert acknowledged the rebuke was well deserved. "In a moment of weakness, and appallingly poor judgment, I gave her my word I would take her wither she wished."

Montrose's frown smoothed into an expression of resignation.

"When one is in love with a woman, it can be dashed difficult to tell her no and stick to it. Hang difficult, it can be damn near impossible," Anthony added, no doubt recalling his early days with Chelsea. Her schemes to raise Robert's ransom had brought them to the brink of mortal danger more than once.

"I do not believe purloining my purse was their intent. Common cutpurses would not have laid chase as this pair did. Moreover, one of them looked to be the same 'groom' who handled my horse after the ball at Almack's. When I returned the next day, no one fitting that description was employed there."

"Good God, man, that's a devil of a lot to keep under your hat. You should have come to me earlier."

Unlike the prideful hellion of six years earlier, Robert took the mild reproof in stride. "Agreed, but first I wanted to be certain. I need to delve into Bouchart's background. I'm not certain I believe he is who he claims to be. Will you help?"

"I still have a few friends in the War Office. One in particular, the Honorable Bennett Templeton, served in France as an espionage agent during the latter years of Napoleon's reign as emperor. He might be of some assistance."

Robert nodded. "Thank you."

"You are welcome." Swirling his brandy about the globed glass, Anthony asked, "Tell me, if not an exiled French aristocrat-cum-wine-importer, who do you think he is?"

Robert hesitated. "I suspect he's a confidence man of some sort—well-spoken, decently educated but hardly cut from noble cloth."

"I take it you haven't voiced your suspicions to Phoebe or her family?"

"I spoke to Phoebe earlier, and only in the service of urging her to caution," Robert admitted. He declined to add that he'd been too preoccupied with seducing her to press his point. Despite how close they'd come to going to bed, he could tell she'd yet to trust him entirely. "As for her family, given my history with Lady T in particular, I deemed it prudent to hold off pending solid proof."

"Wise indeed," Anthony agreed. "But for our first order of business, let us put our heads together and devise a plan for getting our visiting mermaid out of the bath—and this house—without alerting all of Mayfair."

Startled, Robert asked, "How long have you known she was here?"

Anthony shrugged. "From the moment I set foot inside this evening. Templeton isn't the only one with a background in espionage. In this case I hadn't far to search for my spy. The butler is, after all, in my employ."

Robert set his snifter aside. "I'm all ears. What do you suggest?"

"Firstly we call in your sister if she hasn't already discovered Phoebe for herself. As the last woman I ever brought here clandestinely, she like as not has more than a few ideas on how best to sneak someone out. Only mind she herself insisted upon exiting by way of an upper window. If at all possible, let us try and put Phoebe through an actual door."

Aristide sat before the fire regarding the crystal shards blanketing the bricks. With only the flames for light, the remains of the shattered decanter and glass looked like freshly fallen snow, crystalline and pure. Still, the destruction had done little to soothe him.

Once again, Robert Bellamy had had the bad manners not to die.

And now because of it, the rogue was likely even more of a romantic hero in Phoebe's eyes. Since the betrothal ball, Aristide's sway over her had been steadily slipping.

He'd spent all the previous season wearing down the chit's resistance, and he was not about to withdraw now that his prize was within reach. Nor could he afford to do so. Keeping up the appearance of riches was a costly affair. He couldn't hold off his creditors indefinitely. Sooner or later, word of his mounting debts would leak.

Unfortunately, Bellamy had shown himself to be surprisingly formidable. The horse's cut cinch had been meant only to injure, but earlier at the market Payne and his partner had been instructed to bring about a more permanent solution. But even hampered by Phoebe, the rotter had managed to foil them. Clearly he had underestimated his foe, a mistake he did not intend to repeat. Rather than risk striking out in the same fashion again, he must find another means of dispatching Bellamy.

Once and for all.

Chapter Ten

One Week Later

Seated beside Robert on an empty classroom bench, a chalk slate perched upon her lap, Phoebe was alight with purpose. "If more people could but meet the children and see firsthand how deserving and, well...wonderful they are, I feel certain that we would see a surge in placements, not only apprenticeships but adoptions," she said in a hushed voice.

She cast a quick look across the room to Lulu and Fiona. Sitting cross-legged on the floor, their heads bent to their slates, they appeared absorbed in working out the mathematics problem to which Phoebe had set them.

Hoping that solving it would occupy them for a good while more, he shifted his gaze back to Phoebe. "It sounds as though you have something in mind." He leaned toward her, ostensibly to steal a peek at what she'd so far scribbled upon the slate, though in reality it was her warmth and scent and nearness he sought.

"I do," she admitted, holding it facedown upon her breast. "Why not hold a May Day fair? We can pitch tents and stake a maypole on the hospital lawn and invite everyone in the city to attend, from the Lord Mayor on down."

"I think it's a splendid idea," he said sincerely. Coming of age in the country, he'd celebrated many a May Day in such a festive fashion. "How can I help?"

"Truly?"

Robert suppressed a sigh. One day in the not-too-distant future he swore she would accept his word without question but seeing the uncertainty in her eyes, he acknowledged that day was yet to arrive. "I flatter myself to think my capabilities extend beyond pulling purse strings."

She sent him a sideways look. "In that case, I accept, though you may regret your offer when you see how much work's to be done in so little time. We have to engage the performers, arrange for tents lest it rains—and it's England, so it always rains—ensure there's sufficient food and drink and—"

"My dearest, darling Phoebe," he said, torn between amusement and exasperation, "what do you imagine captaining a ship entails if not those very things?"

"Right, sorry." Picking up the chalk and slate, she released a flurry of scribbling. "We'll keep some of the area open for picnicking and games, food sellers and various entertainers—jugglers, mimes, strongmen, a soothsayer, perhaps."

"A soothsayer," Robert echoed, an admittedly madcap idea taking shape in his mind. "I don't recall that as being part of the tradition."

"Strictly speaking, it's not," she admitted. "But people seem to enjoy that sort of rubbish, and well, it's all in good fun as well as a way to bring in additional monies."

"Rubbish, is it? Mind I recall a certain young miss who begged me to take her to the fortune teller's booth at Astley's."

It had been the week before he was to ship out. She'd wanted them to have their fortunes read, had all but begged him to go inside that tent with her. At the time he'd fobbed off the notion as absurd and found an excuse not to go. Looking back, he saw the request as sweetly romantic, yet another missed moment he'd surrender an eyetooth to relive.

Her gaze shuttered. "That naïve young miss went the way of the smooth-cheeked boy—buried and gone. Now, do you wish to hear more of my May Day plans or do you not?"

"I am all ears. Pray carry on."

Listening, it was impossible not to get caught up in her enthusiasm—or her smile. She was smiling more and more of late, and Robert was not the only one to notice. Chelsea, Anthony and Reggie had all remarked upon it. Though she'd yet to give Robert any indication that she meant to break off her betrothal, neither had he heard anything further about setting a date. Surely all this sudden smiling must be a providential sign.

Still, life was too short to waste, as well he'd learned. If need be, he would not hesitate to provide Providence with the necessary push.

"This is a terrible idea," Chelsea said to Robert on May Day morning. Standing behind his chair, she reached down and gave his witch's wig a testing tug.

Seated at her mirror-topped dressing table, he peered back at her from the plated glass. "So you've said a half dozen times. Pass me the spirit gum, won't you?" Had he not applied the concealing cosmetics himself, he couldn't say for certain he would recognize the face staring back as his.

She passed him the tiny jar. "Are you certain you should use so much?"

"Certain, no, but otherwise I'm afraid my nose may slide straight off." He touched a testing finger to the fake nose tipped by a wart bristling with hairs. The costume and novelty shop in Piccadilly had been a treasure trove for disguises. Between it and the colorful cashmere shawls borrowed from his ship's cabin, his gypsy guise was set. "I want Phoebe and the other fair-goers to think me an old witch woman, not a leper."

"I thought Uncle Robin was a pirate, not a witch," Tony called out from his perch upon Chelsea's four-poster.

Seated beside him, legs swinging over the side, Daphne snapped, "Men can't be witches."

"If girls can be pirates, then men can be witches, can't they, Mama?" Tony demanded, clearly determined to sort the current conundrum.

Chelsea heaved a sigh. "To be perfectly precise, men are warlocks, not witches, but as neither exists I shouldn't fret over the distinction."

Turning, Daphne reached out and thumped her brother upon the forehead. "See, numbskull, I told you so."

"Daphne!" Chelsea admonished. "Mind you keep your hands to yourself and cease calling your brother unkind names." Dropping her voice so only Robert could hear, she added, "By the by, these days that epithet is reserved for Uncle Robin."

Robert scowled, which did truly dreadful things to the visage meeting his in the mirror. "Are you here to insult me or help me?"

"Oh, very well, have at it." She handed him the set of wax teeth.

"Thank you."

She shrugged. "What I cannot comprehend is why you will not simply speak the truth to her as yourself."

"If she knows it's me, she'll be on her guard, disputing my every word. Better the sentiment comes through a stranger." And who better to serve as an impartial messenger than a kindly old woman with purported clairvoyant powers?

Despite their détente, Phoebe had yet to trust him entirely. Since their near bedding in the lodging house more than a week ago, she'd gone out of her way not to be alone with him outside of the school. Even there one of the students or matrons almost always happened in on them. Robert was coming to wonder if those "interruptions" were entirely accidents. Despite his best efforts, it seemed she meant to go through with marrying Aristide. Robert had to do something to turn the tide, and quickly; otherwise Phoebe would find herself leg-shackled for life to a man no better than a murderer.

He opened his mouth and positioned the prop. Biting down, he turned back to her. "How do I look?"

The teeth, tinted yellow and molded into a mismatched and broken configuration, altered the shape of not only his mouth but of his jaw as well. Chelsea's hand flew to her own agape mouth. "Positively ghastly. If I hadn't helped you with your disguise, I wouldn't know you for my own brother."

Robert smiled or at least he tried to. "That's the very point."

"Have you considered what you'll do if this half-cocked scheme of yours backfires?"

"It won't." He stood, adjusting the drape of shawl and hunching his shoulders as though once more bearing broken rocks upon his back. "This will work, Chels. It *has* to."

May Day saw the Foundling Hospital lawn transformed into a tented fairground, a beribboned maypole set at its center. Phoebe hadn't seen Robert since the crack of dawn when, true to his word, he'd arrived to oversee the pitching of the food and entertainment tents. He'd left directly thereafter, pleading a pressing engagement to do with the ship that would, most probably, consume the day. Tamping down her disappointment, she'd sent him off with a manufactured smile.

These past three weeks, he'd given generously not only of his money but also of his time. Ulterior motives notwithstanding, he'd been a very great help. He did, after all, still have his captain's duties to keep up. The Swan was apparently out of dry dock and returned to harbor in preparation for loading. In another few weeks, she would sail back to India with or without Robert at her helm.

He still awaited her answer. Would she go through with marrying Aristide or would she not? Though she still found his claims about her fiancé to be farfetched—there was as yet nothing to link Aristide to either the severed cinch or the footpads in the market—the prospect of plighting her troth with him seemed less and less appealing. So far he'd spent most of the afternoon in the beer tent lamenting the lack of decent wine.

That Reggie was there with him no doubt accounted for the beer man going through more kegs than anticipated.

For now what mattered was that the fair was a success. The event had opened under cloudless skies and coming on twilight, the weather still held and the crowd showed no sign of thinning. At Phoebe's direction, the torches had been lit. In a little while, the dancing would begin. Meanwhile, the pie man continued doing a brisk trade, his song-and-dance showmanship as popular as the sweet and savory pies he sold off his tray. So far the juggler, the cook's husband pressed into service, had broken but one set of plates and the clown had made but one child cry. A game of quoits set up on the lawn had drawn men young and old, gentleman and laborer, all eager to test their skill for tuppence a toss.

By far the most popular attraction was the fortuneteller Robert had found for them. The crone had drawn a nonstop stream of patrons all day. Receiving word through one of the children that "Mother Geneva" wished to speak to her—alone—had given Phoebe a start. Pushing past the queue of fairgoers still waiting to be called within the striped tent, she hoped the impromptu request hadn't to do with the gypsy seeking to renegotiate her fee. Determined to hold firm to the fifty-fifty terms Robert had negotiated, Phoebe lifted the tent flap and ducked inside.

A single tallow candle served as the sole source of interior illumination. A round table draped in fringed scarves and two chairs had been brought in for the readings. Occupying one of them, the gypsy sat in shadow, hunched frame huddled beneath a patterned wool shawl despite the weather's warmth. A glass divining ball rested in a footed stand atop the table's center, tarot cards arranged about. Set off to the side, a glass jar brimmed with coins and bank notes. Though Robert had vouched for the gypsy's honesty, Phoebe made a mental note to ensure that the foundlings saw their share of it.

Letting the tent flap fall closed, Phoebe cleared her throat.

"You wished to see me, Mother?"

The crone looked up from the runes she passed back and forth between her broad-backed hands. Casting the carved stones aside, she said, "Indeed, you have sharp ears, dearie, and a third eye nearly as canny as mine."

Crossing the carpet-covered ground to the table, Phoebe was hard pressed not to roll her eyes. "And you a wing-footed messenger, in this case the foundling child, Fiona, whom you dispatched to fetch me. How may I be of help?" she prompted, thinking of the myriad tasks requiring her attention.

A snaggletooth smile greeted the question. "It is I who shall be of help to you, as the great Hecate wills it. Sit, sit!" she commanded, flagging Phoebe to the vacant chair.

Phoebe slipped into the seat. "If this is about the money, I—"

"To her who gives so selflessly and asks naught for herself, I shall perform my soothsaying for no greater cost than a smile bestowed by your pretty lips."

Relieved she wouldn't have to haggle after all, still Phoebe hadn't time for parlor games. Her gaze flickered to the tent flap. "That is very kind of you, but the amusements are meant for guests. There are...quite a few standing in queue," she added by way of a broad hint.

"Bah, let them cool their heels a while longer. A serious-minded young maid such as you could do with a bit of fun."

Odd, Robert had said the same to her only the other day. "I am hardly young, Mother."

"From where I sit, you are fresh as the dew on a spring rose." The witch leaned in, one bushy brow lifting. Despite her rotted teeth, the scent wafting toward Phoebe was both pleasant and familiar, that of anise, licorice or was it perhaps fennel? "As to the maid part, if you wish to unburden yourself, know that Mother Geneva listens but does not judge."

Thinking of how she and Robert had disported themselves

the other week at the lodging house, how she had as much as begged him to make love to her, Phoebe clamped her mouth closed.

Reaching around the candle and globe, the gypsy stuck out a broad hand webbed in wrinkles. "Pass me your palm, pretty. You may well think this is all rubbish, but what harm is there in indulging an old woman's whim?"

"I never said reading futures was rubbish," Phoebe protested.

The crone cocked a canny look. "Did you not?"

Belatedly she recalled that indeed she'd repeated the almost exact phrase to Robert the other day. Had he passed on her objections to the gypsy? She hardly thought so.

Phoebe turned over her hand and laid it in the crone's broad, warm one. "Hmmm, what have we here?" Bending close, the old woman made a show of pouring over Phoebe's palm, tracing the lines and creases with a single straight, tapered finger. "Your life line is elongated and unbroken. It foretells a long and hearty life. And the heart line is likewise long. It shows you to be of a sensual nature."

Thinking again to the other afternoon in the lodging house, Phoebe felt her face heat.

"Though there is a break early on. And...oh no, this is not good at all."

Caught up despite herself, Phoebe asked, "What...what is it?"

The gypsy released a long breath. "Alas, your heart and head lines intersect. In point, they are in violent opposition." She looked up. "There is a war within you. Heart or head, which shall win, I wonder?"

Phoebe snatched her hand away. "I rather think I oughtn't to have to choose."

"Life is all about choices, dearie. Now I shall grant you one wish. Tell me what is it that you most desire?"

Robert, I want Robert.

But how could she ever wholly trust a man, a husband, who by his own admission had chosen to stay "dead" for six years? Despite the time alone they'd spent, he'd yet to offer anything beyond a vague explanation.

She shook her head at the sheer hopelessness of it all. "I'm afraid what I most desire is not within your or anyone's power to grant."

"I'd not be so certain of that were I you. 'Tis true that no one has the power to turn back time to alter the past, but the future remains to be writ upon."

Phoebe sat back with a sigh. "Very well, then, I wish for loving homes for all of my orphans," she said, thinking of Lulu especially.

If ever there was a child who would make someone a wonderful little daughter, Lulu was she. Were Aristide willing, she would take the girl herself. Alas, the one time she had suggested they might do so, he had squelched the subject, assuring her he would keep her breeding far too frequently to have time for a charity child.

The soothsayer scowled, or certainly she seemed to. "Most noble, milady, but tell me, do you wish for nothing for yourself, something of a more...*intimate* nature?"

Had she told the crone she was a peer's daughter? Phoebe didn't think so. Then again it was hardly a secret. Perhaps Robert had mentioned it in passing.

"You mock me, Mother."

"Fie, I do not!"

The witch's deep timbre had Phoebe drawing back.

More mildly, the gypsy said, "Come, dearie, cease your dissembling. I've no need of an orb to tell me that you've been disappointed in love."

Dear Lord, was she truly so transparent? "Very well, I was in love once. We were to be wed, and he went away." She must be mad to make Mother Geneva her confessor, and yet she and the witch scarcely traveled in the same circles.

A triumphant cackle greeted the admission. "I knew it! And now you fear becoming a spinster."

Phoebe bristled. "Not so. I have met another, a Frenchman who wishes to wed me."

A ferocious scowl greeted the assurance. "Pishaw! Tell me, do his kisses cause your knees to weaken and your breath to catch? At night when you lie abed alone stroking yourself, does the honey flow between your legs as you think upon him?"

Face hot, Phoebe started up. "Really, that is the outside of enough. I am to be married."

This time there was no discounting her companion's expression as anything but a scowl. "When is this...happy occasion to take place?'

"Soon, before the season ends."

The wrinkled face relaxed, appearing almost smug. "Haven't yet set a date, hmm?"

"Unforeseen circumstances have created a delay."

The crone's hand, large and surprisingly strong, clamped atop hers, holding her in place. "Wheesht, 'tis plain as the nose upon my face that your heart belongs to your first love, and a handsome devil he is, tall and strapping with a strong arm and a true heart—a heart that belongs all to you, milady."

Phoebe swallowed hard. "Yes, he is handsome and strong and good-hearted, but he also chose to remain away for...a very long time."

The gypsy gave Phoebe back her hand and bent to the glass orb. "Aye, he did and with good reason. I see storm tossed seas leading to a sad separation of...three—no, five—no, *six* years apart with much tears and pining on both your parts."

Taken aback, Phoebe leaned in to look but beyond clear glass fuzzed with dust, she saw nothing. "How can you know that?"

Ignoring the question, the crone continued, "Have you considered that the obstacle keeping him from you was not of his making?"

"If that is the case, why wouldn't he simply tell me?"

For the first time since Phoebe had entered the tent, the gypsy hesitated. "Mayhap he is...ashamed."

"Ashamed?" Based on all she'd witnessed these past weeks, Robert didn't possess a whit of shame in the whole of his broad-shouldered, beautiful body.

The gypsy answered with an impassioned nod. "Aye, and fearful."

Phoebe couldn't fathom Robert fearing anything. "Fearful of what?"

The old woman's gaze wended away. "Of...appearing less than a man in your eyes."

Phoebe could not comprehend how that could possibly be. Robert was the most virile man she'd ever met. Barring Anthony, the other men of her acquaintance seemed as powder puffs in comparison, Aristide included.

"What surety has he that, should he tell you all, you won't revile him as a coward and foreswear your love?" The crone's gaze locked on hers. Despite the thick bracketing of wrinkles, her eyes looked clear, more befitting a youthful person than a wizened woman. "You do love him, do you not?"

"I told you, I am betrothed to another."

Mother Geneva stared at her askance. "Betrothals may be broken, milady, marriages not so easily. You would do well to think long and hard before plighting your troth with one who may claim your person but will never hold your heart."

A ruckus outside the tent had Phoebe swiveling to the flap. A shout went up. "Fire! Fire at th' Ole Bengal Warehouse!"

The crone bounded to her feet, nearly overturning the table. Her shawl slipped off, showing broad shoulders, a flat belly and tapered torso. Phoebe shot out a hand, capturing the left wrist before it might be moved away. Holding it up to the light, she saw the carved ivory bracelet.

Her gaze lifted to the granny's face. "Robert!"

Before he might answer, the tent flap was thrown back. Billy entered, holding one of the Chinese lanterns aloft. "Th' Ole Bengal Warehouse on New Street is afire and they be calling for all able-bodied men t'elp wi' the bucket brigade. May I go, milady? Please, may I?"

Phoebe couldn't so much as form an answer—or stop staring. Gaze riveted on Robert, she saw that what had passed for wrinkles and warts owed to the clever application of theatrical cosmetics. She thought of all he'd tricked her into revealing and shame spilled over her. Once again she'd trusted him—and once again he'd betrayed her.

Stricken eyes met hers. "Phoebe, I didn't mean...I must away. My cargo is stored there, everything from this voyage and... We'll speak of it, everything, later, once I get back."

Tears stung her eyes, but this time she swore she would not shed them. "There's nothing more to speak of. We're done, you and I. *Done.*"

He reached up and pulled off the wig, his own flattened hair concealed in a net underneath. "Phoebe, please—"

Jaw clenched, she shook her head. "You've asked for my answer and now I am prepared to give it. I am marrying Aristide. And you, Robert Bellamy, have deceived and humiliated me for the very last time."

"Gorm, 'tis really gone."

Swiping sweat from his eyes with the back of his hand, Robert dragged his gaze from the warehouse's smoking ruins to Billy standing beside him. "So it seems."

Despite the fire wagon outfitted with the latest hand pump and leaded hosing allowing for a continuous geyser to be aimed at the flames, despite the handheld tank apparatus known as a fire extinguisher being applied with all due diligence by the uniformed members of the fire brigade, despite the sundry sailors and watermen and good Samaritans such as Phoebe's foundling, who'd pitched in to form a bucket brigade to fight the flames, the warehouse was gone as was everything within it.

A king's ransom in textiles had gone up in smoke, not the company's carpets and cashmeres and silks, all safely stored within the barricaded warehouses on Cutler Street, but Robert's personal cargo. The scene evidenced all the signs of arson. It seemed someone had lit oil-soaked rags and lobbed them through the narrow windows. If not everything then certainly a goodly portion of everything for which he'd worked and yes, *slaved*, was reduced to ash. The destruction was, he reflected, almost biblical.

But material wealth wasn't all he'd lost this night. He'd lost Phoebe—again. And this time there was no bloodthirsty pirate crew to blame. Hell, he couldn't even blame Bouchart. The bilge rat might have tried to have him murdered not once but twice, he might also be the architect of the present devastation, but there was one catastrophe Robert couldn't lay at his door.

He hadn't forced Robert to masquerade as a gypsy. That, and its unintended but likely deserved result, he had brought entirely upon himself.

Staring at Billy, face dripping and gaze aglow, it suddenly occurred to him to ask, "Did Lady Phoebe give you permission to come here?"

Billy hesitated. "Well, um...she didn't say I *couldn't* come."

Improbably, Robert cracked a laugh. "Fair enough, but there's no sense in both of us being in her black books." Clapping a hand upon the lad's shoulder, he steered them away from the sight. "I'll see you home to the Hospital before anyone's the wiser.

The warehouse and its contents were beyond salvage but there was one hope for redemption: Phoebe. Praying he might not be too late there too, he steered Billy away from the wharves.

Chapter Eleven

At first Phoebe thought the pinging upon her bedroom windowpane must be rain. Dressed for bed, she hurried across the room to close it. Seeing that the sky was as yet dry, she started to turn away when she glimpsed a male form step into a shaft of moonlight.

Robert.

One hand fisted about what must be a palm full of pebbles, he made a cone of the other and called up, "Psst, Phoebe!"

She lifted the window sash higher and leaned her head and shoulders out. "Go. Away," she answered as loudly as she dared.

Fortunately her bedroom lay at the back of the house overlooking the garden. Still, if anyone were to observe them, she would be finally and forever finished. Given the lengths to which Robert had shown himself capable, she wouldn't put it past him to try and ruin her as a last resort.

He shook his head. "I'm coming up." He grabbed two-fisted hold of the vines and levered himself up, one boot finding a foothold on the stone facing.

"You're a madman," she called out again, fear pitching her voice far higher than was safe.

A chink in the cement sent him slipping. Heart in her throat, Phoebe sucked back a breath. In light of his earlier performance as Mother Geneva, she should be rooting for him to break his neck, and yet despite everything he'd done to plague her she sent up a silent prayer for his safekeeping.

He caught himself, a smear of blood blooming from the scrape on his forearm. Gaining the balcony, he hauled himself over the rail. A thump announced he'd landed albeit none too gently. The French doors were bolted from within, preventing him from going through them to the house. To get to her, he would have to climb one more story. Ironwork Juliet balconies extended from the chamber windows, including hers. Losing sight of him, she surmised he must have grabbed onto the metalwork and levered himself onto the ledge. A whoosh of breath announced he'd made it. Craning her neck, she saw him once more. Back flattened against the house, he skirted the narrow shelf toward her.

"What the devil are you doing here?" Even in the open air, she could smell the charring that clung to him.

"I'll answer in good time, but first let me in, will you?" He stretched out a sooty hand.

For a fraction of a second, she considered shutting the window in his face. Instead she leaned out, took hold of his wrist and guided him toward her. Once he was level with the window, she let go and moved back to make room.

Holding onto the frame, he climbed in and leapt down. "Milady." Landed at her feet, he sketched a brief bow. Straightening, he glanced about. Phoebe tried seeing the chamber through his eyes—the delicate furnishings and prodigious quantities of flounces and chintz, the chased silver mirror and brush set, the mementos from childhood, including a worse-for-wear china-faced doll. "I always wondered what your bedchamber must be like," he admitted, gaze going back to her.

"Now that you've satisfied your curiosity, you may be on your way."

His stark gaze struck hers. "I'd rather satisfy you."

Such leading language left her abashed. Before she could think what if any reply to make, Pippin bounded over, tail thumping. "There's a good fellow," Robert said, stooping to stroke him.

Pippin's tail wagging picked up pace and his black lips

pulled back in a blissful doggie smile—traitor. "He likes you," she said albeit grudgingly.

Expression rueful, Robert glanced down at the droplets of drool upon his boots and back up at her. "I'd rather he liked me less." Holding her gaze, he added, "And that you liked me more."

Phoebe crossed her arms over her breasts, the posture the best she could manage in the way of a shield. "After the deceit you affected at the fair, you should count yourself fortunate I didn't close the window in your face—or upon your fingers."

Straightening, he asked, "Why didn't you?"

She unfolded her arms and waived a hand in the vicinity of his face. Though most of his theatrical cosmetics had worn off, his warty witch's nose stuck on stubbornly. "Given the fire, making you part with your digits seemed crueler than even you deserve. By the by, your nose is melted."

Flush-faced, he tore the faux feature off and tossed it aside. "I suppose thanks are in order."

Phoebe hesitated. "Did you lose much?"

Tight-lipped, he nodded. "I lost everything, all my personal cargo from the past two years."

"I am so sorry," she said, meaning it.

He shook his head. "No, I'm the one who is sorry. Playing at Mother Geneva seemed harmless enough in the moment, but now I see it for what it was—an abominable abuse of your trust."

Phoebe didn't disagree. "Why did you do it?"

His gaze wavered. "I suppose I had things I wanted to say to you, and it seemed simpler to do so whilst hiding behind a disguise."

"Dressing up as a gypsy woman and playing me for a fool seemed simpler than speaking to me honestly?" It was only after he'd left that she'd recalled "Mother Geneva" as Cockney cant for gin.

He hesitated, swallowing hard, the motion pulling at the muscles of his throat, a throat that despite everything Phoebe badly wanted to press her lips upon. "The only person who played the fool today was me. I'd like to make amends, if I may."

Phoebe forced a shrug. "None of us have the power to turn back time, or so says 'Mother Geneva.'"

Robert's lips curved into a smile. "True, but as that wise woman also remarked, the future remains to be writ upon." He looked beyond her. "That's an awfully large bed for one slender woman. I wonder, is it as commodious as it looks?" Without waiting to be invited, he crossed the carpet toward it.

Once a rogue, always a rogue, Phoebe thought, following him over. "Pippin sleeps with me. For a small dog, he requires a great deal of room."

He settled on the foot of the mattress. "But soon he will have to cede his place, surely? Bouchart doesn't strike me as much of an animal lover."

Phoebe hesitated and then sank down beside him. "When he...visits me, I suppose Pippin will have to make do with his basket."

Amused eyes found their way to her face. "When he *visits* you?"

Shushing him, she answered, "I fail to see what you find so astounding. That is how most married couples rub along."

"Is that what you want from marriage—to *rub along*?"

Phoebe didn't answer. She thought of her parents' marriage, passionless and perfectly polite, the roles and rules clearly delineated, nary an eyebrow or a voice raised. It was as if they existed in wholly separate spheres. In so many ways that mattered, their lives never truly touched, and yet in society's eyes, they were deemed a success. Phoebe had always sworn she would never settle for such a state, and yet if she went through with marrying Aristide, wasn't that precisely what she'd be doing?

His gaze locked upon hers. “Were you my wife, there would be no separate bedchambers and skulking through some creaky adjoining dressing closet in the middle of the night. I’d keep you by me, in my bed, and make love to you every morning and every night, and when we were finally too exhausted to do aught but sleep, I’d clasp you to my breast and hold you so close that it would be hard to know where I ended and you began.”

The bloom of heat between her thighs confirmed she’d slipped back into dangerous territory, once more in his thrall and separated from both her morals and her sense. Retreating, she shook her head. “That will serve.”

“Will it?” He slid his gaze over her, reminding her of the matronly nightcap she wore, along with what Belinda never failed to assure her was her least flattering night rail. A faint smile lifted his lips. “Do you always go to bed so...armored?”

She forced her chin up. “Proper Englishwomen always dress for bed.”

To her chagrin, he chuckled. “The bedchamber is the very last place a woman should worry about being proper.”

Images from their interlude at the inn flashed before her mind’s eye, and she felt herself heating with embarrassment and something...more. “Did you come here solely to insult my nightwear?”

“No, I came here to do this.”

He took her face between his hands, his callused fingertips skimming her jaw, all that rough gentleness shooting a strange thrill through her. And then he was kissing her, his supple lips pressing gently but firmly upon hers while his other hand did the most amazing things to her right breast, things she didn’t want to think about but gloried in the feel of.

He lifted his mouth from hers and pulled back. “I ask for nothing beyond a taste of forbidden fruit—and the chance to make good on the promise of pleasure I made you that day at the lodging house.”

Phoebe hesitated. After her talk with Chelsea, she had called upon every whit of her willpower to withhold herself. Robert had yet to explain let alone justify his choice to remain "dead" for six years, a choice that had brought not only her but also Chelsea immeasurable heartache.

And yet she had wanted to lie with him last week. Had they not been interrupted, she would have done so. Even with a week to reconsider, she still badly wanted to be with him. In that moment, she stopped wavering. She decided. She would go to bed with Robert, not because he wanted it, but because she did. Because, propriety be damned, she *deserved* to.

Holding his gaze, Phoebe reached up and untied the ribbon beneath her chin. She lifted the nightcap off and tossed it aside. Her braid hung over her shoulder. Without a word, she pulled the ribbon from the tip and threaded her fingers through, reveling in how the simple gesture made his eyes darken.

Robert swallowed hard. "Lay back upon the bed," he said, not a request but a command.

Phoebe hesitated, unused to hearing that tone from him, hating how much she liked it. "Why?"

"I've promised you pleasure and pleasure you shall have." His jaw tightened. "Trust me this once more, and I swear on my life you shall not regret it."

Phoebe lay down. The mattress creaked as Robert joined her.

Turning toward him, she asked, "What do you want in return?"

"I want pleasure too, the pleasure of watching you lose yourself," he assured her, maneuvering himself onto his knees. "Now reach up with both hands and grab hold of the bedrail." Again, the ring of authority in his voice had her heart thrumming.

"Why?"

A smile whispered across his lips. "Because I've said you

must."

That hardly seemed a reason. Still, intrigued, Phoebe scooted up to the head of the bed and took hold of the metal bars. Robert followed her to the top. He threw one leg over, straddling her.

"Pretend I'm a housebreaker who, upon seeing you, is minded to thieve more than the silver." His big hands braced about her wrists, shackling her to the bedposts. "Tell yourself that I'm taking you against your will, forcing you to feel the pleasure you wouldn't otherwise dare."

Phoebe swallowed hard. She nodded. Whatever game he was about held an undeniably wicked appeal.

Releasing her wrists, he rested back upon his heels. "Under no circumstances are you to remove your hands from the posts. If you do, I shall have to punish you," he added, and inexplicably the warning sent tingling warmth shivering through her.

"But what if I wish to touch you?" she finally asked, looking up into his set face. He'd promised her pleasure and touching him was most certainly that.

His gaze hardened. He shook his head. "You may not lay so much as a finger upon me without me first granting you leave."

Was that because of the game, she wondered, or a ploy to protect himself from being touched? Since his return, she couldn't help but notice how being touched put him on edge. "This feels rather one-sided. Don't I get to make any rules?"

Staring at her, he shook his head. "Mind we observed your rules the week last. Now it's your turn to abide by mine. Unlike yours, mine come with consequences: punishments and rewards."

Feeling a bit breathless, she asked, "What, uh...sort of rewards?"

"Pleasure, for one. There is a freedom in surrender, freedom to give in to your deepest, darkest desires. To ask for anything, *everything,* you want, and know it will be granted."

"Are you saying that so long as I keep my hands above my head holding these bars, I may have whatever I want?"

Robert didn't waver. "Yes. The catch is that you must be very clear, very explicit, in stating your desires. Can you do that, Phoebe?"

She wasn't entirely certain, but she nodded nonetheless. "And the punishments?" Merely asking the question had her feeling flushed and breathless.

His eyes glinted. "You shall discover those too…in time. For now, we'll focus on the rewards. What do you want?"

She hesitated.

"Tell me. Say the words."

"I want you to…to kiss me again."

Robert smiled. "With pleasure." He bent and brushed his lips over hers, very slowly and very softly, back and forth. His tongue's tip slid across the seam, and she opened on a moan. He entered, his tongue flicking against hers, filling her mouth with the taste of anise—and her heart with heightened desire.

Pulling back, he reached down and traced her bottom lip with a clipped nail, the slight scratching sensation drawing her shiver. "You've the most beautifully shaped mouth, a perfect Cupid's Bow. I could go on kissing you all night, but I've a suspicion you might have something else in mind. Yes?"

"I'd like for you to…" She released her hold on the bedpost and reached for his wrist. A smart slap upon her palm had her drawing back. "Ouch."

"That would be a punishment, a mild one as you're just learning the rules."

Hand stinging, she wrapped it back about the bedpost.

"Good girl," Robert said with obvious approval. "Now was it you'd like to happen next?"

Good Lord, he really did mean to make her spell out her desires—to the letter. Reaching for her courage, she looked up into his darkening gaze and admitted, "I'd like you to touch my…my breast."

"I'd like that too, but first let's drop these absurd buttons."

Phoebe lay still as his nimble fingers made short work of the queue of cloth-covered buttons. When he'd finished, her night rail lay open to her waist. Not since their night in the garden six years ago had a man seen so much of her. As it had that long ago night, cool air brushed her belly and breasts, Robert's regard as much as the breeze bringing her nipples pebbling.

"You wear it again." His gaze grazed her throat and clavicle, and she felt its heat as she would a caress. "The lockets we exchanged before my leaving, you're back to wearing yours." His eyes blazed with male satisfaction.

Flustered, she followed his downward gaze. The padlock-shaped locket had become almost a part of her, scarcely more foreign than her God-given flesh and bone. As much as she'd tried casting it aside, in the end she'd weakened and snuck back to her father's study to retrieve it.

Caught out, she lifted her gaze back to him. "Why wouldn't I? It's a pretty thing and so light that oftentimes I forget to take it off."

Tracing the outline of the chain, he shook his head. "You love me. You may not own it yet but you shall soon enough."

She opened her mouth to demur, but before she could, he scratched his nail about her areola, very lightly and very slowly. "Only think if we were wed, you could have this every night."

Phoebe didn't answer.

"You'd like me not just to touch you but to kiss you here too, wouldn't you?"

Cinching her hands more tightly about the rails, she managed a "Y-yes."

He bent his head to her breast, lapping at the slight scratch he'd made and then teasing the taut nubbin of nipple into his mouth.

Phoebe thought she might split in twain, so stunning was the pleasure his "kiss" there gave. Arching to meet him, she fought the temptation to tear her hands away from their tether—and rake her nails down his back.

Lifting his head, he asked, "More kisses?" his hot breath bathing her breast.

Pleasure poured through her. In the midst of it, she nodded.

He obliged, trailing kisses down her abdomen and teasing his tongue into her belly button. Pulling back, he blew a soft breath onto the dampness. "Amazing things, navels, and yours is the most adorable indentation. But as delectable as you are there, I suspect the true succulent forbidden fruit is to be found lower. Does that embarrass you?"

"Yes, but..."

"But?"

Squeezing her eyes closed, she admitted, "But it excites me, too."

"I can tell. Your pupils just before you shut your eyes were huge even in this low light, and your cheeks, sweet Phoebe, are limned in blushes the very hue of those roses outside your window."

Phoebe opened her eyes. "I think you won't be satisfied until you've turned me into a wanton."

"Not a wanton but a woman," he corrected, palming her mons through the fabric. "I told you the other night that I meant to make you feel again, and I do. Trust me?"

Not with her heart, but with her body most definitely.

He snared the hem of her night rail and slid it slowly upward, his hand gliding from ankle to thigh. "So pretty." Combing his fingers through the thatch of coarse curls, he smiled at her sudden, sharp inhalation.

Light, circular strokes coaxed her thighs open. Fingers,

firm yet gentle, teased apart the sensitized folds. Having once viewed herself there with a hand mirror, Phoebe knew what he was seeing. Petal-like lips damp with dew. An inner wine-colored ring crowned by a pearl of firmed flesh. Over the past six years, she'd learned that were that pearl to be stroked and massaged and manipulated with a single moistened finger, great gratification could be brought about. A man's mouth there, Robert's mouth, was a pleasure she'd never expected to experience outside the realm of her fantasies. Now, it seemed, he was poised to prove her wrong.

He lifted her legs and instinctively she locked her ankles over his shoulders. "You can't know how many nights I've lain awake imagining you like this, your texture, your taste."

Phoebe felt as though someone touched a torch to her face. "Are you quite certain you wish to kiss me...*there?*" As exquisite as she knew his doing so would feel, she couldn't fathom what benefit it could possibly bring him.

In response, he slid a callus-coarsened finger inside her, testing her channel. "There are many ways to make love, my sweet. Aren't you the slightest bit curious?"

Phoebe was more than curious. After six years of waiting, she burned to know his every sensual secret. Not just know but experience, *feel*, all that she'd missed.

A low laugh rumbled up his throat. "I'll take your silence as a yes."

His head disappeared between her thighs. He brushed his cheek against her there, letting her feel his beard's roughness. Holding her open between his fingers, he tongued her channel. Impatient, she lifted to meet him, but Robert refused to be rushed.

Anchoring a hand to her hips, he pinned her to the mattress. Drawing back, he lifted a hand to his mouth and moistened his third finger. Phoebe watched, mesmerized, her heart skipping beats and her clitoris pulsing. Bending to her once more, he drew that warm, wet finger through her nether lips and backward—to her ass.

Phoebe's breath seemed to stall and with it her heart. In all the times she'd touched herself, it had never once occurred to her to touch herself *there.*

She lifted her head from the bank of pillows. "Robert, I—"

"Yes?"

His stroking digit roused a delicious tingling. She collapsed back against the bedding, the protest she'd meant to make staying unspoken. The small, wet circles he drew sent her senses soaring, the puckered flesh pulsing beneath his tracing finger. The slight, deliberate scratch of a nail sent her gasping, not because it hurt but because it made her want something she couldn't yet name. Smiling, he pushed a gentle path inside her. Remembering the "rule", she tightened her hold upon the metal bars, her arms straining to break invisible bonds. Perspiration filmed the backs of her knees. The quivering at her core once more began to climb. Responding to primal instinct, she squeezed against the finger working inside her and impossibly, the pleasure spiked.

Still fingering her, he bent his head and covered her quim once more with his mouth. His tongue's velvet sweep sent her world spinning. The pearl that in the past had been the portal to her solitary satisfaction was suckled and sipped. Circles, slow and rhythmic, carried her close to keening. The contrast between the soft fluttering of his tongue and the firm insistence of his finger was an exquisite mystery she could no longer wait to solve. Reaching for release, she bucked her hips and lifted up from the bed, gasping when he slid out—and then drove deeper.

The orgasm struck like a summer storm—swift, violent and darkly beautiful. Pleasure bolted through her, both her quivering woman's flesh and her twitching tail. Spasms convulsed her, releasing a rush of wet warmth. Hard as it was to keep hold of the bars, it was even harder not to scream.

Robert lowered her legs from his shoulders and slid up the length of her. He covered her mouth with his, absorbing her moaning, his lips tasting of anise and her own pungent juices. Drawing away, he unfurled her hands and pressed a kiss into each palm. Weak and boneless, she lay beneath him as he brought the night rail once more about her ankles

"Forbidden fruit tastes even sweeter than I'd imagined," he said with a smile.

A soft knock outside the chamber door set Pippin barking. Robert and Phoebe exchanged fraught looks. Sitting up and closing her gown front, Phoebe called out, "Y-yes?"

From the hallway, her maid, Betty asked, "I heard a noise. Is all well, milady?"

Phoebe scraped a hand through her hair, her fingers catching on tangles. "Yes, perfectly fine. I dropped my…book."

"Shall I bring you something? Some warm milk to help you sleep?"

"No! I mean, no, thank you."

"Goodnight, then."

"Goodnight."

The interchange returned Phoebe to sanity—and remorse. She looked back to Robert. "You should go now."

Rather than fight her, he rolled off the bed and stood. "I've waited six years to have you. If need be, I can wait another few weeks."

Phoebe followed him to her feet. Now that the pleasure had ebbed, she felt physically sated but emotionally battered. The pleasure he'd brought her had exacted too great a toll. In opening herself to receive it, she had reopened six years' worth of wounds. Morality, hurt, outrage—all her defenses failed her. There was but one way to protect herself and her future, to ensure he walked away once and for all.

A direct blow to his peacock's pride.

"Claim my maidenhead, you mean? You sound awfully certain. What makes you so convinced I've kept it all these years?"

Predictably his face fell. “You waited for me, didn’t you? Aristide, you haven’t let him...” His voice trailed off.

“What of you, Robert? Did you wait for me? Given that skillful...performance, I cannot think that you did.”

His gaze shuttered and his color heightened. “Six years is a long time for a man.”

She lifted her chin. “Six years is a long time for a woman too.”

“Shall I take that to mean you’ve given yourself to the Frenchman?”

Looking away lest he read her lying, she said, “And if I have? He is my fiancé, is he not? If any man can claim the privilege of lying with me, it is he.”

His gaze narrowed. “I was your fiancé once. I recall you begging me not to press you and promising that our wedding night would be all the more special for our having waited.”

Now that she was on her feet, her body was tellingly tender but that was nothing compared to her heart, which felt as though it were being wrenched wishbone style in two polar directions.

She spun about to face him. “And so it would have been, only you left me. I never would have left you, but you left me—and then stayed away for six *years.*”

He threw her an exasperated look. “How many times must I say it? I was a bloody idiot, far too simple and arrogant to come close to deserving you. If I could rewind the clock six years and choose again, I’d never leave your side, I swear it. But what is done is done and, trust me when I say this, I’ve more than answered for the consequences. Now all I can do is ask—*beg*—you, to forgive me. Forgive me, Phoebe, for both our sakes.”

She shook her head. “I forgave you weeks ago. But how can I begin to trust you again? What assurance do I have that you won’t hare off when the fancy takes you?”

His brows snapped together. The corners of his mouth

dipped. "Because I tell you that I won't, that I'm here to stay if you'll have me. We can be happy together, I know it. If only you'll stop pushing me away, stop fighting your own heart, it can be right again between us, a hundred times better than before. If only you'll ask me to stay, the promise of a hundred fortunes could not lure me from your side."

Near panic, she gave a fierce shake of her head. "I begged you once before to stay with me, and yet you left. I won't ask you again. I won't risk your hurting me."

"You're desperate. That's why you're giving yourself to this Frenchman, isn't it? Your mother has convinced you he's your last chance, only he's not."

"Don't be insulting," she answered much too quickly. "You of all people have no right to censor me."

"Who says I'm censoring you? It was simply a question."

Her temper flared. "A question you have no right to ask." Leaving the bed behind, she marched past him to the window. "I was a fool to allow you here in the first place, an even bigger fool to so much as consider crying off my engagement."

Following her over, he looked as though she'd slapped him. "In that case, you might ask yourself what you're about here with me."

"At the moment, I'm showing you the door—or rather the window." Giving him her back, she struggled with the window sash, which suddenly seemed to be sticking.

A huff sounded behind her. Moving her out of the way, he pulled up on the frame and slid the window open with apparent ease. Turning toward her, he demanded, "Is this truly what you want from life? Marriage to a man who means to set you upon a pedestal and treat you as though you have no more will or intellect than...than that china doll?" Mouth twisting, he jerked his head toward the shelf holding the toy and several other childhood mementos.

Phoebe turned to him, her chin lifting. "There are worse fates."

At least china dolls didn't have hearts to be broken.

Chapter Twelve

For two years Robert had endured the hell of slavery, of waking up each morning and falling asleep each night to the knowledge that his body, his being, was the property of another. There'd been violations upon his person both great and small, floggings that had flayed the flesh from his back and robbed him of the barest shred of dignity. Over time, he'd become convinced that his heart must be as scar-toughened as his skin. That one slight female, Phoebe, could fell him with little more than a word or look was nearly beyond belief.

Her declaration the previous night of having been with Bouchart had nearly driven him to his knees. Nor was the blow only to his pride. Climbing down from her window, he'd felt as if his heart had been slashed to ribbons and his hopes burned to ash. The image of her lying naked beneath his rival—touching him, pleasuring him, loving him—was almost beyond bearing.

As tempting as it was to cede the field to the Frenchman and walk away, this time for good, he couldn't. The fact remained that he loved her still, as much—more—than ever. At this point, thwarting her marriage to Aristide was no longer a battle of wills, a contest to be won. It was a rescue mission. Even if he couldn't claim her for himself, the least he could do was save her from a monstrous marriage. If only he could find a way to penetrate the seemingly impenetrable armor she'd put up about her heart...

Propped upon pillows in bed, he was working his way through an urn of coffee when Caleb entered, interrupting his brooding.

"What have you there?" Looking up, Robert gestured to the

silver tray upon which a single cream-colored square rested. "Don't tell me some old biddy actually came to pay a social call? If so, pray tell her I am not 'at home.'" It seemed he had waited the entirety of his adult life to say those words and now that he finally had, they brought him little relish.

Jaw set, Caleb continued holding out the tray.

Robert waived him off. "I'm in no mood for society of any sort."

Caleb didn't budge.

"Burn it for all I care."

A disagreeing grunt answered.

"Oh, very well, seeing as you insist." Robert reached for the note—and nearly upended his glass.

The Hanover Square direction was the Tremonts'.

He broke the seal and unfolded the personalized vellum.

Sir:

Pray call upon me at two o'clock. Be assured that you will be welcomed with all due warmth and cordiality.

Yours, Phoebe

He read it again, this time aloud, pausing to ponder each word as though it represented a hieroglyphic from the Rosetta Stone.

"What do you think it means, Caleb?"

The manservant rolled his eyes.

Beyond the oblique assurance of welcome, it was as if the previous night's verbal bloodletting had never taken place. Though a relief, the inconsistency made him curious. It had been six years since he'd seen anything in Phoebe's hand. Her last letter had been the one in which she'd enclosed her miniature. Unfortunately, paper and ink had not survived the sea waters nearly as well as metal and glass, leaving him to rely on faulty memory. He recalled her handwriting as spare and orderly, the only affectation the little flourish she gave to the "P" when signing her name. The present note seemed to hail from a less sure hand and one prone to extravagant loops and the odd splashes, yet the "P" in "Phoebe" was left perfectly plain. But then a person's penmanship often changed over time. His certainly had.

A broad-backed brown hand tapped his arm. "What is it?"

Caleb set the tray down upon the bedside table and signaled what by now Robert knew meant, *I will go with you.*

Robert shook his head. "Thank you, my friend, but no. This is something I must do alone."

A flurry of grunts and flailing hands followed. At times such as this, Robert could feel his friend's frustration, his anger, as though it were his own.

"Calm yourself, Caleb. 'Tis only tea."

The Arab answered with a firm shake of his head.

"You act as though I'm about to hurl myself at the lion's mouth, and I can't say that you're mistaken. True, Lady Tremont may detest me as much as she ever did, but her husband and son tolerate me well enough." The only person with whom he need curry favor was Phoebe.

The gaze honing in on Robert's was unmistakably imploring.

Giving in, Robert said, "Very well, you may drive me, but I go in alone."

He dressed with care and realized he was almost nervous. Bloody hell, he *was* nervous. By now, navigating his way through Mayfair was second nature. Turning over the team's reins to Caleb and confining himself to the carriage interior was bloody torture, but he kept his word. Despite the meandering pace Caleb set, he still reached Hanover Square a full quarter of an hour early. He climbed down from the carriage and proceeded to the columned entrance. Ascending the few short steps to the door, he saw that the knocker was turned down, signifying that the inhabitants were not "at home" to visitors. If Phoebe had in mind another clandestine call, midday was an odd time to arrange it. Robert hesitated and then took hold, bringing metal bashing against wood. Scurrying footfalls answered within. The door opened. Instead of the very proper butler, a buxom housemaid stood on the threshold.

"I'm here to see Lady Phoebe," Robert announced.

She stepped back for him to enter. "She's just popped out for a bit, but she bid me say she'll be back in a nonce."

Her voice, though nondescript and bearing a Cockney's broad vowels, struck him as familiar. Seconds later, he realized why.

"You're Lady Phoebe's maid, are you not?" He scoured her apple-cheeked face, wondering how much she might have heard.

She bobbed a quick curtsy. "Name's Betty, sir, though I've been considering changing it to Bette. It's French, you know."

Unorthodox as it was for a servant to chat up a guest, Robert couldn't find it within him to fault her for it. Whatever notions of privilege he'd begun with, the years of enslavement had knocked out of him.

Stepping inside, he said, "I am pleased to make your acquaintance, Miss Betty but tell me where has Wilson got to?" Stickler for propriety that Phoebe's mother was, Robert couldn't imagine her countenancing a mere maid answering her main door.

She shrugged. "He takes the stage to see his sister every other Wednesday. He won't be back before nightfall."

Robert hesitated. Something didn't feel quite right. With no other servants in sight, the house was shrouded in a tomb-like hush. "In that event, I should call another time." He took a backward step in preparation for leaving.

A firm hand fell upon his forearm, yet another untoward liberty. With her foot, she kicked the door closed behind them. "Oh no, sir, you must stay. My lady will be back at any time now, and she'll have my head if she misses you. Now follow me, and we'll get you settled cozy as can be whilst you wait."

He nodded and followed her through the foyer and into a side parlor. She led him over to a wing chair by the window, all but shoving him into the seat. "Will you take a sherry to ease your wait, my lord?"

"No, thank you. And I'm not a lord. Not even an honorable."

Had he possessed the preferred pedigree, there would have been no need to "hare off to parts unknown" six years ago. Looking back, he allowed that a stronger man would have stood his ground—and fought for his lady.

She giggled. "You seem right lord-like to me and handsomer than most."

Was the chit flirting with him? The bold eye she was giving him certainly made it seem so. For the first time, he studied her as something more than moveable scenery. Most of her fair hair was tucked beneath a lace-edged cap, but wisps had worked loose to frame a face that was, he supposed, passably pretty. If she were in the market for a protector to supplement her wages, she would have to look elsewhere. He'd never so much as considered taking a mistress into keeping. Regardless of how matters hashed out with Phoebe, he didn't mean to take up the practice now.

His gut instinct, his *third eye* as those in the East often spoke of it, called for him to leave at once, and yet he lingered. What Phoebe had to say to him must be vital indeed for her to call him to her when both her mother and the butler were out. Brash plans flooded his mind. Perhaps it wasn't too late. So far as he knew, Gretna Green still operated its chapel. Or, if Phoebe preferred, he would head for Doctor's Commons at once to procure a special license and they could marry wherever they wished. In two or three days, they might be sharing a bed as well as the rest of their lives.

Aside from the ticking of the ormolu clock perched atop the mantel, the atmosphere was eerily quiet, steadily still. "I believe I'll take that sherry after all." More so than him desiring a drink, pouring it would give the girl an occupation other than hovering.

She brightened. "I'll fetch it straightaway." She darted across the Persian carpet toward a Pembroke table, upon which a decanter and several glasses had been set. Back to him, she busied herself with pouring the drink.

Turning away, Robert took the opportunity to peer out the window, willing the carriage conveying Phoebe to return.

Betty bounded over and held out a very full glass. "To your health, sir."

Robert accepted the drink. "Thank you."

Rather than withdraw, she waited.

"You needn't stay to stand guard. I promise I shan't snaffle the silver or make away with the Dresden figurines beneath my coat," he quipped, his puzzlement tinged with annoyance. Beyond anything, he detested being made to feel a prisoner.

She rolled back her lips and laughed, the sound putting him in mind of a nag's braying. "You're a caution, sir."

Clearly Betty was determined to take full advantage of her unsupervised circumstances. "In all seriousness, won't you find yourself in trouble for being here?" He couldn't fathom Lady Tremont would look kindly upon one of her house staff lolling about the parlor making free with a guest, even if the guest in question wasn't precisely welcome.

The girl lanced him a sly look. "What her ladyship doesn't know shan't hurt her—or me, either." She laughed again.

"I suppose you have a point." Settling back against his seat, he fortified himself with a swallow of sherry. "Where did you say Lady Phoebe went?" She hadn't said but that was beyond the point.

"Lady Tremont all but dragged her and Miss Belinda to the shops—fittings for her wedding gown and trousseau and such—and well, you know how determined her ladyship can be."

Indeed he did. Dispirited by the reference to the upcoming

wedding, he swallowed another mouthful of the spirit before asking, “Are either Lord Tremont or Lord Reggie about?”

She shook her head. “At their club, I’m afraid.” It seemed there was not a single family member at home, hence the downturned door knocker.

“Pray don’t let me keep you from your duties,” he said, casting his gaze to the door leading back into the hallway.

This time she seemed to take the hint. “As you wish, sir.” She bobbed a quick curtsey and backed out of the room.

Relieved to be left alone with his thoughts, Robert sipped at his drink. In her note, Phoebe had promised him welcome, a most cordial reception. He could only think that she must mean it. Despite the bad turn things had taken last night, playing the coquette wasn’t in keeping with Phoebe’s character.

Yet again, he wondered how the previous night had gone so horribly awry. The fair fiasco he fully owned as his fault, but after... He couldn’t shake the feeling that the revelation that she’d allowed Bouchart to bed her had been aimed at pushing him away. Had his lovemaking frightened her so much? Or was it her own feelings that she feared?

Once he would have known the answer without question, but those simple, halcyon days were in the past. Then she’d trusted him with her body and her heart, precious gifts he’d tossed aside for the sake of a boy’s puffed-up pride. To reclaim her confidence, he’d cheerfully cross a bed of hot coals as once he’d seen a Sufi fakir do. The holy man had managed his passage without acquiring a single blister, an amazing feat of...feet. If only making amends might be as simple as fire walking.

Setting the empty glass aside, he felt his head begin to grow weighted and his thoughts muzzy. How could one small glass of spirit have such a potent effect? Not only could he curse like a sailor, but when called upon to do so he could drink like one too.

I need to leave—now.

Betty rushed inside the room. "Sir, come quick, I pray you."

Robert rose and made his way toward her on leaden legs. "What is it?"

"Milady's dog is suffering some sort of...fit. He's crawled beneath the bed and I can't get him out. Oh, do hurry, sir. He's strangling. I think he may have swallowed his tongue!"

Phoebe doted upon Pippin. If Robert stood by and let Pippin strangle, she would never forgive him. More to the point, he would never forgive himself.

Seizing upon his hesitation, Betty grabbed hold of his hand and towed him out to the hallway and toward the central staircase. Reaching its foot, he planted a hand on the polished rail and mounted, trying not to mind how each ascending step seemed to set the damnable thing canting. Winded, he reached the top. His head swam, and his limbs felt at once liquid and leaden. The sensation fell somewhere between a mild bout of malaria and the serene ecstasy of opium intoxication, both best experienced whilst lying down. This time when Betty took his hand, he didn't resist. Leaning heavily upon her shoulder, he allowed her to take him toward what must be the door to Phoebe's bedchamber.

She opened it and he fell inside. "He's under the bed, you say?" he asked, feeling sweat trickle between his shoulder blades.

Standing on the threshold with arms folded, she seemed far less frantic. "Aye. Have a look, why don't you?"

Too woozy to wonder at her surly tone, he flattened a palm against the papered wall and made his way over to the bed. Stopping at the foot, he braced a hand to the counterpane and lowered himself to his knees.

"Pippin, come out, lad, and let me have a look at you." On all fours on the carpet, he lifted the bed skirt and groped beneath, but his hands met with empty space.

"Turn up a lamp, will you?" he demanded, dimly aware that

the words sounded slurry and thick as though pushing past a mouthful of marbles. Marbles—how he'd loved shooting them as a child—as well as playing ducks and drakes and...

The door clicking closed brought him back to the moment. He twisted around to see Betty pull a key from the lock. Turning back to face him, she wore a sly smile. "Nay worries, my fine sir, we'll be safe as houses."

"What trickery is this?" Pushing himself up on his palms, he seized hold of the footboard and stood. Wrapping a steadying hand about the bedpost, he maneuvered around to face her. "Unlock the door this instant."

She shook her head. "All in good time."

"N-now." He shoved away from the bed and staggered toward her. Reaching her with arms outstretched, his clumsy grab elicited nothing more than a fistful of air and her triumphant laugh.

Easily sidestepping him, she dropped the key down her bodice. "Come and fetch it," she invited with a saucy smile.

Robert shook his head as if doing so might clear it. "What have you dosed me with, you witch?"

"Sticks and stones," she answered, her fingers fastening onto his trouser buttons. "You'll find far better bed sport with me than milady, I promise you."

The flap fell open. Through his smallclothes, her hand cupped his cock. He grabbed for her wrist, but suddenly he felt weak as a kitten. Her kneading strokes had him hardening, albeit against his will. Still holding him thus, she steered them toward the bed—Phoebe's bed.

Though he'd never struck a woman in his life, the present situation called for an exception. He reached out and shoved at her shoulders, losing his balance as he did. She caught him against her, pushing his head downward so that his nose and mouth were buried in her bosom. Black spots beetled his vision. Her cloying scent filled his nose and mouth to gagging. The room upended. They fell back onto a surface that was firm and yet far softer than the floor—the mattress. Betty rolled and, like an insensible sack, Robert followed, landing atop.

Ample thighs opened beneath him. Dimpled knees cinched about his torso.

Must...get...key!

Willing himself to wakefulness, he pulled at her tight-fitting bodice. She moaned and brought broad hips bucking against him. Battling the urge to backhand her, he pinned her arms as best he could and concentrated on his search. Betty was a substantial armful, the frock, likely a castoff of Phoebe's, a poor fit. The bloody key must be stuck in her stays. There was no help for it. He yanked her bodice down. Stretched to its limit, the fabric rent.

Commotion from below captured his attention. Female voices carried upward from the front hallway, accompanied by high-pitched yipping. Pippin! The dog must have been absent all this time. Robert had been duped indeed! On the heels of that revelation came one worse or equally bad. Phoebe had returned as well.

The barking grew louder. Scratching outside the bedchamber door confirmed Pippin had closed in, likely desirous of his bone and basket. Light-stepped footfalls, human ones, followed after him.

His fingers found flesh-warmed metal. He pulled the key free, hardly caring whether or not the serrated edge scraped her. Feeling on the brink of blacking out, he levered himself up on one elbow, holding his prize aloft and out of her reach.

"Have a care with that bandbox, it holds the wedding bonnet."

Lady Tremont!

"And Phoebe, can you not exert some control over that infernal beast of yours? He's all but pawing the paint from the door."

Phoebe!

"Why is the door locked?" a young girl, possibly Belinda, demanded. "My feet hurt."

More scraping ensued, only this time the source wasn't a determined little dog but a lock turning in the keyway. Heart pounding, Robert rolled onto his side. Before he could stagger to standing, the door opened.

Pippin leapt over a hatbox, one of myriad, and bounded inside. Phoebe, her mother, Belinda and two footman bearing boxes stared inside, eyes popping and mouths agape.

Robert didn't require a mirror to realize how damning the scene within must seem. He levered himself off the bed and gained his feet. Face aflame, he followed their downward gazes to his trouser front, the unbuttoned flap hanging at half-mast. "I can explain. I—"

A sob from the bed cut him off. He looked back at Betty. Shoulders hunched and hands holding together her torn bodice, she scooted off the bed. "Ohhh mi...milady!" she wailed, dashing toward the threshold and casting herself at her mistresses' feet. "Please don't turn me out. I'm a good girl, I swear it. I told him no, but he tried to force me anyways."

"Force you!" Robert echoed, horror-struck.

Betty twisted around to look at him. Had Robert not known better, he might have been gulled into believing himself guilty as well. "Aye, 'tis plain as day he's drunk as David's sow. You've only to look at him to see it's so."

The brunette, Belinda, cocked her head, scrutinizing him as though he were a zoological exhibit. "He does look foxed."

"Belinda, language!"

"Sorry, Mama," the chit answered, looking anything but.

"Belinda, to your room—now!" The directive came not from Lady Tremont but from Phoebe.

Face shocked, Belinda spun about to their mother. "Mama, must I?"

"Yes, you must. Now, run along."

"But, Mama—"

"*Go!*" Lady Tremont shooed her away.

"I don't see why I alone in this family must always be banished." Grabbing a bandbox by the string, she turned and sulked off.

Lady Tremont whirled on Robert. "You always were something of a savage, Bellamy, but this puts you beyond the pale. How dare you barge into my home and molest my maid."

"I m-molested no one," he protested, though it didn't help that his thickened tongue hesitated over every word. He took a step toward them and reeled. "And I didn't b-barge in. Phoebe invited me." He turned to Phoebe, but her ashen face confirmed his presence was as much a surprise to her as it was to her mother. "Your note—"

Tears welling, she shook her head. "I sent no invitation."

"S-someone did and posted the...letter from this household." He slipped a hand inside his coat and felt about the pockets, but he must have left the bloody thing behind. That or Betty had picked it off him during their struggle. Unfortunately, it was his only proof.

"Please, you must believe me." Bypassing the weeping maid, he took a step toward her and teetered. Falling back against the plasterwork, he sought to find purchase on the seesawing floorboards.

Lady Tremont shoved her face close to his, the ostrich feather from her bonnet flicking him in the face. "Leave at once or I shall call for a constable."

Turning to Phoebe, he tried one last time. "D-do you smell the reek of...s-spirits upon my breath? A single s-sherry is all I've had, and that at her insistence." He jerked his chin toward a cowering Betty, the small movement sending the room spinning. "Do you s-suppose one...d-drink would render me so...s-soused?"

Expression crestfallen, she shook her head. "I can't speak for how much you've had or what other intoxicants you might have partaken in, but I have eyes, Robert, and unlike your honeyed tongue they do not lie."

"Someone's lied." He whirled on Betty, nearly falling over. "Who p-put you up to this t-trickery?"

Prone upon the floor, Betty shrank away. "I'm but a poor, simple country girl. Please, don't strike me again."

She was such a fine actress that for a few seconds Robert could do naught but stare at her in amazement. Were he a bystander instead of her dupe, he might have sided with her himself.

She hugged her arms about Phoebe's knees. "Milady, I pray you, don't let him touch me again."

Lady Tremont huffed. "I have had quite enough unpleasantness for one afternoon." She beckoned to her footman, his brawny arms weighted by packages. "Charlie, show Mr. Bellamy out."

"There'll be no need," Robert retorted, this time without a stumble. The drug was beginning to wear off, albeit too late. Focusing on Phoebe, he added, "I'll go now and never trouble you again, if that's truly what you wish."

She hoisted her chin. "It is."

Robert's heart plummeted. He couldn't fight them all. Bouchart and his confederates, Lady Tremont and now even Phoebe herself were united against him. But because he loved her, truly loved her, he swallowed hard and braced himself to bear it. "Have a happy life, milady."

Restless, Aristide roamed his let rooms, his pacing threatening to wear out the already threadbare carpets. He despised waiting, especially upon a woman, and cooling his heels on behalf of a common slut such as Betty pushed his patience to its limit. Where was she?

A soft rap outside his flat door announced her arrival. Still, determined to demonstrate which of them was master, he forced himself to hold back, leaving her to cool her heels on his steps.

On the fifth frantic pummel, he opened the door. "You are late."

"I got away as quick as I could." Betty whisked inside in a cloud of perfume, no doubt pilfered from Phoebe, and the gin that she'd likely quaffed for courage.

Reaching around her, he drew the door closed. "Well?"

She broke into a broad grin. "It worked."

Aristide felt the corners of his mouth lifting. As satisfying as it would be to kill Bellamy—and he still had not abandoned the possibility—disgracing him would serve his purpose as well or better...for now.

"I wish you'd have been there to see their faces. Their jaws fair near fell to the floor. Lady T had the footman escort him out."

The news brought relief—and a cock stand that required immediate attention.

"You did well." Closing the space between them, he pulled the pelisse from her shoulders, not bothering with the satin-covered buttons.

She batted his hands away. "Have a care, you'll tear it. 'Tis real silk straight off your lady bird's back the week last."

He'd thought it looked familiar. Phoebe's scent still clung to the fabric. Not about to be dictated to, he pulled the front open, sending silk-covered buttons spraying the floor. "Soon I will bespeak you a wardrobe of clothes far finer than this rag. You'll have no need of wearing her castoffs ever again." He tore off the coat and tossed it upon the floor.

Despite his rough handling, she beamed. "In that case..." Glancing down, she ground her heel into the silken pool at their feet.

Later, they sat up in bed, Aristide smoking. Leaning back against the banked pillows, Betty pulled up the sheet with a satisfied sigh. "That was the best yet. That bit with your tongue, what do you call it again?"

He turned to her. Now that they'd shagged, she was beginning to bore him. "Cunnilingus."

"Is it French?"

He shook his head. "No, it is Latin."

"What does it mean?"

Aristide took another pull on his cheroot. Exhaling, he answered, "It means exactly what it is."

She let out a laugh. "In that case, it's my new favorite word. I'm keeping a list of the words you teach me so I can talk proper—like a lady."

He raked his gaze over her. Full-breasted, broad-hipped and easily pleased, she served as an ideal mistress. Nor was she the simpleton she at first seemed. So far she'd carried out his instructions more or less to the letter. If only she didn't squeal like a stuck sow every time she came he might consider extending their arrangement beyond the following few weeks. Once he wed Phoebe, he would have no further need of her. For now...

Blowing out another perfect smoke wreath, he said, "Tell me everything and see that you omit no detail."

Betty dutifully recited the tale.

"And they never questioned how he came to be in the bedchamber with you?"

She let out a laugh. "With my bubbies more out than in and us tangled up together atop the bed, they didn't think to question me. I was worried that powder you gave me to dose his drink might make him soft, but even fighting me off, he was hard as Hercules."

He noted the admiration tingeing her tone and felt his

bonhomie begin to slip.

"Alas," she said with a sigh, "I never did get 'round to the shagging bit."

Anger boiled up inside of him. Bellamy—it was as if women could not resist him. Aristide should have maimed him when he had the chance. Schooling his voice to steadiness, he said, "You seem disappointed."

She hesitated, only for a heartbeat, but long enough.

He leaned forward. "Why did you restrain yourself?" When she still hadn't answered, he lowered his voice and honeyed his words. "Tell me, ma petite. *Between us*, there should be no secrets, only truth—and passion."

Relaxing, she shrugged, the action causing the sheet to slip, baring the tops of her bosom. "I wouldn't have minded a go at him, but he only has eyes for her."

He pulled the cheroot from his lips and exhaled slowly. Summoning a mien of sympathy, he turned toward her. "A pity." He reached over and pressed his smoke's searing tip to the swell of her breast.

Betty screamed. Clutching the sheet as a shield, she shrank back. "Crimey! What'd you go and do that for?"

Seeing her welling tears calmed him. Satisfied, he dropped a kiss atop one heaving shoulder, thrilling when she flinched. "To remind you where your loyalties lie." He dragged the remains of the cheroot, no longer lit, slowly down her one arm. "The next time you consider betraying me, look upon my brand and know that you are mine."

Chapter Thirteen

Seated at her escritoire, a blanket draped over her shoulders, Phoebe stared down at the untouched pot of chocolate and buttered toast cooling upon the teakwood tray. It had been years since she'd taken breakfast in her chamber as her mother and Belinda fancied doing. Her custom was to rise early and join her father in the breakfast parlor, but that morning she hadn't had the appetite—or the heart—to do so. Despite her insistence that she wasn't hungry, Betty had brought up the tray anyway, almost as if she were seeking to make amends—a foolish thought, of course.

Looking back at her from the open wardrobe, Betty asked, "Will you want the printed cotton spencer or the square muslin shawl, milady?"

Phoebe glanced down at the loose-fitting, roller-printed house gown she wore. Other than to bathe, she didn't intend to take it off. "Neither, thank you. You may cancel the carriage as well."

Betty closed the wardrobe doors and turned about. "You don't mean to go to the Hospital?" she asked, not bothering to hide her surprise. In the nearly five years since she'd begun volunteering, Phoebe could count the weekdays she'd missed upon the fingers of one hand.

She ran her gaze over the maid as if seeing her for the first time. Blessed with full breasts, round hips and a tiny waist, Betty had the sort of figure associated with actresses and opera dancers. Rather than spoil her smile, her crooked front tooth lent a certain piquant appeal.

Until the other day, Phoebe had never given much thought

to Betty beyond the functions she performed, but now she found herself wondering what thoughts went on behind the girl's slanted green eyes. Phoebe knew little about her. When her previous maid, Martha, had left service to marry a coachman, Betty had moved up the ranks to replace her. Affable and efficient though Betty was, Phoebe had never warmed to her. With Betty, there were no cozy chats over a shared pot of tea, no exchange of late-night confidences as she brushed and braided Phoebe's hair. Clever with her sewing needle and gifted with an eye for fashion, Betty gave no reason to dismiss her. It was hardly her fault that Phoebe felt ill at ease around her.

The scene she'd witnessed in this very room made it impossible to look upon Betty and not see her intertwined with Robert—not the Robert she knew but the stupefied, rutting beast she'd caught disporting himself on her bed. Even her counterpane reeked of the eau de cologne with which Betty doused herself. Phoebe swore she'd move to one of the guest rooms before the sun set on another night.

"I shall write and inform them that a substitute shall have to be found for the week." Even the Hospital was inexorably intertwined with recollections of Robert—riding Lulu upon his shoulders, coaxing Billy's first smile, presenting Mary with her mother's precious letter.

The week off would also afford her time to complete the fittings for her trousseau as well as to accompany Aristide in viewing townhouses for let, including one in the smart Italianate terrace of the new Regent's Row. Ere now, she'd come up with a steady stream of excuses for putting off both, but it was time to set a firm footing in the future—a future that could no longer include Robert.

Betty's eyes widened. "You don't mean to go for a full week?"

Wondering why Betty should care one way or the other, Phoebe responded firmly, "I shall ring you when it is ready to be sent." She followed the broad hint by pointedly peering at the door.

"As you wish, milady," Betty said meekly. Creeping closer, she gestured to the tray. "Shall I take this away?"

Phoebe nodded. "Please." For the present, looking upon food sufficed to make her stomach heave.

The maid bent to collect the tray. Through the fine lawn fichu filling in her bodice, Phoebe spied the angry red weal branding the top of her left breast. Thinking back to the previous day, she did not believe it had been there then. With Betty's bodice all but riding her waist, the mark would have been hard to miss.

"That burn upon your breast, how did you come by it?" she asked, waiting to see if the girl would cast the blame on Robert.

Straightening, Betty dropped her gaze to the tray. "Cook asked me to take a turn stirring the porridge pot this morn and a cinder popped up from the hearth and burned me on the bubbie."

The farfetched explanation didn't fly. Running the household was entirely Phoebe's mother's affair; still she knew sufficient to say with certainty that a cook imposing upon an upstairs servant to help at the hearth would be a severe breach of domestic spheres.

And Betty's burn, while fresh, wasn't nearly raw enough to have happened that morning. The fichu itself was unmarred. "Ask her for one of her salves to put on it," she said, seeking to reconcile all the details that didn't seem to sum.

Whatever else he was—rake, scalawag, adventurer—Robert was no ravisher. That first night in her father's study, angry though he'd been, he'd claimed no more than a kiss. Compared to most of the men in her circle, her brother included, he didn't even drink that much. Despite all the occasions over the preceding weeks when she'd gone out of her way to provoke him, he'd held on to his temper. The other night when he'd climbed inside her window, he could have easily forced himself on her, and yet he'd given her pleasure whilst taking none for himself. Despite all that had taken place since, the memory of his carnal generosity had her heart fluttering.

And then there was the matter of the invitation she'd purportedly penned. Even inebriated, he'd seemed so sincere about receiving it. Why else would he present himself at the calling hour of the day? It wasn't as if he was on warm terms with her mother.

Seeing Betty backing toward the door, Phoebe couldn't resist one final question. "The other evening I went in search of you to ensure myself of your well-being, but you weren't in your room. Wilson said he saw you go out. May I ask where?" She'd granted Betty the evening off, thinking the girl could do with some solitude.

Gaze flitting to the empty bed, Betty bit her lip. "I went for a walk, milady. There's nothing quite like a stroll for clearing the cobwebs, aye?"

"Quite." Phoebe forced a smile. "It certainly seems to have worked. Despite your ordeal, you appear most refreshed."

"Er, thank you, milady. May I go now?"

"Yes, of course. I shall call you in a bit when my letter is finished."

Looking less bright-eyed than she had earlier, Betty slipped out, bringing the door closed behind her.

Relieved to be finally alone, Phoebe focused on the note she needed to write. Now that the tray was taken up, she noted the splashes of ink, globs of sealing wax and dusting of sand left upon the surface. If she discovered that Belinda had been in her room without permission, she'd have the scamp's hide.

She pulled the quire of folded foolscap from one of the interior compartments and placed it on the blotter. The paper too seemed disarranged, the watermark of the fool on the top sheet left upside down. Turning the paper right side up, she felt certain she had not left things so untidy. She pulled her goose quill from the stand, dipped it into the inkpot and began to write. The nib was blunted as if someone had borne down overly hard. She set the pen aside and held the sheet up to the light streaming through the window. The imprint of a previously penned note, not in her hand but in one that was large and loopy, was barely discernible but discern it she did. Belinda might not possess the most studious of minds, but she was rightfully proud of her pretty penmanship.

Whoever had used her desk last was not Belinda.

Fierce energy spiraled inside her. Some innate sense told her there was no time to dally, even less to waste. She pushed her chair back from the desk and stood.

Dear Lord, Robert, what have I done?

More to the point, how could she ever make it right?

Less than an hour later, Phoebe paced the four corners of Chelsea's parlor waiting for her friend, and God be willing, Robert, to come down. Facing Chambers so soon after her previous stealthy visit had tested her courage but, to the butler's credit, he had greeted her at the door and led her inside without so much as a raised eyebrow. Determined to compensate for her recent brazenness, she'd included Chelsea in her request for an audience, entrusting herself to her friend's tact. Once the formalities of the social call were observed, she felt certain she could count upon Chelsea to withdraw and leave her and Robert to their privacy.

Approaching footfalls sounded from the hallway. Heart on her sleeve, she spun about.

Alone, Chelsea crossed the threshold. "I'm afraid you shall have to salve your conscience elsewhere. Robert isn't here." The viscountess's curt tone and stiff stance were not lost upon Phoebe, nor was the pink rimming her eyes.

Heart dropping, Phoebe didn't spare time or words to

dissemble. "I'm sure I'm the very last person he wishes to set eyes upon, but I must see him if only to beg his pardon."

Subsiding onto the sofa seat, Chelsea's gaze narrowed. "Is making an apology the only reason you came?"

Biting her lip, Phoebe admitted, "No, it's not. I also need to tell him that I love him."

Chelsea eyed her. "Shouldn't such fond feelings be reserved for your future husband?"

Phoebe didn't dare presume at this point, but she dearly hoped her future husband would be Robert. "I have broken off my betrothal to Aristide."

Resolved at last, she had placed the brief letter in the hands of one of her most trusted family footman herself before setting out for Berkley Square. Crying off an engagement by way of correspondence hadn't been the most courageous of acts, but considering her need for haste, it had seemed the lesser of evils. She would return his betrothal ring in person once she informed her parents of her decision. For the time being, the ruby hung from the heavy chain about her neck, a reminder of the matrimonial fetters she had escaped albeit narrowly. She would have far preferred to remove it from her sight and person altogether, but in light of how her desk had been rifled, she hadn't dared leave it behind.

Chelsea's starchy demeanor dissolved. "Oh, Phoebe, can it really be so?"

"It can—and is. But please, Chelsea, for the sake of the love we bear your brother, stand as my intermediary this once more and call for him."

Chelsea released a heavy sigh. "I would that I could, but he truly isn't here. This morning he packed what few things he'd brought and left for Blackwall to supervise the loading of his ship."

Heart drumming, Phoebe crossed the carpet and sank down on the sofa cushion beside her friend. "Do you know when he means to set sail?"

Chelsea shook her head. "He said nothing for certain, but I suspect soon." Shifting to face Phoebe, she added, "When he returned home yesterday, he was in a very bad way, seemingly stupefied but with scant spirits on his breath. He maintains he was lured there by a note falsely made out to be from you, dosed with some potent but short-lived intoxicant, and trapped into appearing to deceive you with your maid."

Hearing Chelsea summarize the story, it no longer sounded nearly so fantastical. "Earlier today I discovered that someone has made free with the contents of my writing desk. At first I thought it might have been Belinda, but I have begun to suspect it was my maid."

Chelsea turned to look at her. "The same servant who the other day swore he'd set out to rape her?"

Ashamed at having been so easily duped, Phoebe admitted, "The very one." Plucking at her bonnet ribbons, she shook her head. "Oh, Chelsea, I've made a horrible hash of everything. Since Robert's return, I've done all I can to push him away and now it seems I've succeeded." That thought led to one equally bad or worse. "Surely he wouldn't set sail without saying goodbye...would he?"

Have a happy life, milady.

"I honestly can't say. But if there's even a chance of persuading him to stay on—"

"I have to take it." Phoebe shot to her feet. Rounding the sofa, she made for the door.

"Wait!"

She turned back. Seeing Chelsea struggling to rise, she retraced her steps and helped her friend up.

Bracing a hand to her back, Chelsea said, "I shall go with you. Were you to be seen alone at the docks at this hour—"

"I'd be ruined," Phoebe finished for her. "But that is a risk I am prepared to take." If the past six years of separation had taught her anything, it was that there were worse fates than social exile. "Besides, you are too near your time to go anywhere but back to bed," she added sternly.

Her gaze went to Chelsea's protruding belly, prompting a pang of longing. How wonderful it would be if she were to find herself likewise laden a year hence—but only if the babe was Robert's.

"Then you shall take one of our footmen with you. On second thought, you shall take two."

Phoebe shook her head. "That will make things quite crowded in the hackney, I'm afraid." Waiting at the stands for a hired carriage hadn't been precisely convenient, but it had been preferable to going about her scandalous business in a conveyance marked with her family's crest.

Chelsea's brow lifted. "In that case, you shall take the carriage as well."

Phoebe sent her friend a look of deep gratitude. "Thank you for believing in me despite...everything."

Chelsea shrugged aside the sentiment. "Mistakes have been made all around. There is nothing to be gained by pointing fingers—for any of us. I shall be content to see the two of you settled once and for all. Now off with you and bring my brother back home."

Cradling a glass of Madeira, Robert reclined on the black lacquer divan in his cabin, spoils from a palace in...well, he'd quite forgotten where. Commotion from above deck caught his attention, a woman's voice pitching above the typical sailors' rumpus. One of his crew must have run afoul of his doxy, or so Robert surmised. Women, even the loose sort, seemed to have a sixth sense when a man was poised to pull out of port. Tantrums and full-out fits weren't uncommon. A few went so far as to drive home their hurt feelings at knifepoint. Then again, he supposed it was human nature not to want to be left behind.

You left me. I never would have left you, but you left me—and then stayed away for six years.

Not for the first time, Robert wished he'd found the courage to confess the truth to Phoebe. He'd told himself he was acting in her best interest. Only now that it was over, now that it was pointless, did he own his silence for what it was—pure and simple cowardice.

He'd found his courage but too late. After the other day, she wouldn't believe a bloody word he said. Given the damning scene arranged by her maid, no doubt at Bouchart's behest, he couldn't blame her.

His hopes, his dreams, were as dashed as a ship broken upon the rocks. His gilded surroundings, his storehouse of wealth, even his ship meant nothing to him now. The one treasure he cared to claim was the one he could never have: Phoebe. After the previous disastrous day, there was no new course to chart, no sparkling second chance for which to strive. Star-crossed lovers they'd remain. It was finally and forever too late for them—and the fault was once again his.

But there was a great deal more at stake than his personal happiness. Once she wed Bouchart, she wouldn't only be beyond Robert's touch. She'd be beyond his help as well. Short of kidnapping and sailing away with her, there would be nothing he could do to save her from what he was convinced would be a monstrous marriage.

Montrose was his sole hope. His former spy associate in the War Office had dispatched a man to Paris to dig for details on Bouchart's past—if indeed Aristide Bouchart was even his name. Even knowing he'd lost all hope of having Phoebe for himself, Robert was determined to see the wedding stopped for her sake.

In the interim, there was nothing more to be done beyond holing up in harbor and feeling sorry for himself. Since boarding the night before, he'd camped out in his cabin, leaving word he wasn't to be disturbed unless the bloody boat sprang a leak—several. Whatever was amuck on deck, Caleb or Sandy would have to handle it.

A sharp rap outside his cabin door brought him out of his brooding. It seemed he was not to be left in peace after all. Whatever the hubbub, it must require his personal attention. Trouble with the harbormaster? Another lumper caught stealing? A rat catcher who'd planted fat rodents in order to ratchet up his price? The possibilities for problems whilst docked were depressingly diverse.

"I told you I wasn't to be bothered," he barked, determined not to budge if he could help it.

Sandy, his boatswain, called out, "Captain, there's a lady to see ye."

Releasing an oath, Robert rose. Chelsea, it must be. What was Montrose thinking to let his pregnant wife go haring about the docklands at night? But even an alpha male such as his brother-in-law could exert but so much influence. Despite being mere weeks away from her time, his sister remained as intrepid as ever. She must have given her servants the slip and struck out on her own.

Resigned, he drained the snifter and stood. Wiping his mouth on the back of his hand, he called out, "Very well, Chelsea, come in and say your piece, but be forewarned, as soon as you do I'm sending you back to Anthony." He turned away to pour himself more of the spirit.

The door groaned open. Softly soled footsteps padded inside. Perfume, a light floral fragrance intermingled with citrus and vanilla, wafted within.

The clearing of a feminine throat announced the petitioner's presence. "It isn't Chelsea, I'm afraid."

Robert whirled, sending the spirit slopping onto his forearm. "Phoebe, what in God's name—"

Dropping her cloak's hood, she sent him an uncertain

smile. "Surprise."

Shock was more like it. A tumult of emotions welled within him. Doing his damnedest to force his feelings back down, he flung a look at Sandy, sagely holding back by the door. "I should flay you alive. What the devil were you thinking to bring her below?"

Ever unflappable, Sandy shrugged. "Would you rather I left her on deck for any passerby to remark upon?"

Robert brought his gaze back to Phoebe. Sandy had the right of it—there'd be no passing her off as either a dockside whore or a stevedore's missus. Even without the fashionable bonnet and pelisse, there was no disguising what she was: a lady.

He shifted his gaze to Sandy. "Leave us."

The boatswain looked happy enough to comply. "I'll be topside if you need me." He ducked out, pulling the cabin door closed.

Left alone with her, Robert stared into the pale oval of her face, delved into the quicksilver eyes searching his, and the anger and humiliation from the day before suddenly melded into one bright, pulsating point of pain. "This had better be good."

"I'll do my best not to disappoint."

"If you don't give a whit for your reputation, then at least consider your safety. The docks are no place for a lady to prowl alone. Anyone possessed of a peahen's brain would know that." Even in the throes of wanting to throttle her, he found himself sending up a silent prayer of gratitude to whatever Powers That Be for seeing her to him safely.

Any appearance of sheepishness left her. She firmed her mouth and lifted her chin. "I wasn't prowling and I didn't come alone, so there's no need to ring a peal over my head. Chelsea sent two of her manservants with me. They saw me safely to the bargeman who brought me from shore."

Small surprise, his sister was involved albeit as a confederate. "Oh, well, in that case, I suppose it's all perfectly fine."

"There's no cause for being sarcastic." She started toward him.

For once let her come to me, Robert thought. Midway to reaching him, she lost her footing. Seeing her sway, he was instantly contrite. Her hand shot to the grab rail. Before she could reach it, he was beside her.

Bracing an arm about her waist, he anchored her against him. "Has anyone ever told you you're a menace?"

A smile tipped up the corners of her mouth. "Sorry," she said, looking anything but. "I suppose I don't yet have my sea legs."

"We're docked," he pointed out, in no mood to be gracious. Seeing her gloved hand wrap around the rail, he withdrew and moved away.

Holding on to the bar, she sent her gaze circuiting the cabin's four corners. "I feel as though I've stepped into Ali Baba's cave."

Robert followed her gaze, attempting to see his quarters through her eyes. An intricately decorated filigree attar casket once belonging to Tipu Sultan, one of the Company's most formidable opponents, rolls of colorful hand-woven Persian carpets piled against a cabin wall, a life-size mechanical organ fashioned in the form of a tiger mauling an English redcoat that, when wound, released a most realistic roar.

"I've never much thought about how it must seem to a woman," he admitted. "To me it's simply...home."

She looked at him askance. "Would you bamboozle me into believing I'm the first female to set foot upon your ship?"

"The first female to come aboard this ship, hardly, but you are the first to see the inside of this cabin."

Her steady gaze probed his. "Is that true?"

Dry-mouthed, Robert nodded. "It is."

She glanced to the glass in his hand. "Are you planning to offer me refreshment?"

"My stores of champagne and ratafia have run low," he said, a deliberate sarcasm. "Grog, brandy or Madeira, pick your poison. I suppose I could have the ship's cook boil water for tea, if you want it," he added grudgingly.

"Madeira will serve, thank you." Untying her bonnet strings, she added, "I've acquired something of a hollow leg over these last six years."

Recalling her legs as he'd last seen them, perfectly shaped and spread wide open to him, Robert felt as if he'd swallowed cobwebs.

As if privy to his salacious thoughts, her mouth curved ever so slightly upward. "We've a great deal to settle between us, Robert Bellamy, and I expect we shall both find ourselves in need of a strong dose of Dutch courage before this night is through."

Chapter Fourteen

They sat across from one another in throne-like chairs, the claw feet of which were nailed to the floorboards. They didn't touch and yet Phoebe felt as if her entire being was awash in Robert—his passion, his secrets, his pain.

She hadn't spoken in jest when she'd said she'd need courage. Only now that she was here, alone with Robert, did the enormity of what she'd done strike her. She'd cried off her betrothal, her *third* betrothal, and come aboard an otherwise all-male ship to seek him out in his pirate's lair. Were word to get out, not even her parents' standing would save her. She'd be a fallen woman, doomed to pass the remainder of her days in social exile. Worst of all, she'd be dismissed from her position at the Foundling Hospital. There was, to put it mildly, quite a lot at stake.

Reaching for her resolve, she swallowed a mouthful of the Madeira, forgetting to sip. The spirit scored her throat, making her feel like one of the fire-eaters she'd seen at Astley's Circus. A cough escaped her. She covered her mouth with her gloved palm. So much for her attempts to appear as a sophisticated woman of the world.

Robert studied her with steely eyes. "Why the sudden desire to seek out my company? You didn't seem much interested in speaking the other day."

She set the glass down atop a three-footed table encrusted with gemstones. Really, who lived like this? "You were hardly fit and I was not... When I saw you with...her...on the bed, where you and I...I couldn't begin to think beyond being so terribly hurt."

He blew out a breath. "I was tricked into calling when the house was empty and once arrived was drugged. I don't expect you'll believe me, but 'tis true."

"But I do believe you."

He stood. "Brilliant, now that we're sorted, I'll have Caleb see you safely back to shore and to your carriage."

He made as if to usher her out, only Phoebe was having none of it. They were not, in point, sorted. He needed to talk—and she needed to hear. "I'm not going anywhere and neither are you." She shot to her feet. "This once at least, what's sauce for the goose is sauce for the gander."

Posing her a puzzled look, he asked, "Meaning?"

Her fisted hands found her hips. Hardly caring that the stance must bring to mind a fishwife, or better yet an oyster woman, she sallied forth. "It's all well and good for you to materialize after six years—at my betrothal ball, no less—and to climb through my bedroom window like a house-breaker, but now that I've taken the reins and visited myself upon you, I am supposed to leave for home like the biddable girl you once meant to marry. Best you think again. I have come to you at great risk, both to my reputation and my person, and you should know that I have no intention of setting foot outside this cabin until we've come to terms."

He had the audacity to look amused. "Terms?"

She shrugged. "An understanding, if you prefer."

He spread his arms. "If this is some reprisal of your bloody rules—"

Her fingers unfurled, her arms falling to her sides. "It's not."

"Very well, let's hear it. What do you want from me, Phoebe?" A weary-sounding sigh followed.

She hesitated, moistening her lips. The inside of her mouth felt as if sprinkled with sawdust. "Quite a lot, but I should like to start with your forgiveness."

From his widening eyes, she gathered he hadn't expected that. "If you're seeking absolution, you'd do better to search out a priest than a pirate."

She reached between them and dealt his chest a shove. "I'm trying to apologize, you ninny."

His expression darkened. He let out a laugh, its sharpness slicing at Phoebe's heart like a razor. "Can it be that Lady Phoebe, pillar of London society and paragon of all the virtues, is condescending to apologize to a low fellow like me? Surely my ears deceive me?"

Hurt though it did to hear, she supposed she deserved that. "I was a fool to take Betty's word over yours, an even greater fool to judge you without a fair hearing. I should have known you'd been tricked, that never would you force yourself upon a woman no matter how provoked you might be."

Thinking of the night he'd climbed through her bedroom window, of the dark sensuality he'd given her a glimpse into, she felt heat climbing her throat. Though he could have easily ravished her, he'd chosen to hold back and simply and generously give.

He leaned toward her, so close she could all but taste the anise and Madeira on his breath, a spicy, intoxicating combination. "Ah, yes, but then how can you be so certain? Mind you can't possibly ever bring yourself to trust me."

Determined not to allow herself to be drunk on him, not yet, she sipped her bottom lip and did her best to keep a clear head. "I do trust you. I didn't before, but I do now—wholly."

He pinned her with a skeptical stare.

"I trust you, Robert. I do. I wouldn't have come here like this if I didn't." She hesitated and then reached for his hand, feeling as though she were laying hers in the lion's paw. "Now it's your turn to trust me—with the truth."

Phoebe's quicksilver gaze held his. "It's time you told me

exactly how you've spent these past six years, *why* you stayed away, and don't attempt to fob me off with that rubbish about needing to make your fortune first. I may have accepted that feeble excuse as fact when you first returned, but I shan't now."

His chest tightened as though a vise cinched him. "It's not a pretty tale."

Her chin firmed. "I didn't come here for a tale. I came for the truth." Seeing her strip off her gloves, Robert surmised she was indeed settling in.

He braced himself with a deep breath. "I told you my ship was boarded by pirates."

"Yes."

He fell back into his chair. "Everything I said was true, but there are things I left out, things I'd hoped never to have to admit to you."

She cast the gloves aside, closed the space separating them, and knelt at his feet. "Tell me," she said, taking his cold hands between hers.

He hesitated. How did one confess the consummate cowardice? "I told you that once the pirates boarded us, I escaped and made my way to land, but that was a fiction, a lie. I did attempt it, but they caught me as I was trying to set out in one of the hatch boats and brought me back. Their captain was an Englishman by the name of Arthur Trent. Even for a bandit, he was the very worst of sadists. It wasn't enough for him to kill. He took his greatest pleasure from inciting his crew to torture. As one of the few survivors who was neither a young boy nor an old man, the price I'd fetch in the slave markets made me too valuable for killing, but that didn't mean..." His voice broke off.

Pained eyes lifted to his. "But you must have gotten free eventually."

"I resolved to make my escape, but not in the way you're thinking. Once they...broke me, I made up my mind to take my own life." He hesitated and then held out his left hand, the wrist bare of its concealing bracelet. Done with subterfuge, he'd taken the thing off and tossed it into the water upon boarding.

Phoebe's soft hand banded his wrist. She turned it over to the scar inside. "They didn't do this, did they? You did."

Throat knotting, Robert didn't deny it. The angry wound had been made by him, the scar that was supposed to have brought release, only it hadn't, not because he hadn't cut clean and sure but because the Powers That Be had once again intervened.

Her stark gaze lifted to his. "Why?"

"I was sick in body and soul. I loathed my captor, but that was nothing compared to the contempt I felt for myself. I spent every free moment working out a plan in my head. There was a rusted bit of shaving razor that had been tossed aside and every day I'd take it up and work on the rope at my wrist. The moment my hands were free, I'd slash the main artery and there'd be nothing he or anyone else could do to bring me back."

He'd steeled himself for recrimination, but instead she bowed her head and pressed her sweet, healing lips to the scar. Robert's heart turned over. Though he'd loved her for more than six years, he'd never fully owned her worth until this moment.

She turned her face up to his once more, and the love shining from her quicksilver eyes humbled and heartened him, lending him the courage to continue. "Only I couldn't manage to get suicide right either. The blade was dulled and just as I'd steeled myself to have at it in earnest, he walked in and stopped me. The ship's surgeon was called in to suture and bandage the wound, and they forced something bitter down my throat that made me sleep." He felt wetness on his cheeks and realized he must be weeping. "When I awoke, two days had passed, and we were putting into port at Madagascar. I was taken ashore and kept overnight in a filthy hole somewhere between an oubliette and a storage cellar. The next day they dragged me through the streets to the market square and sold me to a quarry owner for what I later learned was a paltry sum. It seemed they'd pegged me for a dead man. But I didn't die. I lived to slave in that bloody pit for two full years."

She lifted her hands to cover her mouth. "Oh, Robert!"

He forced a shrug. "It wasn't all bad. It was there I met Caleb."

She lowered her hands and laid one along his thigh. Though she couldn't know it, she touched the very spot the brand had scored. "Was he...mute when you met?"

"He was. Apparently one does not require a tongue to pull a cart."

"You said before you saved his life?"

He nodded. "I've always been quick upon my feet. I shoved him clear from being crushed by a falling boulder, and we've been together ever since. When I was sold again, this time to a silk merchant who wished for a tutor to teach him English, I persuaded him to take Caleb as well." He paused, sucking down a shaky breath.

Phoebe squeezed his hand. "Go on, I'm listening."

"My new master was a man of considerable means, learned and not unkind. Fortunately for me, he also had enemies."

"Did one of them aid you in escaping?" she asked.

He shook his head. "I never escaped, though I grant you mine would be a worthier tale if I had. Quite the contrary, I saved my master from an assassin's dagger and in return he granted me my liberty. I took it, the purse of gold he'd pressed upon me and Caleb and together we made our way to India."

She hesitated. "And so Robert Lazarus was born?"

He nodded. "Once I arrived at Fort William, I came to understand I'd been written off as dead for nearly three years. My attempts to persuade the powers that be that I was who I said only made me out to be a charlatan or a madman. After a few days, I gave up, went elsewhere and enlisted at another

Company outpost for maritime training as Robert Lazarus."

Phoebe let out a long breath. "And the pirate captain, whatever became of him? Has he been brought to justice?"

Blowing out a breath, he admitted, "So far as I know, he remains at large though should we cross paths again, not even the love I bear you would stay me from slaying him."

Her eyes widened. She grabbed for his hand and pressed a fervent kiss into the callused palm. "Then let us both pray you never do." Drawing back, she asked, "What happened to you...is that why you can scarcely stand to be touched? Why you prefer pinioning me to leaving me at liberty to lay hands upon you?"

"I'd hoped to keep hidden that much from you, but yes." He scraped a hand through his hair, the fingers trembling against his scalp. "So there, you have it, all my dark, shameful secrets spread out before you, a grim little picnic of the grotesque."

"I'm glad you told me."

He laid a hand upon her elbow and stood, bringing her with him. "So am I. I'm only sorry it's taken me this long." Confession might be good for the soul, but that didn't mean it was pleasant for the hearer. He'd asked so much of her already that inflicting himself any further struck him as the quintessence of selfishness. Before he utterly fell apart, he'd do well to see her out. "I've kept my promise. Now it's time for you to go back before you're discovered gone. I've entrusted my life to Caleb on more than one occasion. You'll be in safe hands."

Phoebe lifted her chin, meeting his gaze with her steely one. "I'm not going anywhere. I'm staying here with you."

"You don't know what you'd be committing to, what it means."

She cut him off with a look at once determined and wise. "I know full well what it means."

Only she didn't. He'd bared his soul but he'd yet to bear his body. Hearing he'd been tortured had to have been hard, but witnessing the result would test in her ways for which she might not yet be ready. Her pity was not something he was prepared to face.

Only it wasn't sympathy he saw on her face now but a scowl to rival her mother's. "Ever since you returned, you've done all that you possibly could to claim me, making a bloody nuisance of yourself and nearly getting yourself murdered in the bargain. And now that you've won your way, now that you've won *me*, you're hell bent on sending me away. It makes no sense and even if it did, this isn't six years ago. I shan't stand for it."

She was offering herself to him. It was what he'd wanted all along, wasn't it?

A better man would persist, but Robert had never been that, not where Phoebe was concerned. "If you stay with me, know that taking you to my bed shall mean as much as vows said in a church. Once we've lain together, once you've let me inside you, I won't step aside, not for Bouchart, not for any man."

"Dear fool," she said, shaking her head and laying a gentle hand upon his jaw. "I wrote to Aristide earlier, ending our engagement."

Half afraid to believe, he covered her hand with his. "Can it be true?"

A smile trembled across her lips. Slipping her other hand into his, she nodded. "I would not have come to you otherwise."

"There will be talk, you know—scandal."

"All that matters is that I'm free—free of Aristide, free of the past, free to be with you." Pinning him with tearing eyes, she smiled again. "Now take me to bed, you foolish man, and claim me as yours in every way."

Phoebe wrapped her arms about Robert's neck and pulled his face down to hers. Standing on tiptoe, she matched her lips to his, her body to his, her *passion* to his, until it was no longer possible to tell where he ended and she began.

He pulled away. Holding her at arm's length, he swept her with his gaze. "Look at you," he said again and again. "How is it you're so beautiful and I so lucky?"

Bit by bit and piece by piece, he freed her from her clothing, his fleet fingers making short work of her tapes and pins and buttons. Finally he slipped the shift from her shoulders. It shimmied off, landing with her other clothes in a pool at her feet. Aristide's ruby betrothal ring still hung about her neck. Quickly, she pulled the chain over her head and set it aside.

Catching sight of herself in the peer glass across the room, she scarcely credited the reflection as herself. Wide-eyed and berry-lipped, the wanton woman peering back at her was in no way akin to the prim and proper lady she'd once taken such pride in presenting to the world.

"You can't know how many times I've imagined you like this. Even so, you're a hundred times lovelier than you ever were in my fantasies." The breadth of his smile sent her heart somersaulting.

"Fair is fair. If I'm to stand about courting lung fever then so must you." As deliciously wicked as it felt to stand naked whilst he still wore his shirt and trousers, she too had waited long enough. Pulling back from his embrace, she reached for the buttons fronting his shirt.

Robert's smile dissolved. He reached out to take hold of her wrists. "Trust me, Phoebe, you'll enjoy this a great deal more if I keep my shirt on. I'm not fit for a lady's eyes."

Her heart stilled. Whatever it was he wished to keep her from seeing must be bad indeed and yet she couldn't imagine him other than healthy and whole.

She glanced from her manacled wrists back up at him. "I'll be the judge of that."

His hands fell away. "All right, but remember that I warned you."

Phoebe answered with a mute nod. Willing her clumsy fingers to cooperate, she worked at the queue of cloth-covered buttons fronting first his waistcoat and then his shirt. The open shirt revealed a glimpse of sun-bronzed flesh dusted with dark hair that narrowed into a queue down his ridged belly to disappear into his pants waist. She sucked down a relieved breath. He wasn't only pleasing. He was perfect, a classical statue brought to life.

She guided the last button through the loophole and slid her hands beneath the cambric, sliding it off his shoulders. It was then she felt it, the webbing of mottled flesh spreading like a net across his shoulders.

His mouth firmed. "I have...a lot of scars."

Skimming her fingers along his back, fingering one especially deep gully, she steeled herself to be brave for them both. If she wanted to make a life with Robert, and she did, she must accept all of him, body and soul, not only the light but also the shadows. "The pirates?"

Rather than answer, he turned away and reached for his shirt. "I'll keep it on. I don't mind." He shoved one sinewy arm through the sleeve.

She shot out a staying hand, landing it hard upon his arm. "Bollocks you will! *I* mind."

He dropped the shirt. His chest rose and fell with each rushed, rapid breath. Thick white scars slashed across his shoulders. A particularly deep one curled over his left shoulder like a serpent's tail. Stepping behind him, she held back a gasp. He'd been not only whipped but burned. Tamping down her shock, she skimmed her hands over the terrain of ruined flesh. Judging from the deep gutters, the area between his shoulder blades had borne the brunt of the lashings.

The image of Robert, *her* Robert, flayed bloody and raw caused her to sway but only for a moment. Knowing she had to be strong, that their future might well rest on how she reacted now, she drew a steadying breath.

"I tried to warn you."

"I don't need warning." Anchoring a hand to his hip, she pressed her lips to the worst of the scars and trailed moist kisses over it.

"Phoebe—"

"Hush," she said, deliberately brushing her breasts against his scarred back. "If anything, these marks but make me love you all the more, for they prove all you endured to find your way back to me."

He turned his head to look back at her. "You're not horrified?"

She crossed around to the front of him and reached for his hand. Taking it, she guided it to the triangle between her legs. She didn't need to look down to know that her nether curls were damp with dew. "Do I seem horrified to you?"

His hand curved about her, his palm warming her in the most deliciously of ways. "No."

"Good, because what I feel when I look upon you is very warm and very wet and very lucky to have you back with me."

Scarred or not, he was beyond beautiful. Roped with muscle, his biceps were even bigger than she'd supposed from seeing him in his rolled-up shirtsleeves, his stomach washboard flat and rippling with sinew. Behind the buckskin trousers what promised to be a truly magnificent erection strained to be set free.

A slow fire smoldered in his eyes, burning away the wary look he'd worn earlier. Emboldened, Phoebe reached out to unbutton his trouser flap. She slid both hands inside to the taut buttocks beneath. He wasn't wearing smallclothes. Knowing him as she now did, she supposed she shouldn't be surprised. Surprised or not, she felt glad—eager—nor was she alone. Robert took a swift step to the side and quickly shucked the garment off.

He turned back to her with a tentative smile, but then he

knew what she was seeing. More scars hacked across his hips and buttocks; the outside of his right thigh bore a mark where he'd been branded, whether by pirates or slavers she couldn't yet know. Sometime in the future near or far he would tell her, she supposed, but for now it scarcely mattered. The time for talking was past, that for loving upon them.

His cock was thick and full, the engorged head damp and luscious. Scarcely knowing what she did, she reached for him. Her fingers cinched around him. He groaned and pushed himself hard into her hand. Encouraged when he neither flinched nor moved away, she stroked him, learning his shape and texture and strength. He was sheathed in satin and forged of steel, and thinking of how soon she would cover him with more than her hand raised a beautiful budding ache.

A bead of moisture blessed her palm, and she had the sudden mad notion to go down upon her knees and taste him there, to love him with her mouth and tongue as he had her. Before she could, he moved out of her grasp.

"I need to be inside you," he said and lifted her into his arms. "I can't wait any longer. I don't want to wait."

Phoebe laid her hand along the plane of his jaw. "I don't want to wait either."

Planks creaked as he crossed the cabin to the bed, a huge canopied affair covered in fringed pillows and draped in scarlet velvet. Reaching it, he laid her upon the center and came down atop her, his powerful arms and thighs banding her body.

Staring up into his taut face and feral eyes, she reached for her courage. "Before we...do this, I have a confession to make too. The other night, I allowed you to believe I'd lain with Aristide. I didn't."

Stroking the hair back from her temple, he said, "You waited for me?"

Phoebe swallowed hard. The subterfuge seemed silly now, a last resort to salve wounded pride. "I did. Even believing you were dead, I couldn't bring myself to be with him or anyone else. I knew it was mad, I told myself *I* must be mad, and yet I waited."

He broke into that smile she so loved, the smile that she now knew was for her alone, the broad-faced grin that brought out the little crinkles at the corners of his eye. "It's bloody selfish of me, I know, but I'm glad, Phoebe, so glad."

"So am I," she admitted, those six lonely years suddenly seeming worthwhile, for they had led her to this. "Are you quite certain you won't mind having a virgin on your hands?" Not that she imagined she would remain that way for much longer. The penis pressing against her seemed to say that her time as a virgin was down to mere minutes.

Robert's smile wavered. "I am honored to be your first and, God be willing, your only. I only hope you won't mind your first time being with a virgin as well."

Scarcely able to credit her ears, she said, "Robert?"

He nodded. "I waited as well."

"Why didn't you tell me before?"

He shrugged. "It's scarcely the sort of thing a man brags about."

"But the other night in my bedchamber, you seemed so—"

"Eastern societies are more open about sexual congress than ours is. Being a slave means living in close quarters. I've witnessed others engage in lovemaking acts I was mad to try but only, *only* ever with you."

Awed and aroused, Phoebe looked at him, unable to believe her great good fortune. His rippling muscles, the coarse hair blanketing his breastbone and thighs, even the scars webbing his shoulders and back, everything about him was unbelievably erotic and sublimely beautiful—and he belonged entirely to her. Beyond modesty, she spread her thighs and tented her knees. He moved to kneel between them. He braced his hands beneath her buttocks. She hooked hers upon his scarred shoulders and lifted herself against him.

His swollen member pressed against her inner thigh. With his fingers he spread her wide, teasing apart the folds of flesh and dipping into her channel as if testing her readiness. Phoebe had never felt more ready in her life. Liquid pooled in her belly. A humming ache emanated from the place his fingers probed. A callus-thickened thumb swiped over her pearl, drawing a delicious staccato ache.

Reaching between them, he fitted himself to her, his engorged shaft pulsing against her. Glancing down, Phoebe didn't see how they could begin to fit, but she trusted he would find a way. "I may be a virgin, but I shan't be an oaf, I swear it. I'll hold back and show the restraint that a woman's first time merits."

"Don't hold back. I don't want you to hold back."

It was the truth. She didn't want him to withhold any part of himself, not even if it meant hurting her. Heart pounding, she could scarcely wait for him to breach her, to be joined together in the most intimate of ways.

He entered her in one clean thrust, burying himself to the base. Pain knifed through her. Phoebe sucked in a breath, feeling as though she'd been torn in twain.

Robert stilled. "Are you all right?"

Looking up into his concerned face, Phoebe mustered a smile. "I am." Even in the midst of it, the hurting was a small price to pay for such profound connection.

Robert began to move slowly back and forth inside her. A warm and quite pleasant tingling replaced the pain. Phoebe closed her eyes, relaxing into the rhythm. His strokes came faster. The inner barrier she'd first felt seemed to have broken away. Instead she savored the sense of being replete, filled.

The blunt pressure built, *deepened.* Lifting herself, Phoebe met him stroke for stroke. Soon they were moving in unison so sublime that it was impossible to tell where he ended and she began. She lashed her hands to his scarred shoulders and cinched her legs about his torso.

Suddenly Robert withdrew. Reaching between them, he slipped his thumb into the center of her slickness. Swift circles brought her buzzing. Digging her nails into his ruined flesh, she felt herself spurting. He slid his cockhead along her slickness and stroked into her once more. Her body trembled. Her heart trilled. Her mind shut off to anything and anyone beyond the magnificent man making her his. Clutching him hard, she came, her body and world splintering.

A final thrust carried him over the cliff edge with her. "Phoebe, Phoebe, Phoebe..."

He pumped into her, his hoarse shouts filling her with feminine triumph. Limbs still wrapped about him, she squeezed her eyes closed and surrendered to the pleasure and peace of being well and truly claimed.

"Regrets?" Robert asked a while later, slipping back into bed with a flagon of wine and Phoebe's discarded betrothal ring and chain in his fist. He'd found the latter lying on the floor near her clothes.

Phoebe lifted herself on one elbow. "I wish I'd let you ruin me six years ago. I rather fancy being a fallen woman."

Laughing, he pulled her back down beside him. "Enjoy it while you can. A special license will allow us to marry in two or three days anywhere we wish. For now I think it's time you returned this, don't you?" He unfurled his fingers, revealing Aristide's chain and ring.

Lifting her head from his shoulder, Phoebe looked down at it with obvious distaste. "I shall do so with pleasure. If I had my druthers, I'd toss it into the Thames, but I suppose I really ought to see it returned. The ruby really is quite fine, but I never could bring myself to have it sized."

She raised it to show him, the distinctive foiled-gold shank freezing his stare. From their first encounter at the betrothal ball, something about Bouchart had raised his hackles, and not only because of their rivalry for Phoebe. There'd been something both familiar and unsavory about the Frenchman that had made Robert's belly clench and the hairs at the back of his neck rise almost as if...almost as if he had some prior cause for fearing him.

"She's a pretty piece, your woman. What's her name?" the pirate captain had asked, pointing to Phoebe's miniature, the heavy ruby ring, too large for his finger, slipping about his slender digit.

"Phoebe Tremont, Phoebe Tremont, Phoebe Tremont..."

Aristide Bouchart. Arthur Trent. They were the same man!

Heart hammering, Robert turned to look full on at Phoebe. "This ruby is the same worn by the pirate captain who tortured and killed without mercy. Sailing under the black flag, he went by the name Arthur Trent, but you know him as—"

"Aristide!" Phoebe shoved a fist against her mouth.

Robert nodded, swallowing against his throat's knotting, the enormity of what he'd done only now beginning to sink in. "He discovered my padlock locket and seized it. From the moment he set eyes upon your miniature, the questioning began. Who were you, what were you. He made it clear he meant to have your name. At the time I couldn't think why; still I was determined not to give it up. Indeed, everything in me screamed to withhold it even if doing so meant my death."

"Oh, Robert, no!"

"Your meeting him in London was no happenstance. Don't you see? He sought you out because of me, because I gave you up."

Bouchart, or rather Trent, must have thought to retire from piracy and marry into wealth. Eventually he'd made his way to London and sought out Phoebe. How delighted he must have been to discover that the miniaturist had, if anything, understated her beauty.

Eyes huge, she shook her head. "I almost wed a pirate. You warned me that he was dangerous, but I was so stubborn, I refused to credit it."

"Don't thank me just yet. It was my fault that he sought you out. Fifty lashes in, he broke me and I gave you up. I shouldn't blame you were you unable to bear the sight of me."

She reached out and laid a hand along his jaw. "You were under torture. You had no choice."

"Did I not? There is always a choice." Too ashamed to meet her gaze, he stared up at the ceiling timbers.

Slender arms banded about him. Soft lips pressed against his cheek. "There is naught to forgive and much to be grateful for. Had you not returned and been so intractable in your pursuit of me, I would be bound to a ruthless pirate in a few short weeks. Cannot you see—you *saved* me."

Heartened and humbled by her generosity, he turned to face her. "Earlier you asked me again why I stayed away for six years and let you think me dead. Now you have the whole of your reason. What I'd done was already unforgivable. How could I compound my sin by inflicting you with the wreck I'd been reduced to?"

"Is that what 'Mother Geneva' meant by saying you feared I might see you as less than a man?"

"Yes."

Framing his face between her palms, she said, "Look into my eyes and tell me what you see."

Probing her eyes' misty blue depths, Robert found only love. Phoebe's love for him shone brightly as any northern star, as fathomless as the sea itself.

"Once and for all, there is naught for you to feel guilty about and nothing for me to forgive."

He shrugged. "That is a subject of some dispute, but what is clear is that there is a great deal to be done. When I first returned to London, I made my report to your brother at the

Admiralty."

Her face registered shock. "Reggie has known all along! But he's never breathed a word."

Robert hadn't imagined he had, and yet it was heartening to hear that his trust had not been misplaced. "I know he's a bit of a black sheep, but so far as his diplomacy and discretion, I believe he's deserving of more credit than he's given."

"What do you mean to do?"

"I was a coward six years ago, but I will be a coward no more. I cannot leave a pirate on the loose in London. I must see justice served."

"Promise me you won't kill him—not for his sake but for yours."

He shook his head. "I wish I could, but I cannot. You see, I have learned one lesson. Heretofore, I am done with making promises I may not be able to keep."

Chapter Fifteen

Dawn was but breaking when Robert handed Phoebe down from the hackney carriage. "I know it's hard to part, but until I can bring Bouchart to justice, your parents' house is the safest place for you. Plead a headache if you must and remain locked in your room until I come for you."

Phoebe wasn't at all certain she would need to "plead" anything. Knowing the atrocities of which Aristide—or rather Arthur Trent—was capable, and that Robert meant to rout him out, had brought on the beginnings of one already. "What of you?"

He shrugged, as though his safety were of secondary concern. "If all goes as planned, by the day's end your former fiancé will be clapped in irons and under guard in the Old Bailey facing charges of murder and piracy on the high seas."

"*If* all goes as you plan. What if it does not?"

"It shall. Know that I am not alone in this. I have Caleb at my side and Montrose too."

"I'd feel better if you'd let me go with you as well." Waiting seemed to be a lady's lot. Just once she wished she might be in the thick of things and truly useful. "I could help, draw him out perhaps. He does not yet know I am aware of his true identity. I could say I've rethought breaking off our engagement and—"

"No!"

Phoebe blinked. Despite all their sparring of the past weeks, this was the first time he'd raised his voice to her.

In a milder tone, he said, "I love you for your loyalty and your lion's heart, but a man of Trent's ilk is not to be trifled with. You've seen his handiwork emblazoned upon my body, and it is far from the worst of the atrocities he's committed. Once I reveal him to the magistrate as an imposter and a pirate, he will not hesitate to use those I love against me both from spite and to secure his safe passage out of England. Promise me you'll do as I ask and stay within until I return?" He gestured to the townhouse, the windows as yet dark.

"Very well, I *promise*."

Expression easing, he nodded. "And for God's sake, do whatever you must to send that maid of yours packing."

"With pleasure," she said though she had a feeling that after the other day Betty might well have decamped of her own accord already. If she was indeed Aristide's mole, now that their betrothal was broken, she must know her mischief-making on his behalf was done.

He leaned in to kiss her. Phoebe lifted her face and met his seeking mouth with hers. Despite the passion they'd shared aboard ship, the closemouthed kiss jellied her knees and set her heart aflutter.

Taking a shaky step back, she smiled up at him. "A kiss in plain view of my parents' house, s'faith sir, you've grown bold to take such liberties with a lady's reputation. My father might well make you marry me for it," she added with a wink.

Robert grinned. "Had I known that was all that was required, I would have kissed you on the street weeks, no, *years* ago. Let what tongues wag that will. Before the week is out, you will be my wife in every way. For now, bear up, be brave."

Bear up. Be brave. Six years ago, he'd taken his leave with fair near the same words.

"You should go inside now," he said, tucking the pelisse about her. "I will wait here until you are safely within." Dropping his hands, he stepped back and turned to climb into the carriage.

Heart sinking, Phoebe caught at his sleeve. "Have a care, my love. I don't believe I could bear it were you taken from me a second time."

"I shan't be," he said with conviction.

She swallowed against her throat's knotting. "Mind no more making me promises you cannot be certain to keep."

He laid a hand upon either of her shoulders. Holding her at arm's length, he looked deeply into her eyes. "Do as I bid, and I *swear* upon our love and all that I hold most sacred and dear that I will come back and claim you as my bride."

Head reeling with the discoveries of the past twenty-four hours, body deliciously tender from their night of loving, Phoebe nodded. "Very well, then I will do as you say—this time."

Tears pooled in her eyes. Before he might see them, she turned swiftly away. Intimately aware of his gaze following her, she crossed to the house's fenced front yard.

The gate opened near soundlessly, likewise her key turned smoothly in the front door lock. Offering up a rare sentiment of gratitude to her mother, who was ever after the servants to oil all hinges, Phoebe pulled the door quietly closed behind her. Tiptoeing through the foyer, she saw that not quite all the rooms were dark. Relying on the light of a single Argand lamp, a housemaid knelt at the grate in the front parlor, laboring with brush and dustbin.

Thankful for her soft-soled slippers, Phoebe made to slip past. A board's creak gave her away. The girl twisted her head around to the open doorway, her eyebrows shooting up when she caught sight of Phoebe. Phoebe's heart stopped and then started anew. Provided Providence was willing, she would be a wife in another few days, her nocturnal wanderings of note to none. Still, much like good manners, discretion hurt no one and cost nothing. Lifting a finger to her lips, she crept toward the stairs. Ascending, she fought a silly sense of foreboding prompted by how quiet it was. The silence was so complete she might have detected a pin's dropping. She was being a goose, of course. Naturally the house was uncommonly hushed. It had just broken dawn. Even her early rising father would still be snoring in his bed. Stepping off the landing, she bypassed her parents' and Belinda's rooms and hurried down the hall to hers.

She slipped inside, brought the door closed behind her, and sank back against the paneled wood. "Pippin," she whispered, gaze searching the dimness. "Mummy's home." Her gaze went from the bed to the basket and back again, but no furry face appeared in greeting. "Pippin," she said again, more loudly, too concerned to care whom she might awake.

Crossing to the bed, panic climbed her throat. Hers was a modest-sized chamber. There were only so many places a small dog might conceal himself. She threw her reticule upon the counterpane and went down on all fours. Pulling up the ruffled bed duster, she peered beneath. Empty. Rising, she searched his other favorite hiding place, the wardrobe, but he was not there either. Her gaze snagged on her writing desk, the tool for Betty's duplicity! Dreading what she might find, she walked over to it. A single sheet of written-upon foolscap lay atop, penned in what she now recognized as Betty's coarse, looping hand.

If you want your dog back alive, come to Serpentine Bridge in Hyde Park—alone.

Phoebe froze. Her thoughts whirled back to the burn she's spied atop Betty's breast. No popping cinder had struck that intimate spot, but for a lover with a sadistic streak access would present no problem. Aristide must have bedded Betty as a first step to persuading her to spy for him; otherwise why on earth would she commit such wanton cruelty?

Gone was the loving glow that had warmed Phoebe but a few minutes ago. Knowing the lengths to which Betty was capable, she felt as though her veins bore ice water in lieu of blood. Her hope for getting Pippin safely back lay in persuading the girl that she no longer stood as her rival. Once Betty learned of the broken-off engagement, she would have no cause to act out of spite. Provided Phoebe retrieved Pippin before Betty learned of Aristide's capture and arrest, all might yet be well.

She would need to act swiftly.

But Robert would never countenance her meeting the maid alone, nor would she blame him. Still, if her plan went awry, someone should know of her whereabouts. Dipping the much-abused quill in the inkpot, she scratched out a brief addendum directly below Betty's threat. Heart drumming, she sprinkled sand to set the ink, folded the paper and penned Chelsea's direction on the outside. There was no time to spare for heating the sealing wax—then again, the contents weren't meant to be private.

She hesitated, turned back and picked up the silver-handled pocketknife used for sharpening the quill. Hoping she'd have no need of it, she nonetheless dropped it inside her reticule and hurried out, carrying the letter with her.

The household would be awakening soon. There was no time to waste. Alighting from the landing, she headed back into the parlor where the sleepy-eyed maid seemed to have nodded off, her bin and brush discarded.

Phoebe bent, rousing her with a gentle shake of shoulders. "I need you to go below to the kitchen and find a footman to deliver this without delay," she said, pressing the letter into the girl's sooty hand along with a coin from her purse.

The girl's heavy lids lifted. "Gorm, a guinea!"

Straightening, Phoebe supposed it was a great deal of money to give as a gratuity, but so long as the parlor maid saw the service discharged, she would have earned every shilling. "Tell Charlie or Freddie or whomever delivers it that there'll be one for him as well once I return."

She spun away and stepped back out to the foyer. Footfalls fueled by fear, she cut across the black-and-white tiles to the door. Reaching for the knob, the irony of her circumstances wasn't lost on her. This time she, not Robert, was the one to break her promise.

But with Pippin's very life at stake, there was no help for it. She could only hope that her beloved pirate would prove swifter to forgive than she.

Standing outside Aristide's rented rooms, Robert exchanged a charged look with Anthony. "Now."

At Robert's nod, Anthony summoned his most lordly tone. "Aristide Bouchart otherwise known as the pirate Arthur Trent, I command you to open this door by the authority vested in me as a peer of the realm and a loyal subject of His Majesty King George."

Anthony's War Office contact had confirmed that while the Bouchart name was indeed one of Normandy's oldest and most noble, the revolution had also rendered it extinct. The last of his line, the true Aristide Bouchart, seventh Count of Beaumont, had come to his end at the kiss of Madame Guillotine at the ripe age of eighty.

They waited in silence. Not surprisingly, there was no response from within. Robert turned to Anthony. "Are you thinking what I'm thinking?"

"We're going to have to break down the door?"

Robert nodded. "If it's all the same to you, I'd appreciate doing the honors. The fellow did try to have me killed twice, perhaps thrice."

"Be my guest," Anthony said, drawing the dueling pistol from his pocket and backing away to make room. "With my gamey leg, my door-breaking days are done. I am, however, an excellent shot."

Planting his weight on his left leg, Robert hauled back and drove his boot heel into the door. Several more well-placed kicks in the vicinity of the lock plate saw the wood splintering and the knob left hanging at half mast.

Robert unsheathed his cutlass and charged within. Anthony followed, pistol at the ready. The unnatural quiet sent Robert's stomach sinking. A room-to-room search confirmed their quarry had fled.

"Bloody hell," Anthony cursed, lowering his weapon. "Shall we away to the magistrate's?"

Robert shook his head, the sinking feeling segueing to full-on dread. "You go on, and I'll meet you there as soon as I may. I have to warn Phoebe."

The city was still cloaked in fog when the hackney left Phoebe off at Hyde Park Corner. Blunt-featured and fatherly, the driver cast a concerned look down from the box. "Ye sure ye should be strolling the park at this 'our? A lady such as yerself could run afoul o' footpads or worse."

"Thank you for your concern, but I shall be fine," Phoebe answered. Passing him the funds for her fare, she prayed that promise at least would be proven true.

Approaching the entrance gate, she paused to take a quick look about. Satisfied that no one followed, she continued through. Barring a few solitary horsemen, the park was deserted at this early hour. She took one of the railed footpaths skirting Rotten Row and leading toward the lake. Chiding herself for not taking the time to change from slippers to boots, she forged ahead, the dampness seeping into her soles. Fifteen or so minutes later, the Serpentine came into view. Skirting it, she swallowed against the lump constricting her throat. The lake with its stock of waterfowl had been Pippin's preferred promenade from puppyhood.

Coming up on the arched bridge bisecting the lake, she allowed that her footwear wasn't the only preparation upon which she'd skimped. Her papa's pair of dueling pistols would have been a far more practical armament than a quill sharpener. Then again, the one time she'd fired a flintlock, the kickback had nearly felled her.

A dog's high-pitched bark had her picking up her skirts

and quickening her steps. Gaining the bridge, she took a set of side stairs to its top.

Squinting through the mist, she called out, "Pippin!"

The barking was by now more muted but still coming from close by.

"Pippin!"

A heavy body slammed into her from behind, throwing her forward. Feeling as though she'd been struck by a boxing bag, she struggled against the wiry arm banding her. She opened her mouth to scream but before she could, her attacker shoved a balled-up cloth inside. The coarse sack pulled over her head robbed her of sight and any smell beyond must.

Trapped, still she struggled, kicking out with legs and feet, but it was no use. Her soles left the ground; seconds later her body upended as she was hefted high and hung headfirst over a hard shoulder. Heavy footfalls bore her forward. Head knocking against her kidnapper's backbone, she fought back panic. From the first she'd known Betty's note was meant to trap her, but she'd thought that, as long as she stayed in the open, she might prevail in rescuing Pippin and getting them safely away. Only now did she realize just how gravely she'd underestimated her enemy.

Her kidnapper must be descending by way of the bridge steps. They reached the bottom, his stride leveling. His soles no longer scraped stone but were muffled as if treading on some spongier surface.

"She's a cunning one is milady," a woman, Betty, called out, her Cockney accent thicker now that she was out of service. "Mind you hold on tight."

Resolved to make the best use of the senses still left to her, Phoebe cocked an ear to listen.

"I don't need a stupid bitch like you telling me my job," Phoebe's captor shot back.

Phoebe would wager Robert's locket that the man holding

her was one of the two who'd pursued them through the market. Robert had tried convincing her they were Aristide's henchmen, but as usual she'd been too stubborn to heed him. *Oh, foolish Phoebe!*

"You'll keep a civil tongue and take the box if you know what's good for you," Betty snarled.

The box—so they were at a carriage. Determined to mark whatever other clues she might, she caught the creak of what must be the opening of a door prone to sticking.

He shifted her to his opposite shoulder as if she were as senseless as the sack shrouding her. "Bugger off." A hard hand clamped down upon her buttocks.

Fighting dizziness, she felt herself being passed up.

A second set of arms received her. "Have a care you don't muck up my cargo," a familiar male voice spoke up.

Aristide! Gone was the French accent, yet the voice was unmistakably his.

Had he eluded Robert? Or perhaps he hadn't eluded him at all but had escaped by doing him some harm? The prospect struck terror into her heart. Robert had not been back for a full month and yet she couldn't imagine her world without him in it. Whether they sparred or made love scarcely mattered. She needed him to feel fully alive. Thinking of how much of the past precious weeks she'd wasted in attempts to push him away brought her awash in regret. Assuming they survived to find their happiness together, she'd not make the same mistake again.

They settled her upright. Hands, none too gentle, pulled off the sack. Blinking, Phoebe stared across to Aristide and Betty sharing the seat opposite her. The former maid held a cocked flintlock aloft. Thinking of the myriad times that same hand had passed a brush through her hair or poured her a cup of tea, Phoebe shuddered.

"You scream and I off the dog," Betty warned, pointing the

pistol downward.

Phoebe followed its direction to the carriage floor to Pippin at her feet. Meeting his wary brown eyes, her heart lurched. She reached out, and he nuzzled his wet nose into her palm. So far as she could tell, they hadn't hurt him, but who could say how long that would last? Fighting tears, she was reminded that hers and Robert's lives weren't the only ones her stubbornness had placed in peril.

Looking back at her captors, she answered with a mute nod before removing the gag.

"Pippin, darling."

Rising onto his hind legs, he planted his front paws upon her knee, tail wagging. Lifting him onto her lap, Phoebe assessed her choices, admittedly slim. Her limbs had been left unbound. Was it possible that she might jump down from the carriage and flee? With Pippin in her arms, how could she break her fall? It was full daylight now, a rather brilliant spring morning. The park would be filling fast. If she screamed, someone might well hear her.

Eying Betty, she put aside that possibility as well. The maid's finger was on the trigger and her bearing suggested that she would require little in the way of persuasion to pull back. Firing at point-blank range, she couldn't miss. No, Phoebe's only course was to sit tight and await a safer opportunity. Once her letter arrived at Chelsea's, Robert would come searching for her. He *had* to.

Arms about her dog, she focused on Aristide, or rather Arthur Trent.

"Why not simply let me go?" she asked, hoping to appeal to his reason. "What can you possibly have to gain by holding me? You shall never get away with this."

A smile slanted his lips. He rapped his knuckles on the carriage ceiling and the vehicle lurched forward. "Never, my girl, is the very devil of a long time."

Robert arrived at the Tremont townhouse as the household was settling into its morning routine. The butler led him to the breakfast room occupied by Lord Tremont alone. A napkin tucked into his neck cloth, the older man pushed back his chair and rose.

"Bellamy, I hadn't thought to see you within these four walls so soon," he said and despite his affable smile, the oblique reference to the debacle with the maid wasn't lost on Robert. "I was coming to believe Phoebe and I were the only denizens of Mayfair to begin their day before noon. But don't stand about. Fill a plate and join me." He gestured to the sideboard set with the ubiquitous covered serving dishes.

Under other circumstances, Robert would have been delighted to accept. But with Aristide on the lam, there was no time to waste. "Has Phoebe come downstairs yet?"

He waved Robert toward a chair and resumed his own. "No, she has not, which is bloody odd. Barring the other day after your...call, she takes breakfast with me every morning."

Robert remained standing. "About that—"

"For what it's worth, that business with our maid strikes me as balderdash, but I'd rather hear you say so."

Robert sucked down a deep breath. "On my life, and the love I bear your daughter, I swear that it was."

His lordship gave a gruff nod. "Good, splendid. Have you sworn as much to Phoebe?"

"I have. But to the purpose of my visit, I have reason to believe she may be in danger." As much as he wanted to believe that she'd sequestered herself in her room as promised, his sinking gut suggested otherwise.

Salt-and-pepper brows shot up. "Danger! What sort?'

As parsimoniously as possible, Robert relayed the happenings of the past weeks leading to the discovery that Bouchart was no French aristocrat but the Manchester-born pirate, Arthur Trent.

Lord Tremont raked his thinning hair with a trembling hand. “Do you mean to say I nearly gave my daughter’s hand in marriage to a pirate?”

“I’m afraid so, sir. But you mustn’t blame yourself. Even I who have been much abused by him failed to recognize Trent and Bouchart as the same man. But we can speak at length later. For now, kindly send someone to fetch Phoebe. I would assure myself of her safety before I continue my pursuit.”

“Of course.” Lord Tremont crossed the room to the bell pull.

Before he could reach it, Wilson appeared, towing along a young housemaid by her sleeve.

Coming up to the table, Wilson addressed his master. “Pray forgive the interruption, milord, but this chit has something to say to you.”

Red-faced, Lord Tremont shook his head. “Really, Wilson, you should know that any household concerns are to be taken up with my wife.”

“It concerns Lady Phoebe, milord.” The butler nudged the girl. “Go on, tell his lordship exactly what you’ve told me, and mind you do not omit so much as a syllable.”

Toeing the carpet, the girl began, “Well, ’tis like this. Lady Phoebe went... That is to say...”

Impatient with her hemming and hawing, Robert opened his mouth to deliver a much-needed prompt, but he was preempted by Lord Tremont. “Out with it!” he thundered, not sounding at all like the mild-mannered man Robert knew. “What have you to say about my daughter?”

“She’s not here.”

Robert’s heart froze.

“What do you mean she’s not here?” Lord Tremont demanded. “Of course she’s here. At this hour, where else would she be?”

“Well, er, I don’t want to get anyone in trouble, mind, but I was blacking the grates in the parlor in the wee hours this morning when I chanced to see Lady P passing by on her way upstairs—fully dressed," she put in pointedly, cutting Robert a look. "A few minutes later she hastened back down and bade me find a footman to deliver a letter forthwith, but I...I got so caught up in ferrying breakfast trays up to Lady T and Miss B that it clear slipped my mind 'til now."

"Where is the letter?" Robert demanded.

"In me pocket, sir."

She dipped a hand into her apron, pulled out the folded paper and passed it to him. Robert unfolded the sheet. The large looping handwriting at the top was the same as before and obviously belonged to Betty. Reading it, his anger ratcheted. Using Pippin as a lure, he should have anticipated it. He skipped to the sparse message penned below in Phoebe's neat, spare hand.

Robert, I've gone for Pippin. I pray God that by the time you receive this, we will both be safely home. If not, please come as quickly as you can—and forgive me for breaking my promise. Yours Always, Phoebe.

Heart in his throat, he handed the note to Lord Tremont. Casting a meaningful look toward Wilson and the girl, he said, "Is there anything else?"

The maid shook her head. The butler ferried her out and closed the door behind them.

Left alone with Lord Tremont, Robert said, "The maid, Betty, is in league with Bouchart—Trent. I'm afraid Pippin is but bait to draw Phoebe from safety."

Lord Tremont regarded him with frightened eyes. "Why should he bother when he still believes they are to marry in a month?"

"Phoebe broke off their betrothal yesterday. I imagine he's feeling desperate." And a desperate man was a dangerous man, as Robert well knew.

"Where do you think he's taken her—and to what purpose?"

"I'd wager my last farthing he's taken her aboard his ship. Once he clears the harbor and reaches open sea... Well, we can't let that happen."

"No," Lord Tremont agreed, expression grim, "we cannot."

Robert hesitated. "I am aware this may well seem premature, even inappropriate, but as Phoebe's father I would have you know that your daughter has consented to become my wife."

"Did she?"

Robert nodded. "She did. While we both hope that you will once more grant us your blessing, you should also know that we are prepared to wed without it. *I* am prepared to wed her without it. And this time 'round, I shall dedicate my days to proving myself worthy of her." Having said his piece, Robert turned to go.

"Bellamy."

Heart drubbing, Robert turned back. "Yes, my lord?"

Crossing to the foot of the table, Lord Tremont stuck out his hand. "Welcome to the family."

Feeling like he'd aged to eighty, Lord Tremont took the stairs up to his wife's room. As he often did, he found her wearing out the Aubusson carpet with her pacing.

She caught sight of him on the threshold and paused. "I wish you would speak to your daughter. The wedding's a fortnight away and so far she refuses to show the slightest interest in the fittings for her trousseau. And the bridal veil—Honiton or Brussels lace, she simply must decide."

Seeing her still in curling papers and her wrapper, he hesitated and then crossed into the room. "I'm afraid there isn't going to be a wedding."

Her head shot up. "Don't be absurd. Of course there is."

"No, there is not."

"But—"

"Beatrice, *sit.*"

To their mutual shock she obeyed, subsiding onto the fainting sofa. Once he imparted his news, the furniture might well earn its name.

She looked up at him with frightened eyes. "Something's happened. Tell me...please."

He settled stiffly beside her and not only because his gout was acting up. It wasn't often he joined her in her sanctum. Despite thirty years and three children together, he still sometimes felt like an interloper. "Phoebe's been taken—kidnapped."

"*Kidnapped*!" The word emerged as a strangled sob. She steadied herself with a breath before asking, "Are you quite certain?"

"Regrettably I am."

She balled her slender hands into fists. "I'll have Bellamy strung up and—"

"Bellamy didn't take her. Bouchart did."

Her gaze flew to his. "To Gretna Green?"

"To his ship, or so we believe."

"We?"

He nodded. "Bellamy just left. He and Montrose have been looking into Bouchart's...background."

Calmer, she rolled her eyes. "As if we should credit the word of either of those bounders. Like as not this...elopement is a misguided, romantic gesture on Aristide's part to hasten the wedding."

As much as it hurt to make her see the truth, for all their sakes he steeled himself to do so. "Make no mistake, Phoebe is a hostage, not a bride, and Bouchart is no count but a bloodthirsty pirate by the name of Arthur Trent." There, he'd said it.

Her face crumpled. “A pirate! Our child is in the clutches of a—”

“Bellamy believes he means to hold her for ransom. If we refuse to pay it, he is likely to...sell her to the highest bidder once he clears British waters.”

Folding forward, she buried her head in her hands. “Our daughter’s life is in danger. She may be lost to us forever, forced into a life of degradation, and it’s my fault.”

“My dear, that’s simply not true.”

“Isn’t it?” Straightening, she fitted a hand over her brow. “She didn’t want to wed Bouchart or...whatever his name may be, but I pushed her. I’ve gone about this marriage business all wrong, and with calamitous consequences.”

Tremont sighed. As was the case with so many top-drawer families, they’d dealt too strictly with the daughters and too leniently with the son.

“You didn’t go wrong. *We* went wrong.”

She lifted her head and turned to face him. “But Tremont—”

“No buts, my dear, not this time. I’ll hold my peace no more. I’ve kept silent far too long as it is. If I’d stood up as a man should six years ago, the tragedy might have been averted. As matters stand, it looks as if Phoebe and her young man may have a second chance at happiness, and I mean to see that they get it.”

Her eyebrows shot to her brow line. “Tremont, whatever are you suggesting?”

“I’m not suggesting anything. I’m telling you plainly that once we have Phoebe safely back I mean to give her and Bellamy my blessing—and this time I intend to see that it sticks.”

“You wouldn’t!”

“I would—and I shall. Moreover, as of this moment, your

meddling machinations shall cease."

Lady Tremont covered her face with both hands. "Have I been that bad?"

Rather than answer that, he said, "I am as much to blame as you, perhaps more. I have shirked my duties as the man of the house for far too long. Whenever a problem arose, whether it was Reginald being sent down from Oxford or Phoebe threatening to elope, I ran off to my club or barricaded myself in my study and left you to bear the burden alone. For that, m'dear, I am truly sorry."

Uncovering her face, she stared at him with stricken eyes. "I'm the one who should be sorry. Only mind the mess I've made. Our children despise me. *You* despise me."

"That is simply not so." He hesitated and then reached for her, his hand hovering above her shoulder just short of settling. "Our children may not like your methods, but they love you." He drew a bracing breath and added, "*I* love you."

"You...*love* me?"

He didn't hesitate. "I do, with all my heart." His hand met her shoulder, fingers curving around the top.

"I...I suppose I love you too."

He hadn't expected that. "You do?"

Mouth trembling, she nodded. "Yes, I do."

They'd shared a roof for three decades and yet neither had said the words until now.

"Come here, wife."

"But, Tremont, 'tis full light."

"Yes, it is, isn't it?" Heedless of who might happen by, he took her in his arms and kissed her fully, passionately and resoundingly on the mouth. When he finally released her and rose to his feet, it was with the vigor of a much younger man.

She followed his progress to the door with her eyes. "Tremont, where are you off to?"

"To fetch my old cavalry sword."

"Whatever for?"

"So I can assist young Bellamy in bringing our girl home."

Chapter Sixteen

Robert, with Caleb, Anthony and Lord Tremont, stood on the wharf staring at the empty ship's berth. According to the harbormaster's log, Aristide's ship had departed an hour ago. Even though Robert had prepared himself for as much, hearing that his fear was not only founded but the reality came as crushing news.

Cursing a blue streak beneath his breath, he dragged a hand through his hair. "I need a boat."

Lord Tremont turned to him. "Isn't yours here in the harbor...somewhere?"

Steeling himself to patience, he shook his head. "The Swan is built for carrying cargo and weathering rough seas over long voyages, not speed. Bouchart has an hour's lead on us. Even with her hull empty, she'd never catch up, not in time."

Anthony spoke up. "Will a clipper ship do?"

Everyone turned to him.

"How did you come by a ship?" Robert asked. Chelsea's husband was a source of seemingly constant surprise.

Expression sheepish, Montrose admitted, "I won it in a game of faro at White's. Tell your sister I played that deep, and I'll be obliged to—"

"Where is she moored?"

"Rotherhithe."

"What are we waiting for? Let's away."

"What's your plan," Lord Tremont asked, hand on his sword hilt.

Robert exchanged looks with Caleb. "I don't as yet have

one," he admitted. "But while we're queuing up for clearance to depart, we'll have ample time to devise...something."

With the wind in their favor, the lithe little clipper ship overtook Aristide's frigate by twilight; however, Aristide's vessel carried sufficient guns to blow them out of the water. As much as Robert might want to board with weapons drawn, he held back.

"How is that plan coming along?" Anthony asked, approaching the wheel.

One hand resting upon it, Robert looked up. "The good news is I have one."

Anthony cocked a brow. "And the bad news?"

"I'm not at all sure it will work."

Seated, Phoebe faced her captor across the ship's cabin, resolved not to reveal how utterly terrified she was.

"What facile dupes you and your fine family proved to be," Trent taunted, his Manchester accent ringing forth from every vowel. "My one regret is that I must miss the opportunity to kill Bellamy after all—unless he's fool enough to follow."

Once they'd pulled up anchor, her heart had sunk. As long as she was in London, she'd held onto the hope that Robert would find her or that she would discover a means of escape. Now that they'd cast off and cleared the harbor, she felt adrift in every way.

Sending up a silent prayer that her beloved was somewhere safe, she demanded, "What do you mean to do with us?"

She cast a nervous look down to the "us" in question, Pippin curled up in her lap. She was doing her best to keep him out of the way. So far Trent had been kept too busy charting their course to make good on his various threats to drown or cook him. Betty had dealt him a kick in passing. The squeal he'd let out had made Phoebe want to tear out every hair in the maid's head. Were it not for the presence of the primed pistol, she might have done so. As it was, she'd scooped him up into her arms and ran her hands over his body, assuring herself that no lasting damage was done—yet. With the sun fast setting and the rum flowing above and below deck, Phoebe couldn't say how much longer her or Pippin's luck would hold.

Left alone for long periods, she'd managed to slip the letter opener from her reticule into her bodice. Even to her untrained eye, the hastily mustered crew looked to be a ragtag lot. If she could manage to overcome her captor or even Betty, perhaps the others might be persuaded to turn the ship around or at least to let her and Pippin off at the next port? Unlikely as that scenario was, she refused to give up hope, not now when she had so very much to live for. For perhaps the first time, she fancied she understood something of what Robert must have gone through all those years ago. Every knot they traveled took her that much farther from everyone she cared for and loved.

His gaze bore into hers, his mouth quirking. "Exactly that which I set out to do from the first: marry you."

After the events of the past twenty-four hours, Phoebe had thought she was beyond shock but apparently that was not so. "You must be mad to think I would marry you now."

He shrugged. "Mad? Hardly. Before Betty left, she slipped my note beneath your dear Papa's study door. Who knows, perhaps he is even now reading it, including the sum I require to make an honest woman of you."

"You expect my parents to *pay* you to marry me? You must be even madder than I'd thought. After all you've done, I shouldn't count on receiving so much as a farthing."

He shrugged. "They are free to refuse, of course. Should they elect to do so, I am acquainted with a certain Middle Eastern pasha who has a penchant for blue-eyed blondes."

Phoebe lifted her chin. "He could not possibly be more monstrous than you."

Smiling, he crossed toward her and instinctively she drew Pippin as close as she could. "Trust me when I say that marriage to me would prove the lesser of two evils." He glanced pointedly down to Pippin. "Along with the flesh of English roses, the pasha has a great appetite for tender little dogs."

At Robert's direction, they waited until full dark, and then he, Anthony and Caleb rowed out in a dinghy. It had required several assurances that the decision had naught to do with his age or gout, but Lord Tremont was finally persuaded to stay behind and "guard" their boat.

The plan in place, no one spoke, the tension within the small boat as thick as the soupy mist. Caleb's hands stayed fixed on the oars. Drawing up beside the frigate, they heard the raucous sounds of revelry filtering down from the lower deck. The noise neatly masked the splash Robert made when he eased himself over the side of the craft into the water. Surfacing, he dragged wet hair from his eyes and grabbed hold of the side.

"Good luck," Anthony whispered, breaking their communal silence.

Robert divided his gaze between his brother-in-law and Caleb. "Thanks, I'll need it." He gave Anthony the agreed upon signal.

"Man overboard!" Montrose shouted in his best army command voice.

Robert released his grip, swam toward the frigate and made a show of flailing.

On board, chaos ensued. Lanterns were directed out onto the water. A rope and ladder were cast out. Robert grabbed hold and let himself be reeled in.

Like a hooked fish, he flopped upon the deck. A half dozen pairs of feet rushed up to him. Light blinded him. A booted toe poked his side. The odor of unbathed bodies mingled with that of rum and rotting teeth. Once Robert would have found himself fighting the urge to wretch, but by now he was well-accustomed to such stenches.

"Ho, 'e's not one o' ours," someone in the crowd called out.

Prepared, Robert pulled himself upright. "No, I'm not." Gaining his feet, he cast a quick confirming glance beyond them before adding, "And neither are they."

Anthony and Caleb had gained the deck behind him. Flintlocks drawn, they strode up to the crew's rear. Unlike Robert, Montrose was scarcely damp. "Couldn't risk wetting the gunpowder," he said with a smile. Addressing himself to the others, he shouted, "Hands in the air!"

"Why should we?" one man called out. "C'mon lads, we outnumber them."

A few others balked—and then Caleb came forward. Gazes rounded. Smiles fell. Slouched postures straightened. Arms shot skyward—and stayed there. Looking pleased with himself, the Arab stopped at each man, patted him down and relieved him of his weaponry. By the time he'd finished, an impressive pile of knives, razors, brass knuckles and even a cutlass or two was amassed on deck.

Robert picked the gold-toothed man out from the outskirts of the pack. "You." He advanced on him.

Showing his coward's stripes, the villain began backing up. "Twas nothin' personal, mate. I was only 'ryin' ter make ends meet. *Thee* see 'ow i' is."

Robert rounded on him. "Oh, indeed I do."

He hauled back—and let his fist fly. The blow struck the henchman squarely in the mouth, sending blood spurting. "That's for cutting my cinch."

Grabbing him by the hair, he lobbed another blow, this one to the nose. The crunch of cartilage beneath his knuckles was an immensely satisfying sensation. "And that was for ambushing us and beating my friend at Billingsgate Market."

The man tried throwing up his arms to shield his face, but it was no use. "And this is for burning that warehouse and destroying my property. Correct me if I'm mistaken, but I'm thinking that was you as well." Robert seized the opportunity to land another blow, this one to the gut. "Oh, and I believe I owe you one more—for kidnapping my lady. By the by, where the hell is she?"

"She be in...one of the cabins below." Air whistled through the gap where his gold teeth had been.

Robert grabbed him by the collar and hauled him to his feet. "Which cabin specifically?"

"The...the quartermaster's, I think 'tis."

"Think?"

"Nay, 'tis the quartermaster's for sure."

Robert released him and he staggered back. Reaching down, Robert scooped up the bloodied gold teeth from the deck and flung them toward him. "You'd best hold onto these. Count on bed and board at Newgate Gaol costing you dearly—mate."

As planned, Anthony stood guard over the prisoners while Caleb went off to foul the ship's guns.

Heart hammering, Robert headed below to search for Phoebe, a version of his erstwhile prayer drubbing his head with every step taken.

Dear God, let her be well.

Dear God, let it not be too late.

Not too late, not too late, not too late...

Pacing the cabin's four corners, Pippin watching her from the place he'd claimed upon the straw pallet, Phoebe allowed that activity, even pointless activity, was preferable to sitting about brooding upon her unhappy fate. Now that Robert and she had made love, she couldn't begin to imagine sharing that ultimate intimacy with anyone else. The threat of Trent's touch sent her flesh crawling.

Footfalls outside her cabin had her sliding the letter opener free from her bodice. Standing behind the door, she braced herself to attack.

"Phoebe, are you within?"

"Robert?" Lowering the knife, she sagged against the cabin side.

"It is I, love. Are you able to open the door or are you bound?"

"I am unbound, but Aristide—Trent—has me locked within. To my knowledge, he has the only key."

"Listen carefully. I need you to stand back from the door, as far away as you can manage."

"I shall, only pray hold for a moment. I have to get Pippin." Quickly she picked up the dog, who had followed her over, and moved to the rear of the room. "We are ready," she called out.

Outside it sounded as though a battering ram was at work, but she suspected it was nothing more substantial than her lover's much abused body. Dear Lord, he meant to break down the door. More than meaning to, he *was* doing so. A dozen or so swift kicks saw the wood about the lock plate splintering. The door swung open and Robert stepped inside.

Phoebe set Pippin down and rushed to Robert. Reaching him, she wound her arms about his neck, hardly caring that he was still dripping seawater. "I thought I might never see you again."

A crooked smile skated cross his mouth. He slid an arm about her waist. "I'm trying to be better about keeping my promises." His gaze scoured her face. "He hasn't harmed you, has he?"

"No, though that witch, Betty, kicked my dog." She glanced over to Pippin, who'd climbed back onto the berth. "He's a bit stiff-legged, but I'm hoping he's only bruised."

"Don't despair. I'm going to get you both out of here."

Answering her unspoken question, he said, "Anthony and Caleb are with me, and your father as well. Anthony is standing guard over the crew."

"You overcame them, then?"

"We did, all but Trent." He hesitated and then admitted, "The rum helped."

Pippin's snarling sent them whipping about to the door. Trent stood on the threshold, a primed pistol in hand. "I should have killed you when I had the chance."

Phoebe gasped. Robert tightened his hold on her. "I could say the same."

Trent pointed the pistol at Phoebe. "I am offering you a choice—marry me or join your brash lover in Hell."

Before she fathomed what he was about, Robert shoved her behind him, shielding her body with his. "Any bullet of yours will have to pass through me first."

Trent smiled. "Fortunately I have no shortage."

Heart pounding, Phoebe tried pushing herself forward, but with arms flung out to his sides and legs akimbo, Robert had made himself as impassable as a mountain. "Pull the trigger if you must. I would rather endure a thousand deaths than spend a single day married to a monster."

Robert shot her a warning look over his shoulder. Dropping his voice, he pleaded, "Phoebe, please do not incite him. You must save yourself; otherwise I die in vain."

Adamant, she shook her head. "And I live in vain without him whom I love with all my heart. I think not. I've known that life for six years, and I have no wish to repeat it in earnest."

Trent shrugged. "So be it." He raised the cocked pistol, his finger easing back on the trigger.

Boom!

The ship teetered, knocking them all to their knees. Seizing on the distraction, Robert righted himself and rushed the pirate. They crashed to the floor. The pistol skittered across the planks.

Phoebe ran to retrieve it. Hands shaking, she trained it on the two combatants rolling about. Firing at point-blank range, she was bound to strike someone, but would it be Trent or Robert? Pippin joined in the fight. The spaniel sprang off the bed, tore over to where the two men struggled, and sank his teeth into Trent's calf. The pirate howled and rolled off Robert. Bounding to his feet, he pulled a razor from his boot and came at Robert at a crouch, slashing toward his torso.

Phoebe screamed, "Robert, look out!"

He dodged, and the slashing stroke meant for his eye grazed his forearm instead. Even so, seeing the scarlet staining his shirtsleeve, Phoebe let out a sob. Sweat streaked down her back between her shoulder blades; her hands holding the pistol were damp. She'd never willfully harmed a living soul in the whole of her life and yet looking on, she could see Aristide—Arthur—had no intention of giving up until Robert was dead.

What phrase was it Chelsea was fond of saying? *Desperate times call for desperate measures.* The struggle playing out before her was desperate indeed. Praying that her aim would prove true, Phoebe laid her finger on the trigger and slowly pulled back.

Pistol fire ricocheted through the cabin. Trent went slack. He folded face-first to the floor, blood and brains gushing from the hole at the back of his head.

The *back* of his head?

Choking on smoke, Phoebe dropped her gaze to her weapon, as yet unfired, and then looked across to the cabin threshold. Betty stood in the open doorway, a pistol in either hand, one smoking and the other primed.

"You've ruined everything," she said, shaking her head at Phoebe.

"Betty, please."

Gaze fixed on Phoebe, she fired.

The bullet whizzed by Phoebe's head, stirring the hair at her temple. Robert lunged, grabbing Betty's arm before she could reload. "Never doubt that I will break it," he threatened, and Phoebe fully believed that he meant it.

Arm locked about Betty, he forced the flintlock out of her hand and held it out for Phoebe to take.

Shaking, she approached. Taking the pistol and holding it at her side, she asked, "Why, Betty?"

The maid stared at her with cold hatred. "Why, what?"

Phoebe hesitated. "Why...any of it?"

Betty's firmed jaw slackened. Her mouth trembled. Tears filled her eyes. "He promised to make a lady o' me. Once we got hold of your fortune, he said we'd marry and go anywhere I fancied. And he might have too, if it wasn't for you."

"He was only using you, Betty," Phoebe said, feeling almost sorry for her—almost.

"I think it's time we rejoined the others," Robert said. "Your father especially will want to know you're safe."

Despite Betty between them, Phoebe found her smile. "Yes, let's go home."

Robert dragged the maid on deck. Phoebe followed, Pippin in her arms. Now that the danger was past, she felt a bit shaky. That they were all safe, as well as finally and forever together, seemed almost too enormous a boon to accept as real. Despite all the odds weighted against them, their love had prevailed, not only hers and Roberts but that of their family and friends as well. Even dear little Pippin was out of danger. It seemed a happy ending was to be theirs after all.

Anthony and Caleb held pistols on the crew, most of who had subsided to sit cross-legged on deck. Looking up as they approached, Anthony said, "I heard shots. Where is Trent?"

Robert tugged Betty forward. "Leaking his brains onto the cabin floor, thanks to this one."

"No honor among thieves, I suppose," Anthony said with a wry smile.

"More a case of 'hell hath no fury like a woman scorned,'" Robert remarked, casting the maid a glance.

Holding a lantern aloft, Anthony glanced down at Robert's sleeve. "You're looking the worse for wear." He shifted his gaze to Phoebe. "You, my dear girl, are braver than most commissioned officers I've known. How are you bearing up?"

"I could do with a bath and a nap," she admitted, "but mostly I'm feeling enormously fortunate to have the males in my life come to my rescue. Thank you all," she added, her grateful gaze encompassing Caleb. Holding back at the rail, he returned her smile.

Pippin spotted Caleb, or rather his turban, and let out a yip. Tail wagging, he sprang from her arms. Betty's earlier kick had left him stiff-legged. Seeing him skid toward the rail, Phoebe's pulse ratcheted. "Pippin, come back."

She started toward him. Before she could come nearer than a step, Betty took advantage of the distraction to break free. She snatched Pippin up, ran to the rail and hauled him over.

Heart in her throat, Phoebe stalled. "Betty, please don't do this."

"Why shouldn't I?" Holding the flailing dog over the side, the maid glared back at them. "You've taken everything from me—*everything*. I'm not stupid, you know. I ken what's coming. Once we make port, you'll turn me over to the magistrate. While you lot are tucked up cozy-like in your fine beds, I'll be tossed into a cell at Newgate. My next rendezvous will be with the hangman. Drowning this mangy mongrel is the least I can do."

Throat dry, Phoebe wasn't prepared to give up, not yet. Out of the corner of her eye, she spied two male shapes—Robert and Caleb—moving toward Betty. Determined to distract her, Phoebe said, "It doesn't have to be like that. Give Pippin back, and I swear I'll speak on your behalf, explain that Aristide—Arthur Trent—coerced you into acting as his accomplice. The burn mark on your breast shall stand as proof of it." Though stalling for time, still she meant every word.

Betty's anguished cry better befitted a cornered beast than a human. "Coerced! It wasn't only the future and being treated as a fine lady that bound me to him. I *loved* him."

Coming at Betty from opposite sides, suddenly Robert and Caleb sprang upon her. A scream rang out.

Heart hammering, Phoebe started toward them, prepared to join the fray, but a firm hand closing about her arm held her back. "Trust me, they know what they're about," Anthony said into her ear.

Phoebe nodded and directed her gaze ahead. With their backs to her and darkness shrouding most of the deck, all she could make out was flailing limbs and entangled clothing. A splash announced someone had gone overboard.

"Nooooo!" This time the anguished exclamation tore forth from Phoebe's throat. In that moment she would have given an eyetooth to be able to swim.

Two of the three silhouettes turned about: Robert and Caleb. Silent, Robert held out Phoebe's former cloak, which Betty had worn. Turban knocked askew and smile stretching from ear-to-ear, Caleb likewise proffered a bundle of some sort—only his moved.

"Pippin!" Phoebe raced to the rail. "Oh, Caleb, it is I who am forever in your debt." She reached out and took Pippin, shivering but otherwise unharmed, into her arms. Cradling him close, she divided her gaze between her two saviors. "Thank you."

Robert answered with a rueful smile. "We saved Pippin from Betty, but our talents did not extend to saving her from herself."

In unison, they turned toward the rail. Looking over it, Phoebe scoured the inky water, but beyond the breaking ripples, there was no sign of movement.

It seemed Betty had elected to cheat the hangman and join her pirate lover in death on her own terms.

Home, finally we're home.

The following morning, Robert stood on the deck of the clipper ship with Phoebe, Pippin wrapped up in a blanket in her arms. Hand-in-hand, they watched the London Docklands come into view.

"We're home, my love." He turned to her, his heart overflowing with an abundance of love and gratitude. For the first time since his return, he felt well and truly as if he was home for good.

Arm bound in a makeshift bandage, Robert gestured ahead. "Once we set foot back in London," he said, including Pippin in his gaze, "you may consider my adventuring days strictly in the past. Any future travels will be undertaken with you at my side."

The promise won him her tentative smile. "I am heartened to hear it, though it may be quite a while before I will want to look upon water again."

Winding his good arm about her waist, he drew her toward him. "What do you wish for as a wedding gift?"

She hesitated. "There is one thing."

"Name it."

"I want you to propose to me."

Robert stared, wondering if somehow he'd misheard. "Phoebe, love, how can you say that? I must have asked you to marry me a score of times these past three weeks."

She tilted her head as if studying him. "You didn't ask. You *told* me. They're not quite the same thing."

"Ah, I see. There are rules to this sort of thing, are there?"

"Not rules precisely, more in the way of ritual."

"I see." And so he did. Phoebe hadn't wanted to be claimed.

She wanted—deserved—to be courted.

Only too happy to oblige, he slipped down onto one knee. Looking up into her lovely, flushing face, he searched his soul for the words that he'd waited six years to say. He was no poet, but for the sake of the love he bore her, he resolved to do his best.

"I love you, Phoebe Elizabeth Tremont, with all my heart and all my mind and all my body. Rough fellow that I am, will you do me the honor of consenting to be my life mate, my soul's companion, my wife?"

"I shall upon one condition."

"And that is?"

She slanted him a shaky smile. "How quickly do you suppose you can procure that special license?"

The society column of The St. James's Chronicle, *one week later*

Despite its impromptu nature—and shocking lack of lace—the wedding of Lady P to Mister B was a lovely affair. The bride wore a gown of fine white muslin, the overskirt shot with primroses, and a garland embossed with white satin roses; the bridegroom a frock coat of dove gray, a dark blue waistcoat and a smile to rival the sun's brilliance. A wedding breakfast was held at No. 12 Berkley Square, the in-town residence of the groom's brother-in-law and sister, Viscount and Lady M. (Persons inclined to indulge in gossip will recall that Viscount M and Lady P were themselves once affianced.) Vast quantities of lobster patties and pates, jellies and puddings were consumed. Most unusually, a great mound of freshly shucked oysters took pride of place on the buffet table. Circulating among the celebrants were a tall, turbaned Arab, a menagerie of foundling children and the bride's spaniel dog, the latter with a blue satin bow festooning his collar.

Phoebe in his arms, Robert kicked the bridal chamber door closed behind them. Crossing to the bed, he set her down upon the rose-petal-strewn counterpane.

He dipped a hand into his coat pocket and brought out one of the two fluted glasses he'd procured. "Champagne, Mrs. Bellamy?"

Shaking the last remnants of rice from her skirts, she beamed back at him. "Yes, please, Mr. Bellamy."

He set out both glasses and reached for the chilled bottle of champagne setting in a bucket of ice on the bedside table.

Glancing at the door, she lowered her voice to ask, "Do you think anyone will come in search of us?"

Robert paused in pouring to look over at her. "They bloody well had better not."

"But they're bound to notice we've gone missing sooner rather than later. We are the guests of honor, after all."

He turned to hand her a full glass. "Let them. As I recall, Chelsea and Anthony scarcely made it through the first toast on their wedding day. Why do you think she insisted upon having this chamber prepared in advance?"

Accepting the champagne, she tried for a look of innocence. "To ensure we would be well rested before tomorrow's journey?"

In the morning, they would set out for Robert's estate in Sussex. Since the loss of his last cargo, he was no longer rich as Croesus, but he'd assured her he had more than sufficient funds set aside to restore his fields to profit.

He let out a laugh. "I hate to disappoint, Mistress Bellamy, but once I see you free of that very fetching gown, you shall receive little rest this night."

Phoebe smiled back. Resting was the very last notion upon her mind. With six years for which to make up, she was hard-pressed to keep her eyes, or hands, off her handsome husband for very long. "I shall take that as a promise."

They sealed the pact with a saluting of glasses, the crystal meeting with a soft clink.

Phoebe took a sip and set her glass aside. "After all your seafaring life, are you quite certain life as a country squire will suit?"

Robert pretended to ponder. "Hmm, let me think. Squalls, off-shore reefs and hidden shoals, fouled equipment, leaks and threats of fire, the perennial worry over replenishing drinking water and perishable foods and, of course, pirates—it is a great deal to give up. But with you by my side, I shall be most happy to live out my days as a landlubber." He pulled back to look at her. "What of you? Shall you miss London and the foundlings?"

Phoebe hesitated, feeling a pang in the vicinity of her heart. While she was fond of all her students, dear little Lulu would be by far the hardest with whom to part. The child had made the most adorable of flower girls. Knowing that on the morrow she must bid her goodbye for the foreseeable future was the one damper on an otherwise perfect day.

"As it happens, I've been thinking of establishing a sort of rural retreat for former charity children, an agricultural academy where boys and girls both might learn farming and animal husbandry. I'd start with a small group at first, of course—Lulu and a few of the others. What do you think?"

Biting her lip, she searched his face for some sort of reaction. Most husbands would frown upon a wife committing herself to such industry. Some might even forbid it.

Fortunately for her, Robert was not "most" husbands. Unruffled, he sat on the edge of the bed beside her. "It's a splendid idea. As soon as we've settled, I shall set up a time to present your plan to my steward."

"Oh, Robert, truly?" Beyond relieved, she reached out to embrace him.

"Yes, truly."

Pulling back to look at him, she saw that his earnest eyes confirmed he meant every word. "I too have given thought to our near future. I know that you have some quite...modern notions of how a marriage should go, no doubt seeded by my sister, but what say you to us setting up our nursery without delay?"

She pretended to prevaricate, though in truth nothing would delight her more. Joined in marriage to the love of her life, she was more than eager to begin their family forthwith. They'd already waited six years. Why delay so much as a single day?

Still, she couldn't resist teasing him just a bit. "Ah, so I see how it is, sir. I'm not even out of my bridal gown and already you're scheming to see me barefoot and breeding before our first six months are out."

"Well, yes to the breeding bit, but I have something specific in mind as well."

"I know that look, Robert Bellamy. What secret are you keeping from me this time?"

"Not a secret so much as a surprise. A wedding gift, one I'm particularly anxious to present."

Phoebe couldn't imagine what more in the way of gifting he might have in mind. The warehouse arson had been a great loss, but it had hardly beggared him. He'd already given her more pearls, emeralds and diamonds than her jewelry case could accommodate. By tacit agreement there'd been no rubies, though. Invariably intertwined in her mind with her last disastrous betrothal, the scarlet stone was one Phoebe vowed never to wear again.

"Considering it's from you, I'm sure I shall love it whatever it is."

"Not what, but *who.*"

She hesitated, turning the possibilities over in her mind. "Pippin is a bit jealous-natured where I am concerned and somewhat inclined to cling since his kidnapping. I'm not certain adopting a second dog is such a good idea."

He broke out in a laugh. Taking her face between his

callused palms, his eyes smiled into hers. "Dearest darling Phoebe, it's not a pet I have in mind, but a child. What say you to us adopting Lulu as our daughter?"

Amazement and, above all, joy struck Phoebe simultaneously. Grateful to be sitting, she was not at all certain her legs would have held her otherwise. "Do you mean it?"

"I do. I've already approached the board with my—our—petition. If you want her, she can be ours within a fortnight."

Tears gathered. Smiling through them, she reached out and folded her hands over his. "*If* I want her! Beyond you, I've never wanted anyone more. Oh, my love, how can I begin to thank you?"

"You already have." Gaze gentle, he traced his thumb along her smiling mouth. "Your happiness is all the thanks I shall ever want or need." He lifted the garland from her head and set it aside. "For now, I should very much like to get on with the business of making love to my wife. That is, if she does not object overmuch." Angling his face to hers, he tipped up her chin.

Feeling the delicious throbbing beginning to build, Phoebe laid her hand along his jaw. "I know for fact she does not object in the least." She wound both arms about his neck and pressed close, glorying in his solid warmth and the newfound sense of perfect, impenetrable connection they'd forged. "I have it from a reliable source that Mrs. Bellamy is most eager to begin her wifely duties posthaste."

About the Author

Hope Tarr is the award-winning author of twenty-five historical and contemporary romance novels including *Operation Cinderella*, the launch to her popular *Suddenly Cinderella* Series, optioned as a major motion picture by Twentieth Century Fox. Hope is also a cofounder and current curator of Lady Jane's Salon®, New York City's first and only monthly romance reading series now in its sixth year with nine satellite salons nationwide, all of which donate their net proceeds to a 501c(3) charity. (The original New York Salon supports Win, formerly Women in Need).

Most recently, Hope launched *Scribbling Women and the Real-Life Romance Heroes Who Love Them*, a charity anthology of twenty-eight essays by popular romance authors on how they met, wed, and love their real-life spouses and significant others. Net proceeds are donated to Win.

Hope lives in Manhattan with her real-life romance hero and their rescue cats.

You can visit Hope online at www.HopeTarr.com, as well as www.LadyJaneSalonNYC.com, www.Scribbling-Women.com, www.Facebook.com/HopeC.Tarr & www.Twitter.com/HopeTarr.

Desire as essential as breath...deception as fragile as sanity.

Beauty and the Earl

© 2014 Jess Michaels

The Pleasure Wars, Book 3

Liam, the Earl of Windbury, had everything when he held his secret lover in his arms. Until a feud between their families left her dead, his body broken, and his sister married to his bitterest enemy.

Wracked with guilt, simmering with rage, he's spent a year in seclusion, seeing no one except a few servants as he does his best to forget the past and patently refuses to think about any kind of future.

When courtesan Violet Milford enters Liam's lair, she's on a secret mission to gather information for Liam's desperate sister, who fears for his sanity, even his life. What she finds is a man scarred inside and out, whose dark, controlling sensuality hides the kind, wounded man within.

Violet awakens a sexual desire more powerful than Liam has ever known, and her stories weave a spell that begins to work its way past his defenses. But when the truth inevitably comes out, it could well destroy the love that is saving them both.

Warning: This book features a sexually experienced woman who will use every trick in her book to save a man from himself.

Available now in ebook and print from Samhain Publishing.

CPSIA information can be obtained at www.ICGtesting.com
Printed in the USA
BVOW01s0045040315

390164BV00002B/7/P